TEMPTED BY THE SINGLE DAD NEXT DOOR

AMY RUTTAN

MILLS & BOON

For all the doggos, kittens, chickens, horses,
cows and alpacas I know and love.

Each animal in this book represents
an animal who owned my heart or owned friends'
and family's hearts.

A special shout-out to my doggo,
the best writing buddy ever, Willow.
You are the bestest girl.

Special thanks to Christine,
for suggesting the cat rescue name
after trying to generate a random name,
with horrible results. Thanks for laughing it off
with me and coming to *my* rescue.

Thanks to Cathryn for our shared cockerels.

And thanks to my sister-in-law Theresa,
vet extraordinaire. You are an inspiration
and this former city mouse loves you.

Born and raised just outside Toronto, Ontario, **Amy Ruttan** fled the big city to settle down with the country boy of her dreams. After the birth of her second child Amy was lucky enough to realise her lifelong dream of becoming a romance author. When she's not furiously typing away at her computer, she's mum to three wonderful children, who use her as a personal taxi and chef.

Kate MacGuire has loved writing since for ever, which led to a career in journalism and public relations. Her short fiction won the Swarthout Award and placed third in the 2020 Women's National Book Association writing contest. Medical romance has always been her guilty pleasure, so she is thrilled to publish her first novel with Mills & Boon's Medical Romance line. When she's not pounding away on the keyboard, Kate co-runs Camp Runamok with her husband, keeping its two unruly campers in line in the beautiful woodlands of North Carolina. Visit katemacguire.com for updates and stories.

TEMPTED BY
THE SINGLE DAD
NEXT DOOR

AMY RUTTAN

RESISTING THE
OFF-LIMITS
PAEDIATRICIAN

KATE MacGUIRE

MILLS & BOON

First published in Great Britain 2024
by Mills & Boon, an imprint of HarperCollins*Publishers* Ltd,
1 London Bridge Street, London, SE1 9GF

www.harpercollins.co.uk

HarperCollins*Publishers* Macken House, 39/40 Mayor Street Upper, Dublin 1, D01 C9W8, Ireland

ISBN: 978-0-263-32151-7

02/24

This book contains FSC™ certified paper
and other controlled sources to ensure responsible forest management.

For more information visit www.harpercollins.co.uk/green.

Printed and Bound in the UK using 100% Renewable Electricity
at CPI Group (UK) Ltd, Croydon, CR0 4YY

CHAPTER ONE

"DON'T LOOK AT me like that!" Harley Bedard stared down into the big, round, saucer-sized brown eyes of her black-and-silver-colored cockapoo. The only reason Willow was staring at her like that was because Harley was finishing up her quick breakfast of a scrambled egg before starting her morning rounds. Willow always begged for eggs, cheese, chicken, tuna. Basically anything she ate, her dog wanted.

Badly.

Willow shifted, but her gaze was still intense. She stuck out her little pink tongue, wetting her black nose and silvery beard.

Repeatedly.

Harley groaned, but smiled at her goofy little dog. It was hard to resist that adorable face. She held a piece of scrambled egg in her palm and Willow eagerly ate it up.

"Don't say that I don't do anything nice for you," Harley muttered as she patted and scratched Willow's ear. The dog sneezed a couple of times, her feathery tail wagging. "You ready to do our chores?"

Willow sneezed again, shaking her head.

She took that as a yes.

There was a lot to do today. She had to check on the dogs that were in the kennel. Today wasn't a doggy day care day, so there wouldn't be an influx of clients with their pups driving down her gravel lane, but she did have a grooming session booked in. Her client had three dogs known as the wild bunch, so she tried to schedule that groom on a day when doggy day care wasn't running. Her friend Christine, who ran the local cat rescue, needed her help assessing a new load of kittens and older cats that had been dumped, and then there was a summer renter coming to sign a lease for the tiny home that she had on the other side of her yard behind the chicken house. When she bought the property three years ago, the small cabin had already been there. She'd refurbished it. Usually, she would get the odd tourist who wanted to be in the heart of Huron County for a couple of weeks and loved her little guest home tucked away on her thirty acres just outside of Opulence, Ontario. This time it was different. The house was booked for the whole summer.

The person renting her property was the son-in-law of local vet Dr. Michel Van Dorp. He was semiretired and didn't hide the fact that he wanted said son-in-law to take over his practice.

The vet clinic was integral to this part of Huron County as it was an agriculture community. Harley worked there when needed as a veterinary technician. Only when she had the time, though. Her kennel and grooming business were growing larger every year. Thankfully, she had hired help.

A new vet and a revitalized clinic would be so good for the community. Michel wanted to keep working, Harley knew that, but he couldn't keep up. He was getting older, and his health hadn't been the best since his daughter, Daphne, died two years ago.

Daphne had only been three years older than Harley. It shocked everyone when she died, and it nearly killed Michel.

He had been trying to retire for five years and had brought in other vets, but none of them stayed. People from the city said they liked country life, but they liked it when it was sunny and nice and perfect. No one liked delivering a cow in minus forty weather.

It wasn't her business. It was up to Michel to figure it all out. All that was within her control was her business Cosmopawl-itan Opulence, her animals and her summer rental. She had worked out a reasonable deal with Michel to house his son-in-law, Dr. Ryker Proulx, for the summer. Michel was optimistic it could be longer. He was so certain Dr. Proulx would want to stay. Harley had her doubts, she really did. Unless you were from here, no one really stayed.

She knew that firsthand.

Four years ago, she'd fallen for a veterinarian who had come to Opulence. They'd met while Michel was showing him the ropes, and Jason had completely swept her off her feet. He'd said that he loved her and the country life, and after a whirlwind romance, he'd proposed.

She should've known it was too good to be true.

They planned a big, white wedding. Family and friends from all over Huron County came to see her marry her very own Prince Charming. They had dreamed about extending the veterinary practice, buying land, raising a family. Jason had promised so many things.

Love.

Partnership.

Trust.

Harley had bought the most extravagant, sickeningly fluffy white wedding dress. She was so excited for the fairy tale, floating down the aisle to the man of her dreams.

She'd showed up at the church, ready for her happily-ever-after. Except, Jason hadn't.

He'd jilted her at the altar.

When she got back to their home, she saw his bags were packed. Jason came out of their bedroom. He looked apologetic, but clearly his mind was set. She knew that look of determination well.

"Why?" she asked, hugging her arms.

"I'm going to Toronto. I have an opportunity there that I could never get here."

"But what about us?"

Jason picked up one of his bags, hefting it over his shoulder. "You wouldn't be happy in the city. You weren't even happy in Hamilton, and that's smaller than Toronto. You told me that. It's better this way."

"Is it?" Her voice was breaking.

"It is. You're happy here. You have big plans. I'll be happier in the city, and I have goals that I want to reach. Marriage, right now, isn't a good idea. This was all a mistake."

She didn't respond. She just stood there, numb.

"Bye, Harley."

It had absolutely crushed her heart.

He didn't want the life they had planned together.

She had been an idiot, and she was never going to get her hopes up again. Never going to put her heart on the line again.

No way.

No how.

She had worked hard to buy her thirty acres on her own after Jason left her. Before she met Jason, when she was working in Hamilton she'd put in hours of overtime, scrimping and saving. Then she returned to Opulence, her hometown, met Jason and they fell in love. She'd taken some of her savings, spending money on the wedding that never happened. After that, she'd tucked anything she made away again. Since then, she'd been building her business slowly in Opulence, and now she'd finally got her feet back under her.

Things were looking up. She had her animals, her farm, that's all she needed.

Wasn't it?

Willow barked, getting her attention, and Harley glanced down at her.

"Message received. We've got work to do." Willow sat down.

Harley slipped on her rubber boots and grabbed her noise canceling headphones, because it got loud in the kennel.

She had to take care of Toby and Gordo, the two dogs currently boarding with her, and then make her way out to her barn to check on her rescue alpacas, Gozer, Vince and Zuul, aptly named after characters in one of her all-time favorite movies. She needed to feed her flock of maniacal chickens that liked to lay eggs all over the place and chase her. She let Willow out, who followed her.

Willow was only twenty pounds, hardly a good security dog. She had been with Harley for eight years now, since she'd helped the veterinarian at the clinic in Hamilton repair Willow's shoddy knees. The runt of the litter, Willow was the one puppy the breeder couldn't sell and Harley promptly fell in love with her.

She made her way to the kennel. As soon as she walked in there Toby and Gordo made it clear they were excited to see her. The headphones helped drown out the excited barks and yips. She loved it when dogs were so happy to see her, but her eardrums didn't love it so much.

"Come on," she called out over the excitement. As she opened the door to the fenced backyard Gordo, Toby and Willow all bolted. Thankfully, the three of them got along so she didn't have to separate them. She refreshed their water and put food in their bowls.

She'd let the dogs play while she made her way to her alpacas. Her rescue alpacas snuffed and stood up in their pen, happy to see her. Harley made sure the pasture gate was secure before she opened the stall door.

Once everything was done, she let the alpacas out to munch on fresh grass. Vince, Zuul and baby Gozer trotted from the barn, frolicking in the morning sun, while she grabbed a pitchfork to muck out their stall.

"Bonjour." There was a gentle tap on her shoulder from behind.

Harley screamed, tossed the pitchfork to the floor, spinning around to grab the lapels of the stranger, meaning to flip the guy, but instead she slipped on some excrement and fell into a pile of dirty hay. The stranger fell on top of her, or rather between her legs, landing with an "oof!"

Harley ripped off her headphones. "Who the hell are you?"

Intense gray eyes, with a hint of yellow, met hers as he shook dark hair from his face. Her breath caught in her throat, her face prickling with a rush of heat as their gazes locked.

Her heart skipped a beat and she forgot for one fraction of

a second that this guy she had just tossed to the ground, who was lying almost on top of her, was in fact a stranger.

"I'm Dr. Ryker Proulx. Your tenant for the summer," he said, climbing off her.

"Oh!" Of course.

She had just tried, very unsuccessfully, to Krav Maga her new renter. Hopefully, he wouldn't give her little rental a bad Yelp review.

She was a bit taken aback. She had never met Michel's son-in-law before.

Daphne had moved to Montreal after university and got married when Harley had been in school. Like a lot of people who left their small town for greener pastures, Daphne had never returned other than to visit family.

Looking at her husband, Harley could see why.

There was no doubt in her mind Ryker was handsome, but she'd been bamboozled by good looks before.

"Sorry! Couldn't hear you." She groped around in the straw to find her headphones, holding them up as if to say ta-da.

At least she didn't say that out loud.

"See?" she said, wanting to point out that she didn't just pull random guys on top of her in the barn. "I didn't hear you arrive."

Ryker brushed some of the straw off his shoulder. "I figured as much."

"Welcome," she blurted out, still sitting in a pile of alpaca poo.

Oh. My. God. Harley, get ahold of yourself.

Her brother David always said she rambled and blathered around dishy men. So did he. She could feel the warmth of the flush rising up her neck to her cheeks. It was the ultimate tell in the poker game of trying to hide your attraction for someone you just met.

She sucked at the card game too.

A small smile lifted his lips. He held out his hand to help her up. She took it, her pulse quickening, a knot starting to twist in her belly as he pulled her up. He was taller than her, and her heart raced as she looked up at him.

Ryker was exactly her type. His dark hair was longer, but not so long that it brushed the top of his shoulders. His generous mouth was set in a hard line, as he gazed around her barn. There was a hint of a five o'clock shadow on his chiseled jaw.

He was dressed in a black leather jacket, a white T-shirt and well-fitted jeans that had not seen a day's work in the field. His black leather boots were polished too.

Everything about him screamed city, that he didn't belong in Opulence, and that further solidified her belief, in that moment, that he would not be staying. He was a summer visitor.

"Shall we go sign the agreement?" Ryker suggested.

"Yes. Is Michel here?"

"*Oui.* He was knocking on your door when I saw you slip into the barn," he replied in a distinct French-Canadian accent.

"Okay." It wasn't the best way to meet a new tenant, throwing him into a pile of poop, but it was what it was. She quickly made her way out of the barn and saw Michel standing by his red pickup truck.

"There you are!" Michel exclaimed.

"You're early," she replied, hoping Michel didn't notice that his son-in-law was covered in straw, dirt and manure.

"I thought you might be up," Michel said brightly as she approached his truck.

"I'm always up early." She grinned. "I am glad you swung by. I have a busy day. I have to go down to Blyth and help out at the cat rescue this afternoon."

"I figured as much. I heard they got a bunch of strays in," Michel said.

"They did," she confirmed, looking back over her shoulder at Ryker uneasily. He was still wiping off straw and dried crap.

"Harley, I would like to introduce you to my son-in-law, Dr. Ryker Proulx from Montreal. Ryker, this is the vet tech I often bring in and as you know, she's your landlord for the summer too!"

Ryker turned to her, those gray eyes fixing on hers with a momentary widening of shock and a quick travel up and down her person that sent a shiver of anticipation through her.

"The vet tech?" Ryker asked.

Michel nodded. "Yep."

Her gaze locked with Ryker's again. He still looked surprised. She knew she looked a fright, wearing her baggy overalls, rubber boots that came up to her knees, a grungy tank top, and her hair barely brushed and put up in a very large top knot. At least they were both covered in alpaca crap and straw.

Get a grip.

Her inner voice was right. Who cared what she looked like? And the way she looked had nothing to do with her ability as a certified and well respected veterinary technician.

She wasn't here to impress him, even though there was a part of her deep down that wanted to… She locked that niggling thought away. Dr. Proulx was her tenant, a widower and Michel's son-in-law.

Most important, Harley was fairly certain Ryker was here temporarily, and she wasn't interested in dating anyone. Especially someone who wasn't staying.

"Pleasure to meet you properly, Dr. Proulx," Harley said, clearing her throat and shaking all those thoughts away as she extended her hand.

Michel's eyes widened as he realized the state she and Ryker were in. "What happened?"

"I surprised her. We both took a tumble," Ryker explained coolly, accepting her proffered hand. She felt a little zing of warmth shoot up her arm and quickly pulled her hand back, annoyed at her reaction to him.

"Well," Harley started, clearing her voice. "I just need to go let Toby and Gordo back in their kennel. The tiny home is on the other side of the yard. It's unlocked, so do have a quick look around and make sure it's what you want and I'll meet you both back here."

"Sounds good, Harley," Michel responded.

Harley needed to focus on her work and not the way her body had reacted so traitorously when she met Ryker. He was off-limits. That way there was no risk of a broken heart. Like what happened with Jason.

However, it had been some time since she had had that kind of physical attraction to a man. Ryker Proulx was dangerous to her equilibrium and even though he was technically about to become her neighbor, at least she could keep him at arm's length. The only times she had to interact with him would be if she saw him on the property or if he needed her at the clinic.

It would be totally professional.

Besides, she liked Michel too much to get involved with Daphne's widower, and after what happened with the last vet she fell in love with, she was never, ever going to date a veterinarian again.

No matter how hot the vet was.

Ryker watched Harley walk away. He had spied the fences of the kennel and saw the sign at the head of the driveway. Cosmopawlitan Opulence.

He'd cringed at the cutesy name, but Michel had huge respect for Harley.

Honestly, when Michel had mentioned that he had a friend who had thirty acres, ran a kennel and owned a tiny home that they rented out, he had assumed the woman was closer to Michel's age. He had been shocked to see a younger woman, maybe in her early thirties, running such a successful business and owning quite a bit of farmland.

He was also taken aback by her stunning beauty, even covered in muck and straw. She looked a wreck in baggy overalls and her golden hair tied up in a messy bun, but when their gazes locked, his heart had beat just a little bit faster and when he landed on top of her, his blood had heated at the brief touch. Yet it was her eyes that had shocked him. They were so blue, and he saw a spark of strength buried deep in that cerulean color, before his gaze traveled down to her soft, pink, plump lips. For one brief second, he thought about what it would be like to kiss them.

Only for a brief moment, and then the guilt overcame him, for a split second.

Daphne had been gone for two years. She had been his world, they had a beautiful son, Justin, and then when they thought they were pregnant with their second, her pregnancy turned out to be ectopic. Her tube ruptured and she bled out so fast there was nothing to be done.

All he could do was take care of their son.

The problem was, they were isolated in Montreal.

After Daphne died Ryker had thrown himself into work and taking care of Justin. Friends had drifted away. Even Justin's friends, because he no longer wanted to play sports or do anything without his dad.

So no, maybe not fully isolated, but it mostly was just Justin and him.

He had no family left. Ryker had been an only child, and his parents were dead. They had talked for a couple years about moving back to Daphne's hometown, to be near her parents and so Justin would have cousins who lived close by.

It would be family, but now Daphne was gone and he wasn't completely sure that he could leave everything behind and live here. Montreal was his home. Justin's home. He'd told Michel he would stay for the summer, to see how it worked out.

The truth was Justin was struggling. Montreal reminded him of his mom and he never let Ryker far out of his sight. Ryker was actually surprised that he'd been able to come here to sign the lease, but Nanna was occupying Justin for now. He was hoping the summer here in Opulence would help the boy heal.

Justin thought they were on an extended summer vacation. He was nine and just so excited to be near his grandpa, his nanna and some cousins. Ryker hadn't seen Justin this happy in so long.

To keep himself busy, Ryker had offered to work for his

father-in-law. A small-town vet practice would be a break from the hustle and bustle of a city practice.

So when Michel offered up his friend's tiny home as a rental for them, Ryker thought it was perfect, until he learned that the so-called friend was a good-looking, sexy blonde. Maybe, he needed to find another place to rent.

"Well, let's go see the place. It's just on the other side of that coop," Michel said, walking toward the chicken house in question.

"Maybe we should find somewhere else," Ryker said cautiously.

Michel paused and raised his bushy eyebrows. "This is the closest rental to the vet clinic, at a decent price. There's not much for rent in Opulence."

"Right. So you've said," Ryker groused. He had no choice.

"I know Harley looks a little rough around the edges, but she is a smart, savvy businesswoman and part-time vet tech."

"Part-time?" Ryker asked, all too aware that Harley was not only his landlord, but someone who would be working with him.

"Yes. She works sometimes at the clinic. Just part-time as she's really busy here. There's a shortage of good, reliable and bondable pet services. When I'm not at the vet clinic, people do have to drive thirty, sometimes forty minutes. There are wait lists for groomers."

Ryker was shocked.

Wait lists?

He took for granted the city life, where there was always some artistic doggy or pet spa popping up.

"Besides," Michel said, interjecting through Ryker's thoughts of doubt. "This is the only place that has a lease term that you're looking for. The rest are cottages that rent an enormous amount week to week and are mostly fully booked, sometimes a year in advance."

Michel was right. Ryker was stuck. The vet tech and working at the clinic part worried Ryker, but if she worked with him, then she was definitely off-limits. As long as he compartmentalized her in his mind like that, maybe this could work out.

He couldn't tell Michel his real hesitations for wanting to stay here. He couldn't let his father-in-law know that for the first time since he lost Daphne he was physically attracted to someone.

That wasn't going to happen.

"*D'accord*, let's go see this place then."

Michel nodded and Ryker fell into step beside him.

There was frantic barking and he glanced over his shoulder, pausing to watch as Harley opened the door to the gated play area of her kennel. Two dogs came bounding over to her, tails wagging happily, before finding their respective places to do their business. Harley's little dog trotted in front of her.

She had her noise canceling headphones back on. She was tossing balls and other soft toys at the dogs as they bounded around happily outside, running all around her and demanding her attention.

Harley was smiling and laughing as she took a ball from the big, horse-like dog and tossed it again. It was clear she was passionate about what she did, and Ryker couldn't help but smile, watching her.

That passion was what he felt for animals, too.

Before he got married, he had a red setter that had been his best friend. Daphne had loved his dog, Temart, too and even in his old age the dog had been so protective of Justin as an infant. A lump formed in Ryker's throat as he thought of his old dog.

These were memories he thought he'd locked away, but watching Harley out in that kennel with those happy dogs brought those memories rushing back and it overwhelmed him. There was a part of him that wanted to join in on the fun—he couldn't remember the last time he'd let loose and tossed a ball to a dog. It surprised him how she affected him so.

Someone he barely knew.

Don't think about her. Don't let her in.

And he had to keep reminding himself of that. All he had

to do was rent a place from her and possibly work with her on a professional level. That's it. Just because he was attracted to her, it didn't mean anything. He was not opening his heart to the prospect of pain.

He couldn't deal with that kind of loss again. It was too risky.

All that mattered to him in this world was Justin's happiness.

He'd loved and lost. And he was never going to go through that again.

CHAPTER TWO

ONCE SHE HAD got somewhat cleaned up, taken care of the dogs and got them settled back into their kennels, or doggy suites as she liked to call them, Harley made sure they both had a nice pupsicle to smooth over the wound of being put back inside. Even Willow got her own doggy suite and pupsicle so she wouldn't be underfoot as Harley went out to the tiny home and dealt with the lease.

That's if the fancy veterinarian from Montreal thought her summer rental was good enough. She laughed to herself as she thought about how she sounded like some of the older members of Opulence, casting derision at the out-of-towner. And she felt slightly bad for ruining his nice clothes.

When was the last time she dressed up? She couldn't remember.

Life on her farm, running her business and dealing with animals, didn't leave her too much time to go out. And she had never been one for dance clubs, or even a girls' night. She was a bit of a loner.

Her phone buzzed. It was her older brother, David.

"Yo," she answered, stepping out of the noisy kennel.

"Hey, Nerd," David replied. "Wondering what you're up to today."

"Cat rescue, a groom and dealing with a summer tenant."

"Usual then."

"Summer tenants are hardly usual," she remarked.

"Oh! I missed that part. A summer tenant?" David asked, intrigued.

"Michel's son-in-law from Montreal."

"Is he cute?" David asked.

Her stomach did a little flip. *That was an understatement.*

"No," she blurted out.

"Liar," David chuckled.

"Do you actually need something, David, or are you just calling to pester me?"

"Yes, I do. My vet's away. I'm dealing with a horse that has a gastric ulcer. He's on omeprazole, but he's still not wanting to eat. Any suggestions?"

Her brother and his partner owned a horse ranch up near Inverhuron. They bred racehorses and were quite adept at minor equine medicine. They were a fully equipped operation.

Harley frowned. "How long has he been on the omeprazole?"

"For a couple of weeks."

Harley frowned. "His stomach could still be irritated. There's not much I can do over the phone. You'd have to check with a scope to see if the stomach has healed, but it could also be a case of his being afraid to eat."

David sighed. "Afraid? He could be."

"Alfalfa. You got any?"

"Yeah."

"Hand feed him. I also heard, once, beet pulp, but you really have to let it soak in the feed for at least twenty-four hours. I can't come up today, but I could come tomorrow. Do you need me to come?"

"No. It's okay. I know you're swamped. I'm going to try those suggestions and see if it helps him. Our vet will be back in a couple of days, before he goes on his next whirlwind vacation," David said.

"Vacation, what's that?" She laughed dryly.

"Something you need to take once in a while."

She knew it, but when would she have time? At least David

had a partner. She was alone here, besides her two employees. "Call me if there any more problems."

"Will do. Love you, brat," David said affectionately, then hung up.

Harley slipped her phone back in her pocket and she hung her noise canceling headphones up over her desk. Her assistant, Kaitlyn, would be coming in soon to watch the dogs while Harley made her way to Blyth and the cat rescue for the afternoon. She glanced at herself briefly in the mirror, just to make sure she didn't have some paw prints or slobber on her, grabbed her tablet with a copy of the lease and then made her way out into the yard, past the chicken house.

Whatever Dr. Proulx decided, she hoped it was quick.

She had other chores to do.

There was a small part of her that hoped he wouldn't stay, because she hadn't been overly excited about how she reacted to him when they shook hands. Dr. Proulx was a danger to her good judgment.

He was so the type of guy she was in to.

Tall.

Dark.

Refined. Even covered in alpaca mess, he was still classier and more sophisticated than her.

Her draw to him reminded her of that instant connection with Jason, and she wasn't going to make that mistake twice. She had learned her lesson.

Have you though?

She thought she had, but work was her life. Maybe that was part of the problem. Perhaps she was lonely. She ignored that little twinge as she approached the tiny house. Ryker and Michel were standing on the covered porch. The deck was something she had added last year, so visitors could enjoy the vista of her seventeen acres of forest and the sound of the small creek that ran across her property. Ryker had clearly slipped off his dirty shoes to look inside and was putting them back on, on the porch when she found them.

Harley winced. Hopefully the leather wasn't ruined, but she did appreciate him keeping the house clean.

"So?" she asked, coming up the stairs. "What do you think?"

Ryker nodded. *"Très bon.* It will do for my needs."

"Great." She forced a smile on her face. He just lived on the property. She didn't have to provide him breakfast, just had to make sure that he had power and water. They could be neighbors. They didn't have to be friends. "So you have to bring your own bedding."

"That won't be an issue," Michel said. "Maureen has plenty of extra sheets and stuff for Ryker and Justin."

"Justin? Who's Justin?" Harley asked.

"My nine-year-old son," Ryker answered.

And then she remembered. Michel's grandson. Daphne's boy. She hadn't been able to attend the baby shower nine years ago, because she had been in school, but she had sent a gift. A no-sew quilt she had made. It was fleece and had dogs on it.

Everyone in Opulence had been invited.

"Of course," she responded softly. "I remember now. Michel always brags about him."

Michel smiled broadly, nodding and a faint half smile tugged at a corner of Ryker's mouth.

"It won't be a problem with him staying here, will it?" Ryker asked.

"No. Not at all. Sorry if I seemed shocked. It's good to know. Lots of places to ride his bike, if he has one. There's a basketball hoop. It's not overly exciting here."

Ryker smiled at her warmly. "It's perfect."

A blush crept up into her cheeks again. She could feel that flood of warmth. She had to agree with him; her place was kind of perfect.

"Well, I'm glad," she added, not sure what else to say as she stood there grinning like a fool.

"Is that the lease?" Ryker asked, pointing to the tablet in her hand.

Right. The lease. He needs to sign it. Focus, Harley.

"It is." She unlocked the tablet and handed it to him with a stylus. Ryker flicked through the simple contract. His face was serious as he scanned the document, and she just stood there, watching him, rocking back and forth on her heels. Not sure what to do with herself.

Ryker signed it quickly and handed it back to her. "When can we move in?"

"As soon as possible." She reached into her pocket and held out the key. "I hope you enjoy your summer here. I know I do!"

She winced again.

Yep.

Nerd.

Ryker reached out and took the key, their fingers brushing momentarily. Heat coursed through her, and again she quickly snatched her hand back and stuck it in her pocket.

"Thank you," Ryker replied stiffly, holding the key awkwardly.

"Great. Well, I have to go into Blyth in a couple of hours and offer my assistance to some rescue cats."

"Do they need my help?" Michel offered. "I mean, I have a doctor appointment first…"

"No. It's fine. I can handle it," she said.

Michel looked at his son-in-law. "Ryker can go!"

Ryker's eyes widened, and she didn't know what to say. She couldn't say no, but she didn't want to say yes.

"I'll go," Ryker stated, breaking the tension.

"What about your son?" Harley asked.

"He's with his nanna for the day. If I am to work in this community for the summer, I should get to know the local rescues," Ryker said.

Harley was flabbergasted. The new vet hadn't even moved into his home yet and he was offering to come to Blyth. Granted, Michel had offered him up, but he agreed. Albeit reluctantly.

"Well…" Harley stammered. "I have to be there in two

hours. Michel knows the address and yeah, it would be great to have you there to meet the rescue volunteers."

Ryker nodded. "Excellent. We better get back home so I can change and then I can grab what I need. Right, Michel?"

"Of course." Michel grinned, then frowned. "Maureen needs your car though, Ryker. I have my appointment, and she promised to take Justin to the beach."

"Ah. That's right." Ryker frowned.

Without thinking Harley blurted out, "I can pick you up and take you there."

Ryker's eyes widened. "That won't be a problem?"

"Nope. Not at all."

You're being very aggressively friendly.

"All settled," Michel stated brightly. "Thanks, Harley."

"Thank you," Harley replied. "I mean, you're welcome."

She was still stunned she'd offered to go out of her way to pick up a virtual stranger. However, it was good for the cat rescue. A veterinarian volunteering their time was amazing. It would be worth the awkward car ride.

"I'll pick you up in an hour or so," Harley said.

"Sounds good," Ryker replied.

She watched them walk across the yard and get into Michel's pickup truck. She meandered back toward the house to put away her tablet. Michel honked and waved, but Ryker didn't look back at her.

Not that she expected him to.

Ryker could've said no. He was kind of bamboozled into helping out by a well-meaning, but oblivious Michel. Either way she was glad. Her offering up a ride, well, she still didn't understand what came over her when she said that. As Michel drove out the driveway, Kaitlyn's little car turned in and she honked in greeting to Michel before parking in her usual spot beside the kennel.

Harley made her way over to the vehicle. Kaitlyn was eighteen and was saving up money to go to university and then eventually veterinary college. She was Harley's right-hand woman at Cosmopawlitan Opulence.

"Who was that?" Kaitlyn asked excitedly.

"It was Michel," Harley responded sarcastically.

Kaitlyn rolled her eyes. "Not Michel, the dark handsome stranger in the passenger seat."

"Michel's son-in-law and the new veterinarian in town. He's staying at the tiny house with his son. At least for the summer."

"How exciting. Do you think he'll stay for good?"

"No," Harley replied frankly.

Men like Ryker didn't stay in small towns. A day would come when Kaitlyn would leave for school, and Harley seriously doubted she'd come back. Kaitlyn would move somewhere a little more exciting than Opulence.

Barely anyone stayed here.

"Bummer. It'll be some time before I get my degree and can take over."

Harley smiled at her. "You'll do great, I'm sure. I'm going to go put this tablet away, and then I have to go feed the horde of chickens and the alpacas."

Kaitlyn nodded. "Good luck. I like chickens, but your flock should be storming the beaches of England like some vikings."

Harley chuckled at that image. "You think they need horned helmets?"

"No! They peck my ankles enough." Kaitlyn headed inside the boarding barn and Harley went back to her home. She couldn't stand here in the driveway all day muddling over Dr. Ryker Proulx. She had chores and commitments. She couldn't give an extra second to a man who was only here for the summer.

A temporary resident.

At least, that's what she told herself. Her mind had other ideas.

Why did I agree to this?

Ryker kept asking himself that question over and over in

his head as he gathered his gear out of his suitcase along with some equipment that Michel had graciously loaned him. He should've said no, but he didn't have much of a choice since Michel had volunteered him. Giving his time to a nonprofit was a no-brainer, but what was difficult for him was the fact he'd be working closely with Harley. If she was just his landlord, he could avoid her, but she worked in his sphere.

A vet tech.

Now, he'd be traveling in a car with her. He wasn't sure how long it was to get to Blyth or this rescue. Could he even remember how to make small talk? These days he either talked work or talked parenting with other people. He'd completely lost touch with adult chatting with friends who either weren't married or didn't have kids.

His whole life had become work and making sure Justin was okay.

Which he wasn't.

Justin rarely played anymore. He was always by Ryker's side and was struggling in school. It was like Justin was afraid to let him out of his sight.

Ryker hoped this summer would get Justin out of his funk and help him remember how to play. He hoped it would heal him before they headed back to Montreal.

Working at Michel's clinic would be a slower pace than the city, but at least he could do something useful and spend more time with family.

He'd thought this was going to be an easy summer. Until he met Harley.

When Ryker had got back to his in-laws' small condo, where he and Justin had been couch-surfing for the last couple of days, he'd showered and changed into an older pair of jeans and a flannel shirt, and now there was nothing to do but wait for Harley to pick him up.

Sure, there were beautiful women, but there was something about Harley that he quite couldn't put his finger on, that drew him in. Ryker found it disconcerting.

Extremely so.

He paced on the driveway and for one brief moment he thought of backing out. Which would look terribly unprofessional. It's not like he could run and hide. She knew where he lived, at least for the summer.

Ryker chuckled to himself at the absurd idea of running away and hiding just because he was attracted to Harley and would be working closely with her.

A blue pickup truck pulled into the driveway and Harley waved at him from the front seat.

Did everyone drive pickups around here?

His luxury sedan already stuck out like a sore thumb with his Quebec license plate in a sea of dusty trucks and Ontario plates. He loaded the gear into the bed of her truck. He opened the passenger door.

"Howdy! Ready to save cats?" she asked forcefully.

"That's enthusiastic," he teased.

Pink tinged her cheeks. "Well, it's a great rescue. You have to be enthusiastic about that!"

"I'm sure." He buckled up and she pulled away from Michel's house.

An awkward silence descended between them. Ryker sneaked a glance at Harley. She still had her blond hair piled on the top of her head, but it was now neatly braided into a bun. The rubber boots were gone and replaced by sneakers, and she was wearing scrubs that were branded with her doggy boarding facility. They were covered with little cartoon animals in various poses, attending a spa. A couple of poodles were getting their "hair done," and he saw a cat doing yoga poses. There were many more little pets on her scrubs, but he had to tear his gaze away before she thought he was staring at her.

Which he was.

And it wasn't just the cartoon animals that were drawing his gaze. The scrubs were loose, but not as generous as the overalls she was wearing this morning.

He could make out the curve of her hips, the swell of her

breasts, which was not what he should be focusing on now. Especially as she was doing him a favor by driving him.

It was inappropriate.

"Thanks again for picking me up," he said, breaking the silence.

"It's no problem. Thank you for volunteering your time. It really is a big deal with this community. Rescues are a great thing."

She was talking a mile a minute, and he couldn't help but smile as she quickly glanced at him. She grinned, a wide, fake, set smile that didn't reach her eyes.

Not that he could blame her. They hadn't really talked much so far. He'd been a bit aloof with her. It was easier that way.

For who?

He ignored that thought. It was best he kept everything professional. He didn't need to make friends with her. All he had to do was be cordial. He'd see to these cats quickly and put Harley out of his mind. Still, she agreed to pick him up. He couldn't be a jerk.

"Thanks again for agreeing to help out," she said.

"Well, I think you mean thank you for being volunteered by Michel, *oui*?"

Harley smiled, that cute little grin that made his heart beat just a bit faster. "Right. Still, it's appreciated."

"You've thanked me three times, but again, it's no problem. You're right, rescues are important."

"I tend to repeat myself. A lot. Especially around people I don't know. So my apologies for the overabundance of gratitude. I mean, you could be terrible and I'll regret thanking you later."

Ryker chuckled again. "You have so little faith in me then?"

"Of course not. I don't know you at all. But I've been around vets. Good and bad."

"I assure you, I'm good."

"Do you have your own practice?" she asked.

"No," he said, sighing. "It's expensive to manage and run a clinic in Montreal. I am an associate at a busy urban clinic."

He also didn't have time to run his own practice, not when Justin needed him.

"Running a business takes a lot of time. For sure. I know."

"You managed to buy a business and a farm. It's impressive."

Pink flooded her cheeks again. "Thanks."

"That's four times now," he teased.

He liked the way she smiled at him. It made him want to get her to smile more, to have her blue eyes twinkle. To make her happy.

Get ahold of yourself.

He needed to regain control of these thoughts running through his mind. He was not here to make Harley happy.

"How many cats are we looking at today?" Ryker asked, trying to steer the subject onto business, so he didn't have to make small talk or think about how cute she did look in those ridiculous scrubs.

"Eight."

"Eight?" he repeated, surprised.

"There's also a couple that are feral and most likely could be considered for the feral barn cat program," Harley admitted. "They still need their shots and to be checked out to make sure they're healthy. We'll most likely have to sedate the feral ones, so it's actually good you're here."

"So eight fairly domesticated cats and two or three feral cats?"

"And five kittens."

Ryker's eyes widened. "So, about sixteen then?"

So much for a quiet day. Why did he think summer here would be a slower pace?

This is just a rescue. Rescues are always full.

Harley looked up at the sky and was mouthing numbers silently. "Yes. Is that too much?"

"No. It's fine. I just like to know what I'm dealing with."

They'd be there awhile.

Harley pulled into the parking lot next to a newish looking barn that was very similar to her kennel. It was long, kind of like a modern milking barn, but with walls, instead of open sides for the cattle.

"We're here," Harley announced, parking.

"Looks respectable."

"It is. It's very well run. I'll introduce you to the couple that runs the rescue."

"D'accord." Ryker got out of her truck and they grabbed the gear from the back. He then followed Harley. There was a big sign out front that said Fluffypaws Rescue, and there was a huge cartoon cat painted in the style of chibi. It was all so cutesy. Too cutesy for his sensibilities, but he knew that would help attract potential adopters.

The barn door opened and a blonde woman in kitty scrubs came out, smiling, relief washing over her face. "Harley, thank you for coming."

Harley hugged her. "No problem, Christine. Always happy to assist."

Christine turned to look at him. He smiled and extended his hand. *"Bonjour, mademoiselle."*

"This is Dr. Proulx from Montreal," Harley informed her. "He's Michel's son-in-law who is here for the summer. He wanted to meet you and help out today too."

Christine smiled brightly at him and took his hand. "Pleasure to meet you, and I'm so glad for an extra pair of hands!"

"I'm glad to be of assistance," Ryker answered. He glanced over at Harley, who was smiling warmly at him. There was a genuine warmth, and it made his heart skip a beat. As much as he wanted to keep her at arm's length and keep it professional, he couldn't help but smile back at her. For some reason it made him happy to see her smile so warmly at him and know that he was making her happy right then.

Focus.

He really had to pull himself together.

He wasn't here to please her. He was here to do a job and

that was it. The whole purpose of his summer out here in south-western Ontario was to have Justin near some family. He was hoping the summer here would cheer Justin up. That's it.

He wasn't here to flirt or even think about getting involved with someone. He wasn't going to put his heart on the line. He wasn't going to lose in love.

Again.

His heart couldn't take another shattering. It had hurt too much.

"Let me show you around," Christine said, interrupting his thoughts.

"Please," he said, quickly and tightly locking away his smile.

Right now he had to just focus on the task at hand and that was assessing the cats and kittens. Harley was a vet tech and he was a veterinarian; they were just here to work.

CHAPTER THREE

CHRISTINE SHOWED RYKER and Harley where they could set up and do their work for the afternoon. Ryker was extremely impressed with how the rural rescue was set up and so well run. The barn had a small exam room, which had an exam table and a weight scale. Christine stated she was going to slowly bring the cats in to them from where they were housed in their kennels. He could see the kennels through a window. They were clean and spacious.

In the exam room and supply room there were vaccines and other medicines that he would need, all generously donated by various vet clinics around the county. Even private members of the communities and businesses gave to the cat rescue. He could see names of benefactors listed on a plaque on the wall— and by plaque he meant a beautiful cross-stitch that Christine had stitched herself. She had explained this all during the tour and how she did it to show her gratitude to those who donated and volunteered.

He saw Harley's name there. Just below Michel's.

Harley Bedard.

Reading her last name, he wondered if she had French origins too.

You need to pay attention.

Here he was, letting his thoughts wander toward Harley again. He had only known her a couple of hours and he was devoting all this time to thinking about her. What he needed to do was focus on the job at hand.

But it was apparent how well liked and respected Harley was in this community.

"So," Christine stated. "I'll let you two get to work. Harley knows where everything is."

"Merci," Ryker said.

Harley spun around on her heel. "So what's your plan of action?"

"Plan of action?" Ryker asked, cocking an eyebrow.

"Yes. This is the first time we're working together. I need a plan."

"Okay." He ran his hands through his hair, trying to think. "Well, I'll vet the cats and make sure they're healthy."

"Of course. We need veterinarian certifications so Christine and her husband, Dave, can start working on finding foster families or forever families. Or as we like to say, fur-ever."

He grimaced. "Ooh, that's a terrible pun."

"I ramble. Sorry." She shrugged.

"I noticed," he mumbled. "So, we are going to get the cats ready for adoption then. *Oui?*"

"That's the goal for the nonprofit."

"I would assume so." Their gazes locked and his heart skipped a beat. He quickly looked away and tried to focus on getting his equipment ready and not the fact that he was now alone in a room with Harley. Neither of them said anything to each other as they got everything ready for their furry friends.

He found her rambling and her incessant nervous chatter charming. The more he talked to her, the more he liked being around her.

It was distracting.

This is ridiculous.

He always talked to his vet techs. It was all business. So why was he reacting like this? Harley was no different from any other vet tech he worked with. Except she was. Harley was his new landlord, and he was really drawn to her. He thought he was long past this awkward tension with a woman he found attractive.

He had been a fool when he first met Daphne twelve years ago. He had been so awkward when he met her in Guelph at school, and she had laughed at him. They'd fallen deeply in love and never stopped laughing.

Well, he stopped laughing after she died. He couldn't stop the memory from sneaking in.

"Daphne?" Ryker called out. Justin was dragging a grocery bag up the steps.

"Look, Pappa," Justin shouted proudly.

"I see, buddy." He headed back into the house. It was quiet, except the shrill whistle of a kettle.

Where was Daphne?

Ryker set the rest of the groceries down as Justin dragged the smaller bag in. He made his way to the kitchen and turned off the kettle, then he saw Daphne unconscious, lying on the floor. Like she had collapsed on her way to the kitchen.

"Daphne!" He was on his knees, calling emergency services as he checked for breathing, for any sign of life. There was no pulse.

There was a scream in his head.

"Mama!" Justin cried out. Then he began to sob and there was nothing Ryker could do. He was powerless.

Ryker shook that memory away. He didn't want to think about it today.

"Are you okay?" Harley asked, interrupting his thoughts.

"Fine," he replied stiffly, annoyed that he had let that thought creep back into his mind. Daphne had died two years ago. He thought he had locked all that grief away. He had Justin to take care of. He had spent two years trying to be strong for his son.

This was not the time or place to let that memory back in.

What he needed to do was to keep talking about work.

"So, this feral barn cat program? Tell me about it."

Harley's blue eyes widened, but only for a moment. "Well, it's not called that officially, but basically it's designed for feral cats—cats that don't want to be inside cats and want minimal contact with humans. You provide them shelter outside, a bowl of food and clean water. We neuter and spay them, vaccinate them and all that good stuff, and then they come and go as they please. Local farmers love it. Helps keep down pests."

"It sounds like a good idea. I think I heard a bit about it, but I worked mostly in a city veterinary clinic. There weren't many feral cats that I had to treat."

"Upscale clinic?" Harley teased, a droll half smile tweaking her mouth.

"Why would you ask that?"

"Well, Montreal is a cosmopolitan type of city. Plus you were dressed *très chic* compared to my rustic grunge."

He laughed. He wanted to tell her how cute she had looked in that rustic grunge look, as she called it. "I guess it does serve a more metropolitan type of clientele. Not many feral cats for the barns in Le Plateau-Mont Royal."

"Is that where your clinic is located?" she asked.

"Oui." He nodded.

"Neat. Well, a lot of the cats in this program are found in the city as well. Street cats. It's not just a rural problem."

"Really?" Ryker was surprised. "Well, yeah, I guess I never really saw that. Maybe my clinic was too posh." Now he was teasing, but it wasn't too far from the truth.

Harley smiled at him. "Don't worry about that. You're not too posh to help here, and that's what matters. It means so much to Christine, Dave, the community and me."

His heart skipped a beat and he smiled at her. "And you? It means that much to you?"

There was a tinge of pink that crept up her slender neck and pooled in her cheeks. She looked away quickly. "Well, animals mean a lot to me and so does this rescue. There's only so much I can do, but having you here today we can get more done."

He nodded, pleased. "Well, as I said, I'm glad to help out and be a part of the community this summer."

That's when he saw that her grin changed just a little bit and the twinkle went out of her eyes. Like she was disappointed that he was only there for the summer.

"Right. Well, I'll go tell Christine to bring in the first cat."
Harley quickly exited the exam room.

Ryker sighed. He felt bad for disappointing her, but it was
the truth.

Right now, there was nothing permanent about his situation.
He was here for the summer. Montreal was his home, but he
was glad to bring Justin here. Even for just a couple of months.
It was nice to be close to family.

Hopefully to help knock Justin out of his funk.

When he first decided to spend the summer here in Opulence, he had a pretty clear vision in his head: cheer Justin up
and help him connect with his late mother like he needed.

Now, looking at Harley and feeling those first stirrings of
attraction, something that he never thought he would ever feel
again for another person, he wasn't so sure where this summer
was going to take him.

All he knew was he had to protect his heart, because he
was not staying.

Christine brought in the cats one by one. Harley really wasn't
sure how she and Ryker were going to work. That was why
she asked him to lay out his plan, so she'd know what to expect. She had trust issues with veterinarians she never worked
with before. Michel and Jason had trusted her completely, but
other vets that had come and gone, either through volunteering here at Fluffypaws or at the clinic, sometimes treated her
as a glorified coffee girl—at least until she stood up to those
who doubted her skill, because she knew what she was doing
and when Michel wasn't available, she would often step in and
help where she could.

She'd taken three years to earn her veterinary tech diploma
through a prestigious college, then a year in animal science and
then a certificate in grooming and kennel maintenance at night.

Some people, like Michel, had questioned why she just didn't
fully become a vet and the truth was because she wanted this.

She loved being a vet tech. She loved grooming and her dream of a farm and her own business.

Harley had worked so hard to scrimp and save so she could buy her own land and run her dream business of Cosmopawli-tan Opulence. She didn't need a doctorate or the title to prove anything.

No matter what some other vets thought. Which was why some temporary vets had deemed her as "difficult." Harley didn't see herself as that.

Rambly.

Awkward.

Chatty.

But damn good at what she did.

Ryker had only seen the weird side of her so far, so she was slightly nervous to see how he was going to be when Christine brought in a beautiful orange-and-black cat that had been named Nia. Would Harley be pushed to the side? Or would Ryker actually work with her?

"Can you weigh the cat for me, please?" Ryker asked.

"Sure," Harley replied, relieved that he was apparently going to utilize her skills.

Nia was a love bug, but skittish when Harley took her from the safety of Christine's arms and held her against her chest. Instantly, Nia began to purr.

Ryker grinned; there was a twinkle in his dark eyes as their gazes locked. A little frisson of excitement zinged through her.

"She seems to like you, eh?" Ryker remarked.

"I think so," Harley agreed.

"Maybe you need a barn cat?" Ryker teased as Harley weighed Nia on the scale.

"I have a feeling that this cat is not part of the barn rescue."

"She's not," Christine interjected. "She's a house cat—she was definitely someone's pet. She was found on the side of the road."

"Is there a microchip?" Ryker asked, opening up his laptop to make notes.

"No. There's never a microchip when they come here, but we do microchip them before we send them out to foster or be adopted," Christine stated.

"Would you like that done today then?" Ryker asked.

"Microchipping?" Christine asked excitedly.

"Oui," Ryker replied.

Christine beamed. "If you could?"

"I think Harley and I can manage that," Ryker said, returning to his notes.

"I'll leave you both to it. Just holler when you're done with her." Christine slipped out of the room.

"Nia weighs two point nine kilos," Harley stated, picking up the meowing cat once more.

Ryker pressed his lips together in a thin line. "She's underweight, especially if she was a domestic cat."

"She probably lost some when she was abandoned." Harley couldn't help but nuzzle Nia's fur.

"You sure you don't need a cat?" Ryker asked slyly, his eyes twinkling again.

"I like animals. That's obvious. But no, I have enough at the farm already..."

"Does Fluffypaws solicit the cat pictures to see if the cat was lost and is missing?"

Harley nodded as she set Nia down on the exam table. "They try, and they contact shelters and everywhere they can think of, but without a microchip it's hard to track anyone down."

Nia arched her back and rubbed herself against Harley's arm, her little tail ramrod straight and flicking.

Ryker smiled again and chuckled as he reached out to pet Nia's head. *"Comment vas-tu ma chérie?"*

"Did you just ask her how she was?" Harley asked.

"Oui. Actually, I asked 'how you doing, my sweet girl,' because she is very affectionate."

Nia was rubbing herself against Ryker now, and Harley could feel her insides warming by the way he was looking at the cat.

Jason may have been charming and swept her off her feet, but he hadn't been this way with the animals.

He'd been gentle with them, but it was all business.

Harley was a firm believer that animals knew when there was a decent human around. They could sense who was kind and caring. Nia obviously liked Ryker, and Harley couldn't help but smile as she watched him examine her.

The way he was gently talking to her and comforting her when she would let out a little meow... He loved animals just as much as Michel did.

Just as much as *she* did.

Their gazes locked once more, and she could feel the warmth creeping back up into her cheeks. She knew that she was 100 percent blushing in that moment. Why did she keep blushing around him?

It was highly annoying.

Well, you're not rambling. Take it as a win.

She looked away quickly, mortified that she had blushed in front of him again.

"She looks healthy. She's been spayed, I would guess about five years ago. So, we can age her at five years, given her teeth and the state of her coat, but that is just an approximation without previous vet records," Ryker said, petting Nia.

"If there were any," Harley mumbled.

Ryker cocked an eyebrow. "She's domesticated."

"Doesn't mean she was actually taken to a vet. Much. She's been spayed, but maybe not regular checkups and vaccinations."

Ryker nodded. "True. We'll give her a series of her regular vaccinations, if you could prepare them, and then we'll microchip her."

"You want me to vaccinate her?" Harley asked.

"Were you not going to do just that before I agreed to come along?"

"Right, it's just usually when a vet is here that's not Michel or..." She paused, because she'd been about to say Jason's name, and she didn't want to think about her ex. Not in this moment and not any moment of the day.

Ryker's eyes widened. "Or?"

"I mean, besides Michel, other volunteer vets just have me fetch things," she said instead.

Ryker made a face, one that looked like he didn't quite believe her. "That is not right. You're qualified?"

"Yes."

"Then you can do it and I will make notes. Have you done a microchip on your own before?"

"Actually, no," Harley admitted. Microchipping was fairly easy and vets she worked with did that job.

"Well, I will show you how. Then when I am not around and no other vet is, you can help the rescue out and do it yourself."

Her heart sunk a bit when he said that he wouldn't be around, and she really didn't know why. She barely knew him and no one really stuck around in Opulence, so why was she so surprised? Why did it bother her so much? He was only here for a short time. The fact he wasn't staying shouldn't affect her, but it did and she was annoyed at herself.

Get it together, Harley. He's showing you a valuable skill.

Ryker held on to Nia while Harley prepared all the medicine and then grabbed some treats to help occupy Nia from her shots. Ryker petted and soothed Nia as Harley injected the cat for rabies, FeLV and FVRCP, which was a combo vaccine that helped with feline rhinotracheitis virus, feline calicivirus and feline panleukopenia. The FeLV was to help protect Nia against the feline leukemia virus. Next came the Bordetella, which was administered by drops in the nose.

Ryker held Nia's head and she protested. Harley leaned over him, trying not to think about how close he was to her, how she could smell his clean hair, feel the warmth of his skin or how his breath tickled the side of her neck. How her insides were flipping around, her pulse racing and her ears drumming with the beat of her quickened heart rate.

She administered the drops as quickly as she could. Nia

sneezed a few times, not liking the feeling of the drops in her nose, but it was important. She needed Bordetella because Nia was boarding with other animals and they didn't want kennel cough to spread through everyone at the shelter. It was highly contagious.

Nia took the vaccines in her stride and Ryker fed her some treats.

He got the easy part of the job.

Harley disposed of the used syringes and the Bordetella eye dropper in the yellow medical waste bin and then washed her hands.

"Can you hold Nia?" Ryker asked. "And I'll grab what's needed for the microchip."

Harley nodded, not making eye contact with him, because her heart was still racing as she recalled how it felt to be so close to him, how her body reacted.

This was not how a professional behaved, and she was annoyed at herself.

Ryker grabbed everything needed, including the little chip that he loaded into a little blue syringe with a long needle and then a scanner to read the chip once it was implanted. The chip itself was the size of a grain of rice.

"Michel lent this to me," Ryker said. "This is the easy part of microchipping."

"What's the hard part?"

"Paperwork." He winked at her.

"I see," she said, chuckling. "So you want me to register it?"

Ryker grinned, a little devilishly, and it made her heart beat a bit faster. "That would be most helpful. First though, you can inject the chip."

He held out the syringe and Harley took it.

"Grab some of the loose skin on Nia's shoulder," Ryker instructed.

"Like this?"

"*Bonne*. Now, insert the needle and inject the microchip. It's very quick."

Harley inserted the needle and Nia barely flinched. She pushed the depressor of the syringe down and then pulled the needle out.

"That was easy. I don't know why I thought it would be harder." Probably because Jason always insisted on doing it. Even the paperwork, because she wasn't a vet. Back then she never thought anything of it.

Ryker scanned the chip and the information popped up on his computer, everything to register Nia.

"It populates with the chip information," Ryker stated, pointing to the computer screen. "We'll register it all over to Fluffypaws and Christine, then when Nia is adopted it will be transferred over to the new owner."

Harley leaned over him to get a better look at the computer screen.

She was aware again of being so close to him, but when she realized that her breasts were pressed against his back, she froze.

What are you doing?

Ryker's body tensed under hers and she jumped back quickly.

"It looks great. All official and stuff. Registration is so cool," she said.

Really, Harley?

Ryker looked amused. "*Oui.* Very official."

"Do you want me to fill out the information?"

"No. I'll fill this out. Why don't you take Nia back to Christine. Fill her in and then bring the next cat?" Ryker turned and looked back at his computer screen.

"Of course." Harley scooped up Nia and headed to the door.

She had made it awkward and uncomfortable by getting too close.

Ryker had no interest in her, and she needed to keep things professional.

And she certainly didn't want to fall for someone else who might leave. She was not going to put her heart on the line again for anyone.

If she made time to date, she kept it casual and brief.

She had learned her lesson. There were no happily-ever-afters. There were no fairy tales.

Not for her.

Even if she was starting to suspect she secretly still wanted there to be.

CHAPTER FOUR

THEY FINISHED WITH the cats at Fluffypaws Rescue and got into a good rhythm of working together. It was seamless and comfortable. Nice, even. The rest of the cats and the kittens were in fairly good health. Vaccines, drops and other medicines were administered. Other than instructions of what needed to be done and some more microchipping, all banter and unnecessary chatting ended.

It was cool.

It was professional.

Isn't that what you wanted?

Which was true.

Ryker was a stranger. Even if he was Michel's son-in-law, Harley had never met him before today. She only knew him through stories Michel had told her, which hadn't been much. She never got too physically close when she was working, especially with a man she barely knew. What had she been thinking?

She hadn't been. That was the issue.

Ryker had spoken with Christine and Dave about spaying and neutering the cats that needed it at Michel's clinic in Opulence, free of charge—Fluffypaws didn't have the operating room he needed to do it.

Ryker had said that he wanted to win over the locals, and offering free veterinary services to a beloved cat rescue was the right way to do it. If Harley didn't know any better, she could've sworn Ryker was going to end up with his name on Fluffypaws's gigantic cross-stitch.

The cats for the barn program were too agitated, and Ryker had made arrangements to also have feral cats seen at Michel's clinic for later in the week. They finished at a decent time at the cat rescue, which Harley was relieved about because she had to head home for that grooming appointment. And the sooner she left, the better. The tension was getting to her. She was tired of blushing and rambling on when she did open her mouth.

She groaned inwardly thinking about the mess she had made by pressing her breasts against Ryker's back. By getting too close with a man she barely knew.

It had obviously made him uncomfortable, from the way his spine stiffened, but she was grateful that he'd brushed it off, like nothing had happened.

Harley was kind of mortified by how she acted. She never usually acted that way around men, even if she found them attractive. Not since Jason.

When she met Jason she'd thought he was so sexy, so handsome and charming. The only difference was Jason hadn't backed away from her awkwardness. He had asked her out to dinner the first night they met and completely romanced her.

Physical attraction did not equal love. She knew firsthand.

She had learned how to keep her heart safe and protected, by not putting herself out there.

So why couldn't she stop thinking about Ryker? Probably just because he was the first man since Jason she had been attracted to.

She had to get over this.

Do you? What if you date him and find out?

Harley snorted at that foolish thought. There was list of several reasons she couldn't date Dr. Ryker Proulx.

1. He was her tenant.
2. He was Michel's son-in-law and Daphne's widower.
3. He was a vet.

4. He wasn't staying beyond summer.
5. Because she really just couldn't take another heartbreak.
6. They had to work together.
7. And who said he was interested in her?

She could probably go on and on, but really there was no good reason to even dream of the idea that they could be together. It just wouldn't work.

Why not?

Harley ignored that little voice in her head. After Jason, she never even considered getting back into a relationship. She focused her energy on building her business. And she didn't really have time to date anyway, which was fine by her.

She wouldn't trust anyone else with her heart.

It had taken a couple of years to really get over the embarrassment of being left at the altar, of having her heart broken in front of her friends and family. Wherever she went for the first few months after the breakup, people would give her a sympathetic look or pat her on the back and tell her to cheer up.

People pitied her, and she hated that with every fiber of her being.

So, no. She was not going to fall into that trap again. Ryker was an out-of-towner, which meant all the big red flags for her heart were standing at attention and waving the word *NO*.

She waited out in the parking lot as Ryker made some arrangements with Christine.

"Everything sorted out?" she asked as he loaded a bag in the back of her truck.

"Almost." He hesitated for a moment. "Would you like to get a drink?"

Her breath caught in her throat. She wanted to, but she had a groom.

"I can't. I've got to get you back to Michel's because I have a client. Maybe another night? We could do a barbecue or something." She winced. A drink was a lot different than a dinner.

"A barbecue would be nice," he said, climbing into the truck. "Your place or mine?"

She laughed. "I'm sure we can figure it out."

They both waved at Christine and she started her truck.

"It's peaceful here," Ryker remarked a little way into the drive. "I grew up in the city. My parents didn't have much use for the country."

"Didn't?" she asked, glancing at him. "Did they pass away?"

He nodded. "My father died while I was in school. My mother passed away just after Justin was born."

"I'm sorry." How horrible for him. First his parents and then his wife.

"What about your parents?" he asked.

"Alive. Plus my older brother David. He lives north of here. They're very much into interfering in my life."

Ryker snickered. "That's what family does."

"I'm sure Michel meddles too, since he does with me and I'm not even family."

"You know my father-in-law well."

"He's been my biggest supporter. I hate that he's going to retire."

She pulled into Michel's driveway.

"Thanks for the ride," Ryker said. "I'll see you tomorrow."

"Yes." She nodded quickly.

"Good night." He closed the door, grabbed his gear and headed around the back of Michel's house.

Harley raced back home and as she pulled into her driveway Ross was waiting for her. His dogs, Mookie, Aspen and Denver were all waiting in the back of his truck. Mookie was an energetic chocolate Lab that thought she was more horse than dog. She loved everyone, but she'd run you over without a second thought. She barrelled through unsuspecting people all the time, but always followed up with a tail wag and a lick.

Aspen was a yellow Lab with a pink nose, elderly and respectful, but she liked to steal loaves of bread and get sick from snarfing them down in one sitting. She was a smart dog, but not when it came to eating food she shouldn't, especially food that would give her stomach troubles.

Denver was the Boston terrier and sort of the alpha hole of the odd little pack of "mutts" that Ross and his wife owned. Denver was a spoiled prince, cute as anything with big googly eyes and a scrunched-up face, but he could be a bit of a dick.

"Sorry I'm early," Ross said as she pulled up beside his truck. "My wife is working late and I have my little girl to pick up. I was just about to bring them in to Kaitlyn."

"No problem. Sorry I'm a little behind. I was at Fluffypaws helping out the new vet."

Ross cocked an eyebrow. "New vet?"

"Michel's son-in-law is here for the summer to help out," Harley explained.

"That's good to know," Ross said, rubbing a hand over his bald head before slamming a Jays ball cap back on. "I hate driving forty minutes to a vet when Aspen eats something she shouldn't."

"Well, maybe he'll stay," Harley offered optimistically. Maybe if Ryker saw how awesome the people were here and how much he was needed, he'd take over the practice. She still doubted it—why would he leave everything he knew in Montreal?—but Ross didn't need to know that piece of information.

Kaitlyn came out with leads and leashed Mookie. Aspen was a smart old gal, and she just followed her energetic little goon of a sister into the barn. Harley scooped up Denver, who snorted at her with his smooshed-up face and sort of rolled his big, bulgy eyes at her in derision at being manhandled.

"Same treatment as usual?" Harley asked, knowing that Ross needed to rush off to pick up his daughter.

"Please. When should I come back?" Ross asked.

"Give me three hours," Harley responded, glancing down at Denver whose buggy eyes were now giving her serious side-eye…which meant that it might take a wee bit longer. "On second thought, can I get three and half?"

Ross chuckled. "Sure. I'll come by after dinner."

He got into his truck and drove away. She carried Denver into the kennel and got him settled with his siblings, so that she could prepare her room for the groom. She liked to take one dog at a time, or else it would be utter chaos. Especially with this group.

The outside security camera chimed that another car was turning into the driveway. She checked her security camera to see that Toby's mom had pulled up in her truck.

"Don't worry, I got it," Kaitlyn called out as she raced by to the reception area. "I can stay late tonight to help with the Ross crew too."

"You're a gem, Kaitlyn!" Harley shouted over her shoulder.

She was really going to be sad when Kaitlyn left, even if it was inevitable.

No one stayed.

Except her.

And even she had left for a time, but only to work toward her dream. She'd always planned to return.

Harley released Willow from her pen, and the little dog trotted along happily behind her, but sneezed a few times to let her know that she wasn't particularly pleased to have been hanging out in the kennel for most of the afternoon.

Not that Harley could blame her.

"Sorry," Harley offered apologetically. "It's been a busy day."

And it still wasn't over.

After her grooms were done, she and Willow would go check on the alpacas and make sure that they were bedded down for the evening and then make their way to the mob of chickens. Willow would usually sit back a fair distance as the chickens were contemptuous and Willow wasn't that much taller than the rooster.

Her last job for the night would be to make sure the rental was ready to go for the arrival of Ryker and his son tomorrow.

Then she could have a late supper, a shower and start this whole process all over again…which just solidified the resolve in her brain that she didn't have time to date, let alone give more than a passing thought to an attractive man.

Her animals, her business and her farm were more important.

Her brain didn't have time for thoughts of romance.

Doesn't it?

Stupid brain.

Ryker wasn't sure what made him ask Harley out for a drink. He dwelled on it as he watched her drive away, needing a moment to collect himself before heading inside to see his son. It had been a long time since he even thought about going out for a drink after work.

Maybe it was because Justin was with his grandparents. It had been hours since his son had last texted him, and even then it had been different from his usual texts, which all worried about where he was.

So he forgot himself and asked Harley out.

It was freeing.

Maybe bringing Justin here would be good for *him* too? Ryker knew he would have a job. Michel wanted him to take over the clinic in Opulence. It could be *his* clinic.

That's absurd.

He couldn't leave Montreal. It was their home. And he certainly couldn't uproot his son unless Justin wanted it.

He shook those thoughts away.

Ryker had texted Michel earlier to confirm a good time to do the remaining feral cat procedures, but Michel had replied that he needed to clear the date with Harley, because she was the vet tech that Michel had hired on an as needed basis. If she wasn't available to help then it was all a moot point, since the other vet techs that he had employed in the past had either retired or moved on to other clinics that could offer them more hours.

Then, distracted, Ryker had completely forgotten to ask her before she drove off.

Maudit.

That was unusual for him. He just got so caught up in being himself around her.

Not a vet.

Not a father.

Just him. It was refreshing. Coupled with the fact he was so drawn to her and he didn't know why.

When Harley had leaned over him, it had caught him off guard only because it had ignited every nerve end in his body. She was so warm, so soft, and he'd resisted the urge to spin around in that office chair and pull her onto his lap. Which was a very bad thought to be thinking about someone he barely knew, but it had crossed his mind. Every touch, every look, everything she said made him like her more and more.

He wanted her and that surprised him. Even though he'd only known her a day, it felt like he'd known her longer. He wasn't sure why.

It was easy to work with her. And he enjoyed her incessant chatter.

Michel had not been wrong. Harley was excellent at her job.

Honestly, he thought she belonged in a clinic full time and he couldn't help but wonder why she didn't continue her studies and become a vet. She had a way with animals.

That's none of your business.

For one brief moment he thought about what it would be like to run the Opulence clinic alongside her.

It thrilled him and terrified him at the same time, but he was being silly thinking this.

Harley wouldn't give up her successful business to work solely with him. No matter how much he would like that.

It wasn't his place to question her, and usually he wouldn't really concern himself with what another person was doing. But for some reason he really did want to know more about Harley. And that was troubling to him.

He'd never thought he would ever really think about another woman again, at all. He'd had passing fancies for women he found attractive, but never acted on them because his whole world was Justin and making sure that his son had everything he needed because he had lost his mother.

Justin needs a family.

Ryker sighed deeply as that thought skittered across his mind. Justin did need a family.

It had been just him, Daphne and Justin in Montreal.

And when Daphne got pregnant with their second, they'd talked about living a simpler way of life. They talked about moving to Huron County, but then Daphne had died and Ryker just threw all those plans and dreams he had made with her away, because it was too painful to think about carrying them on without her.

Yet, here he was, in the place they'd talked about moving to, because Justin was lonely. Justin had been only seven, but the grief was so real for him still. Ryker tried to be everything for Justin, but he saw that his son needed more.

Montreal was a great city. It was their home. He had his career there, and so many precious memories were layered in every fiber of their life in that city. Yet, it was the same here. He had visited Michel and Maureen with Daphne; he remembered her stories as she'd go over pictures.

There had been Christmases in Goderich with Michel, Maureen and Lexi whenever Lexi had flown in from out west.

Daphne's older brother, Tomas, was only an hour away in the city of London, and Tomas had four boys who Justin loved playing with.

Ryker was the foreign one here.

Unfamiliar.

He just hoped this summer could help cheer Justin up. Maybe a trip back here could become an annual thing.

Ryker walked up the driveway of Michel and Maureen's condo, a semidetached bungalow that was just outside the town of Goderich. It was an adult lifestyle community, which was why Justin and he couldn't couch surf for too long. They couldn't stay the whole summer—neither one of them was fifty-five plus.

The community of condos, like his in-laws' and some larger single modular homes, was on top of the bluff. From Michel's place there was an unobstructed view of Lake Huron and the west coast of Ontario's spectacular sunsets.

The community also had its own private beach and from the beach towels waving in the evening sun, he could tell that Justin and Nanna had had a beach day. Maureen had needed his car to drive down the bluff to the beach.

Michel was on the back deck, and Ryker could see smoke rising from his barbecue.

Oh no.

Michel was a brilliant veterinarian and surgeon, but he was no cook.

"Dang!" Michel cursed.

"Did you burn yourself again, Gramps?" Justin called out.

"Just a small scorch," Michel answered jovially.

Ryker chuckled to himself, spinning his key fob around his index finger as he opened the back gate to head into the backyard, dreading whatever burned dinner Michel was cooking up.

"Pappa!" Justin shouted happily.

Ryker set down his gear and held out his arms as his son, still wearing his swimming trunks and still damp, jumped off the low level deck for a hug.

"You are still damp, my friend," Ryker teased as he set his son down. "Have you turned into a fish?"

Justin laughed. "A little. Gramps told me that you rented us a cottage! Is it on the lake?"

"No, it's close to town. Where your mama grew up," Ryker replied. "It's on a farm though, with dogs, chickens and alpacas."

Justin's eyes widened excitedly. "Really?"

Ryker's heart melted. It had been a while since he had seen Justin this excited.

This happy.

This was a good sign.

He let out an internal sigh of relief. It felt like all this weight had fallen off his shoulders. There was a faint glimmer of the little boy he remembered.

Unburdened and having fun.

Ryker nodded. "There's a forest and a creek. There's a trail to ride your bike."

"That sounds great! When are we going there?" Justin asked.

"Tomorrow morning." Ryker tousled his son's hair, relieved Justin wasn't upset about moving out of his grandparents' condo. He climbed up the steps of the deck with Justin bouncing up and down excitedly beside him, completely thrilled about the idea of a farm.

"I'm going to tell Nanna!" Justin bounded into the house and Ryker took a seat in a wooden Muskoka chair to watch Michel butcher dinner on the barbecue.

"So, have you cleared a time that Harley can come help you at the clinic for the cats?" Michel asked.

"No. I texted her, but she has not responded."

"She's probably grooming. She mentioned having to groom three dogs tonight."

"Hopefully she'll get back to me," Ryker said offhandedly. He was hoping it could be a simple text exchange so that he didn't have to talk to her, because he could not get her out of his head.

The softness of her skin, the way her breasts had pressed against his back. It had ignited his blood. He had wanted to taste her pink lips and run his hands through her golden hair. It had overwhelmed him, how much he wanted her in that moment, so he'd pulled back as fast as he could.

Yet, even now, just thinking about that, it all came rushing back, lighting his blood on fire.

"I doubt she'll get back to you tonight. She'll have chores. If you need to confirm with her tonight, you might as well drive out there after dinner and talk to her face-to-face," Michel stated, interrupting his thoughts.

"Talk to her?" Ryker asked, surprised.

Michel gave him a quizzical look. "Yes. Is that a problem?

I thought you two would get along. You worked well together this afternoon, right?"

"*Oui*. She's competent…and she's…" He trailed off, not sure what to say next. As much as he wanted to keep his distance from Harley, it would be hard to do that when he was living at her farm and working with her and when he apparently randomly asked her out for a drink.

And he wanted to fix an appointment for the cat rescue. He needed to firm up the date for Fluffypaws, and if he had to discuss it with Harley in person, then so be it. Tomorrow was all about moving and making sure that Justin settled in all right. He wanted to answer Christine and let her know about those dates as soon as possible, so he could give his son his full attention tomorrow. He wanted it all sorted and booked, and he didn't want to leave an awkward phone message, so there was no real reason not to go and get the appointment figured out.

Perhaps he could bring some of his things over tonight too, and save them an extra trip tomorrow.

"*D'accord*. I'll go to the farm after dinner."

Michel was chuckling to himself.

"What?" Ryker asked.

"You said she's 'competent.'" Michel made air quotes.

"So?" Ryker asked, puzzled.

"She's more than competent. Don't ever tell her she's mediocre and don't have her fetch coffee."

Ryker smiled. "I know. She warned me."

Michel closed the lid of the barbecue and headed into the house for something.

Ryker sat back in the Muskoka chair and stared out over the lake and the sun that was slowly setting. It wouldn't fully set until well after eight, so it's not like he would be headed to her place in the dark.

Even though he really didn't want to see Harley tonight, he would. He knew deep down the best thing for him to get her out of his thoughts was to keep her at arm's length, and going to her place after dinner was doing the exact opposite of that.

Still, this was a professional discussion. It was work related and nothing more. They would be friendly coworkers. He would keep it completely platonic.

He could do that. Couldn't he?

CHAPTER FIVE

AFTER ATTEMPTING TO eat Michel's rubbery, burned steaks for dinner, Ryker headed over to Harley's farm. He felt somewhat foolish driving out there tonight, especially when he was moving in tomorrow morning, but he really needed to focus on making sure that Justin adjusted to the move, and he wanted to also make sure that everything was set up and arranged for Fluffypaws at Michel's clinic.

There were a lot of moving pieces and Harley was the most important, it seemed.

He had to make sure she had time on her schedule as well. And he was still kicking himself for not asking about it on their drive back to Michel's place.

When he parked in her driveway, he could see that she was outside. The sun was setting behind a line of towering spruce trees, casting a golden orange light across the yard. There was a rustling sound, whispering through the low hanging boughs of the spruce trees. He always liked that sound. It made him relax, and it just made the world feel so serene.

He could listen to the wind in the trees for hours. Maybe it could be peaceful for him and Justin here.

Maybe you could be happy here?

The perfect image was interrupted by a couple of curses, and he watched the scene outside the chicken house in amusement as Harley attempted to herd a very unruly flock of hens and a couple of roosters. It was anything but the perfect pastural snippet of serenity.

"Cluck Norris Jr., you son of a..." Harley shouted as a large gingery-and-black-colored rooster flapped his wings after her. Then it hit him—did she say Cluck Norris...junior?

"Bonjour," he called out, so he didn't startle her and end up on top of her again.

Would that be so bad?

He groaned at the thought. It wouldn't be, but that's not what he was here for.

Harley's head snapped up, and the chickens took the opportunity to continue their scratching and pecking at the ground instead of heading into the henhouse for the night to roost.

"Dr. Proulx, can I help you?" she asked, surprised.

"Please, just call me Ryker. I prefer that to the formal." Which was true. Only new patients called him Dr. Proulx. Once they got to know him, it was Ryker and that's the way he liked it. It was a bit odd to hear her call him Dr. Proulx. Especially given they were going to be living on the same property and most likely interacting on a regular basis.

As much as he'd like to keep her at arm's length, he wasn't sure how that was going to work out. Not when he needed a vet tech. Friends was a good compromise.

Pink flushed in her cheeks, only momentarily. "Ryker, then. How can I help you?"

"Actually, I need to talk to you about something."

"Now?" she asked, glancing back at her chickens and giving a glare to the rooster who had cornered her.

"If we could. I did drive all the way out here."

"You could've texted." She crossed her arms, stating the obvious. There was a whisper of a smile playing on her lips.

"I did, but you didn't respond and I need an answer sooner rather than later."

"Sure," she replied quickly, but he could tell she was just being polite. She was annoyed that her chore was being interrupted, and he did feel slightly bad. She had changed out of her scrubs and was now wearing overalls, with an oversize purple hoodie that had an outline of Lake Huron plastered on the back.

She stepped over the fence and walked toward him, her arms crossed over her chest. He turned his gaze away so that he wasn't looking at her chest directly, or remembering the way her breasts felt against his back.

He wasn't going there again.

He was here for business, not to think about how adorable she looked in that oversize hoodie or how humorous it was to see her conversing with her chickens.

"Is it about tomorrow?" she asked, breaking through his thoughts.

"Tomorrow?"

"Move-in day," she reminded him.

"What? No," he said. "It's about scheduling a time for you to come into the clinic to help me with the Fluffypaws feral cats. We have to neuter them and sedate them to give them a thorough health check."

"Oh," she said, letting out a sigh that sounded like relief. "I was worried it had something to do with moving in tomorrow. Wondering if you needed boxes or a cart."

"No. I'm good. Move in is still a go."

She cocked her head to the side. "Why didn't you just ask me this tomorrow?"

"Fair point," he agreed, smiling gently. "Honestly, it's because I have to make sure that my son settles here tomorrow, so I need to be there for him. And I thought it would be good to get it on the calendar tonight. I know your business and farm keeps you busy."

A strange expression, almost one of gratitude mixed with surprise washed over her face. "Thanks. Other vets Michel brought in, in the past, would just schedule things without my input. So I appreciate you asking."

"What happens if you can't make it in?" he asked, curious.

"They find another vet tech or they reschedule." She grinned wickedly and then pulled out her phone. "I can do this Friday, in the morning. I don't have any grooms that day, and both my employees are here to watch the dogs I will have boarding for the weekend."

Ryker typed it into his phone. "Do you think six in the morning will be too early for Christine and Dave to bring the cats?"

"No, they'll be fine."

"You're sure?" he asked, hesitating because not too many people liked early-morning appointments.

"Christine and I are good friends. She'll be thrilled you're doing this for her. I'll text her and let her know."

"*Merci.* That's fantastic." He turned back toward his car, but then turned around and before he could stop himself from offering, he blurted out, "Do you need my help herding up the chickens? I mean, I did interrupt you."

Her blue eyes widened. "You're offering me help with my horde?"

"Don't you mean flock?" he asked, trying not to chuckle.

"Sure, I mean that's what a big group of chickens is technically called, but these chickens are a horde in every sense of the word. They're mean." Harley had put an emphasis on the word *mean.*

"Then why do you have them?" Now he was amused by this whole prospect.

She shrugged. "Well, I like them. They're dicks, but I like having them around. Plus eggs are good. So, yeah, sure, if you want to help. I need to get them into their chicken coop for the night so that they're not carried off by foxes or coyotes or whatever else wants a bloodthirsty chicken."

Ryker laughed. "This description of them is not really helping your case."

Harley grinned wide, her blue eyes twinkling in the dimming light. "No, but I want to be transparent."

"Fair enough." Ryker followed her and climbed precariously over the fence.

A couple of the chickens stopped pecking to watch him warily. He noticed that there were three roosters. Which was unusual.

"Watch out for Cluck Norris Jr. He kicks a mean…kick," she warned as she walked toward the far edge of the flock.

"Which one is—" A shock wave of pain went up his shin, and he spun around to see a rooster clawing, scratching and flapping his wings. *"Merde!"*

Harley was laughing to herself. "See, Cluck Norris Jr. Aptly named because of his high kicks."

"Why junior?" he asked.

"He has an uncle out east called Cluck Norris. So I had to name him after his uncle."

"And the other two roosters?" he asked, taking a step back before Cluck Norris Jr. could line himself up and plant another kick to his already bruised leg.

"Count Cluckula is that fancy rooster. Actually he's an Appenzeller Spitzhauben, which is incredibly rare here in Canada."

"A what?" Ryker asked, as he looked at Count Cluckula who was a white-and-black-speckled rooster with a high coif of beautiful speckled caramel feathers, almost like a pompadour on top. It was very fancy indeed.

"It's a Swiss breed, but I figure Switzerland is famous for chocolate." Harley dived for a couple of hens and got them headed up the ramp. "And it's near Transylvania…sort of. Anyways, he's really no threat. He just likes the ladies."

Ryker chuckled to himself as he herded Count Cluckula into the chicken coop. "And the final rooster?"

"Wyatt Chirp, because he doesn't crow. He just chirps," Harley stated as they were herding the last of her horde into the coop.

"He chirps? Is he injured?"

"No, but Cluck Norris is a jerk and every time Wyatt would crow he'd get a kick and a peck. So, now he chirps and mostly keeps the peace among the hens."

Wyatt let out a pathetic half crow, half chirp before flapping his feathers and heading inside.

"There," Ryker proclaimed triumphantly. "They're all in."

Just as the words came out of his mouth there was a fluttering of feathers and then he felt a sharp jab to the back of his knee, a peck, and he fell down, straight into a pile of chicken excrement.

Why did this have to happen again?

A string of expletives left his mouth, and then he regretted using such strong language. It had been some time since he really cursed like that. He couldn't cuss around Justin, though there were times when he felt like it.

Harley grabbed Cluck Norris Jr. "One day, my friend, we'll make sure you're fried Texas style."

She tossed the rooster into the chicken coop where he flapped his wings to a gentle landing. He looked back at them and made eye contact with Ryker before Harley locked the chickens in their coop for the night.

"That bird," he mumbled.

Harley was grinning, her eyes twinkling as she held out her hand. "Come on, you can clean up in my place and I'll make you a tea. I'm sorry you've fallen twice at my place into a pile of poop in less than twenty-four hours."

"Yes. It seems like a coincidence."

Or a curse.

Harley chuckled. "Come on, let me help you up."

Ryker took her hand and she pulled him up. They were standing so close, he could see the top of her head, just below his chin, and he could smell the clean scent of her shampoo. It smelled like melons and something else.

It reminded him of summer.

His pulse was pounding between his ears and he was fighting that overwhelming urge to kiss her in the middle of this chicken yard. It almost could've been considered a romantic moment, if he wasn't covered in chicken crap.

What're you doing?

This was not keeping it professional. Far from it. Instead, he took a step back.

"I don't think you want me in your house," he said. "I'm disgusting."

"And I don't think you'll want to sit in that nice luxury sedan of yours and have it smell like chicken crap. I can give your clothes a quick wash and dry. While you're waiting I'll scramble you eggs and you can imagine that you're eating Cluck Norris Jr. for revenge. Or I could make you some tea."

Ryker laughed. "I don't want to picture that, but tea would be great. I just had dinner, so I'll pass on revenge eggs."

Although he shouldn't go into her house, she was right. He didn't want the leather seats of his car to get ruined and have the lingering smell of barnyard in his car for days after. Then again, given how the tiny home was not that far from the chicken coop, he was probably going to smell it anyways and he would have to get on good terms with Cluck Norris Jr., Count Cluckula and the very bullied Wyatt Chirp.

Why did I invite him in?

That's what she was asking herself as she put the kettle on to boil while Ryker's pants were in the dryer. It hadn't been too bad to clean off the chicken mess, so to save time and on his insistence, Ryker hand-washed his jeans in her laundry sink and then tossed them in the dryer for a quick cycle.

Now, he was sitting at her kitchen table with a beach towel wrapped around his waist. Willow, who had already greeted him and got several pets, was now snoring away on the couch, on her back with her legs wantonly spread out. Ryker had just laughed at her and called her a little goof.

She had only been half paying attention to that because she was very well aware that he was pants-less, in her kitchen. When he had pulled up in her driveway he was dressed casually, but his jeans were pressed and obviously designer.

It was a city mouse, country mouse situation. She couldn't

remember the last time she thought to iron jeans. Probably never. Actually, he was the first person she'd met who did.

She hadn't expected him to offer help with the chickens. No one ever did—at least, not more than once. No one ever offered again after Cluck Norris Jr. was done with them. She felt bad about his clothes, but it had also been quite comical.

Then she'd helped him stand up and he had been so close. She could smell his cologne. It was subtle, but she liked that spicy scent of his and she had just stood there, the pit of her stomach swirling, half expecting him to kiss her. Even though she wanted nothing romantic to do with him, she was shocked that she had wanted his kiss.

Harley had been relieved when he stepped away, breaking the spell.

At least, on her end. Because she was pretty sure that he wasn't feeling anything toward her, and why would he?

The kettle whistled and she shook away all those invading thoughts about kissing him.

"How would you like your tea?" she asked, hoping her voice didn't catch.

"Just black is fine." Ryker was flipping through one of her farmer reports.

She poured hot water over the tea bag and then brought him the mug. She wasn't going to have tea this late, because she wouldn't be able to sleep at night if she did, so instead she poured herself a glass of water and then joined him at the kitchen table.

Ryker was still engrossed in the report.

"Find anything interesting?" she asked.

"A lot, actually." He set the report aside. "I've always been fascinated by farming. I'm sorry I helped myself. Rooting through your magazines."

"It's fine."

"Are you a farmer then too?"

"No. I don't really do farming," she said. "I rent out the

fields. Someone else plants whatever they want. I do have a tractor though."

"My son would like to see that," he said, smiling.

"I can show him." And she would be glad to show Michel's grandson around.

"I don't want to disrupt your life."

She shrugged. "It's no bother. I'm close with Michel, and you're both important to him, so I'd be glad to. I used to be friends with Lexi Van Dorp, but we've drifted apart. I knew Daphne a little too, but she was older."

His expression softened, but she could see the brief flicker of pain behind his eyes. "Did you?"

"I didn't know her well, but this is a small town."

"*Oui*. It is. I'm not used to it."

"It's peaceful. Maybe it'll grow on you."

He smiled, taking a sip of his tea. "So tell me, does Michel's clinic get a lot of large animal patients?"

"Some. Blyth's vet clinic is exclusively large animal, but Michel gets some. Have you ever had to do a C-section in minus forty?"

Ryker winced. "No."

"Stick around until calving time next February and you might," she teased.

"I think that is a pleasure I will miss out on." He sighed. "In my city clinic, C-sections are done in a comfortable operating room."

And there it was. Confirmation yet again that he didn't plan on staying. She knew that it would disappoint Michel that he couldn't hand over the reins of his clinic to Ryker and properly retire. The clinic would probably close, which would be so awful for the community.

It really wasn't her business, but maybe there was some way that she could convince Ryker to stay.

And why would you want that?

Harley ignored that little voice, telling herself that it wasn't for her, but for Opulence and the animals here. Someone needed to replace Michel full-time, but would Ryker really uproot his child? Probably not.

"So have you worked with large animals?" she asked, changing the subject from him leaving at the end of summer.

"A bit. I have delivered a few cows and a horse," he admitted, finishing his tea. "What kind of animals are farmed around here?"

"Mostly chickens," she joked, picking up his empty mug and taking it to the dishwasher.

He cursed under his breath, laughing softly. "And?"

"Pigs, but they're highly regulated. You won't really see them out wallowing in the muck."

"Biohazard risks. Swine flu, *oui*?" Ryker asked.

She nodded. "So, large animal vets fully versed in biohazard safety handle those pigs. There's also some dairy and cattle."

"I like cows."

"Me too. But my 'farm' is limited to the chickens and my rescue alpacas."

"I am aware," he remarked, dryly.

Warmth bloomed in her cheeks as she thought of their first meeting in the alpaca pen. "Right." They shared a smile.

"It can't be easy to look after all those animals and run your business. You are a woman of many talents."

She could feel the heat creeping up her neck. "Thanks."

The dryer dinged. "I guess that is my cue to go."

"Right. Thanks for your help with the chickens."

"My pleasure." He bowed slightly, in an exaggerated way that made her giggle quietly.

"So what time should I expect you and your son?" she asked, following him to the dryer.

"I think after breakfast. Around eight. Thank you for renting us the tiny home. It's perfect for us." He ducked into the bathroom and came out with his pants back on and placed the towel in the hamper.

"It's no problem." She crossed her arms again, taking a step back while he slipped on his shoes and jacket. It was dark out now, and there were fireflies fluttering in the long grass next to her barn. Their little lights winking on and off.

"I'll see you tomorrow. Good night, Harley," he said quietly.

"Good night, Ryker."

He waved as he stepped outside. She closed the door and watched him climb into his car and drive out onto the lane. Willow came trotting in from the living room and sneezed. Harley turned to look at her.

"You missed him."

Willow sneezed and shook her head again.

"You'll see him tomorrow. He's our new neighbor."

Temptation was her new neighbor, and someone she was going to be working with very closely over the summer. She had to keep reminding herself that she couldn't get caught up with someone who was going to leave. She was over Jason, but was she over the hurt of having a life-changing decision made for her, all because she was happy with life in Opulence?

No.

She wouldn't do that to herself ever again.

She couldn't open her heart to a temporary resident.

CHAPTER SIX

DESPITE AVOIDING CAFFEINE before bed and even though she was bone-weary exhausted, Harley's mind refused to shut down. She just tossed and turned. It was highly frustrating. All she could think about was Ryker and how she acted like a fool around him.

At least, she felt like she acted like a fool and that made her angry. At herself. She was better than this. Yes, her tendency to ramble was quirky and overly friendly, as her friends sometimes said, but she was usually able to keep it professional. It was only when Ryker was around that she felt kind of giddy and nervous and lost control completely.

Almost like she had a crush.

The last thing she wanted. There was no way she was going to let that happen again. She was way more guarded now. More protected.

More alone.

Yeah. There was no denying that. She had her animals, but no one to share her life with. This business had always been her end game, but part of that dream was also to have a loving partner, kids.

That was something she had mourned when Jason shattered her heart.

Even though she repeated the mantra in her head, all night, that Ryker was off-limits, she still couldn't sleep. Not well, anyway. Eventually, annoyed with her non-sleeping, Willow got up, heaved a huge sigh of disdain and left the bedroom for the couch downstairs.

When Harley got up that morning to do her rounds, she headed straight for the coffee and received some serious side-eye from Willow, who was looking at her with extreme accusation that she had interrupted her good night's sleep in the cushy bed.

"Sorry," Harley muttered to Willow as the dog trotted ahead of her outside so that she could relieve herself.

Usually, Willow would come to the barn to check on the alpacas and dogs, if they were boarding any, which they weren't at the moment, but after Willow did what she needed to do, she headed back to the mudroom door where Harley let her in.

"Traitor," Harley grumbled, as Willow slipped past her back into the house and headed straight for her comfy spot in the living room.

Harley was slightly envious because she would love to have a nap right about now, but the animals always came first and it was almost nine in the morning. The alpacas would be wondering where she was, and the chickens would have to be let out soon.

She dragged herself slowly across her driveway when she heard the sound of wheels on the gravel lane. Her heart did a little pitter-patter in the pit of her stomach as she recognized the dark sedan with the Quebec license plates.

Why is he here so early?

And then she remembered it was move-in day, and it wasn't that early. She was just late with her chores. He had even told her he'd be there early. What she needed to do right now was pull herself together.

Ryker slowed and rolled down his tinted window, and she tried to stifle a nervous yawn.

"Good morning," he said brightly, his gray eyes twinkling. "How are you?"

"Good." She was lying. She was exhausted. "How is your leg?"

"My leg?" he asked.

"From your attack last night," she teased.

"He has a big bruise!" A little voice spoke up from the back.

Ryker groaned and then rolled down the window in the back seat next to him. A little boy with reddish hair and big green eyes stared up at her. It took her breath away for a moment, because she saw Michel's eyes—Daphne's eyes—staring back at her.

"You must be Justin," Harley said, fighting the overwhelming emotions bubbling up inside her.

He looked so much like his mom.

"Yep," Justin responded.

"Justin, this is Harley Bedard." Harley waved as Ryker introduced her. "She's our landlord, and she owns this farm."

"Can I see the attack chicken?"

"Later," Ryker replied patiently. "We have to move in first."

Justin looked crestfallen.

"I promise, you're here for the summer so you will meet all the chickens," Harley said, trying to ease Justin's disappointment.

Justin smiled again and pumped his fist.

Harley turned back to Ryker. "Do you need anything from me?"

"I don't think so. Oh, the water and electricity are on, yes?"

Crap.

That's what she'd forgotten to do.

"No. So let me release my alpacas, and then I'll make my way to your place and show you how to power it all up."

"Sounds good." Ryker pulled away, slowly, headed down the lane to behind the chicken house where the bright turquoise tiny home sat.

Harley quickly made her way to her livestock barn, which housed the three rescue alpacas. It was only supposed to house two of them, Vince and Zuul, but then they had Gozer and honestly for one brief moment Harley thought, given the characters they were named after, the end of the world might actually come.

It didn't, but they were dramatic nonetheless and made their displeasure about her lateness well-known. She made sure they had feed in their outside trough, and water, then she climbed into their pen and let them out into their small outside pasture.

She wasn't wearing her headphones this time, so she wouldn't be startled by anyone sneaking up behind her.

She chuckled remembering that. So humiliating. At least Ryker had a good humor about it.

Then her blood heated as she remembered him on top of her.

Those gray eyes gazing into her eyes.

Get a grip.

After she took care of Ryker's needs at the rental, she'd come and muck out their stall and put down fresh bedding for the night. Thankfully, in summertime, there wasn't a whole lot she had to do. They were very content grazing in the long grasses of her small pasture.

She was going to be very quick about getting everything at the tiny house all set up so that she could give Ryker the space he needed with this son and keep her distance from him.

For a moment she thought again that it might be nice to have a nap, but then she snorted and laughed to herself as she made her way to Ryker's place for the summer.

A nap. What's that?

Ryker had the front door open and there were a couple of suitcases still sitting on the front porch. There was also a bike leaning up against the side of the house, and Justin was bouncing a basketball on the gravel lane.

He glanced up as she came over.

"There's a basketball hoop hanging off the side of the old barn with a small concrete pad if you want to play," Harley offered.

It had been there when she bought the property. The basketball hoop didn't have a net, but she just never bothered to take it down.

"Really?" Justin asked.

Harley nodded. "You don't have to just hang out in front

of this house. The only places I don't want you to go without adult supervision are the green building near the road and that fenced-in area. Oh, and the old barn has my rescue alpacas. It's best to keep away from them. Zuul is a bit protective of her baby right now."

"Dad," Justin shouted. "Can I go play basketball at the barn? Ms. Bedard said there's a hoop there."

Ryker stepped out of the house, ducking slightly. "You're okay with that? I don't want him to get in your way."

"It's fine." Which was true. Someone better get use out of the basketball hoop.

Justin looked so eager. Ryker pursed his lips together. "*D'accord*, but I want you to bring in the last of your things and set up your bed first."

Justin groaned and set his basketball down. "Fine."

Harley watched as he opened the back seat and pulled out a knapsack and a very weathered fleece blanket. Covered with dogs.

A lump rose in her throat as she saw it.

It was the no-sew fleece blanket that she had made for Justin, or rather she had sent it to Daphne for the baby shower she couldn't attend because she had been in school. Daphne had loved it and wrote her a lovely thank-you letter. When Justin had been born, Michel had sent her a baby picture.

"Can I see that?" Harley asked.

Justin nodded and handed her the blanket. The fleece had pilled, but it was still soft and it was obviously well loved. It made her overjoyed to know that.

"It's been my blanket since I was a baby," Justin said softly.

"I know," Harley whispered.

"How do you know?" Justin asked.

She grinned and handed Justin back the blanket. "I made it for you."

Ryker wasn't sure he registered what Harley was saying at first. He had been standing there processing how happy Justin seemed to be and how well he was interacting with Harley.

Justin often struggled with new people. He shied away. The fact that he was conversing with her, especially about his blanket, gave Ryker hope, and then she said she made it.

Her expression had sobered when she saw Justin's baby blanket. Daphne had received it at her surprise baby shower. They had been in Goderich visiting her parents and there was a baby shower, with a lot of friends and family. Presents had been sent from those who couldn't make it, and Ryker distinctly remembered when Daphne had opened that blanket. She had loved it so much and the day they had brought Justin home from the hospital, he had come home in that blanket.

It was Justin's safety and security. The thing he clung to the most, besides his dad.

And Harley had made it?

The blanket that Justin clung to when he learned his mother had died. The comfort and love that had been shared with that blanket. Ryker was trying to fight back the tears that were threatening to spill, because he didn't want Justin to see him cry.

"You made this?" Justin asked excitedly. "You knew my mom?"

Harley smiled at Justin. Ryker's breath caught in his throat. Watching her with his son melted his heart. Seeing his son so engaged, like he used to be.

Don't, a little voice warned.

She was off-limits.

"I did. Though, she was older than me. We grew up in the same town. Everyone knows everyone here."

Justin looked down at his blanket lovingly. "That's so cool."

"I think so," Harley remarked and then looked up at Ryker, and he couldn't help but smile at her tenderly. Even though he shouldn't, he couldn't help himself. It was cool, as Justin had said. Justin was so engaged. He couldn't remember the last time Justin had volunteered to play outside on his own. They'd only been here, in Opulence, a couple of days and Justin was almost back to his normal self.

He was happy.

Maybe it'll last? Maybe you can stay?

Ryker shook that thought away. There was no sense in getting ahead of himself. Better to take things one day at a time.

"Come on, Justin. Bring your stuff inside and then you can go play basketball," Ryker said, hoping his voice didn't break with all the emotions rushing around inside him.

"Right!" Justin grabbed his knapsack off the ground and tore into the house.

Ryker stepped outside and approached Harley, not sure of what to say. "I didn't know you were there at the baby shower."

"I wasn't," Harley said quickly. "I was at school, but I sent the gift. Bought the fabric from a fabric store on Queen Street, in the fabric district no less, then I put it together in my dorm room and mailed it to my mom, who took it to Michel's for the baby shower."

"Well, your present meant so much to Daphne and to Justin."

And to me.

Only he didn't say that part out loud.

"Well, I'm glad." Pink tinged her cheeks. He loved the way she blushed. It was endearing.

Enchanting.

"Right," he said hesitantly, breaking the tension that was simmering between them. "Power?"

"Yes," Harley responded. "Let me show you how to switch on the tiny home and all the buttons and stuff for the septic, water and solar panels."

"Solar panels?" Ryker asked in wonder.

"It's a tiny home," Harley teased. "Of course there's solar panels. It's a whole movement, this smaller scale living. It's environmentally friendly and green."

He chuckled. "Lead on."

Harley slipped off her rubber boots and he followed her into the house, confused about all these emotions she had stirred up in him with just a simple memory. Ryker wasn't one to believe in fate, but now he was questioning that disbelief, because it felt like something was tying him to Opulence.

To her.

Even after just a day. And he wasn't sure how he felt about that, because whether it was fate or not, he wasn't sure that this could be a forever home. Montreal was home.

Opulence wasn't.

CHAPTER SEVEN

RYKER HAD FOOLISHLY thought that Justin would want to spend the day with him. But the moment the bags were set in their respective rooms, or rather lofts, Justin grabbed his basketball and ran outside.

Ryker was pleasantly surprised. Actually, flabbergasted was a better word.

It took Justin a while to warm up to places and people now, and that was hard to watch, especially when Justin had been so adventurous before.

He thought it would take Justin longer to get settled into their new residence, because when they had been coming to Ontario to spend the summer Justin had been slightly nervous to leave Montreal.

Yet, there was a part of him that wasn't surprised by Justin taking to the tiny home on the farm property as fast as he did, because the moment they had pulled into Michel and Maureen's driveway after their eight-hour car ride, Justin was no longer nervous and had appeared to take to the idea of this summer in Huron County with gusto.

Apparently, this was no different. How could he say no when Justin eagerly asked to play basketball again?

Ryker couldn't.

It thrilled him to hear Justin's laughter again, the excitement in his voice about where they were staying.

Justin said he loved it.

All of it.

Ryker thought it would do.

He had to sometimes duck, in the cramped space, but surprisingly it was laid out quite smartly.

There were two lofts. One of them had stairs with storage drawers under each step. The other loft, which Justin had claimed as his hideaway, had a folding ladder. Ryker was fine by that, as he preferred the stairs.

The main floor of the tiny home had a modern kitchen with an island and there was a cozy living room with a couple of chairs, a television on the wall and a small wood burning stove that Ryker doubted they would be using. Under his loft, there was a beautiful bathroom that overlooked the fields and the forest.

Outside there was a covered porch with a wraparound deck and brightly colored Muskoka chairs. When he walked around the side, he found a small propane barbecue.

It was the perfect summer hideaway.

Ryker took a seat in one of the Muskoka chairs, where he could see that Justin was making use of the basketball hoop. He could hear the rhythmic dribbling and the sound of the ball bouncing off the backboard.

It had been a long time since he heard that sound. He closed his eyes, just listening to that sound. It was the first time in a while where Justin wasn't glued to his side, moping and fearful.

"Pappa! Look at me," Justin shouted.

Ryker cracked open an eye. "What, buddy?"

Justin did a trick shot. It bounced off the backboard and dropped in the hoop.

"See that, Pappa?" Justin exclaimed.

"C'est magnifique!"

Justin turned back to his game.

It was nice to have a moment to relax.

He could also hear the chickens, and for a moment he glared in direction of the chicken coop, knowing that Cluck Norris Jr. was there. Then he laughed as he thought of that ridiculous scene from last night, and then he thought of Harley again. Thought of her constant chatter.

Her smile.

Her laugh.

He couldn't help but wonder where she was.

He could hear some soft humming. Almost like a droning.

He got up and walked toward the old barn that had a fenced-in pasture. He could see that Harley was out there, and she was dragging a mineral lick. There were three alpacas in the grass, very interested in her and her work. The mineral lick looked heavy.

When he had startled Harley and she had pulled him down into their pen, he hadn't noticed how many alpacas usually occupied that space.

Now, he could get a good look at them. Leaning over the fence, he watched Harley interact with them.

Two adults and one little one.

He smiled as he watched the alpacas gently nudge her. Harley then dug in the pocket of her overalls and pulled out some carrots, which they happily lapped up from the palm of her hand with their waggling lips.

She had the touch when it came to animals.

It had been really apparent to him when they had worked together in the cat rescue. He didn't have to give her much instruction. Once he had shown her how easy it was to microchip the cats, she did it like a pro.

It was like she understood exactly what he needed in each moment. He had never worked with someone like that. Usually it would take years of working together before a vet tech could anticipate what he needed, but with her in that moment at the cat rescue, it was like they were in tandem.

She looked up and saw him leaning against the picket fence. "Everything okay?"

"It is. Do you need help?" he asked.

He'd thought he'd be hunkered down with Justin all day.

Now, he was unsure of what to do. Ryker had a hard time keeping still.

Harley cocked an eyebrow. "You're still dressed too nice. I will not be responsible for you falling in poop for a third time."

He laughed. "Fair enough."

She waded through the long grass toward him. "Where's your son?"

He nodded over his shoulder. "Basketball."

"Oh, good!" She crossed her arms. "I hope he likes it here."

"He seems to."

A car came roaring up the driveway; he could hear the gravel crunching.

Justin dropped his ball and came running toward him, spooked because it was someone he didn't know.

"Pappa!"

Ryker turned and walked quickly toward him. Justin cuddled up against him.

A farmer in green coveralls parked his truck. He looked like he had just come straight from the barn. There was straw all over him.

"Have you seen Harley?" the farmer asked.

"She's in the pasture." Ryker motioned over his shoulder.

"Thanks!" The farmer took off quickly, waving and calling Harley's name.

"What's wrong, Pappa?" Justin asked nervously, clutching his basketball closer.

"I don't know. Stay on the porch, *oui*?"

Justin nodded and ran toward their deck, but Ryker could tell Justin's anxiety was amped.

He made his way over to the farmer and Harley. She had her hands on her hips and was frowning, nodding.

"What's wrong?" Ryker asked.

"His cow is calving," Harley said tensely. "Or she's trying to."

Ryker was surprised. It wasn't calving season.

"I need your help, Harley. The large animal vet is on another farm. You've delivered calves before," the farmer pleaded.

"I have, but if she needs a C-section, I can't help you, Mel," Harley stated.

Mel nodded. "I know, but please come. I don't have the strength the pull the calf myself."

"Do you have a jack?" Ryker asked.

Mel nodded and then asked. "Who are you?"

Harley glanced at Ryker. "Mel, this Dr. Proulx, Michel's son-in-law. He's a vet. Can he tag along?"

Relief washed over Mel's face. "Please. Harley knows where I live. Hurry."

"Go, we'll be there," Harley reassured him.

Mel nodded and ran off to his truck.

"What about Justin?" Harley asked.

"He can come too," Ryker stated. There was no way he would be able to leave Justin alone with him so anxious, let alone leave him in a new place.

Justin often came with him to his practice when he had to work a weekend shift. Justin was not grossed out by veterinary medicine or squeamish at all.

"Do you have coveralls?" Harley asked.

"Ah, no."

"I do. Follow me."

Ryker motioned to Justin to come with them, and they followed Harley into the mudroom of her farmhouse. Willow came over and before he could say anything, boy and dog were on the floor and suddenly best friends forever. All that anxiety Justin had built up since Mel arrived seemed to melt away as his son buried his face in Willow's fur.

Harley was chuckling. "Willow loves kids."

"I can tell." A smile was tugging at the corners of his mouth as he watched his son and Harley's ridiculously tiny farm dog make friends. Willow was wagging her tail, or more to the point, her whole back end was wagging back and forth as she licked Justin's face. Justin was giggling and petting her.

"What's her name?" Justin asked.

"Willow," Harley replied as she turned to the armoire that was in her mudroom. "She seems to like you!"

"I like her!" Justin announced, his eyes shining as he petted Willow.

"So it seems," Ryker murmured.

"Can Willow come with us?" Justin asked hopefully.

"She sure can," Harley replied.

"Are you sure?" Ryker asked.

"You're bringing your kid. I'll bring mine." She winked. "It's fine."

"Yay!" Justin kissed Willow, which surprised Ryker.

Harley finished rummaging and handed him some green coveralls. "You can change in the bathroom. I have boots about your size too."

"Merci."

"I don't have boots for Justin though." Harley placed her hands on her hips, grinning as she smiled at his son and her dog.

"He won't come into the stall. He's come on calls with me and with Michel before," Ryker explained. "Besides, he has to stay with Willow, *oui*?"

Justin finally extricated himself from Willow's affection and dusted himself off. "I know what to do. I won't get messy, but I do have rubber boots at the tiny house!"

"Go get them then," Ryker said quickly.

Justin nodded and ran out the door. Willow whined, missing her new friend.

"You'll see him later," Harley replied to the dog, but Willow just sat at the back door, watching it and wagging her tail.

"I'll change." Ryker slipped into the small bathroom and quickly pulled off his nice clothes and then pulled on the one-piece coveralls. They looked like they hadn't even been used. He zipped them up.

He stepped out of the bathroom and she set a pair of rubber boots down in front of him.

"Merci," he said, slipping them on. "These are new coveralls. Why haven't you worn them?"

"Uh. They weren't mine," she said quickly. "They were my ex-fiancé's. He left them with me. I should've given them away, but moved them here when I bought this place."

A flare of jealousy coursed through him. He was surprised by the green-eyed monster rearing its ugly head.

She'd been engaged?

He wondered what had happened.

It was none of his business, of course. They were friendly, but they were still strangers.

"They're nice coveralls," he said, unsure of what to say and trying to change the subject, but not doing it well.

"Exactly. Come on. We'll take my truck. I already have a bunch of vet gear packed in the lockbox."

There was no arguing with that. Justin was waiting outside, so Ryker walked out of the house, allowing Harley to lockup. This wasn't the day he planned at all, but that didn't matter.

All that mattered was getting that calf safely delivered.

Harley didn't know what came over her, mentioning who'd owned the coveralls. She'd forgotten they were even there, but as she didn't have any other coveralls to lend Ryker, there was really no choice. At least he didn't ask her questions about her ex or the fact she was engaged. Not that she had anything to hide. She just didn't want any pity from him. She didn't need that.

Justin was happily chatting about Willow and the calf that wasn't born yet as they drove the two kilometers down the road to Mel's farm. Willow was leaned up against Justin, staring up at her new buddy adoringly.

Ryker glanced over his shoulder. "I think you've been replaced in your dog's affections."

Harley peeked in her rearview mirror and giggled. "I think so."

It warmed her heart to see Justin with Willow. It was nice.

"So this is not the usual time of year for a calf," Ryker remarked.

"No. You're right. It is a bit odd to have a cow calving in the summer, but Flossie is a new heifer and Mel's bull escaped and now they're having a summer calf. Flossie is a prize dairy cow."

Ryker grinned. "An escaped bull and a prize cow. Oldest story in the book."

"Flossie is worth a lot. The calf is probably worth something too, because the bull that is Flossie's baby daddy is a prize stud as well."

"I didn't realize there was so much farmyard drama around here."

"It's a regular Days of Our Livestock here." She laughed awkwardly at her own joke, but she was the only one who did. She could almost hear crickets from the silence that descended. Even Willow cocked her head to the side in confusion.

Ryker raised his eyebrows. "What?"

"A soap opera pun." She had to stop punning all over him.

"You tell terrible jokes," Justin quipped. "I like them."

Harley and Ryker both laughed at that.

"Well, I'm glad someone does," Harley said.

They pulled into Mel's yard and parked. He was waiting for them in the barn. Flossie had been fenced off in a pen with lots of hay, and right away Harley could see that the bag that contained the calf had burst.

"It's big," Mel stated. "I've delivered calves before, but none this big."

Ryker frowned and grabbed one of the gloves that Mel handed him. A long glove that he rolled over his sleeve and up his arm.

"Hang back here, Justin, with Willow," Harley instructed as she grabbed a glove and followed Ryker into the pen. She was very familiar with Flossie, and Ryker was a city vet with less large animal experience. She didn't know if he'd understand the nuances.

It only took a minute for her to realize that Ryker knew what he was doing. He was talking calmly to Flossie as she mooed, trying so hard to deliver her calf. He gently placed his hand up inside Flossie and felt around, then removed his arm.

"Well?" Harley asked.

"I can feel the head and the legs. The calf is in position, but it's large. Quite large. I think I'll use the calf puller."

"I'll get it," Mel said. "Come on, young man, you can help me. Bring Willow too."

"Okay." Justin leaped down from where he was hanging off the fence and followed Mel. "Come on, Willow!"

"Feel," Ryker suggested to Harley.

Harley nodded and slowly approached, following Ryker and doing what she had done countless times when she helped check local cows for pregnancies. She could feel the calf there—it was alive, for now, and Ryker was not wrong. It was a large calf. Flossie's womb contracted just then and Harley slipped her hand out.

A foot came forward, but then slowly went back.

It was clear that the calf was stuck.

"We're back, Pappa!" Justin called, following Mel as he brought the calf puller, sometimes called a calf jack.

"*Bonne.* Harley, hold Flossie while I get this ready."

"Right." Harley disposed of the glove and went around to Flossie's head, stroking and comforting the suffering heifer. "It'll be okay."

Ryker seemed to know exactly how to set up the jack behind Flossie. Harley always thought it looked horrible. There were metal poles, a lever and rope that went around the calf's feet. The lever cranked on a pulley, making a grinding sound. Harley preferred to tie a rope around the calf and use her body weight to help pull the calf from the heifer with each contraction, but since this calf was in distress and might die, the calf puller was needed in this instance.

Ryker readied it, pushing the handle, and there was a creaking sound. "I'll wait for another contraction."

It didn't take long. When Flossie was pushing again, Ryker used the lever, working with each contraction to carefully guide the calf out.

"I see the nose!" Justin shouted.

Harley craned her neck. Ryker was working with Flossie and once the nose had made an appearance it didn't take too long before the calf puller did its job and a calf dropped out of Flossie onto the hay bed.

Harley tied Flossie up so they could check the calf.

Ryker removed the calf puller and dropped down on his knees, rubbing the new calf with his hands vigorously. Harley joined him, their hands working together as they rubbed the newborn. Their fingers brushing. She watched him in awe, his strong hands working to keep the calf alive. There was a blink of a large brown eye and a breath.

"It's a girl," Ryker announced to Mel. "She's alive."

Harley stood up and released Flossie, who was mooing and calling to her young one. Ryker stepped back as Flossie attended to her new calf, licking and mooing to her as the large heifer calf stood up, tentatively, big eyes blinking in shock.

Harley's heart swelled with pride, seeing how much Flossie loved her little surprise calf. She met Ryker's gaze again, and his gray eyes twinkled at her. She knew he was feeling it too.

New life.

A calf that surely would've died had they not been able to come.

"This is the best part," Mel said softly. "When they love their calves so much. When they reject them, it's heartbreaking."

"No doubt," Harley agreed wistfully. "It's my favorite part too!"

"Good job, Pappa and Harley!" Justin said. "It's so cute. What're you going to call it?"

Mel scratched his head. "Don't know. Do you want to name her?"

Justin grinned. "Molly!"

"Okay. Then the calf is Molly." Mel tousled Justin's hair and then turned to Ryker. "Thank you, Dr. Proulx. You have the same love and drive as your father-in-law."

"That is a high compliment," Ryker replied, and he smiled at her again, making her heart skip a little beat.

Ryker might not think he belonged there, but it was becoming obvious to Harley that he did.

Opulence needed him. If only he'd stay.

CHAPTER EIGHT

AFTER THE CALF had been taken care of and they checked over mama cow, they climbed back into her truck. It was well past lunchtime, and Harley's stomach was growling.

"I'm hungry, Pappa," Justin complained. Apparently Harley wasn't the only one.

"How about a burger?" Ryker teased.

Justin laughed but Harley's mouth dropped open.

"Who is telling terrible jokes now?" she asked, indignant.

"It's okay, Harley. I'm used to Pappa's bad jokes too. I wouldn't mind a hot dog though," Justin told them.

"Well, I think I have hot dogs at home," Ryker said.

Harley flicked on her blinker. "Never mind that. I know a place. It's the Freezie Witch!"

"Witches?" Justin gasped, excited.

"Witches of ice cream, hot dogs and fries," Harley announced.

"Yes! Hear that, Willow?" Justin hugged his new best friend.

Willow responded with a happy bark.

"I guess I am outvoted on going home to check for food," Ryker groused playfully. There was a secret smile hovering on his lips. "But I'm treating everyone."

"Including Willow?" Justin asked.

"Only if they have ice cream that's safe for dogs," Ryker said firmly.

"They do. They have pup cups," Harley replied. "I appreciate you offering to pay for lunch, but you don't have to."

"I insist. I greatly appreciate your rental for the summer, and it wouldn't hurt to treat my new neighbor and friend to a hot dog."

Her pulse quickened. "Friends?"

"Sure. We'll be working together. Friends is right."

They shared a smile. She liked the way he smiled at her. It made her feel warm and fuzzy. Friends wouldn't be a bad thing. It was a safer option, and Willow had already taken a shine to them.

She pulled into the parking lot of the Freezie Witch. It was a fry stand, and there was a large grassy area with picnic tables under shady trees. Harley picked the shadiest spot she could to park. She hooked Willow up to her leash while Ryker and Justin went to order.

It wasn't long before Justin came running back with a pup cup, and Ryker followed holding a box that carried three hot dogs and some bottled water.

"I got foot-longs," Ryker stated.

"They're huge!" Justin exclaimed.

"I bet!" Harley responded. Willow was slurping up her pup cup and didn't pay them any attention.

"Thanks for lunch," she said as Ryker handed her a hot dog. She grabbed a packet of mustard.

"You're thanking me again," he teased.

"I can't help it. It's a Canadian thing, right?"

He chucked softly. "I suppose it is. I do it too. Well, you're very welcome."

Justin sat out on the grass next to Willow, oblivious to their conversation.

"He seems happy here," Harley remarked.

Ryker nodded, his expression soft. "I know. It's nice to see it again."

"Again?"

Ryker sighed. "He's had some challenges. I was hoping this summer would cheer him up. It seems to be working."

"Opulence is the best. It's small, but mighty."

"It is…small." Ryker winked. "So, what about you?"

"What about me?"

"You grew up here? Have you always lived here?"

"I grew up here, but no. I haven't always lived here. I spent several years in Hamilton after college. Didn't like the city and came home."

"Did your ex move here with you?"

She choked slightly. "Wow, you're, eh?"

"Sorry."

"No, it's fine. I actually met him here. He was a vet, with Michel. Eventually he wanted city life. I didn't. My life is here. My business is here. So, it ended."

It was one of the first times she had been so blasé about it. But Jason didn't matter, not in this moment with her new friends.

She was glad they could be friendly.

"Did he live at the farm?"

She shook her head. "No. I bought that myself. After."

"Good for you." Ryker nodded.

She released a breath she didn't know she was holding. Usually people pitied her when she told them what happened between her and Jason. They didn't care much that she had accomplished so much on her own, just that she'd been dumped. At least that was the impression she got.

Ryker just seemed impressed that she managed to buy the farm herself.

It was an accomplishment and one she was damn proud of.

They sat there, eating their hot dogs. They didn't have to say anything more.

It was just nice to sit there.

Together.

After lunch they went back to Harley's farm. Ryker went to clean up with Justin at their home, and she went back to her place to do the same.

The rest of the day, she really didn't see either of them. Spending time with Justin and Ryker together made her feel a longing for a family. A feeling she thought she had grieved and moved on from.

You don't have time to think about this.

She had a lot of work to do at Cosmopawlitan Opulence and taking care of her animals.

Ryker had made it clear that he wanted to spend some time unpacking and getting settled into their place. When she got back from her work at the end of the day, she saw that the coveralls were cleaned, neatly folded and on the bench next to her back door.

The rest of her week was busy. She didn't have much time to spend with them, but every time she saw Ryker or Justin she'd wave or they'd exchange a few quick words.

It was nice having them around on the property.

She didn't feel so alone.

At the end of the week she'd spend time with Ryker at the vet clinic, and she was kind of looking forward to it.

When she woke up on Friday, she got ready to head into Michel's vet clinic, knowing that she would see Ryker. What she had to remind herself of was that she was there to do her work and she couldn't let all the swirling emotions interfere with that. Especially the piece of her that kind of missed him. She'd only know them for a week, and they were already weaving themselves into her life, which scared her.

It was an early start to a clinic day, as Christine was bringing in their feral cats for the barn cat program and there were a couple of friendlier cats they had to neuter, so they could be adopted. It was a full, packed day.

Ryker was an excellent vet and she knew she could work well with him, if she could keep all these ridiculous thoughts and notions out of her head for five minutes.

Harley did her chores early and greeted Kaitlyn, who was

dealing with doggy day care. Then Harley went back to her house, showered and got dressed in her scrubs. She quickly braided her hair and poured her coffee into a travel mug.

It was early in the morning, but the farms that surrounded hers were already up and running. Farmers were out doing chores and doing their jobs. It was her favorite time of the day to drive down the road and into Opulence. Tractors in the fields or rumbling up dusty lanes. Shiny milk trucks speeding by her on the way to their next dairy farm.

These were the mornings she loved.

It was a short drive, but she had enough time to finish her coffee by the time she pulled into the clinic parking lot.

Ryker was already there. He was just getting out of his car when she parked her truck beside him. He was wearing dark blue scrubs and a white jacket. It took her aback to see him in those scrubs, which seemed to bring out the color of his eyes and accented his bronzed skin.

Her heart began to beat just a bit faster.

Get control of yourself.

She climbed out of her parked vehicle. "Good morning, Dr. Proulx."

"Ryker. We're friends, remember?" he reminded her, and then smiled. "And good morning."

"Well, I figured since we're at the clinic…"

"No. It's always Ryker." They walked up the couple of steps to the front door so he could unlock it. "How are you this morning?"

"Fine," she said quickly. When really she wasn't, because she could not get him or how good he looked this morning out of her mind. It was way too early to look that good. "Where's Justin today?"

"With his grandparents. They are having another beach day and then going to London to visit his cousins. It's supposed to be hot today."

"Don't worry, the clinic is air-conditioned. We'll be as cool as cucumbers."

Stop rambling.

He nodded as he unlocked the door and punched in the security code. "I would hope so. When does the receptionist get here?"

Michel's receptionist, Sarah, had been with him a long time, and Harley was pretty sure that Sarah would be getting close to retiring soon too. Ryker would have to hire someone else to take Sarah's place.

Then she rolled her eyes. Who was she kidding? Ryker wasn't staying.

"Sarah. She'll be here at nine. By then we should be done with most of the cats from Fluffypaws, and then you can see the new puppy who is booked in later today."

"Good. I'm hoping to keep busy, but also get to know everyone," he mumbled as he went through some of the files that had been left in the inbox on Sarah's desk.

"Why?" Harley asked, point-blank.

He cocked an eyebrow and looked at her. "What do you mean, why?"

"Why bother to get to know them if you don't plan on staying?"

Sure. Just railroad him with awkward questions why don't you?

He was taken aback by that and yeah, she was being harsh, but it was the truth. He had made it perfectly clear that he wasn't sure if he was staying. The lease for her tiny home was only for the summer.

"Well," he told her. "It's polite."

It wasn't a yes and it wasn't a no, but Harley was pretty sure the noncommittal answer was most likely a no. That's usually what happened, but he was right. It was polite.

"I'm sorry for the blunt questions this morning," she said. "I just… I love this town, the people and the animals."

His expression softened. "I know. So, why didn't you become a vet? If you were, you could take over. Michel thinks very highly of you and your work."

Now it was his turn to be blunt with her, it seemed.

"I wanted the business that I have," she stated proudly. "I wanted to work with animals. I worked for many summers, when I was a teenager, for a dog groomer, learned things from her. I loved it. I wanted a little bit more, so I went for vet tech. I paid my own way completely and came out debt free. It was always my dream to have my own land, work with animals and be my own boss. I don't regret anything about my choices, even the not becoming a doctor thing."

Ryker smiled at her, his eyes twinkling. "You should be proud of those accomplishments. I hope you know that I wasn't looking down on the fact you're a vet tech. I would be lost without my technicians."

"I know you weren't." Heat crept up her neck and bloomed in her cheeks, and she was annoyed with herself for blushing. There was a part of her that wished he would stay to take over Michel's clinic, but uprooting a child from his home seemed highly unlikely, and she didn't want to get her—or the community's—hopes up.

"By the way, thanks for cleaning the green coveralls and folding them so nicely. You didn't have to do that. I could've cleaned them. I know the tiny house only has a small washer-dryer combo."

"It's not a problem. Thank you for lending them to me." Ryker hesitated. "Sorry I pried about your ex the other day."

Her stomach knotted and plummeted to the ground. She didn't want to think about Jason, knowing she always felt unsettled when she did.

She swallowed the lump in her throat. "It's okay. I'm over it."

And then it hit her. She was.

It had hurt, she'd been crushed, but for some reason it wasn't weird talking about it with Ryker.

And the more she did, the more she noticed it didn't sting as much to think about her ex.

* * *

Ryker knew he shouldn't have asked about her ex. It was none of his business.

He'd tried to put it out of his mind for the last week, but he couldn't.

They hadn't interacted much since their lunch after the calf was born. That moment when they were sitting at a picnic table having a couple of hot dogs had felt so right. Like it was supposed to be. It felt like they had done that many times before—having lunch and chatting. She lightened the burden and all the stress he'd been carrying when she was around. He was trying to keep his distance from her. But Harley felt like his partner. His equal.

He'd only been in Opulence for a week and here he was constantly thinking about a woman, when that should be the furthest thing from his mind.

He didn't want to push Harley away or make it all awkward. He just liked being with her.

"I'm sorry," was all he managed to get out. "Again, I really didn't mean to pry."

"Don't be sorry. It's okay. It's all in the past." She was trying to sound confident, but she wasn't looking him in the eyes and her voice shook slightly.

She mustered up a brave smile and then looked back at him, but he could see the pain under the surface.

It was a different kind of pain than his, but he recognized the pain of loving and losing. He wanted to ask her more, but he didn't.

He felt bad for bringing it all up again.

"Well, we better get everything ready. Christine and Dave should be here soon."

"Right," she replied quickly, and then cleared her throat. "They'll probably come to the back entrance. I'll go see if they're here now."

"D'accord." Ryker watched her walk away. This wasn't like

him. What was coming over him? All he knew was he had to pull himself together.

Her question about him staying in Opulence had been blunt, but he answered truthfully.

Montreal was home. But working with Harley and seeing Justin thrive daily was making him see Opulence differently.

Justin has been so happy here.

Which was true, but it had only been a short time. The magic of somewhere new could easily wear off, and he couldn't move his son on a whim. Would his son be happy come fall?

Ryker pushed all those thoughts to the side as he got on with his work. He still had a lot to do. The feral cats had to be put under for their general health check, their microchipping and then their neutering. The other two cats he had already microchipped and vaccinated; they just needed to be neutered.

First, he dealt with the feral cats, because they needed the most time. Everything had to be done under anesthetic. To protect himself, but also to not stress out the cats.

Neutering usually only took about fifteen minutes to half an hour, but he had a few more things to do on them.

There was no more general chitchat as he and Harley worked in tandem seeing to the cats in their care. Soon, all of the cats were in recovery, to be released back to Christine and Dave just after lunch, but there was no time to breathe because he had a new puppy wellness check.

When he had a breather, he checked his phone. There was a text from Michel. Justin was having a panic attack and needed him. Just when he thought his son was adjusting.

He sighed.

"What's wrong?" Harley asked.

"I need to leave. Justin needs me to pick him up."

"Well, it's the lunch break and the new puppy check isn't until later, so why don't you go get him and bring him here?"

"You're sure?" he asked.

"Of course," Harley replied.

"I'll be back in time for the later appointment, I swear."

Harley nodded. "You better!"

It was a warning tease, but he appreciated her nonchalance about bringing Justin to the clinic. Not everyone he'd worked with in the past had been so easygoing.

Another point in favor of Opulence.

CHAPTER NINE

IT WAS EASY to work with Ryker. He seemed to trust her to know how to do her job. Other vets who came and went through the years, ones who didn't know her, would hover over her. Even Jason, in the beginning, had done a bit of that.

Ryker seemed to trust her skill and her judgment, which made her feel good.

It was unusual for her to open up and talk about her ex, but she was glad she did. She didn't tell Ryker the whole thing, that she'd actually been jilted, but it was nice to talk to someone who hadn't been there during that time, about her feelings.

About what happened to her.

Best of all, Ryker didn't probe or pry.

She appreciated that.

When Ryker returned with Justin, she could tell the boy was upset. His eyes were puffy, like he had been crying.

"Hey," she said carefully.

"We're back," Ryker replied stiffly.

"Is everything okay?" she asked.

"We're good. Justin wanted to spend the day here. If that doesn't bother you?"

Ryker was asking again, but she got the feeling it was for the benefit of his son.

Maybe Justin needed that reassurance from her.

Harley shrugged. "Why would it bother me?"

Justin smiled then, a half smile, but he seemed to brighten with that. "It's okay if I stay?"

"Of course," Harley replied. "Who said that it wasn't?"

"I just thought…some of the techs and other staff get annoyed when Pappa brings me to the clinic in Montreal." Justin swallowed hard. It hurt her heart to see Justin so upset and anxious. It was so hard to see someone so young hurt like this. To carry such a burden.

All she wanted to do was hug Justin, but she was still mostly a stranger to him.

"I have no problem with it. You can be my assistant for the rest of the day, if you'd like?" Harley asked, hoping it would cheer him up.

"Really?" Justin grinned, his puffy eyes lighting up.

"I'm okay with that," Ryker responded. "You have to listen to what Harley says though."

"I will." Justin jumped up and down before going to drop his bag in Michel's office.

Ryker turned to her. "Thank you."

"For what?" Harley asked.

"For being so caring to my son. He…he has a hard time leaving me some days. Today was one of those days. Then he got worried because some of the staff at the clinic where I work, they're not so kind."

Harley frowned. "I'm sorry to hear that. That's not right. Really, it'll be no trouble. There's a bunch of supplies that need to be put away, and I'm sure that Sarah wouldn't mind some help either."

Ryker smiled, relieved, and nodded. "I'm appreciative nonetheless."

She couldn't even begin to imagine the pain Ryker was feeling, and there was a part of her that wanted to shake some sense and compassion into those people who had been unnecessarily cruel to Justin. There was no need for that.

They didn't say anything else as they both went to find Justin, who was chatting away with Sarah.

"I hear we have a helper," Sarah said brightly.

"We do. He's my helper, but I guess I can lend him to you if you need him," Harley teased, winking at Justin.

"I could show him the shredder, and I do have some letters that we need to post." Sarah smiled tenderly at Justin.

"Yay!" Justin was so excited. At least someone was excited about document shredding.

"When is the new puppy coming again?" Ryker asked Sarah.

"Three," Sarah responded. "It's an urgent one. The puppy is not doing well according to the new owners."

Harley's stomach knotted. That wasn't a good sign if a puppy wasn't thriving. It either got into something it shouldn't, picked up something it wasn't vaccinated for or, well, she didn't want to think about the worst or the idea of it coming from a puppy mill.

"There was also an email from Christine at Fluffypaws to thank you, Dr. Proulx. Apparently, the domestic cats, Bonnie, Bubba, Trouble and Hims were all adopted after they were picked up," Sarah announced. "Nia is still looking for a home."

"Really?" Harley questioned. "Nia wasn't adopted yet?"

"Maybe it's a sign," Ryker teased. "I seem to recall that she liked you very much."

"I was thinking about barn cats…" Harley mused.

"You're getting a cat?" Justin asked excitedly. "Dad, if Harley doesn't get the cat, maybe we should?"

Harley grinned at Ryker who just moaned and rolled his eyes. "I'm going to get ready for the afternoon. Justin, listen to Harley and Sarah."

"Okay, Pappa." Justin saluted his dad, who in return saluted him as he disappeared into the back.

Harley was still laughing to herself.

Maybe she *should* get some barn cats. She needed to keep the alpacas safe, and the old barn was on the verge of being infested with vermin that could pass on diseases. Lady Sif, Loki, Odin and Valkyrie were all available barn cats, so if she wanted to move forward with it, she'd just have to decide which one she wanted for her barn.

"What do you want me to do first?" Justin asked her, interrupting her thoughts.

"I think you should do some shredding with Sarah," Harley suggested.

"And I think Harley is smart," Sarah quipped, standing up. "Come on, Justin. I'll take you into my office supply room."

Justin bounced after Sarah.

Harley was about to get ready for the rest of her day when she heard frantic banging on the front door. She turned around and saw a woman cradling a small brown lump in a towel. Her eyes were wide and her hair was a mess.

Harley ran to the door. "Can I help?"

"It's my puppy. She's listless. I'm so worried," the woman replied.

"Are you the wellness check for three?" Harley asked.

"No, I don't have an appointment. I just got my puppy two days ago. Her name is Brownie," the woman sobbed as Harley bent over and checked on the vitals of the chocolate-colored pup. There was a weak pulse, but the puppy was not responding. Harley's heart sank.

"You better come in." She led the frantic woman straight to the first exam room where Ryker was waiting for the next appointment.

He was typing something on his computer and he looked up at the early interruption, startled. "Harley?"

"Not our expected puppy, but this one is not doing well," Harley explained.

"Bring the puppy here." Ryker stood up and immediately was invested.

The woman laid her wee little pup on the exam table. Ryker put on gloves and a disposable surgical gown. The silence was slightly deafening as Ryker examined the puppy.

"She's dehydrated," Ryker murmured. "How old is the puppy?"

"Her papers say she's seven weeks old. I got her two days

ago from Sharpe Line Farms. They're outside of Dungannon." The woman handed the papers to Ryker.

Harley's stomach knotted and she saw red. Sharpe Line Farms was a known puppy mill. She knew that Christine, Dave and a few other animal rescue places were trying to get that place shut down. The problem was that puppy mills weren't illegal in Canada.

She had no doubt that this little puppy had parvo, and those papers the woman was handing over to Ryker were forged.

Ryker frowned. "I need to run a fecal antigen test, but first things first, this puppy is severely dehydrated. You can tell by how when I squeeze her skin, it doesn't bounce back. I need to hook her up to an intravenous."

"Okay. Please, do whatever it takes to save Brownie," the woman sobbed.

Ryker smiled. "Brownie? That is a nice name for a dog. We'll do what we can. Harley will take you out to Sarah, our receptionist, and get your information sorted. I'll keep you posted."

Ryker scooped up little Brownie and Harley opened the door for him. He was taking Brownie into the back, to the hospital part of the clinic.

The woman sobbed again and Harley put her arm around her to console her. She couldn't tell the woman everything would be okay, because there was no cure for parvo. It was up to the dog to get over it. All they could do was support the puppy's body to give it a fighting chance.

Ryker was just waiting on the result. He'd hooked up Brownie to an intravenous and some antibiotics. Then he was able to collect the small sample he needed to run the antigen test. It wasn't a complicated test, and he was pretty sure that he knew what the outcome would be.

He was pretty sure it was parvo.

The vaccines that were on all the papers Brownie came with were fake. He was checking them now and each came up nil. The vet and the vet's license number were no longer in use.

In fact, the vet in question had died ten years ago and his license had lapsed.

Ryker would contact the deceased vet's family. But first, he was going to contact Animal Welfare Services to send an inspector out to this Sharpe Line Farms. There were most likely criminal charges pending for forging a deceased vet's credentials and using a lapsed license.

No doubt this puppy had no vaccinations and had parvo.

It's why he had put on gloves right away and a disposable gown. It could spread to another dog so quickly. He was actually going to change into Michel's spare scrubs before he saw other patients.

He would have to tell Harley to do the same and then have Sarah and Justin clean the door handles, the floor and anything that Brownie's owner touched.

Harley came into the back room, her arms crossed. "Sharpe Line Farms is a puppy mill."

"Tabarnak," he cursed. "You are sure?"

She nodded. "Positive."

His timer went off and he checked the test. There was a dot. "So is the test."

Harley cursed under her breath. "Okay. So clean everything and have other appointments pushed?"

"I checked the file on the new patient. That's a Sharpe Line Farm puppy too. I would wager same litter. I need to see that puppy, but we need to change. We can't spread this around." Ryker picked up the phone and buzzed the front. "Sarah, please cancel the later appointments. No. I still need to see that other puppy. They both came from the same place. We have a parvo outbreak in the clinic. I need to do a deep clean."

Ryker hung up the phone and then checked on Brownie. She was resting and her vitals had perked up.

"I don't have a change of clothes," Harley said, worrying her bottom lip. "I can't go back to my farm like this."

"No. You can't," Ryker agreed. "Michel has extra scrubs in his office. Take a pair and change, and then we'll put our soiled clothes in a bag and seal it. We'll wash them in the machine in the clinic, *oui*?"

Harley nodded. "Okay. I will."

Ryker watched her scurry from the room. He made sure that Brownie was okay. He set her intravenous drip and set an alarm on his phone after he had safely disposed of his used gloves and gown and sprayed his hands with antiseptic spray.

He left his phone on the desk in the hospital room and then made his way to Michel's office. Without thinking he opened the door and walked right in on Harley, standing there in a bright pink bra and matching underwear. Her cheeks went the same color as her undergarments.

All he could do was stare—it was just for a moment, but it felt like a lifetime.

"Veuillez m'excuser," he said, dropping his gaze and quickly shutting the door.

He was an idiot. What had he been thinking?

He had told her to go change. Of course, he didn't expect that she would change right in Michel's office. For whatever reason he thought she would grab the spare pair of scrubs and change somewhere else.

Where?

Justin came running into the back. He was wearing a disposable gown and gloves. "Pappa, the other puppy is here. Sarah let him in and took him to exam room two. The man didn't touch any doors."

Ryker cleared his throat. *"Bonne.* I will be there as soon as I can."

Harley came out of the room, not meeting his gaze, but she smiled brightly at Justin. "You look the part of a vet."

Justin nodded. "That's the plan. The other sick puppy is in exam room two."

Justin took off, back to the front to help Sarah clean.

"Well," Ryker said, clearing his throat. "I'm going to change and then we need to check out that puppy."

"Right," Harley replied. "I'm going to get some gloves and a paper gown on too."

She walked away quickly, hiking up the too large scrub pants. She tried pulling them tighter, but that just amplified her shapely rear end, of which he'd gotten an eye full in those hot pink panties.

Stop thinking about it.

The problem was, he wasn't sure that he could. It was burned into his retinas and the fact of the matter was, he kind of liked that.

It was easier to get Harley and her pink underwear out of his mind when he saw the second puppy, who did come from the same breeder with the exact same vaccinations, or rather lack thereof.

This puppy's parvo case was worse. The antigen test came back positive and Ryker, with the help of Harley, got puppy two hooked up to an IV for fluids and antibiotics. Now all they could do was wait. Which was exactly what they were doing.

And what he planned to do for the entire night.

"It's closing time," Harley reminded him gently, as she came into the treatment room.

Ryker looked up from his computer, where he'd been typing notes. "Is it?"

"I sent Sarah home ages ago. Justin and I packaged medicine and food orders. We ran a curbside pickup."

He smiled. "Where's Justin now?"

"On Michel's computer, playing games." Harley pulled up a rolling stool and sat, staring down at their two very sick patients.

"Could you do me a favor?" he asked.

"Sure."

"Can you bring Justin a change of clothes and his pillow and blanket?"

Harley's eyes widened. "You're going to stay here?"

"*Oui.* I need to watch these puppies closely. And Justin…"

He hesitated. "He can't be alone. He gets severe anxiety if we're separated, because of what happened to his mother."

"Okay. I can do that."

It was a relief she had empathy for his son. Not everyone did. It didn't seem to faze her.

Her expression softened. "Was he there, when it happened?"

"When Daphne died?" he asked.

"Yes," she whispered.

Ryker nodded. "He was. I came home with Justin after grocery shopping. We found her on the floor. She was pregnant, but it turned out to be an ectopic pregnancy. Her tube ruptured and she bled out."

"I didn't know," Harley whispered. "Michel never said how she died."

Ryker swallowed the lump in his throat. He couldn't believe he was telling Harley all of this, but she was so easy to talk to and it felt good to release it all, to talk to someone.

"I just remember him screaming. He was only seven at the time." He cleared his throat. "It's why we're here. To give Justin a break from his hyper vigilance. He hasn't been a child in so long."

"Well, this is the perfect place," Harley said brightly. "My childhood in Opulence was the best."

"Daphne often said the same."

"It's true."

"Do your parents still live in Opulence?" he asked, wanting to change the subject from Daphne.

"No, they moved into Goderich. Same condo community as Michel. They do sometimes go up to the family cottage in the Inverhuron area and my older brother and his partner have a horse farm in Ripley, which is also near Inverhuron."

"Did you grow up on a farm? Is that why you wanted to buy one of your own?" he asked.

"Nope, I just always wanted to live on a farm. I bought it after…" She trailed off for a moment then squared her shoulders. "It was always my plan. I thought it was my ex's plan as well. We talked about it, but in the end it wasn't. He changed his mind. I'm very proud I was able to do this on my own."

"You should be. Your ex sounds like an *ostie de colon*."

"A what?"

"An idiot." Ryker smiled. "Look, about earlier in Michel's office…"

"Don't worry about it. It's fine," she said quickly, a pink tinge in her cheeks. He liked the bloom of pink on her cheeks, but then he immediately thought of her in her underwear.

What are you doing? Now who's the ostie de colon?

"Anyways," he said, breaking the tension. "If you could bring Justin those items."

"How about Justin crashes at my place tonight?" Harley offered.

"What?" Ryker asked, surprised.

"I'll get him a change of clothes, we'll order in pizza to eat here and then he can come hang out with Willow and me tonight while you watch the puppies and disinfect our exposed clothing."

"I doubt Justin would agree to that." He barely would agree to staying over with Michel and Maureen without Ryker.

"We can ask him," Harley suggested. "This isn't the best place for spending the night, and Willow would love to curl up beside him on the couch."

Justin hadn't spent a night apart from him since Daphne died, but Harley was right. This was a miserable place for a kid to spend the night. He was positive that Justin would say no, but he had to ask and try.

"If he's up for it, I don't see why not," Ryker agreed. "Are you sure?"

Harley nodded. "Positive, and if he really needs to see you, I'll bring him back here."

It sounded too good to be true, and it was very sweet she was offering.

"I'll go ask him. Can you watch the puppies?"

"No problem."

Ryker cleaned his hands and headed over to Michel's office just outside the treatment room. Justin was playing a card game online. He didn't look up from his game.

"Hey, buddy. Look, I have to stay here tonight. Those puppies are really sick."

Justin frowned, disappointed. "We have to stay here?"

"*Oui*. Unless… Harley has offered for you to spend the night at her house with her dog."

Ryker held his breath. He was pretty positive Justin would say no to that suggestion.

Justin paused his game. "Really?"

"Is that something you'd like?" Ryker asked cautiously.

"Yeah!" Justin exclaimed excitedly.

"Okay." Ryker was shocked, but pleased. "Well, Harley will go get you a change of clothes so you don't give Willow parvo. Before you change clothes and leave, we'll have some pizza and then you can go home with Harley."

"Sounds good." Justin nodded and turned back to his game.

Ryker left Michel's office in shock. Justin wanted to spend the night at Harley's away from him?

Maybe it was the change of scenery?

Maybe the change was a good thing?

And maybe Ryker needed a change too.

CHAPTER TEN

AFTER ALL THAT Ryker had told her about Justin, and Daphne's death, Harley was actually very shocked that Justin had agreed to come home with her. She was pleased though, because it had made her so sad to see him upset. A little kid shouldn't have to carry such a hard burden. He should be able to play and just be a kid.

Harley had been surprised at herself when she offered, as she usually didn't babysit, but she was glad Ryker felt comfortable enough to trust her with Justin's care, and she was relieved Justin trusted her enough to accept. She was glad it seemed to have cheered him up.

After she picked up pizza, they ate quickly and Justin followed her out to the parking lot.

Ryker told Justin to be good and the boy nodded before climbing into the back of Harley's truck, eager to get to her place.

He chatted happily all the way back to the farm and once they made sure they'd sanitized, Kaitlyn brought Willow out of the kennel and back to the house. From that moment it was dog and boy, best friends reunited.

Justin absolutely adored Willow and vice versa. Willow seemed to melt away Justin's anxiety.

It actually warmed her heart to see it.

They both went over to the tiny home and collected what he needed for the night and then locked it up and headed back to her house.

She wasn't used to being around kids.

She'd wanted to be a mother, but since she closed her heart to the idea of ever falling in love again, she sort of let go of the notion, the dream of having kids. When she was younger, she used to babysit, but it was a long time since she'd done that, and her brother and his partner weren't planning on having kids, just horses, so she wasn't often around children.

Now, she worried she was going to be too boring for Justin. What did kids even like nowadays? She didn't have any video games.

At least Willow seemed to occupy him, but how long would that last?

"What're we going to do now?" Justin asked, as Willow curled up beside him on the couch.

"Now?" She scratched her head.

Crap.

She didn't know, and Justin was just staring at her expectantly. Which was exactly what she was afraid of.

"Um, well, I have chores I have to do. Then I have to do one walk through the kennel to make sure the dogs that are staying over have everything they need."

"Can I help?" Justin asked.

"You want to help me with chores?" she asked, surprised.

"Yes. I love animals," Justin explained. "I want to be a vet like my pappa and Gramps."

Warmth flooded her heart. Ryker had mentioned that Justin had anxiety and grief that were holding him back, but she was starting to see glimpses of a boy who wanted more, who loved his life with his dad and grandparents. A boy who loved it here, clearly.

Maybe if Ryker sees that he'll stay?

She shook that thought away.

No one stays, a little voice reminded her. Ryker's intentions had been clear since she met him. Their time here was only for a season.

Just because Justin was happy here now didn't mean anything was going to change. It made her sad to think about the end of summer, how empty the tiny home would be with them returning to Montreal.

"So can I help?" Justin eagerly asked, breaking through her thoughts.

"Okay, but it can be messy. You can wear the coveralls your dad wore, but they'll be big."

Justin shrugged and jumped up. "It'll be fine. I brought my boots over here because I knew you would have to deal with the other animals."

Harley smiled at him warmly. "Did you? Well, you're smarter than I thought."

"I'm super smart," Justin stated proudly.

"Okay then Mr. Super Smart, let's go do chores. Willow can come too."

"Awesome."

Harley got Justin fitted out in the very large overalls, but she had a belt and some clips that helped pin it all together. She slapped a baseball cap on his head and he slipped on his boots, following in her steps as they did the last chores for the evening.

He didn't get in her way and did exactly what she told him to.

He was a big help.

Even Kaitlyn took a shine to him before she left for the night.

Willow was completely glued to Justin's side as they bedded down her alpacas, and Vince even let Justin feed him some grapes.

As for Cluck Norris Jr. and his maniacal flock, well, Justin and Willow kept back. Surprisingly the chickens were well-behaved as she bedded them down for the night. Once they were secure in the coop she had Justin help her move the pen, so the chickens would have fresh ground to scratch at and peck the next day.

The sun was starting to set as they finished up.

"Harley!" Justin exclaimed. "What's that?"

Harley looked over her shoulder and could see the bats swooping and diving after bugs. "The bats."

"I've never seen a bat before," Justin said, his mouth agape as he watched them.

Harley laughed. "It's pretty neat, right? I mean, bats can carry rabies, but they're essential to the ecosystem. They do good by keeping the mosquitoes down. Especially when mosquitoes carry diseases like West Nile."

"Gramps told me about that," Justin remarked. "It's so cool. You don't see stuff like this in the city. Or stars."

Harley craned her neck to see the first few early evening stars poking their faces out in the darkening sky.

"No, you don't," she agreed. That was why she hadn't liked the city. She needed to go to school there, and she worked there to gain experience, but she didn't like all the noise, the light pollution, the cramped spaces.

She loved this. Maybe Jason had been right. She couldn't have been happy in Toronto. It was just that he never gave her the choice. He'd made the decision to end it without her input. She was an adult; she could make her own choices.

"I don't like Montreal," Justin said offhandedly.

"Oh?" Harley asked, gently coming up beside him. "But you're from Montreal. It can't be all bad."

"I guess not, but I like it here. The animals and my family." He looked up at her. "Mom was from here."

"I know." She placed her hand on his shoulder, giving it a squeeze. "There's no place like this and your mother did love it here, and she loved you and your father."

Justin nodded. "I miss her."

"I'm sure you do." Tears stung her eyes as she just stood there, staring up into the evening sky with Justin, watching the bats and the stars. "I'm sure she's up there, watching you."

"I feel her more here, Harley." Then Justin slipped his small hand in hers. It surprised her but made her melt inside. She squeezed his hand, letting him know she was here too and he had a lifelong friend in her.

"How about we make some popcorn, build a blanket fort and watch a movie?" she asked, hoping to lighten the mood.

"Yes!" Justin said, jumping, which made Willow jump and bark despite not knowing why she was excited. "Come on, Willow!"

Harley watched as Justin raced toward her house, with Willow following close on his heels, barking and excited. Usually, after she was done her chores, she would catch up on emails and paperwork over a cup of tea.

She couldn't remember the last time she'd slowed down and enjoyed a movie.

It sounded nice.

It would be even nicer, having someone to share it with.

Don't get attached.

She had to remind herself of that. Even though Justin had said how much he liked it here, it didn't mean that Ryker was going to stay. And she already knew she'd miss them terribly when they left.

Ryker was so tired, but his exhaustion was worth it. Both of the puppies had improved dramatically over the course of the night. They just needed monitoring today in the hospital area, and then he could release the puppies back to their owners.

Michel had heard from Sarah about the parvo puppies and how Ryker had spent the night, so he came rushing over in the morning, effectively relieving Ryker for the day so he could get some sleep.

Ryker thought he would be able to come back to the clinic just before dinner to release the puppies back to their owners, but for now, he was planning to have a nap. He was pleased that there had been no calls or texts from Harley about Justin, and he couldn't help but wonder what they had got up to. It was the longest he and Justin had been apart in two years.

After he left the clinic, he swung by the local coffee drive-through and got some doughnuts and a couple of double-

doubles, since he didn't know what Harley liked. Most people he knew liked the double-double version of the coffee.

When he pulled into her driveway, Harley was sitting on the porch, cross-legged on a lounge chair and reading. She was wearing yoga pants and a tank top. Her blond hair was in a braid hanging over her shoulder, and he could see hot pink on her toenails. The reminder of her love of that color sent a rush of heat through him.

"Hey," he said, hoping his voice wasn't too laced with fatigue.

She looked up and set her book down. "How are the puppies?"

"They'll live," he replied, and then he held up the cardboard tray of coffees. "I wasn't sure what you liked."

"I like coffee however I can get it."

Ryker handed her the cup and then took a seat in the lounge chair next to hers. "How did Justin do?"

"Great! He's still sleeping. I left him a note to come outside if he was looking for me. I did my chores early when Willow got up. After she did her business she joined him back in the fort."

Ryker cocked an eyebrow. "Fort?"

"Sure, a blanket fort," she said offhandedly, taking a tentative sip of her coffee. "We both slept in there. He insisted, and I have to say that I'm too old to sleep on the floor."

Ryker chuckled. *"Oui."*

She gave him serious side-eye. "What?"

"I don't mean you're old... I mean I get that feeling of..." He threw his hands up in the air. "I'm not making that sound any better."

"Nope. So I'm old, but not old?"

"Tabarnak," he muttered, pinching the bridge of his nose.

Harley laughed. "I'm teasing you. And hey, it's nice someone else is putting their foot in their mouth. Usually it's me."

"Fine. Still, I don't think you're old." He winked at her, relieved she wasn't offended.

"I appreciate that you don't think I'm old," she responded. "So who is watching the puppies now?"

"Michel. If they continue their improvement, then I am going to discharge them this evening. I've already spoken to both of the owners. They were ecstatic, but are terribly upset about Sharpe Line Farms."

Harley pursed her lips together. "So am I. They've been a thorn in this area's side for years. All the rescue groups are aware of them. We've called bylaw officers, police, but there are no laws against puppy mills. There are no bylaws in this county."

"Well, we have to do something," Ryker stated.

"I've talked to Christine and Dave and some friends at other animal rescue organizations. We're going to put the word out on social media. They'll shut down for a time, but they always regroup."

"I am still going to complain to the solicitor general. Puppy mills are notorious for not giving their breeding animals sufficient food or shelter. I already have copies of the fake vaccination records. They'll send an inspector out."

Harley sat upright. "Really?"

He nodded. "Have you never had this proof from them before?"

She shook her head. "No. Just rumors and run-ins, but nothing concrete."

"I'd say two puppies that should've been vaccinated from parvo that are from the same littler and bought from the same location with almost identical and meticulously copied vaccination reports, plus a fake veterinarian identification, is cause for the inspector to descend on Sharpe Line Farms."

Harley set down her coffee and threw her arms around him. It caught him off guard, but he enjoyed the embrace. Her arms around his neck, the warmth of her body pressed against his. He wanted to hold on to that feeling.

She pulled away, wiggling in her seat. "This is so great."

"I'm glad you're pleased." He stood up. "I should go check on Justin."

"Sure, head right in." She picked up her phone and was no doubt texting Christine at Fluffypaws to let her know. She was so cute when she was excited, and he couldn't help but smile when he looked at her. She was so friendly, warm and it was obvious that Justin liked her, because he hadn't called. He'd made it through the night at her house.

In a blanket fort!

Ryker walked into the living room and Willow let out a little woof and started wagging her tail when she saw him.

"*Tout va bien, ma chérie.* I'm just here to see Justin."

Willow seemed to understand him and trotted back into the blanket fort. Ryker peered inside and smiled when he saw his son spread out across the floor. Pillows everywhere, arms akimbo, and Willow was right in the middle of it. He could see where Harley had curled up, and it was a tiny sliver of a space. Justin had taken over most of the air mattress. The fort was made out of various quilts, and there was a string of battery-operated lights strung up on the chair backs.

Ryker shook his son gently. "Justin, I'm here."

Justin groaned and opened his eyes slowly. "Pappa? Did the puppies live?"

"*Oui.* Your gramps is there now taking care of them, but they should be able to go home later this afternoon."

Justin closed his eyes and smiled. "That's good."

"Did you have a good night?" Ryker asked.

Justin nodded. "Yes. I saw Mamma last night. It was nice. She was happy I'm here."

It felt like Ryker's heart was being squeezed. Tightly. It was hard to breathe, not in a sad way, but a good way. It was unnerving how comfortable Justin felt here and that Ryker could see glimpses of the way his son used to be, before he lost his mother.

This was what he wanted.

And he had to wonder if Justin would be okay, going back to Montreal and their life.

Why do you have to go back?

Instantly he thought of Harley, of not having to say goodbye to her, and it was a tempting thought indeed, but there was no way that he could open his heart again. If he let someone else in, if he ever entertained the idea of falling in love and having Justin love that woman too and something happened to her, well, he wasn't sure that he could survive it.

Or that Justin could.

It was just easier to be alone, and he could put distance between Harley and himself by returning to Montreal at the end of the summer. All he could allow her to be was a coworker and a friend.

That's it.

So he would have to be careful with Harley and Justin, because he didn't want Justin to get too attached to something temporary.

Why does it have to be temporary?

Justin was clearly happy here. Maybe moving to Opulence would be the best thing for him.

For the both of them?

It was a big decision, and Ryker wasn't quite sure what to do.

"I'll be outside." Ryker slowly backed out of the tent and then headed back outside. Harley was on the phone, talking to someone, and she just gave him an enthusiastic thumbs-up, which he returned.

He couldn't allow his heart to melt around her.

He couldn't allow someone else in.

Or could he?

CHAPTER ELEVEN

AFTER RYKER HAD a nap, he woke up to the sounds of laughter and shouting.

Where am I?

It took him a moment for his eyes to adjust and to remember that he was not still at the clinic and that he made it back to Harley's farm. He grabbed his phone and saw the time.

Tabarnak.

He had slept for four hours and it was the afternoon. He didn't mean to sleep for that long, but he had been up all night taking care of those puppies.

Knowing Justin had been okay with Harley overnight had relaxed him. When his head hit the pillow, he was out cold.

He groaned, only because he hadn't intended to sleep so long, but also he hadn't slept that soundly in some time.

Quickly he checked his messages. Michel had texted that puppies were doing really well, which was good. It meant they could go home, but they would still need regular checkups and care. He had to clean up a bit, make arrangements with the owners and head over to the clinic to release the puppies.

He got out of bed and made his way to the window to look outside. Justin was running barefoot across the lawn with a water gun, and behind him was Harley with a seemingly never-ending hose. She looked soaked to the bone and was laughing. And he chuckled softly, watching the two of them, hearing them laugh. It had been a long time since he heard Justin giggle and shriek like that. Also, he couldn't help but wonder where the water gun came from.

It made his heart happy seeing Justin having fun, playing. Justin was at ease with Harley, which was great to see, but it was worrying too. Harley lived here and they lived in Montreal. What would happen when they left? He didn't want Justin to be hurt or get attached to something temporary.

Ryker didn't want to hurt Harley either. She deserved lasting love and happiness.

So do you.

Ryker shook that thought away. Maybe he needed happiness, but he couldn't take a chance on a possibility. Not with his son involved.

Yet watching the two of them made him long for this moment, and he thought briefly about what it would be like if things were different. If he took a chance and stayed. Except he was too afraid to take that risk.

He splashed some water on his face and headed outside, where Justin raced by him.

"Hi, Pappa!" Justin shouted, dashing around the corner of the tiny house.

"Justin..." Ryker screeched as he was blasted with a stream of ice-cold water. He sucked in a deep breath, gasping in shock. He'd thought about having a shower, but not one on his porch, in his clothes. Definitely not a frigid cold one.

"Got ya!" Harley shouted, jumping out from behind a shrub, holding her hose. "Oh crud! Sorry!"

She turned off the nozzle.

Ryker ran his hand through his wet hair. "Well, I'm awake now."

"I'm so sorry," Harley said. "We were having a water fight."

"I figured." He walked inside and grabbed a towel before heading back outside to drip-dry. He saw Harley whispering to Justin and both of them laughing as they glanced his way.

"Pappa, you got hosed!" Justin giggled.

Harley was stifling laughter behind her hand.

He cocked an eyebrow. "I'm aware."

Justin ran off and Willow flew past the house, chasing his son with a happy bark.

"I'm so sorry." Harley apologized again, trying to hold back the laughter.

"Somehow I don't think you are," he groused, but then grinned because it was funny. Even if he was the victim.

"I truly am."

He cocked an eyebrow and she was still laughing. "Really. You seem so contrite."

"Okay. It was funny," she admitted. "Still, I'm sorry. You were not my intended target."

"It's no problem." And it wasn't. It was worth it to hear his son's happy shrieks.

"Have you heard about the puppies' status?" she asked, changing the subject.

"Yes. I'm going to go discharge them." He checked his watch. "In about an hour."

"I'm glad to hear it. At least you've had your daily shower." Her eyes were sparkling with humor. She was teasing him.

"Yeah. I appreciate that." He pulled off his wet T-shirt, not even thinking about the fact that Harley was standing right there. When he remembered, he looked up and she was looking away, her cheeks flushed. He liked that he made her blush, that she noticed him. It excited him.

Don't think like that.

He wrapped the towel around him.

"Well, I'm going to get changed, and then when I get back we'll have a barbecue. I would like to make you dinner to thank you for taking care of Justin."

"You don't have to," she said quickly.

"I want to."

It was the least he could do.

"Okay. That sounds good."

"Bonne."

She was beaming, her blue eyes twinkling. She brushed

some damp hair out of her face, and he noticed tiny rivulets of water trickling over her sun-kissed skin. He resisted the urge to reach out and run his hands over her bare arms.

Both of them were dripping wet and leaving huge puddles on the deck. There was a part of him that wished he could get involved in the water fight, but he had to go change and discharge those puppies.

"Well, I better go change," he announced, clearing his throat.

"Right." She stepped off his deck. "See you later. I promise you I won't hose you again."

"I would appreciate that."

Harley turned and slowly wound the hose around her arm, heading back to her house.

If it wasn't for the puppies, he'd join in on the fun. It was nice to play again, and he was looking forward to the barbecue tonight.

But he needed some space from Harley right now. He didn't know how, but she was weaving herself into his heart, into his life.

A temporary life that could only last the summer.

Who says?

He was beginning to think his inner voice was right.

Harley eventually managed to dry off and got Justin to change out of his wet clothes. When Ryker came back from discharging the puppies, she finished off her daily chores and changed for the barbecue. She put on a nice flowy top and leggings and braided her hair.

When she made her way back to Ryker's, she could smell the steaks and hot dogs sizzling on the grill. She had whipped up a garden salad.

Justin was setting the table that he had pulled outside. The outdoor deck lights were on, and there was a cooler full of ice and pop. Willow let out an excited bark and ran ahead of Harley to greet Justin.

"Hey, Harley!" Justin called, waving.

Ryker peeked around the corner from where he was grilling, waved and went back to the barbecue.

"I brought salad," she announced.

Justin took the bowl. "I'll put it in the fridge. Come on, Willow!"

The little dog followed Justin inside. Harley made her way around the house to speak to Ryker. Although she was feeling a bit shy. She couldn't get that image of him shirtless out of her head. It made her body heat thinking of his muscular chest and those rivulets of water running down his tanned, taut skin.

Get a grip.

Her cheeks were flushing again. She had to stop thinking about him like that. The problem was, she couldn't, and her body betrayed her every time with all the blushing.

"How did the discharges go?" she asked, trying to distract herself with work talk and hoping it would do the trick. She actually enjoyed talking about work with him. They could talk about anything, easily. It was what she liked about their conversations.

"Excellent. I think both puppies will recover." Ryker smiled, flipping a steak.

"That's great." And it was. Now if only the animal welfare inspectors would do their job and shut Sharpe Line Farms down. It was government, though, and they'd take their time.

"I want to thank you again for taking care of Justin. He had a great time. It's been ages since I've seen him this happy."

"My pleasure. He's a great kid," she said.

Which was true. She loved being around him. It was almost like they were this little family. It felt right, which was preposterous because she knew it couldn't last.

Even if she wanted it to.

Her life was here, and theirs was not.

"I've been meaning to ask," Ryker said. "Where did Justin get that water gun?"

"Ah, when we went out for lunch while you were napping. I'm sorry. It was in a discount store and I was impulsive. I'm sorry if I overstepped any boundaries buying him a water gun. He didn't ask for it, not with words."

Ryker chuckled. "It's fine. He really likes you."

Harley smiled. "I like him too."

"You should've bought yourself one," he remarked.

"The hose is so much more powerful to soak someone with."

"I remember," he groused.

"So steaks and tube steaks, eh?" she teased.

"Tube...what?" Ryker asked, horrified.

"Hot dogs." Harley pointed.

"Wieners." Ryker winked.

"Oh no," she chortled. "Why do we seem to have these odd conversations?"

He shrugged. "I don't know, but they're fun, *oui?*"

"Oui!" she agreed, winking at him. "You're easy to talk to." She hadn't meant to admit that to him, but it was true.

"Am I?" he asked, his voice husky.

"Yes," she whispered. All of it was the truth; she liked being around him. "You're a good friend."

Ryker took a step toward her and took her hand in his, pulling her away from the barbecue to a more secluded spot. His strong hand, holding hers, made her heart flutter. Her body tingled and he took another step closer to her.

"It means so much," he whispered. "To have you as a friend too."

"I am glad to be your...friend," she responded breathlessly. Her stomach twisting, she trembled at the thought of him so close. She could smell him. Right now, in this moment, she wanted to be more than just friends.

She gazed into his gray eyes, falling under his spell again. She usually was so strong, but he made her melt. Before she knew what was happening his thumb brushed across her cheek, making her knees weak.

"J'ai des sentiments pour toi. Je veux te serrer contre toi," he said softly.

And she really regretted not remembering her high school

French classes because she had no idea what he was saying, but frankly she didn't care. She couldn't help herself. She was melting in his arms and then under his lips in a kiss that wrapped her up in a hot, longing, embrace. It took her breath away. His hands ran down her back, pulling her closer to the hard planes of his body.

She just wanted to stay here forever, in this moment.

"Pappa, your meat is on fire!" Justin shouted from across the yard.

They broke apart.

Quickly.

Ryker glanced at the barbecue, which was smoking. *"Maudit!"*

Ryker opened the lid and let out the smoke while Harley stifled a nervous giggle.

"Is it…is your meat burned?" she teased, grinning and trying not to laugh.

"You have no idea." He grinned. "It's fiery."

"Right," she said breathlessly. Just as that kiss was. It had been amazing.

She'd completely lost herself in that moment when they had connected.

Why did you let that happen?

She'd wanted it to happen, but she couldn't remember who had stepped closer and who was the first to initiate the kiss. His simple touch on her sent shivers of anticipation through her whole body.

That, she remembered.

She had completely lost herself, when she shouldn't have.

They were friends.

Except friends usually didn't share passionate kisses…

"Harley," he said, his voice low. "I'm sorry if I overstepped."

"No. There's no need to apologize," she reassured him.

Justin came running up to them and their conversation ended.

"We'll talk later," he whispered, motioning his head toward Justin.

Harley nodded. Her body still thrummed with unquenched need, all for Ryker, but she couldn't let that happen again. She couldn't put her heart at risk again. It had hurt too much before. She didn't want to hurt Justin if things didn't work out, and with Ryker only here for the summer, that was inevitable.

She'd rather it be her who lost out over Ryker than his son being hurt.

It wasn't just her fragile heart on the line. There was too much at risk to even contemplate taking a chance, even a chance she wanted so very much.

A couple of weeks went by and Ryker barely saw Harley other than in passing, but they always made time to have a barbecue on Friday night, at Justin's insistence.

Truth be told, Ryker looked forward to them as well.

They hadn't talked about their kiss, but maybe it was better this way.

They worked well together and he had a better experience on the days she could assist him, but she'd been so busy with grooming appointments at her farm recently that they'd barely had a chance to work together, which was why he was looking forward to today.

He was scheduled to see Michel's regular patients, and Harley was scheduled to help all day. Michel was originally supposed to work, but Ryker had volunteered to step in while Michel and Maureen took Justin to visit his cousins in London. The clients were expecting to see Michel, but he would ease their minds.

He took a deep breath as Harley brought in the first patient.

"Sylvie, this is Dr. Proulx and he's filling in for Michel today. Dr. Proulx, this is Sylvie and her cat Bootzie."

Sylvie smiled and set her cat carrier on the exam table. Bootzie meowed from inside.

"It's nice to meet you, Dr. Proulx," Sylvie said as she opened the door to the cat carrier and Bootzie came out, flicking her black tail back and forth.

"A pleasure," Ryker said. "What brings Bootzie in today?"

"I collected a urine sample," Sylvie said, producing a bottle. "Dr. Michel gave me some beads. Bootzie has been emptying her water bowl and drinking so much. I was little worried."

"I'll take that," Harley said, taking the sample bottle away. "Standard tests, Dr. Proulx?"

"*Oui. Merci*, Harley." Ryker examined Bootzie while Harley left the exam room to test Bootzie's urine for an infection or possibly feline diabetes. He stroked the cat, who was quite content, and checked the extra skin on the cat's neck to see if there was a sign of dehydration, which could mean that there was a blockage.

"Has Bootzie been crying while trying to relieve herself?" Ryker asked, making notes.

"No. No crying," Sylvie answered. "She's been licking herself quite often and goes to the litter box more than she should, because of the water drinking."

Ryker produced a small cat treat, and Bootzie took it willingly. He smiled and petted her. "She really is a quiet, calm cat."

Sylvie smiled. "She is."

"Well, let's weigh her." Ryker picked up Bootzie and set her on the scale. She was ten pounds, which was a healthy size for a domestic cat. When he made a note of her size in her file, he could see that Bootzie was right on track.

Harley knocked and entered the room. "Her urine is testing positive for a UTI. Just. So Sylvie may have caught it early."

Ryker nodded. "I'm going to prescribe her an antibiotic, but I am still going to send Bootzie's urine for a culture and sensitivity test."

Sylvie looked concerned and looked immediately to Harley. "Should I be worried?"

"No, Dr. Proulx just needs to know what kind of bacteria is causing the UTI," Harley responded, stroking Bootzie, who purred.

"*Oui.* We're going to give her a script for a UTI, but if it's not just the general Escherichia coli, I'll need to prescribe something to kill that specific bacteria. In the meantime, the general antibiotics will give some relief to Bootzie, and I will also prescribe a painkiller to relax her when she does go to the litter box. Once I have the results, I will call you and we'll go from there. If the symptoms persist, call me." Ryker handed Sylvie the scripts, because they didn't have that particular med in the clinic. He knew she'd be able to fill it out at the local pharmacy.

"Thank you, Dr. Proulx." Sylvie smiled.

"You're most welcome." He picked up the chart and exited the room so that Sylvie could pack up Bootzie and leave.

He made his way to the next exam room and entered it, while Harley went to retrieve his next patient.

Harley opened the other door, which led to the waiting room, and Ryker took a step back as a beagle with a small black chihuahua riding it came into the room, followed by an elderly gentleman with a cane.

"Uh, who do we have here?" Ryker asked.

Harley's eyes were twinkling. "This is Snoopy and Pepper. Best friends forever and this is their owner, Al."

"How are you today, Al?" Ryker asked, trying not to stare at the dogs. Snoopy sat down and Pepper jumped down, sitting right next to her bestie.

"Oh, terrible," Al stated.

Ryker widened his eyes, and Harley laughed quietly behind her hand. "Really?"

"Just ignore him. Al always says that. Right, Al?" Harley chided.

"I'm afraid so." Al grinned and sat down, resting his hands on his cane. "Harley knows me. She watches my other little dog, Gordo."

"You have three dogs?"

Al nodded. "My wife and I do. Donna is at home with Gordo."

"So what can I do for Pepper and Snoopy?" Ryker asked as Harley scooped up Pepper and plopped her on the table.

"Rabies vaccines today. Gordo already had his. He's a bit of a diva, so I bring him on his own. Snoopy and Pepper, they're buddies, so they come together," Al explained.

"Very well. Harley, would you weigh Snoopy and get the vaccines ready while I examine Pepper?"

"Sure thing, Dr. Proulx." Harley made a small whistle and Snoopy followed her out into the hallway where a large scale was. Pepper whined and watched her bestie leave.

"It's okay, Peppercorn Doggy. Snoops will be back," Al reassured the little chihuahua.

Harley returned with Snoopy. "Snoopy is twenty-three pounds."

"Perfect," Ryker said. He weighed Pepper and she came in at ten pounds, which was slightly overweight for her size, but it wasn't too much. Harley was right beside him as they examined the dynamic duo.

He was very aware of how close she was and how he didn't have to give her a lot of instructions. He could smell her clean scent. His blood heated. He liked being close to her, working alongside her.

All he could think of was the night of their first barbecue. The softness of her skin, her smile, her laugh. When he held her close, she trembled under his touch.

Great.

Now he couldn't stop thinking about her lips and how he wanted to kiss her again and again.

For a moment he entertained the notion of staying in Opulence. What if he and Justin moved?

He could run this clinic with Harley by his side. Maybe they could finally talk about that kiss—and whether she wanted to kiss him again as much as he wanted to kiss her.

It caught him off guard imagining that. It was nice to daydream again.

He couldn't help but smile as he watched her with Snoopy and Pepper. Everything she did seemed to make him smile these days. It was her gentle touch with all the animals, and how she was so kind to his son.

She was just a wonderful human being, and these feelings that were hitting him were not as unwelcome as he would have thought, but no matter how much he wanted to explore them, he couldn't. He wouldn't hurt her, because there was one thing he was certain about.

He was never going to fall in love again.

That was off the table.

Is it?

CHAPTER TWELVE

WHEN THEY SAW their last patient for the day, Harley's feet were aching.

Although her days were usually packed full, she'd forgotten what a busy day at the vet clinic was like.

So even though her feet were throbbing and she could use a big glass of wine, it was still worth it for a job well done. Kaitlyn messaged to say that she had done the chores, including dealing with Cluck Norris Jr. and his mob of chickens, for which Harley was eternally grateful. All she had to do when she got home was make something for dinner, put her feet up and relax. She let out a sigh of relief she didn't even know she'd been holding.

Thankfully, it hadn't been awkward not talking about the kiss with Ryker, but it still ran through her mind all day. She just had to keep her distance, which was hard to do when they had a barbecue for the last couple of weeks, but she wouldn't trade those moments for anything.

When Justin was around, it was easier to resist temptation.

"You're still here?" Ryker asked, clearly surprised at coming outside to see her in the parking lot.

"Yes, I just had some stuff to put away." Harley stretched her shoulder, which was a bit stiff.

"Justin's with his cousins, so I was about to go to the local brewery and grab something to eat. Would you care to join me for dinner?"

Say no. Say no.

That was her first instinct, but she wouldn't mind clearing the air about their kiss. Rip the bandage off and get it over with.

"Uh, sure," she blurted out, because she felt like she was taking too long to answer him. She groaned inwardly at her own weirdness striking yet again.

This was a no-brainer. They were friends. He was her colleague and neighbor.

A tempting, gorgeous one at that, but still she could keep her cool. It was a simple meal.

Ryker nodded, pleased. "Good. I'll meet you over there?"

"Okay." She swallowed past the lump that formed in her throat. Her heart was racing, more like hammering in her chest. "See you in a few."

Ryker nodded again and climbed into his car.

She looked down at her scrubs and wished she had time to change.

Which was silly. She'd gone out to dinner with colleagues in scrubs before and it had never bothered her, until now.

Don't overthink it.

This was just a casual dinner. Nothing more.

A kiss hadn't changed anything.

Hadn't it?

She got into her truck and followed Ryker just outside of Opulence to where the small microbrewery was located. It was a popular place to grab some beer and order a casual dinner. She wondered if they would even get a table tonight as it was Friday, and this was a favorite stop in the summer with all the tourists.

Ryker was waiting for her outside the brewery. At least she wasn't the only one in scrubs. Thankfully the restaurant didn't look too busy either.

He waved as she pulled up and parked.

This shouldn't be a big deal.

So why was she so nervous?

You know why.

Because she liked being around him. She enjoyed his company. There was nothing wrong with that.

Harley ignored the sarcastic voice in her head as she climbed out of her truck.

"Do you think we'll be able to get a table?"

"I think so. I was thinking about the patio, to watch the famous Huron County sunset. Does that sound good?" he asked.

"Yes. I think that sounds nice."

"Good."

They fell into step and said nothing. Awkward was all she felt in that moment, because she wasn't sure what to say to him. Which was absolutely silly because they had chatted and worked all day. It was a good day. Long, but excellent. Right now she felt like that shy girl that she'd been when she was very young. It wasn't until she went to college that she found her own voice, her own particular brand of sass.

The kind of gumption that could Krav Maga a guy into a pile of alpaca poo.

She chuckled to herself thinking of that absurd first meeting.

"What's so funny?" he asked quizzically.

"Nothing." She didn't want to bring that incident up again. Especially how he had landed on top of her and between her legs. Heat flushed through her body, and she rubbed the back of her neck anxiously.

"Why is it suddenly so hard to talk normally?"

Ryker's eyes widened. "Is it difficult?"

"I don't know what to talk about. Except work. We could talk about that. We could discuss neutering."

Oh. My. God. Harley!

Ryker chuckled. "That's worrying."

She buried her face in her hands. "I know. I didn't actually want to talk about that."

She was absolutely mortified.

"It's okay. I've never actually discussed that at dinner."

"I'm sure you haven't. It's my brain, it's like yes, that's a good idea, let's talk about neutering and next we can talk deworming. I just tend to… I…" she stammered.

"Ramble. I know. I find it charming."

She met his gaze and his expression was soft, sincere.

Her heart fluttered. This time the flush to her cheeks wasn't embarrassment. He found her charming. "I'll take that as a compliment."

"You should."

They approached the wait-to-be-seated sign.

"Welcome!" a young girl said brightly.

"Table for two. Outside if we could?" Ryker asked the greeter.

The young girl smiled. "Of course. Right this way."

The patio was full of people, but there was a little table in the corner, with a perfect view of rolling green fields and forest. The sun was a little high still, but definitely getting ready to sink.

Ryker pulled out her seat for her. She was not used to men doing that for her. Jason never did.

As she sat down, she could feel Ryker's fingers brush the top of her shoulder, sending a tingle of pleasure down her spine.

"Thanks," she said, hoping her breath didn't catch in her throat.

"I am a gentleman at my core." He winked at her, and she couldn't help but laugh.

"I'm not used to that," she replied.

"Can I get you something to drink?" the waitress asked, interrupting them.

"Just water for me until I figure out which beer I want," Harley responded. She'd call Brenda, the local taxi driver, to take her home if she needed it, but one beer and a good dinner of potatoes wouldn't affect her.

The waitress nodded and turned to Ryker. "And you?"

"Same," Ryker replied.

"Okay, two waters and I'll come back in a few minutes after

you've checked out the menu. The special tonight is the rutabaga salad with cheese from the local goat farm."

Ryker frowned as the waitress walked away, he leaned over
the table. "What is rutabaga salad?"

She laughed. "Like coleslaw, but shaved rutabaga."

"Why?" he asked, wrinkling his nose and frowning.

"It's grown around here. It's very popular, particularly
around Blyth. Lots of rutabaga grown there. They have a whole
festival around it. Bed races, rutabaga man…it's a thing."

"I would've never guessed." He opened his menu shaking
his head. "I'm not sure I want to try it."

"It's fine. Have you never eaten rutabaga raw?" she asked.

"No!" He pulled that grossed out face again. "Is it a thing
people eat?"

Harley smiled. "It is indeed. Have you ever had Huron
County Fries?"

"No…" he said cautiously.

"It's fries, gravy, cheddar cheese—"

"So a poutine?" he interrupted, his mouth twitching like he
was holding back a smile.

"No. Let me finish. It's fries, gravy, cheddar cheese—"

"It really sounds like a poutine." There was a twinkle in his
eyes as he leaned back in his chair and crossed his arms. He
was totally teasing her.

"Last time I checked a poutine didn't have cheddar cheese.
It has cheese curds," she replied saucily. "You know what.
You don't deserve to know what Huron County Fries are, Dr.
Proulx."

They both shared a laugh.

"Go on. Tell me," Ryker urged. "Fries, gravy, cheddar cheese
and…?"

"Ranch dressing, dill pickles and bacon."

Ryker made a face. "Ugh. I'd rather eat rutabaga raw."

"What do you mean 'ugh'?"

"Ranch dressing and gravy."

"Hey, cheese curds and gravy doesn't exactly sound one hundred percent appetizing either, but it's good."

"It's the best, but then Montreal has all the best food. Best bagels, best smoked meat, best poutine."

"Huron County is pretty awesome too. We have rutabaga." She laughed then and acquiesced. "Okay, Montreal is pretty good too."

"It is," he said softly.

"So about that kiss from a couple weeks ago." There was no point in dodging the conversation any longer. She just wanted to clear the air. "I know we probably should have talked sooner, but things have been so hectic..."

"*Oui*. I'd like to talk about that as well, but I understand you've been busy."

"I'm glad we're friends."

He nodded. "Me too. I don't regret the kiss, but I would like to continue on as we have."

She sighed in relief. "So would I."

"*Très bon.*" His smile was so warm that all the awkward tension she'd been feeling melted away. For one brief moment, she wished the summer would last forever.

"Do you mind if I ask you a personal question?"

"Go ahead."

"Why are you here?" He raised his eyebrows, and she hurried to clarify. "I mean, we're lucky to have you, of course. With Michel dropping to part time and wanting to retire, we all feel that loss for our animals. He is amazing, but I have to wonder why you're here and working in the clinic for him this summer."

"It's for my son," he responded softly. "He's still grieving his mother's loss. It's hard and he's not been the same since."

"He seems like a normal kid. Worries a bit, but a great kid nonetheless."

Ryker nodded. "It's wonderful to see, but since his mother's death that normal kid has been missing. All the sports he'd play, he didn't want to any more. He wouldn't go out to play unless I was there. I can't be out of his eyesight. Justin gets so anxious."

"He's not here tonight," Harley said gently.

"No," Ryker replied, his voice laced in relief. "Is it bad if I say it's nice?"

"I don't think so. You need a break too."

He nodded. "It's nice he's having fun with his family and doesn't have to be vigilant about my well-being. That's not something a kid should have to worry about."

"And how about you?" she asked.

"What about me?"

"How have you been?"

Ryker wasn't sure how he was supposed to answer that question. Was he still the same after Daphne's death? No. He was not the same man that he had been, but he was coping. Justin couldn't even spend the night away from him. That was before though. Ryker was thrilled Justin had done so well at Harley's and now this evening he was in London with relatives. It was starting to feel sort of normal again.

Justin even had issues going to school. It was like his son was forever on guard.

Always had to know where he was. Justin hadn't been a kid since Daphne died.

So it was nice that Ryker had a little break because Justin was happy to be with his grandparents and cousins.

Ryker had a moment to breathe.

He was surviving, whereas Justin had not been.

Are you surviving though?

He ignored that little thought and plastered on a fake smile. "I am fine. I am willing to be here for the summer, and see how Justin likes it. I hope our time here helps him remember how to have fun. It seems to be working."

"I hope he isn't too bored at the farm. I know I said that before, but I do worry. We're kind of isolated," Harley admitted. "My nearest neighbor is a kilometer away and their kids are teenagers. Not many kids nearby."

It was sweet that she was so concerned about his son making friends. It was on his mind too.

"He hasn't been bored," Ryker reassured her. "He loves it there. When I first told him there were dogs, alpacas and... I hesitate to use the word chickens when referring to Cluck Norris Jr., but he was very excited. He loves animals. He loves Willow."

"She loves him too. I love how much he loves animals, but we should still keep him away from Cluck Norris Jr."

Ryker pursed his lips together in a frown and rubbed the sore spot on his leg. "Yes. I still have that bruise, weeks later."

"I'm telling you, eat the farm fresh eggs and picture taking out your revenge on Cluck for every peck or scratch."

"That's kind of dark for a vet tech to say."

"What's more twisted is hanging on to him and trying to win his love."

"Can chickens love?" he wondered.

"I don't know, but I try," she said in exasperation.

"So instead of cats you'll have chickens?"

"I suppose so. Why are we talking about my chickens?" she asked, catching her breath.

"It's better than neutering!"

Harley laughed out loud. It was infectious and he couldn't help but laugh along with her. Her blue eyes were twinkling in the setting sun light. She was so charming, so personable. He could see why Michel liked her so much.

Why everyone she interacted with liked her.

It was hard not to.

It was nice just having a conversation about ridiculous chickens. It was also nice to laugh with someone his own age again. It had been some time since he'd done that, had a real conversation with someone outside of work or family. It was hard not to like Harley, to fall under her spell.

Like when he'd kissed her. He was glad she'd agreed to be friends still. Part of him really did want more, so he knew he had to be careful. A boundary of friendship would help.

"Tell me, how did you came into possession of these chickens?" he asked.

She cocked an eyebrow. "It's not that interesting. I like eggs and I thought it would make sense, so I adopted some birds. Then I had this friend who said roosters are killed almost at birth and tossed. She was running a rescue program for unwanted roosters out in Nova Scotia, which is where I was when I acquired Cluck Norris Jr., Count Cluckula and Wyatt Chirp."

"So you drove three roosters from Nova Scotia to Ontario out of sympathy?"

Harley nodded. "Yes, but they were chicks and it's not that long of a drive."

"Um, it's like twenty-some hours."

Harley shrugged. "Well, it was supposed to be my honeymoon at the time and I had all these nonrefundable deposits, so Willow and I went for my honeymoon."

"Honeymoon? So how close did you get to marrying your ex?" he asked.

"Well, he left me at the altar, so pretty close."

He could hear the sadness in her voice. The hurt.

He understood pain, but his was different. Daphne hadn't run off on him, she had died, but still there was heartache there. And he could see heartbreak etched on her face and in her voice. He understood it.

Before he could stop himself, he reached across the table and took her hand in his. Her small, delicate fingers fit so nicely in his. He brushed his thumb over her knuckles and a ripple of gooseflesh broke out up her arm.

Their gazes locked and his heart was hammering as he fought the urge to pull her close and kiss those delectable, plump lips. Pink bloomed in her cheeks and her lips parted, as if she was going to say something to him.

Only she didn't. Their gazes just remained locked. His blood heated and moved through every nerve ending in his body. His pulse thumped between his ears. Her blue eyes gazed at him, full of softness.

She was beautiful. Her blond hair cascaded over her shoulders, and he wondered how soft it was. It had been some time since he'd felt stirrings of emotions, of desire, like this.

And he wasn't sure what to do.

It was nice holding her hand. Feeling that connection with someone again. Even though he should, he didn't want to let go.

"There's a fair next Friday," she said, breaking the silence.

"A fair?" he asked, curious but not letting go of her hand.

"A midway, rides and games. Maybe after we barbecue, we could take Justin?"

"That sounds like a good idea," he agreed.

"Good," she murmured, her eyes sparkling as the sun began to set. It was so hard not to kiss her again. He wanted to.

Badly.

"Ready to order?" the waitress asked, interrupting them.

Harley snatched her hand back. The pink in her cheeks turned to crimson, and she focused on the menu in front of her. Whatever moment they'd shared was gone, and it was probably for the best. "Yes, I'll have the chicken special with a salad and my French-Canadian friend here is dying to trying Huron County Fries."

There was a devilish twinkle to Harley's eyes.

Ryker just shook his head in dismay and looked at the waitress, who was smiling the widest grin he had ever seen.

"Huron County Fries! Awesome. It's just like a poutine, but with bacon!" The waitress took their menus and moved away. He cringed at the "just like poutine" comment, because it wasn't.

"Why did you order me that?" Ryker asked, trying not to laugh.

"Hey, when in Rome, eh?" She winked at him.

"Touché." He leaned back and watched the sun set over a green rolling hill. He wasn't sure what was happening with Harley, and he knew he shouldn't let anything else happen, but when he was with her it was so easy to feel like he was becoming himself again.

The man he used to know.

The fun-loving jokester and not the hollowed-out shell of a person he was now. The one he'd had to become so he could take care of his son and be there for Justin. The one who had to live day-to-day, numbly, so his son didn't have to bear the additional burden of his own grief.

The problem was, no one was there for him.

And no one ever would be, if he had his way.

What if you stayed?

The thought still scared him, but for a brief moment he let himself picture it.

He thought about leaving Montreal, of taking over Michel's practice. Working with Harley. Continuing to get to know her. It would be a risk.

And he wasn't sure he wanted to take a risk like that, at least not for himself. If they reached the end of the summer and it seemed like moving was the right decision for Justin, then he'd have to consider it. But he couldn't think about it for himself.

Not for a fleeting feeling of freedom and sharing a beautiful sunset with a gorgeous woman.

He just had to enjoy the time he had here and not muddle it up with notions of a happily-ever-after because he shared a nice moment in time with someone, because happily-ever-afters didn't exist.

He knew that loss.

He'd felt that loss.

Keenly.

CHAPTER THIRTEEN

THE REST OF the dinner they chatted about the patients they had seen throughout the day. Thankfully, they avoided all neutering chats.

She really enjoyed dinner, even though she had been having reservations about it when she drove over there. Harley had no regrets after. Except that it ended.

When they both got back to her farm, Michel brought Justin home and she said good-night instead of lingering. She had a busy weekend ahead of her and some business stuff to catch up on.

The clinic was closed on the weekend, but Ryker had his number up on the website to deal with on-call emergencies, to give Michel a break. Michel may have only dropped down to part-time hours, but he was always on call for animal emergencies. Another reason why Michel was so loved.

It was nice that Ryker was carrying on with that. Even for the short time he was here.

She had some dogs that were boarding with her over the weekend, so she was busy in her kennel and doing her chores. When she did see Ryker and Justin, it was when they were coming and going from their place. It was just a friendly wave and nothing more.

But all weekend she couldn't stop thinking about their dinner. How Ryker had opened up about Justin and how tender he was about how she was jilted.

It was nice to have a conversation with someone who understood about pain and loss, even though they each had a different kind of loss.

It still hurt them, nonetheless. Talking about it helped.

When he reached out and took her hand, her blood heated and a rush of anticipation unfurled in the pit of her stomach. It was tender and electric at the same time.

She'd wanted to kiss him again. She'd burned with a need to press her lips against his. And the urge had surprised her.

It was a good thing the waitress interrupted them.

It had been a long time since she felt this way about someone. It was freeing, but scary because she knew that Ryker would leave after the summer.

As she moved through her hectic weekend, she found she really did miss talking to both Ryker and Justin, and for the first time in a long time, she was aware of how lonely she felt.

And she didn't like that feeling at all. It was a long, boring weekend, and although that feeling of loneliness persisted into the week, at least she had even more work to distract her. She spent some time working at the clinic with Ryker, but they were both so busy that there wasn't much time to chat, there or at home. Especially since she had clients' dogs and her own animals to care for. There was no more talk about that kiss, but there was no awkwardness either. It was like the kiss had never happened. At least, that's what she was telling herself. She couldn't get it out of her mind, but she didn't let it interfere with work, and she wasn't planning to let it interfere with their Friday plans either!

She woke up on Friday looking forward to the day and going to the fair that night.

The day dragged on, but she got her chores done early so they could head to the fair right after their dinner.

It was such a peaceful evening, with the three of them enjoying food outside and under the locust trees. The wind whispering through the boughs of spruce and the droning sounds of her alpacas out in a field. It was like the most perfect summer day.

After dinner they cleaned up and everyone piled into Ryker's car to head into Opulence for the small midway that had been set up on the fairgrounds. The sun was setting, and she could see the electric and neon lights that were lighting up the darkening sky.

"Oh, wow, look!" Justin exclaimed from the back seat. "A Ferris wheel!"

Ryker and Harley shared a smile.

"Pappa, can we go on the Ferris wheel?" Justin asked.

"Of course. We can go on all the rides," Ryker announced.

"Yes!" Justin exclaimed.

"Maybe not too many spinning ones," Harley said. "We just had dinner."

"We'll walk around first," Ryker agreed.

They found a place to park and then walked toward the ticket booth, so they could buy their passes for the rides. Justin ran ahead, and she could tell he was so excited.

"It's been a long time since I've seen him this excited. He used to get this way about Halloween or Christmas." Ryker sighed.

"This is good. He's healing."

"He is." He glanced over at her. "How long did it take you to heal from your broken heart?"

"A year." Actually, she wasn't sure it was so clear-cut. Would she ever really heal? Did a person ever really get over a blow or a loss like that? She wasn't sure. She was over Jason, but what happened was something she would always carry with her. She didn't miss him. She was just hurt by how it all ended.

She didn't like being blindsided.

"How about you?" she asked.

"I'm not really sure. I think I just focused on Justin instead of grieving, when it first happened, so it was always hanging over me. But more recently I've had time to myself and I've been feeling…lighter. I mean, it'll always be a part of me, but…" He trailed off.

"This is a very heavy conversation for standing in line to buy tickets," she teased gently.

"You're right. No more talk about that. Let's enjoy tonight."

"Agreed. Pinky swear?" She held out her hand, and he hooked his pinky around hers. A zing of electricity passed through her and her body heated, remembering how he kissed her, how he held her hand at the restaurant.

"Pinky swear," he replied.

They shook pinkies on it.

When they got to the ticket booth Ryker bought a whole whack of tickets, and they made their way to the rides.

It wasn't a huge midway; it was one of those traveling ones that went from community to community during the summer, but for Justin it might as well have been a big theme park, he was so excited. His eyes were twinkling and his mouth open as they walked around the grounds, scoping out where they wanted to go first. There was loud music from the games with rows and rows of brightly colored stuffed animals hanging above the booths. There were cotton candy vendors, bright shiny red candy apples and popcorn popping, making her stomach rumble with appreciation.

She couldn't remember the last time she had cotton candy.

"Pappa, they have a Haunted House! Can we go in the Haunted House?"

Ryker cocked an eyebrow. "You want to go on the Haunted House ride?"

Justin nodded. "Yes."

"Okay." Ryker made a face, and she laughed as they walked up to the false front Haunted House ride.

A little cart pulled up. Justin got in the front seat, but insisted he was brave enough to sit alone, which mean that Ryker climbed into the back seat, right up against her. They were crammed there, and he adjusted so that his arm rested on the back of the seat. She had to lean into his body, and her pulse began to quicken.

"I'll keep you safe," he teased.

"Or push me out."

The bar came down and there was a bell that rang. The cart bumped forward with a lurch and the gaudy painted Keep Out doors swung open with sounds of rattling chains. The doors shut and their cart slowly wound its way through glow-in-the-dark-painted ghosts, with a cheap piped in soundtrack of ghosts moaning, chains rattling and screams.

Justin was killing himself laughing as he looked back at them.

All Harley could focus on was the closeness of Ryker's body and how his arm made her feel so safe.

Until a plastic spider dropped down in front of her and she screamed for a moment and then started to laugh.

"Harley, are you scared?" Justin asked.

"I hate spiders," she gasped, trying to calm her racing heart.

Justin giggled and then turned back to the ride.

"I'll keep you safe," Ryker teased, squeezing her closer.

"Thanks," she groused, but she liked the fact that he promised to keep her safe. No one had ever offered her that before, besides her parents and her older brother. She had learned to rely on herself.

No one disappointed you if you relied on yourself, but as she secretly glanced up at Ryker, she really did feel safe next to him. It felt right.

The doors opened and the dark Haunted House filled with light. The cart lurched again and came to a stop. The bar lifted and Ryker removed his arm from around her.

"What did you think of that, Justin?" Ryker asked, standing up.

"Great!" Justin exclaimed, exiting the ride.

Ryker turned to her and held out his hand. She slipped her hand in his and he helped her up. Her heart was racing and her body trembling as they stood there for a moment, before exiting the ride to join an excited Justin.

She had told herself that their kiss was a one-off. They'd both agreed that it couldn't happen again, but it was hard to remind herself of that in this moment, where they felt like a family.

After the fair they headed back to the farm. Justin had passed out, and Ryker had to carry him into their place to put him to bed. But before he had carried Justin off, he had given Harley a soft kiss on the cheek, which made her feel so warm and fuzzy, if a little confused. She had wanted more, but she knew that wasn't an option, so she did the last of her chores and sneaked off to bed herself.

She was trying not to think about how much fun she had with them, but that was impossible. Even though she was physically exhausted Harley spent another night tossing and turning, thinking about Ryker. The way he snuggled closer to her in the Haunted House and how he held her hand when they would exit the various rides together.

She loved the way he was with his son, and she loved being with them both.

It was like they were all supposed to be together.

She played out so many scenarios in her head, but always came to the same conclusion: it couldn't work. Even if Ryker were open to dating, Montreal was too far from Opulence.

When she woke up, she turned on her phone and groaned at the alerts for thunderstorms later in the day, which would be a pain to do her chores in. She saw a few missed calls pop up, but before she could register anything else the phone rang in her hand. She squinted at the screen and saw her brother's number. She knew it was her brother's by the name she assigned to it.

Dingus.

"Good morning, David," she answered, stifling a yawn.

"Harley, I need your help."

She could hear the panic in David's voice. He usually called her nerd. "What's wrong?"

"I have a foal and it's lame. Our vet is away still. Do you think you can ask Michel to come and take a look?"

"Michel is with his grandson today." She knew their schedule without needing to check.

"Damn," David cursed.

"I can see if my…" She trailed off. Ryker wasn't her anybody. "I can see if Michel's son-in-law can come. He's a vet too."

"That would be great. I'm super worried about the foal."

"No problem. If he can't come, I'll come and try to help as much as I can."

"Love you, Nerd," David said, then hung up.

Harley rolled out of bed, had a quick shower and got dressed. She finished her chores, changed out of her barn clothes and by the time she headed outside to face Ryker, Michel was there to pick up Justin.

"Morning, Michel and Justin," Harley greeted. "You got big plans for the day?"

"Morning!" Michel said. "We're taking Justin go-karting and to a museum."

Justin nodded eagerly. "Then Gramps and Nanna are coming here for dinner."

"That sounds fun. Is your dad around?"

"Yeah, he has some work so he's not going go-karting."

"We better go," Michel said, glancing over his shoulder at Justin.

The boy nodded. "Okay, Gramps. Bye, Harley!"

Harley waved as Michel and Justin drove away. She made her way over to Ryker's place. He was on the deck, his laptop open on the small bistro table, and he was sitting in a Muskoka chair.

"Morning," she said, feeling instantly nervous.

Which was silly. They'd shared an amazing kiss and nothing more. He may have kissed her softly when they got home from the fair, but it was just a friendly kiss. A peck on the cheek.

Not a burning, sensual, soul-singeing kiss like they had shared a couple of weeks ago. So she shouldn't feel so nervous around him.

"Salut!" he said when he saw her approaching.

"You're not interested in go-karting?" she asked.

"No. My nephews will be there, so Justin will have company. I love them, but hot sun and go-karts, no thanks."

"How about a trip to a farm outside of town to check out a lame foal?" she asked, wringing her hands, which she always did when she was nervous.

He cocked an eyebrow. "A client?"

"My brother, David, the horse breeder. His vet is away. Michel has helped out before, but I didn't want to ruin their plans."

Ryker glanced at his laptop and then closed it. "*D'accord*, but I'm supposed to cook dinner tonight for my in-laws."

"I think we'll be back by then," Harley reassured him.

"I was… I was hoping you'd come to dinner as well," he asked, his voice hopeful.

"Um…" She wanted to ask him if that was such a good idea. But Michel and Maureen were friends of hers as well, so how could she say no. "Sure."

"*Parfait.*"

"Shall I drive?" she offered.

Ryker nodded. "Please, and in return I will not burn your dinner tonight, like Michel tends to do when he cooks."

She laughed, knowing that all too well. "Deal."

"I'll meet you by your truck in ten minutes."

Harley left. It was going to be hard to be trapped in her truck with Ryker for an hour, but she could be professional.

She had to be professional.

Just because they'd spent a cozy evening pretending to be a family at the fair didn't mean their agreement had changed. And that cheek-kiss last night had meant nothing.

She grabbed her gear and met Ryker at her truck. He loaded her gear and his into the back of the vehicle and then climbed into the passenger seat. He looked really good in his faded denim jeans and his plaid shirt. At least he was better dressed for work at a farm. This time if he fell in poo, she wouldn't feel so bad.

She snickered at that thought.

"What?" he asked. "I got this at the tack shop. Is it wrong?"

"No. It's perfect. I was thinking about poop." She groaned as the words tumbled out of her mouth.

He snorted. "I understand what you meant. Why do you think I bought this outfit?"

"It looks great," she told him. It really did. She was trying not to stare too much.

"How far away is your brother's ranch?" he asked.

"Just over an hour. We're leaving Huron County for Bruce County." She waggled her eyebrows, trying to break the tension with some silliness as they drove away.

"Exciting for a Saturday," he responded drolly. He smiled at her warmly, and her heart skipped a beat. The feeling of his lips, the memories of their kiss and his strong arm around her at the fair last night played on an endless loop in her mind. This was going to be a long, long ride to David's ranch.

Ryker had been hoping for a quiet day to catch up on reports. He'd called to check on the parvo puppies, both back with their owners by now, and they were both doing well. He'd also formulated a letter to get someone to inspect Sharpe Line Farms' breeding facilities. He sent that off right away.

All productive busywork that didn't distract from the fact that he couldn't stop thinking about Harley. He knew they'd agreed to be just friends, and he still knew that was the smart thing to do, but other ideas kept sneaking in: that kiss. He didn't know what came over him. She was standing there and he just couldn't help himself. The kiss had been everything he thought it would be. And it had been on his mind for weeks.

Then he told her that he wanted to hold her close and kiss her in French, and he was pretty sure she didn't know what he said.

It was sweet and overwhelming. She was so soft in his arms, and he wanted so much more. He was glad when Justin had interrupted them. Or so he told himself.

He'd thought a night at the fair would distract him, but instead it drew him closer to her. It was so nice to feel normal again. Him, Harley and Justin. It was like it was meant to be.

They had chatted about how long it took to get over heartache. He wasn't sure if one ever did, rather suspecting that one learned to live with it, but there could be room for another person. Which was silly. How could he even contemplate that?

All night he couldn't stop thinking about her and how he burned for her. She made him feel like he wanted to take a risk again, and that scared him. There was a lot to process. Part of him was saying to leave and head back to Montreal, but the summer wasn't over. Justin would be crushed if they left early. His son was so content here.

He was happy.

It felt like a heavy weight of grief was being lifted off his shoulders, and he didn't know how to process it all. Maybe it was time for a change?

He was falling for Harley and he didn't know what to do.

"Will you tell me about David's ranch?" he asked, trying not to think about her lips. He just wanted to talk about anything so he didn't have to think about how close she was to him, how he could smell her scent of melons and cucumber.

"His ranch?" she asked, not taking her eyes off the road. "Not much to tell. My brother loved racehorses so much he studied equine care and management in Ridgetown. That's where he met his partner, Armand. They fell in love and they started breeding some of the most sought-after racehorses in the county. David also has stud horses that are also in demand, and he also teaches horseback riding. Equestrian and western."

Ryker was impressed. "So he knows his horses."

"Yep. Usually if there's a horse problem, he and Armand can handle it. When he calls me or his vet for help, then it's not good. It's something completely out of his depth."

"You said the foal was lame?" Ryker asked.

She nodded. "I don't know what degree of lameness, just that David sounded really distressed when he called."

"Well, we'll see what we can do."

"I appreciate that." She glanced at him, her blue eyes full of warmth, which made him feel a rush of emotions again.

She was enchanting, and being with her made him feel alive again. He'd been living in a fog for so long, trying to be strong for Justin, it was nice to feel something. Even if it was something he shouldn't.

The rest of the ride was pretty quiet. He looked out the window, enjoying the scenery as they drove north up the Lake Huron coast. He could see windmills, farms, crops and trailers in the distance, and occasionally a tractor on the road, which slowed them up.

Finally, they turned off the main highway and down a gravel road that led to a dead end. There was a huge western-style gate at the end of the gravel road that said Bedard and Soukh Ranch, with a beautiful engraved mustang running across a field with a burning gold sunset of Lake Huron in the background.

Harley buzzed in and the gate swung open.

He raised his eyebrows, impressed.

Harley shrugged. "They do very well. They practically have their own vet clinic on-site."

"Impressive."

Harley knew exactly where she was going, and as she approached a massive, beautiful modern barn Ryker could see there were two men waiting, with a nervous foal in an outside pen, just lying in the dirt. The mother was nearby, but separated so that she wouldn't nip at them. Or at least, Ryker assumed it was the mother.

Harley parked her truck and a blond man came over, his arms wide open. "Hey, Nerd."

They climbed out of the truck and Harley gave the man who called her a nerd, a hug. "Hey, Dingus. So this is Michel's son-in-law, Ryker. Ryker, this is my brother, David Bedard, and that other man coming this way is his partner, Armand."

"Your brother-in-law," David corrected her. He turned to Ryker and the same blue eyes that Harley had shined back at him, his appreciation evident. "I am so glad you could come at such short notice."

"It is no problem," Ryker assured him, taking David's hand.

Armand came and introduced himself next and then gave Harley a big hug.

"So, tell me about this foal," Ryker said, trying to get to the business at hand. Justin was expecting him to be at home tonight and he had promised to cook Michel and Maureen dinner.

And Harley. You invited Harley as well.

The sooner he saw this foal, the better.

"Adele was born about three days ago," Armand stated. "The lameness started this morning—she won't put any weight on her leg, and you can tell she's in pain. I am worried about an infection. I have seen that before, bacteria that gets in through the umbilicus."

"You're not wrong," Ryker agreed as he made his way to the pen cautiously.

The foal in question tried to stand, but it was evident by the way she didn't put weight on that leg and the way she tried to hobble away that the leg was paining her. The foal collapsed on the ground.

She was a young foal, so if it was something infectious like infection of the bone plates or joints, then she would have a fighting chance. What he needed was a blood test, but for now he could help ease some of the pain.

"Harley mentioned you have a treatment space for your regular vet," Ryker asked. "Can we get the foal in there so I can take a look?"

"We sure do," David stated. "We have an ultrasound machine and painkillers. Everything our vet needs."

He was very impressed. They put their animals first, like any good farmer or any good breeder. He couldn't help but think of Sharpe Line Farms and how they were anything but the definition of good.

Armand and David worked to get the foal standing, and then

Armand picked her up to carry her into the barn, while David calmed down the mother.

"I'll show you the way in. They have gowns and everything. Armand took some animal science courses. They are very involved with their horses and all their animals," Harley stated.

"I admire that," Ryker admitted. "To run an operation like this is impressive."

"David is a savvy businessman. I always admired him for that," Harley admitted.

What he wanted to tell her was that she was too, building a grooming and boarding facility on her own from the ground up, while also working as a vet tech. That was something to be applauded for too.

They walked through the main office, and Harley led him to the treatment room. He put on a disposable gown and gloves and then made his way into the spacious and clean room. The foal was lying there again, but then stood in the small pen with Armand soothing her.

Ryker approached Adele and spoke softly to her. He knelt down and got a look at the leg in question. There was swelling and as he gently palpated the area he knew it hurt the horse, but he didn't think it was an infection as he felt her leg and saw the trouble.

"I think it's her coffin bone," Ryker said. "I would need an X-ray to be sure."

"Coffin bone?" Armand asked. "Can that be healed in one so young?"

Ryker nodded. "It can. She'll need rest, but again I would need an X-ray. We'll still do a blood test to be sure, and I will give the foal some pain relief."

"All our meds are in that cabinet. It's unlocked," David said, coming into the treatment room. "We do have a portable X-ray machine."

"I can operate it," Harley volunteered. "Animal radiology was something of a speciality."

Ryker grinned. "*Bonne*. Then I'll give her some pain relief, give her something to calm her down and we'll X-ray her."

"It's in the next room," Armand stated.

"I'll need you to insert the plate," Harley said to Ryker. "I'll get the machine ready and pull out the lead vests."

"*Bonne.*" Ryker hadn't done many equine X-rays, but he knew how they were done. He was glad Harley was here and familiar with how the machine at her brother's farm worked. In Montreal the vet techs were the ones who ran the diagnostic machines, for the most part.

He was way more hands-on here than in the city, and he liked it. It surprised him how much.

After Ryker had done the blood work and given the foal some pain relief, Armand led her out into the next room. It was clear that the pain medicine was already helping, as well as the mild sedatives to help calm her down.

Harley helped him on with a lead vest and then helped Armand on with his while Ryker held Adele. He stroked her muzzle and told her what a good girl she was.

"The plate is on that table," Harley said, quietly before she readied the machine and slowly inched it toward Adele on its long swinging arm.

"*Merci.*" Ryker picked up the plate on a long handle and knelt down slowly.

Armand continued to speak in soothing tones.

A red light flashed on Adele's chestnut-colored leg. She moved her sore foot once, lifting it up, but then gently put it back down and stood still.

"Ready," Harley said.

Ryker slipped the plate between the foal's legs, and Harley counted down and took the X-rays in quick succession.

"All done," she said.

Ryker removed the plate and set it down. Armand led Adele out of the X-ray room and they removed their lead vests to head back into the treatment room.

The diagnostic images had been sent to the computer in the treatment room and David was bringing the images up. Ryker went through the images.

"It is her coffin bone." Ryker pointed to where the fracture was in the front hoof. "See, the distal phalanx or coffin bone."

"At least it's not bacterial," David remarked, although he still sounded disappointed because that fracture was not an easy one to recover from, as Ryker knew firsthand.

"She is small enough and doesn't weigh too much. Adele should recover. She'll need a bar shoe, and we'll have to keep repeating X-rays until it's completely healed. It will take several months."

David nodded. "I do have bar shoes. And I have small ones."

"Well, let's get the shoe on her and then have her rest in her stall with her mother. She's been through enough stress today. Make sure you let me know about the results of the blood work, and I'll leave a note for your regular vet and where he can contact me."

David grinned and shook Ryker's hand. "Thank you again, Doc. Be sure to send me your bill."

"He will," Harley reassured her brother.

David and Armand led Adele out of the treatment room to take her to the barn where they shoed their horses. Adele was young enough that Ryker had no doubt the coffin bone would heal with rest and the help of the bar shoe, which was a circular horseshoe that joined the heel together and prevented movement of the hoof.

Ryker typed up his notes and recording the testing he did on Adele for David and Armand's vet.

"You did really good in there," Harley remarked. "For a city vet."

He smiled, pleased she was happy. "Well, I'm not used to taking X-rays of a horse in the city. It's definitely more hands-on here."

"It is, and that's what I love about it. Remember, I worked in a city too," she reminded.

"I remember you saying how much you don't like the city."

"I don't hate it, I just prefer it here."

He nodded. "I understand that."

"Can I ask you a question?"

"Of course," he replied as he continued to type in his notes.

"Why don't you own your own practice yet?" she teased.

Ryker took a deep breath. "It's been my dream. Justin was born shortly after Daphne and I married, so I was never in a rush to strike out on my own."

Another reason why taking on Michel's clinic was tempting. A practice that had everything set up? Clients, equipment, staff. It was too good to be true. Still, it was nerve-racking to think about taking it over and leaving the safety net of Montreal. Could he carry the burden of his own business on his shoulders? He wasn't sure that he could. Not when Justin still needed him so much.

"Makes sense," Harley agreed.

Ryker finished typing. "There. Now, let's go see Adele and her shoeing. Then we should hit the road. *Oui?*"

Harley smiled and nodded. *"Oui."*

"Well, lunch first somewhere." His stomach grumbled. "Then back to Opulence."

She smiled sweetly. "I think we can make that work. David has already mentioned wanting us to stay. If you're up for that?"

"I think that's fair."

Ryker followed her out of the treatment room, disposing of his gown. There were so many things to love about this area. So many good things, yet he was so terrified of making the leap. But he wasn't as scared of taking that chance as he was when he first came here.

Maybe, just maybe, Opulence could be his and Justin's home too.

CHAPTER FOURTEEN

WHEN DAVID HAD insisted on making them lunch, Harley honestly thought that he was going to make something simple and quick. But when the grill came out and David got cooking, Ryker was completely invested in it and didn't seem to be in such a rush. Not that she could blame him.

David was an amazing cook.

They ate outside the small ranch house, overlooking the farm. David and Armand's ranch was on a hilltop, so they could see a thin blue line of Lake Huron in the distance and all the other surrounding farms. It was one of the most beautiful spots in this area, although she naturally preferred her farm.

Then again, David had over a thousand acres and she just had thirty...but dogs didn't need a thousand acres to run like horses did.

As the lunch went on Harley could see the big, dark, rolling shelf clouds coming over the western horizon and the lake. There were more warnings popping up on her phone, only now it was more serious and there was a potential threat for a tornado and localized flooding.

Ryker and she quickly packed up and said their goodbyes, but the storm rolled in quicker than Harley could drive. Not far into the journey, they were blasted with heavy, torrential downpour making visibility very difficult.

"How far does this storm spread?" Ryker asked. She could hear the concern in his voice. She knew he was thinking about Justin.

She was too.

"It's across most of northern Huron County and western Bruce County," she replied. "It's coming in from Michigan across the lake."

Ryker's phone dinged and he glanced at it. "Michel and Maureen are at your place with Justin. The go-karting got rained out. Justin is upset, but Willow is calming him. I hope you don't mind, Michel used your spare key. The tiny house is kind of cramped."

"Not at all." Harley was glad Willow was calming Justin down and most likely vice versa. Willow wasn't a big fan of thunderstorms. She could tell by the way Ryker's brow furrowed and how he kept checking his phone that he was increasingly worried about Justin.

"I shouldn't have stayed for lunch," he murmured.

"We still might've been caught in it," Harley admitted. "It came in fast."

"I was just enjoying myself. Adult conversations, good food…" He trailed off.

"You don't need to apologize."

A bolt of sheet lightning arched across the sky, along with a crack of thunder that seemed to shake her truck.

"That was close," she murmured. There was a greenish tint to the sky, and it was darkening the closer they got to the lake. She wouldn't be surprised if waterspouts developed.

The wind picked up and had a hollow, eerie whistle to it.

Ryker's phone and hers went off at the same time. Warning alerts telling everyone in their area to seek shelter now.

The rain blasted them sideways, and it became hard to keep control of the truck. She couldn't see through the rain. They were already thirty minutes from David's and forty minutes from home.

"We need to take shelter," Ryker stated, his face hardened.

"I think you're right." As they passed a gravel side road, a bolt of lightning struck a tree, which fell down in front of them.

Harley slammed on the brakes, her truck hydroplaning before coming to a stop.

"You okay?" Ryker asked.

"Yep. My heart rate should return to normal soon," she said, nervously trying to make light of their near miss. "The road to my parents' cottage is a few minutes back the way we came. We can wait out the storm there."

"Good idea." Ryker texted Michel to tell him.

Calming her frazzled nerves, Harley turned the truck around and made her way back a few minutes to the private road that she knew led down the hill to a cluster of cottages. Her parents' place was at the end. Navigating other fallen branches, she made it to her parents' cottage, parked her truck and dug out the spare key on her key ring. Then they made a mad dash to the front door through the pelting rain that was turning to hail.

Her fingers were cold and numb as she unlocked the door, the wind pushing them both inside. By the time they got in and shut the door against the strong wind, they were absolutely drenched.

"Let's see if we have electricity." Harley flicked on the light switch and it did nothing. "Nope."

"Well, at least we have a roof."

The wind howled and the thunder rumbled. They both stared up at the roof nervously, half expecting it to be blown off. There was a crash, and they rushed to the window to see that an old spruce had fallen down, blocking the driveway and the road, and narrowly avoiding hitting Harley's truck.

Great.

They were trapped here.

"I need to tell Justin I'm okay, but that I'll be delayed." Ryker pulled out his phone but cussed, and she saw he had no service. She pulled out her phone and saw she had no bars either.

"Try the old rotary," Harley suggested as she looked for towels and blankets in the linen closet.

"Bonne." Ryker picked up the phone, but there was a loud

crackle of static, which meant the phone line had been struck by lightning.

"Put it down!" Harley shouted, suddenly remembering you shouldn't use a landline phone during a thunderstorm. The risk was small, but if lightning struck it, he could get shocked.

"Tabarnak," he cursed, setting it down quickly. "I wanted to tell them I was safe and where I was."

"Michel, Maureen and Willow are with him. He'll be fine."

Ryker nodded apprehensively, but she could tell he was nervous. She handed him towels and a blanket. *"Quoi?"*

"I'm not sitting around in wet clothes. Modesty be damned," she muttered.

"Agreed. We're adults."

"Exactly. You can use the guest bedroom and I'll go into my parents'. Maybe they have some dry clothes here."

"Merci."

She slipped into her parents' room and got out of her wet denim. She took it all off, because she was completely soaked through. The storm was raging and the wind was howling. She could see the small trees in the yard bent over under the unrelenting wind. It was so dark in her parents' wood-paneled homage to the eighties cottage, that she fumbled.

There were no spare clothes, so instead she wrapped herself up in a quilt and grabbed an emergency flashlight to make her way back to the living room.

Ryker was there. A towel wrapped around his waist. His broad, muscular chest was bare. Her pulse began to race and she tried not to look at him, but it was hard not to.

"Any luck?" he asked, obviously referring to clothes.

"Nope. Nothing. The one time my parents don't have anything." She shuffled toward the couch, shivering. He came and sat close to her, the two of them just sitting there and listening to the storm rage. It wasn't the only storm raging though; her own storm was raging in the very fiber of her being.

Her body was so very aware of how close he was and how alone they were.

"The OPP will come check the cottages here," she said, breaking the silence. "Once the storm is over."

"I hope service is returned soon so I can call Justin."

"I'm sure it will be," she reassured him gently.

Ryker sighed. "I would hate for this to set him back. He's made great strides here. He's more himself."

"And how about you?" she asked.

"What do you mean?"

"You're so concerned for Justin, but have *you* been able to heal, too?"

They had talked about this before, about healing. She had thought she was good, but just spending time with him, she was beginning to realize she was also on her own journey of trusting again. Only she wasn't completely there.

She was falling in love with him, of that she was certain, but she wasn't sure she could trust him not to leave her.

He sighed. "I've never really had a moment to process it all. Justin and his mental health have been my priority, but...yes. I think I have," Ryker admitted, his voice shaking. "I grieved my wife's loss, but my everything was Justin. When we first came here, I wasn't sure what I should feel. I'd just been so numb for so long. I think that being here has helped."

Harley understood that. She'd gone through the same thing with Jason when he left her standing there in her wedding dress. Hurt, crushed and humiliated. It had taken her a while to find herself, to get the strength and courage to move on and to protect her heart and set boundaries.

Boundaries that she and Ryker seemed to cross every time they were together. Her walls kept everyone out but him, it seemed. So when he said that Opulence could heal him, her heart was hopeful.

"What about you?" Ryker asked. "Has Opulence helped your heart heal?"

"I'd like to think so."

"You're not sure?"

"Are you?" she asked.

He shrugged. "You don't date?"

"No."

"Why?" Ryker asked.

"At first I told myself it was because I was too busy, but maybe that was because I was scared of being hurt again. Both were true, because the reality is my business took all my focus. There's not much downtime. But I've also learned that people never stay in Opulence. Not really. It's small, but that doesn't bother me. There's just not a lot of single men around here. I have to be careful. I'm not going to lower my standards because I'm lonely."

She was completely rambling, giving him a thousand excuses why she was alone, but in reality it was fear. Fear of having her life decided for her. Fear of being abandoned and alone. "My choice was taken from me. My ex decided to end our relationship because he changed his mind about where he wanted to live, and he assumed I wouldn't be happy with him in the city. He didn't give me a voice, so it's been better to be alone. I make my own decisions."

Except during these weeks with Ryker, she realized that wasn't true.

"Are you lonely?"

"I am," she admitted.

Ryker nodded. "I am lonely too."

"It's nice to have a friend though." Their gazes locked and her heart was racing, her body began to thrum with need as she thought about their kiss and every touch they'd shared since.

How she melted for him.

Every moment they spent together, she thought about how she wasn't alone when she was with him.

Thunder crashed again, the wind and rain lashing at the cottage, but she couldn't really hear it over her own hammering heart. She longed for him to wrap his arms around her, to hold her close.

To make her feel safe again.

Ryker reached out and brushed a damp curl of hair from

her face. "It is nice to have a friend. Or maybe more than a friend…"

"Yes," she whispered.

"I would like to kiss you, Harley," Ryker said. "I know we said it was a one-time—"

"I would like that too," she interrupted him.

"You're not babbling," he whispered, leaning closer. "No longer talking a mile a minute like you usually do when you're nervous."

"I'm not nervous now." And she wasn't, because this was what she wanted. This was serious. She moved closer and reached out to touch his face, her hand trembling. He took her hand and pressed a hot, searing kiss on the pulse point of her wrist, making a zing of liquid pleasure shoot up her arm.

She wanted to resist him, but it had been so long. She wanted to feel vulnerable with someone. To be held and have that kind of intimate connection she had denied herself in order to protect her heart.

She didn't know what was going to happen after, but it could just be about now. This moment.

Just about connection and comfort.

This was something she wanted. Something she'd been fighting since she met him. She just wanted to be carried away in his arms, in his embrace.

Sure, her heart might be broken at the end of this, but it was a risk she was willing to take to feel something again. She cupped his face, pulling him close, the blanket falling away from her shoulders to reveal her nakedness. Harley pressed her lips against his and melted into his kiss.

Sweet and honeyed.

And completely overwhelming.

It rocked her to her core and she never wanted this to end. Their kiss deepened and his hands were in her hair as he pressed her down into the couch. She was ready, and she wanted this stolen moment of passion with Ryker.

Her desire for him was fierce. It scared her all over again

because she'd never felt this way for another man. Not even Jason. But she had to live in this moment. "Ryker, I want you."

"Harley, I don't think we can," he murmured. "I want to, but I don't have protection."

"I'm on the pill. It's okay." She pulled him close again and he cupped her breast. "Touch me."

Ryker moaned and captured her lips with his, sealing her fate. There was no turning back now and she didn't want to. His lips trailed over her body, leaving a trail of fire as she arched against him, not wanting the connection of heat to break.

She was glad for the storm, so that they didn't have clothes in their way. They were just skin to skin, heartbeat to heartbeat.

Touching.

Melting.

She ran her hands over him. Touching him as he stroked and kissed her, making her ache with need.

"You make me feel alive again," he murmured against her neck.

"Oui." She whispered teasingly and he chuckled. His eyes twinkling in the shadows cast by the storm. Only flashes of lightning allowed her glimpses of his hard, muscular body over hers.

She was lost to him.

Harley opened her legs for him to settle between her thighs. She was wet and ready for him.

So very ready.

She wanted him to take her. She wanted to feel all of him inside her. She wanted him to heal her and to wipe away the past hurts. Arching her back, bucking her hips, she let him know how much she needed him. His hands branded her skin where he touched her, where he stroked between her legs making her thighs tremble.

"You are so wet," he murmured, touching her between her legs, making her burn with need as a coil of pleasure unfurled in her belly.

"I want you," she said again, breathlessly.

"J'ai tellement envie de toi." He blew across the skin of her neck. "I want you so much."

He covered her body with his, his hands pinning her wrists over her head as he licked her nipples. Their gazes locked as he slowly pushed into her, agonizingly slow.

She cried out, emotions of pleasure overwhelming her.

"You are so warm, wet and *tu es si tendu,*" he moaned.

Harley moved her hips, urging him to take her harder and faster. To completely possess her. It scared her how much she wanted him. He let go of her wrists, bracing himself as he thrust faster. She dug her nails into his shoulders, clinging to him as he rode her urgently.

The sweet release was just at the edge, building deep inside her. She locked her legs around his waist as the climax washed over her and she succumbed to the wave of pleasure.

He moaned, and it wasn't long before he joined her in his own release.

She rolled to her side so he wouldn't fall off the edge of the couch. He touched her face, smiling at her so gently. She felt safe with him, but she couldn't tell him that. Instead, she ran her hands through his dark hair, tears stinging her eyes.

It was all so overpowering. The rush of emotions she had worked so hard to lock away for so long. It was like a dam had burst inside her.

"Are you crying, *cherie*?" Ryker asked.

"I'm fine," she said, her voice trembling. "It's just been so long since I…"

He nodded his head and kissed the tip of her nose. "*Oui.* I understand."

She brushed her tears away. "I don't regret what happened."

"Me either," he agreed, then he pulled her close, kissing her and holding her as she trembled against him.

She had sworn she wouldn't put expectations on this, that she could live in the moment. She had to protect her heart. The problem was her heart was already losing itself to a man who couldn't promise her forever. With Ryker, that moment had meant everything, and it was breaking her heart, the idea that he'd leave with Justin and the little family she'd gained would be gone.

The family she didn't know she needed, but had always wanted.

Ryker couldn't believe what had just happened. It had been so freeing that he had shared something so intimate with Harley. He'd never thought that he would ever share a moment like that again with anyone.

His whole life had been focused on taking care of Justin and easing his pain that he locked his own life away, his own feelings. He had been numb for so long. It was good to share something like that with someone like Harley, but there was a part of him that was scared too.

When she had trembled in his arms after it was over and he held her, he started feeling that trepidation of what would happen next. Neither of them had promised each other anything, and he wasn't sure what he could give her, because he still wasn't sure what was going to happen at the end of the summer.

He wasn't sure that he could make his and Justin's life work here, but he wanted it to.

He loved his friendship with Harley, he loved working with her and spending time with her. He'd already suspected he was falling in love with her, but now he knew that he couldn't stop it.

"So what do we do?" she asked.

"We wait." He wasn't sure if that's what she wanted to hear, but he didn't know what to say. He was healing, but was he ready to take a chance on a big move? One that would affect his son? He wasn't sure.

"Do you really need to leave Opulence?" she asked.

It caught him off guard.

"Montreal is home," he admitted. "It would be hard to leave there. You could visit in Montreal."

"I could, though my farm takes time and it's hard to leave for long."

"True. I have thought about moving here, more than once, but it's such a big decision."

"Understandable. It's hard to make a change."

"Oui," he replied tightly.

There was a buzz and then the lights turned on.

"We have power!" Harley exclaimed, jumping up. "I'm throwing our clothes in the dryer."

"That's a good idea." Ryker pulled out his phone, but there was still no service.

Tabarnak.

He was concerned that Justin would be having anxiety about being separated during a violent storm, and he had a bit of guilt for getting lost in the moment with Harley.

He wandered over to the window and stared outside. He could see everything clearly now. There were branches and trees all over the road, but Harley's truck still looked intact. Hopefully the storm wasn't building to a tornado. Or if it was, it didn't hit the farm.

"There, in about twenty minutes our clothes will be dry," Harley remarked, covering herself with a blanket again. "Do you have cell service yet?"

"No." He frowned. "I'm sure he's okay."

"I'm sure he is too. Try not to worry." She glanced at her phone. "Hey, I have service. Want to call Michel with my phone and check on the farm?"

"Oui!" He took Harley's phone and called Michel.

"Harley!" Michel answered, a frantic edge to his voice.

"No. It's me, Ryker," Ryker responded. "My phone still doesn't have service. Is everything okay?"

"No," Michel said. He sounded like he was fighting back tears. "Where are you?"

"We're at Harley's parents' cottage. Outside Inverhuron. What's wrong?" Ryker was bracing himself to hear that there'd been damage to the farm or someone was injured. His mind was running amok, and he felt the same way that he had years ago when he found Daphne unconscious on the kitchen floor.

Powerless.

Helpless.

"When we couldn't get ahold of you, Justin slipped out of the house. Willow followed him, but they're missing." Ryker's stomach dropped to the soles of his feet, and he was having a hard time processing what Michel was telling him. "We went out in the storm, but I don't know where they've gone. The OPP are here, and emergency crews. We need you here, Ryker."

"I'm coming," he said without a second thought. But he swore when he remembered. "The road here is blocked."

"I'll tell the officer where you are and they'll come for you both. I'm sorry, Ryker," Michel sobbed. "I shouldn't have let him out of my sight. I can't lose him...not like I lost Daphne."

Ryker's chest constricted. He was so worried Michel would have another heart attack like he did when his daughter died. "It's not your fault. I will be there as soon as I can. We'll be waiting for the OPP."

He hung up the phone, handed it back to Harley and ran his fingers through his hair, not sure of what to do. It felt like his knees were giving out.

He couldn't lose Justin.

Maybe this change for the summer was a mistake. Maybe it had been too much. He shouldn't have pushed for Justin to be independent of him. He should've gone go-karting with his son.

"What's wrong?" Harley asked.

"Justin panicked and ran away...with Willow. They can't find them. They were lost in the storm."

Harley gasped. "Oh my God."

"The OPP are coming to get us." Ryker swallowed the hard lump in his throat as all this anger just bubbled up inside him. "I should've never come here. I should've never taken him from Montreal. This was all a mistake. I can't stay here."

He saw the look of hurt in Harley's eyes. He didn't mean that she was a mistake, but he couldn't tell her that, because all he could think about was getting to his son, whom he shouldn't have left.

He moved past her to stand in front of the dryer, where he panicked in silence and watched the load spin until it dinged and he could get his clothes.

The moment they found Justin, he was heading back to Montreal and the safety of their small home. He would make sure that Justin would always feel safe. He should've gone go-karting with his son today, or he at least should've stayed at the tiny home.

Hell, he should've stayed in Montreal. Where it was just the two of them. A place where he could keep an eye on Justin. Montreal was their home, and it helped him in this frantic moment to visualize bringing his son back there safely, but somewhere behind the panic in his mind, for the first time, it didn't feel so much like home when he thought about it. Knowing it would be just him and Justin alone.

CHAPTER FIFTEEN

THE RIDE BACK to her farm in the OPP cruiser was silent. Ryker was understandably stressed, as was she. She'd known it was likely that he wouldn't stay, and this incident would definitely drive him away. She couldn't blame him. It hurt so much because despite her best efforts to keep Ryker at arm's length, she had fallen in love with him.

With both him and his son.

Right now, she was having a hard time trying to keep it all together, because she was hurt, but scared and angry too. Angry that they weren't there for Justin and that he was so afraid he ran away. Like his dad, Justin had sort of worked his way under her skin and into her heart. She worried about Justin and Willow. Maybe it was foolish, but her little dog had been her whole world for so long.

As they drove back to her farm, she could see the downed hydro lines and there was a small path in a field of destruction where something had touched down, but none of that would be confirmed until later.

She just hoped that they could find Justin and Willow. That the two of them hadn't wandered far. It was still raining pretty heavily, and the temperature had dropped by the time they pulled onto her property.

Kaitlyn was there, with a few of their clients and some other volunteers from town.

Michel was standing in the rain as the cruiser pulled up. His face was drawn and haggard. As the OPP officer parked,

Ryker got out of the back without saying a word to her and went straight to Michel and Maureen. She followed him and noticed Maureen was openly sobbing. Her arm was bandaged in a sling and there were paramedics on the scene.

"It's my fault," Maureen said, weeping.

"How?" Ryker asked, gently touching her shoulder.

"He saw me get hurt. I slipped and came down hard on my arm. Then he cried out for Willow to come back and...he took off. I tried to chase him, but the wind was so strong," Maureen whimpered.

"We've searched all the buildings, no sign of him," an officer said.

"How about the forest?" Harley suggested. "There's seventeen acres and he's always been fascinated by it. He told me about how he'd like to visit it."

The officer nodded. "We're going to start there, but..."

"What?" Ryker asked, an edge to his voice.

"The creek is overflowing and the footbridge over the creek to the forest is moving fast. We can't get over the footbridge. There's water with a strong current running over the top."

Maureen cried out and Michel pulled her close. Harley's heart sank.

Ryker's eyes were wild and he began to cuss as Harley paced around the yard in the rain. She knew exactly what the OPP officer was suggesting, that Justin and Willow were both swept away. She swallowed a lump in her throat. She didn't want to think about it.

"There's a higher water crossing, farther down about seven kilometers at the side road," Harley suggested. "It's a direct line into my forest, and the water wouldn't be going over that bridge."

"We should go," Ryker suggested.

The officer nodded. "Let's go. He'll be wet and the temperatures are dropping fast. We don't want hypothermia to set in."

They formed a search party.

Michel and Maureen stayed behind, with Kaitlyn and Sarah

looking after them. Harley changed into her rubber boots and threw a raincoat on, giving Ryker boots and a raincoat too. They didn't say anything; there was nothing to say in this moment. She knew he wasn't staying. Nothing would change that now.

She saw this coming. It just sucked that she was right all along and ignored her instincts anyways.

Right now though, all that mattered was finding Justin.

The emergency crews gave them reflective gear and flashlights, and they all drove over to the side road, seven kilometers away, while other rescue crews searched the creek flats.

She didn't want to consider the possibility that something worse had happened, because she didn't believe it for one moment. Justin and Willow were fine. They would be okay.

Once they got to the high water crossing, they made their way through the fields and then they split up. Everyone was calling Justin's name.

"As soon as I find him, we're heading home," Ryker groused.

"He'll be fine," Harley reassured him. "Then maybe if you give it a couple of days—"

"I'm in no mood, Harley," Ryker snapped, cutting her off. "This trip was a bad idea. I let my guard down because Justin seemed happy."

"He *is* happy here," Harley countered.

"And what would you know? You're not a parent. Opulence isn't safe for a child, but you don't believe that because you only see the perfection of Opulence. You're just too afraid to leave."

She knew Ryker was just afraid for his son, and lashing out, but it hurt, because it was true. She wasn't a parent. But she wasn't scared of leaving Opulence.

Aren't you?

She couldn't leave. Her business was here. She was so connected to this place because yes, maybe Opulence had always been her safety net, but it was good to her too. Her life was here, and she wasn't looking to change anything.

"And Montreal is so perfect?" she asked. "I think you use

Justin as an excuse not to take a chance on something. I'm not the only one afraid."

Ryker didn't say anything to her, but he started down one forest path and she headed in a different direction, straight into the middle of her forest, fuming and upset.

The bush lot was owned by several land owners in the area, and she knew exactly where the boundaries of her forest lay. She knew that if he went too far in one direction, there was a steep drop-off, back into the creek flats that wound their way through several properties before joining the main river that flowed toward Lake Huron.

She hoped that Justin wasn't too scared to come when his name was being called by a stranger. She could hear the distant pleadings, calls for Justin, calls for Willow echoing through the forest.

When Justin had stayed over at her house, she had told him in the center of her forest was an old truck and a tree house. He had been fascinated by that. She only hoped that he'd headed there, because that's where she was leading them.

"Justin!" she cried out. "Willow?" She whistled, hoping her little dog would let her know they were nearby. She climbed over branches and fallen trees. It was still raining, and thick droplets from the canopy of trees were sliding down the back of her neck, but she didn't care.

It seemed like the slowest walk ever when she finally caught sight of the truck and the tree house. She shined her flashlight onto the muddy forest floor and saw where small shoes had imprinted the ground, followed by paw prints. They'd almost been washed away by the rain, but they were still faintly visible.

Her heart skipped a beat as she found shoes, stuck in the mud, and socks that were soaked. The footsteps still made their way toward the drop-off, so she quickened her pace. Calling for them.

"Justin! Willow!"

Then she heard it.

A weak bark.

Faint.

She ran, branches scratching her face as she headed to the drop-off. It was getting darker, and another storm would soon start rolling through.

"Willow!" She paused at the edge and heard the barking again, looking down she saw Willow there, sitting on top of an unconscious Justin, who was caught up on branches. His coat snagged and his head was next to a rock. She could see he was injured, but the rock and branch had stopped him from sliding into the rushing water below.

"Oh, God," she gasped.

Willow couldn't climb the steep hill and she was whining something fierce. Muddied and shivering.

"Stay there, girl. Keep him safe. Help is coming." She pulled out the flare gun an OPP officer had given her earlier, found a clearing and fired a flare into the sky to let the rescue crew know where she was.

Ryker was panicking inside. His voice was hoarse from calling Justin's name, and all he could do was beat himself up for bringing him here.

Why did he bring him here?

That's what he was asking himself over and over again. Then he thought of Harley and all the mean things he'd said when he was scared and afraid. He regretted it because he was falling for her. Was he willing to admit that now? He still felt hesitant about his feelings. If only she'd consider leaving Opulence, maybe they could work something out. Was that true? Or would he still need time to figure out his feelings? The thing was, she wouldn't be happy in the city.

He knew that.

He saw the flare and heard the pop. His heart rose into his throat, and he started to make his way over to the source. He wasn't far.

Please let him be alive. Please.

He broke through the brush and saw Harley there, standing over the edge of a drop-off.

God. No.

"Harley?" he asked frantically.

"I found him. They're stuck," she explained.

Ryker ran to the edge and saw his son, bleeding but safe from the rushing water below. Willow was muddied and sitting on him, protecting him the best she could. He frantically looked around, trying to find some way that he could get down there and retrieve them, but it was so steep and muddy. He didn't want to knock Justin loose and have him and Willow be swept away in the creek below.

That feeling of powerlessness became all too apparent again.

All he could do was wait, and it was agonizing.

Why had he left him alone today?

"Over here!" someone shouted in the distance.

Harley turned around, waving. "We're here. We found them!"

Rescue crews and officers came through the brush. Ryker stood back as Harley explained to them that Justin was hanging precariously at the bottom of a steep embankment. They had the gear to traverse the cliff.

A stretcher was brought out and the EMS crew went to work to rig up their rappelling gear to retrieve Justin and Willow.

Ryker stood next to Harley. Without thinking, he reached down and took her hand for comfort, and she squeezed it in response.

"I'm sorry for what I said earlier. I was unnecessarily harsh. But I can't stay here," he said. "We're going to go home. I know I have my own stuff to deal with, but I can't ask you to move for me while I'm still processing everything. You wouldn't be happy in the city. I know that. So you need to stay."

She frowned, her lip trembling. "You're not giving me a choice either way."

"It's for the best," he stated firmly.

He was hurting her, but it was to protect her in the long run.

She pulled her hand away as Justin was lifted to safety and put on the stretcher. Ryker was by the paramedics' side as they lifted the stretcher up and carried it through the brush to a clearing.

Justin was alive.

Injured, but alive.

Harley made her way to the edge as a member of the rescue crew went down and brought back up a very muddy and upset cockapoo.

Tears streamed down Harley's face as she took her sweet little lamb of a dog in her arms. "Good girl."

Willow was trembling, but licking her face.

A paramedic handed her a blanket. "She did good."

Harley nodded and wrapped her dog up, holding her close while they worked to stabilize Justin. He was still unconscious, hypothermic and probably had a concussion. They lifted the stretcher out and took him to the edge of the forest, where the ambulance was waiting, thanks to her neighbor, a farmer, who led them down the lane that he had made for retrieving wood. They got Justin into the back of the ambulance and Ryker followed. He glanced back at Harley, standing there with Willow.

The dog howled mournfully and Harley just kissed her muddy little head. She was shivering now too, and he wanted her to come with him. She could come to Montreal too, but what could he give her there? He made the choice for her, so she wouldn't resent him in the end.

She had a business here. Her family. Her farm. Her animals.

There was nothing he could offer her.

Your heart?

Only he wasn't sure that was enough. It was better to end it before it began and not give her a real choice.

It has begun already. You're a fool. He shook that thought away.

The paramedics closed the doors between them. The lights and siren went on, and he just sat in the back as the paramedics worked on Justin. They were going to the children's hospital in London.

All that mattered right now was his son. Not his heart. Just the safety and security of Justin. He'd been foolish to think that a summer here would help them heal. Justin still needed him, and he was done trying to push Justin out his comfort zone.

He had what he needed.

He had had love before and he was greedy to think that he could have a second shot at it. He just hoped that when all was said and done, when the dust settled, Harley would forgive him. As much as he had fallen in love with her, and he had, he hoped that she would still want to be his friend, even if he couldn't properly give her his heart like he wanted to.

Even though he'd hurt her.

Harley held Willow tight on the ride back to the farm. The OPP officer helped her out, and it felt like her legs were going to collapse under her. When she got there, Michel was waiting. Her phone rang and she saw it was her brother calling.

Harley choked back a sob. "Hey."

"It'll be okay," David replied. Michel came up behind her and put his arms around her shoulders.

"How did you know to call?" she asked.

"The storm. I was worried. I called the house and Michel answered and told me what happened. He said you found them."

"Yes. I'm glad you called," Harley sobbed. "I've got to go. Call me back in a bit."

"I love you, Nerd," David said gently.

"Ditto." She ended the call and saw Christine coming her way with a blanket. She was grateful for her friends.

"They told us you found Justin, a few minutes before you got back," Michel said weakly.

Harley nodded. "They're taking him to the Children's Hospital of Western Ontario in London."

Michel nodded. "Thank God you found him and that Willow was with him. What a good girl."

Willow was still trembling.

"Let me take her. I can take a look at our little hero," Michel insisted.

"I'll help," Kaitlyn offered.

Harley nodded as Michel took Willow from her arms, which were frozen and numb. She looked at Christine, shaking still.

"You're cold and wet. We need to get you warm too," Christine said. "Maureen is resting inside and Michel has Willow. Let me take care of you, like you take care of our pets."

Harley broke down sobbing. She couldn't hold back the rush of emotions anymore. She had cried in private when Jason had left her, but then she stopped crying and continued to make a life for herself, determined to prove to everyone that she was okay. And she was eventually, but right now her heart was breaking all over again, and she couldn't hide that.

She loved Ryker and she had loved Justin, but she'd been having a hard time seeing how it could all work out, even if Ryker hadn't bailed. Maybe it was a good thing Ryker didn't give her a choice either, so she wouldn't be so brokenhearted if it ended when they were in even deeper.

It still hurt though.

It still broke her heart. It angered her to not have that choice. Again.

Christine led her into the house and took her straight upstairs, into her bathroom. Even though Harley was a grown woman, Christine drew her a bath and then helped her out of her wet clothes. It had been so long since she had let someone take care of her.

Harley settled into the bath, but was still shaking. "Christine, can I have my phone? It's in my jacket."

"Sure." Christine left and brought her the phone and shut the bathroom door. She called her brother back, her hand trembling.

"Nerd?" David asked softly.

"I did it again."

"What?" David asked.

"I've fallen in love with the wrong man." She sobbed. "I've fallen in love with his son and—"

"He's not the wrong man, Harley. Jason was. You didn't cry this much when Jason left you. Don't let Ryker go. You need those two as much as they need you."

"But he's leaving…"

"Not everything has to be decided today."

"Okay," she whispered.

"You're okay. As soon as the road opens, I'll be there."

"Thanks."

"Rest, and call again if you need me, sis."

"Will do." Harley ended the call and set her phone down on the vanity.

She sat in the hot bath for a while, until she stopped shaking. She got up and dried herself off. She put on warm clothes from the dryer and made her way into the kitchen. Maureen was sitting at the table, and Harley went over to her and kissed her cheek.

"You saved them," Maureen said.

"Hardly, I just found them."

Maureen looked at her seriously. "Trust me when I say you saved them."

Harley's throat constricted. "Ryker said he's going back to Montreal."

"Because he's mad at himself," Michel said, coming back into the house with Willow, who had been freshly cleaned and dried by Kaitlyn. Willow limped over to her, whining. Harley scooped up her little dog.

"Is she okay?" Harley asked.

"She's sprained a tendon. I gave her some painkillers. She'll be fine. She's a hero," Michel proclaimed.

Harley buried her face in Willow's fur.

No one said anything. Christine placed a cup of tea in front of her, while Willow curled up on her lap. Michel took a seat and sighed.

"It felt like we'd lost Daphne all over again," he said, his voice breaking. "Daphne would be so grateful to you, for finding Justin. We all are. And I think Daphne would want you to keep taking care of Justin. We all love you and Justin adores you. He's told us. You're exactly what Ryker and Justin need. Ryker is angry and scared, and I can't blame him for that, but the worst thing for them would be to go back to Montreal. He doesn't have family there, and Justin loves it here. Both of Ryker's parents are gone. You can be his family, Harley."

Maureen reached out. "Be a part of our family."

"I'm not sure if I'm brave enough for that," she said, her voice trembling. "Or that my life here is what Ryker wants."

"It is," Maureen said. "Don't let my stubborn son-in-law go. Justin and he need you, and Daphne would want it that way."

"You've felt so alone since Jason left you, and he wasn't right for you," Christine said. "You aren't alone, Harley, and you don't have to do this life alone. Love means hurt sometimes, but it's also joy and happiness. When you're ready, go, get your family."

Harley nodded.

She was scared to take a chance on going to London and telling Ryker how she felt about him and Justin, but if she didn't take the chance, she would regret it for the rest of her life. Ryker and Justin belonged here, but most important, she belonged with them.

Her little family.

Even if it meant she had to go to Montreal and prove it.

She was tired of being alone because she was too afraid to reach out and take a chance. She'd been brave about a lot of things in her life, but love was something she was always scared of. Even now, looking back, she had been scared about the unknowns with Jason, and when he left her at the altar it just confirmed all her worst fears.

It was enough of an impetus to say that she was never going to fall in love again. It was enough of an excuse to close herself off from others, from love. She thought she had protected her heart well, but she was wrong.

It wasn't protection.

It was loneliness. It was giving up on dreams.

It was hurt.

She'd taken a chance to make the rest of her dreams come true. She couldn't back away from this dream, her long secret dream of a family.

Of happiness.

Of love.

This was her second chance, and she wasn't going to let it pass her by, because if she did she would regret it for the rest of her life.

He may have thought he took away her choice, but he didn't.

She was going to fight to take back the decision he made for her, because losing the both of them wasn't in her best interest.

Ryker had spent the night in an uncomfortable hospital chair in Justin's room. Actually, it was a leather reclining chair. It wasn't horrible as far as hospital rooms went. Justin had roused, but he was still suffering from the effects of hypothermia, and he had a concussion.

The pediatric doctors planned to keep Justin in the hospital for a few days. Ryker had texted Michel to give him an update and asked if he could bring down a change of clothes and Justin's blanket that Harley had made.

His heart sank as he thought about Harley.

He was in love with her, and he'd hurt her by pushing her away because he was scared.

When that ambulance pulled away and his last view of her was her standing there holding Willow, he could see her heart was breaking, just as much as his.

Ryker never thought that he would ever find love again, but he had.

It was tearing him up knowing that he would have to leave her, because he couldn't ask her to leave Opulence. He'd pushed her to the side and took away her choice, her voice, like a fool. *Just like her ex.*

When he had heard what happened to her with her ex, he couldn't even fathom someone doing that to someone they professed to love. It wasn't right, and he swore that he wouldn't ever be like that, but here he was.

Ending it before it really even began.

And it was just an excuse. He was using Harley's love of Opulence as an excuse to end things, but really it was his own fear. Fear of losing someone special again… But he'd already lost her by pushing her away. *Tabarnak!* He'd really messed up.

"Pappa?" Justin moaned.

Ryker sat up and went to his son's bedside. He took his little hand in his. "I'm here."

Justin opened his eyes. "My head hurts."

"You had a fall. Remember?"

Justin blinked. "Willow?"

"She's okay."

"She fell down that embankment. I was just trying to get back home," Justin whispered, tears running slowly down his cheeks.

"To Montreal?"

Justin frowned. "No, to the farm. Home. We both were."

"That's not our home though," Ryker said softly. "We're going to go home to Montreal."

"I don't want to go back there," Justin cried.

"Justin, you ran away when I wasn't there."

"No! I saw Nanna get hurt and then Willow got out and she bolted so fast, but then I caught up to her and the storm was too bad. I was scared, but Harley told me there was a tree house. I couldn't see how to get back to the farm, so I took Willow to find the tree house."

"You weren't running because I was away?" Ryker asked.

Justin looked sheepish. "At first, but like I said…thunder and lightning and I guess both Willow and I got scared."

"It's okay." Ryker stroked his face. "All that matters is you're okay. I shouldn't have been apart from you."

"Pappa, I'm okay here," Justin said vehemently. "I want to stay in Opulence. Mom is here."

"Justin," Ryker said quietly.

"I know Mom is gone, but I feel her here. Gramps and Nanna love Harley and so do I. I want a family again, Pappa, and I want you back…the way you were. The way we used to be." Tears were rolling down Justin's face. "I want to be near Gramps and Nanna. I'm happy here. Can we stay? You can take over Gramps's practice and I can go to school in Londesborough. Gramps showed me the school. It looks so nice."

Ryker began to cry. Wiping his tears away, he asked, "You're sure this is what you want?"

"I don't want to forget Mom and here I won't. Please can we stay? Maybe Harley will let us stay in her tiny home."

"Hi," a small voice said from the open door. Ryker spun around to see Harley standing there, holding a small duffel bag and a very worn blanket in her hands. His heart swelled and he had to fight back tears again, just seeing her there. Safe and sound.

She had come all this way for them. Maybe he hadn't ruined it all when he pushed her away.

"Harley!" Justin exclaimed.

Harley held up his blanket. "I thought you might need this."

"My blanket!" Justin began to cry. "Harley, I'm sorry."

"No need to apologize." She tousled his hair gently. "I'm glad you're okay."

"And Willow?" he asked.

"She was muddy, but your Gramps took care of her. You saved her and she saved you. You're best friends forever. I'm sure of it."

Justin smiled and snuggled his face into his blanket. "I'm really tired."

"Rest then, buddy," Ryker said gently. He touched his face. "I'll just be outside the door."

Ryker motioned for Harley to follow. She followed, with

one last look at Justin. When they were in the hall he closed the door, just slightly.

"You brought him his blanket," he said quietly.

"He needs it. Besides, it's the best blanket ever." She smiled. "I was worried. I care about him. A lot."

"I know."

Her eyes were filling with tears. "Look, Ryker. I know you said you have to go back to Montreal but...don't. Not because I'm afraid to leave, but because you both belong here. And you know what, if you can't stay... I don't know how things will work, but we'll figure something out, because I can't lose either one of you. I love you. I love Justin."

Ryker brushed away her tears with his thumb. "I love you too and Justin loves you."

She nodded. "If I have to invest in Michel's clinic to keep you here or... I don't know...move to Montreal..."

He shook his head. "That won't be necessary. What I said to you, I was scared. Montreal is all I've ever known. Sure, I have a job and we have friends, but here we have a family. I was so scared about leaving my own safety net, a place where I could control and keep Justin and I both safe, but what we really need is family. It's been so long since I've had more than just Justin in my life. I took away your choice and I hope you forgive me, because I would like to date you."

"So you're staying?" she asked cautiously.

"We're going to stay, and I'll open the practice full-time, make it my own, finally."

"You mean that?" she asked.

He nodded. "*Oui*. I love you, Harley. I never thought that I would find love again, but I have. You've healed us."

"You've both healed me too. I can't picture my life without either of you," she responded. "So much so I would've gone to Montreal with you both. I would've hated it, but to be with you and Justin, it would've been worth it. You're right, Opulence isn't perfect."

"No. I was wrong. It's perfect because you're there, because it's home."

He brushed his knuckles across her cheek and then bent down to kiss her softly, pulling her into his arms. When the kiss was over, she wrapped her arms around him and rested her head on his shoulder, melting into his embrace.

"I do have a problem though," he said.

"What? Closing up everything in Montreal? That won't be a problem. I'll come help."

"No, not that. I'll need to extend my lease until I find a place."

She chuckled. "I can do that, but no rush. This is your home now."

"No. You're my home." And he kissed her again. He'd never thought he could fall in love again, but he realized now that he wasn't replacing Daphne, he was opening his heart, expanding it to include Harley.

"I have some more good news," Harley said.

Ryker was curious. *"Quoi?"*

"Sharpe Line Farms shut down. Criminal charges were laid, and their puppies and breeding dogs are now with appropriate rescues. Christine stayed with me last night and got a text about it. I was thinking, we need one of those doggos. Maybe not a puppy, but definitely a mama dog. And I might've adopted a cat."

Ryker chuckled. "Nia?"

She nodded. "Yep. You can call that adoption emotionally driven."

"Justin will be thrilled. About both the new dog and the cat."

"Well, that's the beauty of country life."

"I wouldn't have it any other way," he said.

"Pappa?" Justin called out.

"Shall we go tell him?" Harley asked.

"Yes. We'll probably have to tell it to him again later, because his head is still fuzzy from the concussion, but he'll be thrilled."

Harley nodded. "We're a family."

"Oui. Family. Forever."

EPILOGUE

One year later

"YOU NEED TO go deal with Cluck Norris Jr.," Kaitlyn insisted as Harley finished sweeping the grooming room. Kaitlyn had her hands on her hips and was very insistent about the whole thing.

"What?" Harley asked, removing her noise canceling headphones.

Willow and her rescue mama dog, Birch, looked up from where they were snoozing on the big dog bed together. They weren't completely interested in what Kaitlyn was saying.

"Cluck Norris Jr. is out, and he's running amok across the yard!"

"What!" Harley set down her broom and headed outside.

Stupid rooster.

Justin had insisted upon handling the chickens. She just hoped she could wrangle Cluck Norris back to the pen before he became splattered across the road. She headed outside and froze in her driveway.

A bunch of people were there, and a weird archway had been erected with lights. Justin was standing in front of her in a suit.

Harley chuckled nervously. "Why are you wearing a suit and tie?"

Justin held out his hand. "It's a surprise. Everyone is in on it."

Harley glanced around the yard, and she could see her parents, Michel, Maureen, Sarah, Armand and David. Harley gasped, her heart hammering, and she spun around to see Kaitlyn standing in the doorway with Willow and Birch. There were little fancy bows on Willow's and Birch's heads.

Nia scooted by, followed by a couple of the barn cats Harley had also adopted.

Justin took her hand and led her through the yard.

Everyone was dressed up but her, and she really didn't know what was happening. She wasn't a huge fan of surprises. Ryker should know that, considering that when he snuck up on her a year ago, she'd tossed him into alpaca poo.

She glanced over at the alpaca pen, and the three alpacas were sticking their heads over the fence. Vince had a bow tie and Gozer and Zuul had bows as well.

"What's going on?" Harley asked again, her voice trembling.

"Surprise!" Justin exclaimed.

Ryker melted out of the crowd, also wearing a suit, and her heart skipped a beat as he reached out and took her hands. Behind him was Cluck Norris Jr. and the rest of the chickens. Somehow Cluck Norris Jr., Wyatt Chirp and Count Cluckula had little tuxedo vests on. That must have taken serious dedication and courage.

"I don't like surprises," she teased nervously.

"Just enjoy it, Nerd!" her brother called out.

She shot him a glare over his shoulder. Behind him was a horse-drawn carriage and Adele, the little foal from last year with the broken coffin bone was standing next to her mother who was harnessed up to it. She swallowed the lump in her throat and looked back at Ryker.

"Harley, marry me." He got down on one knee and pulled out a ring.

"All this for a proposal?" she asked, stunned.

"Well, not just a proposal. A wedding," Ryker admitted.

Harley was confused and she looked around and then down at her scrubs. "What? That is…"

"My idea," Justin said confidently. "Marry Pappa, Harley. We love you."

Tears streamed down her face. "Yes. I'll marry you."

"Bonne." Ryker cupped her face and kissed her to cheers. Justin threw his arms around them both.

"But it's not fair you're all dressed up and I'm in scrubs," she said nervously.

"Your mother has a dress," Ryker said. "Go get changed. The officiant will be here soon."

"And if I said no?" she teased.

"I bet him twenty bucks you wouldn't," Justin said. "And I was right!"

Harley laughed and pulled Justin into an embrace, kissing his head. "So you were."

Harley was whisked away by her mom, who quickly got her dressed in a simple white lace dress and did her hair. Her mom pinned a pink peony in her hair, which was her favorite flower.

Ryker and Justin had moved into the big farm house a few months after they officially started dating.

It had been the happiest year of her life.

Ryker was waiting for her under an archway that was lit up with lights. The sun was setting behind the spruce trees. Her father led her down the short little aisle to where Ryker and Justin were waiting.

Her boys.

Her family.

He wasn't leaving her. The last year had proven that. Justin was thriving at his new school. He had made so many new friends and was loving his life here.

Ryker had revitalized Michel's clinic, allowing Michel to finally fully retire, and Harley's business was booming too.

Ryker took her hands and smiled down at her. "I love you, Harley."

"I love you too."

Justin stood between them as the officiant performed a quick wedding. He handed his dad the ring, and Ryker slipped it on her finger.

"Now you can kiss her, Pappa!" Justin said, interrupting the officiant.

Ryker winked at his son and kissed her, making her melt all over again. She was finally healed, she had her family. Her dreams had all come true and they were all finally whole again, with a whole future stretched out in front of them.

For the first time, since Ryker and Justin walked into her life, she was excited about what was around the corner.

She was excited for the future with her husband, son and a farmyard full of animals at her side.

* * * * *

RESISTING THE OFF-LIMITS PAEDIATRICIAN

KATE MacGUIRE

MILLS & BOON

This book (and my heart) is dedicated to Patrick.

Thank you for believing in me. Love you… Always

CHAPTER ONE

SANDY WHITE BEACHES as far as the eye could see... Early-morning sea-kayaking adventures... An elegant evening at the world-class opera house.

Charlotte thumbed through the images on her social media feed. She knew her friends meant well, but every photo of their amazing vacation in Sydney, Australia, was like an ice-pick to her heart.

Thunder cracked overhead as she waited in line for her rental car. No sandy white beaches here, thank you very much. Instead, she was stuck in her former hometown of Seattle, Washington, right in the middle of one of its legendary rain-storms. She took one last longing glance at her missed vacation before closing her social media feed. That was enough torture for one day.

Every few years she and her friends—all traveling doctors like her—planned an amazing trip to take a break from their locum tenens medical assignments. For their first trip they'd gone to Bora Bora. Then came Madrid, Rome, and Singapore. These trips, along with her doctor assignments, were captured in her travel blog, *GypsyMD*. She had a small but loyal group of followers who loved her work-hard-play-hard lifestyle as a locum tenens physician.

But the Sydney trip had been the hardest to plan. More of her friends were finding partners, getting married, and settling down with full-time permanent jobs. None of which interested Charlotte, but it sure did make it harder to get enough people interested to justify the expense of the Sydney trip.

Just when she'd solved that problem, her life had taken an unwelcome detour. From out of the blue, a man claiming to be her father's estate attorney had called her.

"It's important that you come to Seattle," he'd said. *"There are some matters related to your father's estate that must be settled."*

Your father.

Two words that sounded so foreign to a girl who'd grown up without one. Once upon a time, when she was much younger, she had daydreamed about her missing father. Was he a rock star who spent every night in a different city? Or maybe a navy captain, steadfastly determined to protect her country's borders? Or a reclusive mountaineer who climbed the world's most treacherous peaks and slept in a yurt?

But in her favorite little-girl dream he was a powerful but despondent king, who used every resource at his disposal to find her. No one would rest, he'd bellow, until his precious, long-lost daughter was returned to her family, safe and sound.

Eventually she'd outgrown those silly daydreams and accepted her fate. Her father had no idea she existed. So when her mother was killed in a terrible car accident, Charlotte had found herself orphaned at thirteen, with no one to claim her and nowhere to go.

"Ma'am?"

A voice behind her shook Charlotte from her reverie. She mumbled an apology and moved forward with the line. Another crack of thunder overhead released a torrent of rain that fell in sheets against the windows of the airport rental car office. This unexpected trip home was getting better by the minute.

An hour later, Charlotte had finished an oversized coffee and made her way to the address the estate attorney had texted her. The rain had let up a bit, and she paused to gather her thoughts before meeting him. Her view of the house was partially obscured by the steep sloped front yard and its landscaped features of rocks and vegetation, all there to protect against the soil erosion and landslides that came with living in one of Seattle's hilly neighborhoods. The house appeared to be a two-story split-level, with a large fir tree dominating the front yard.

Someone rapped hard on the passenger window, startling her. A small man with a hooked nose and small, beady eyes peered through the window. "Charlotte? Dr. Charlotte Owens?"

She nodded.

"I'm Jeffrey Bain, your father's attorney."

She nodded, still taking in the home and its upscale neighborhood. She remembered this neighborhood from her childhood. Located northwest of downtown Seattle, the Queen Anne neighborhood was built on a hill with amazing views of the Puget Sound, an inlet of the Pacific Ocean. It was an enclave for Seattle residents who were far more affluent than she and her single mother had been. Once, on a dare, she and a few other teens in her foster care group home had tried trick-or-treating here, to see if they really gave out full-sized chocolate bars, as was rumored. Only one house had.

"Shall we?"

The attorney indicated the house with a short wave of his hand. He seemed to be in just as much of a hurry to get these estate matters settled as she was.

She followed the attorney, navigating the stone steps that climbed the hilly front yard. "You have a beautiful home," she said, noting the professionally designed garden beds and hand-painted ceramic pots along the walkway, though many of the flowers and plants seemed to be languishing.

The attorney gave her a strange glance over his shoulder. "No, ma'am," he said. "*You* have a beautiful home."

Charlotte stopped in her tracks as her brain scrambled to make sense of his words. She had assumed this was the attorney's home, because it didn't make any sense that her father would live here.

"He was just a silly summer fling," her mother had said, when she could be enticed to say anything at all about Charlotte's father. *"He was never going to amount to much."*

All the questions she'd had as a child about her father were swirling in her mind like nosy summer gnats. The attorney unlocked the door and beckoned her inside where the possibility of explanation waited.

She followed him for a breakneck tour of the five-bedroom home. Architecturally speaking, the house was perfect in form and function, design and style. But the wood floors were dull and the windows were dirty. Dust lined the windowsills and spider webs wafted in the corners when she and the attorney passed. Despite touring both floors, she found nothing that explained what her father had become after his summer fling with her mother. There was no evidence of a family. No tick marks on the wall marking a child's growth, no holes in the wall where a teen would have hung posters. Instead, the air was stagnant and sour. Like no one had ever lived here other than ghosts and dust motes.

The tour ended in the kitchen, where the attorney hoisted his oversize briefcase onto the perfect marble countertop, displacing a small cloud of dust. He combed rifled through the files in his briefcase until he found a gray and white folder marked with the emblem of his law firm.

"This is your father's last will and testament, along with

his living trust and other important legal documents for your records. Now, as you may be aware, your father lost a great deal of his wealth due to a series of business failures over the last decade of his life. I'm afraid this home is his only real asset, and he has specifically left it to you."

No, she was not aware of any of this. And how could he leave his home to her when he didn't know she existed?

She was about to ask that very question as she thumbed through the legal documents—there were so many! But one caught her attention: *Form JU 04.0100 Petition for Termination of Parent-Child Relationship.*

Charlotte's breath went shallow as she withdrew the document and read it slowly. She was a pediatrician, not a lawyer, but if she understood this right her father had signed an agreement with the state of Washington to forfeit his parental rights. Time slowed as she searched the document for his signature.

It was dated six months after her mother had died.

She continued staring at the document, but the words were blurred, and a horrible rushing sound filled her ears as if a massive runaway train was bearing down on her. Had he known about her all along? Or not until Child Welfare Services had contacted him, informing him that he had a daughter? Either way, he'd known she was orphaned when he'd signed his rights away.

She set the pages down and stepped away from the counter, her chest so tight it burned.

So, her daydreams hadn't been so far-fetched after all. She *was* the long-lost princess daughter of a quasi-king. But knights had never been dispatched to search for her because the King had never yearned for her return.

Inconvenient. Unwanted. Go away.

Anguish uncoiled from deep in her core, its tendrils finding every painful memory of her foster care years that she wanted to forget. How she'd grown up always feeling like an outsider, unwanted and unwelcome. The social workers who'd shown up without warning, giving her a donated suitcase and ten minutes to pack for her next placement. Knowing she would never, ever, find a home of her own. Because everyone knew that families wanted babies, not teenagers.

She squeezed her eyes shut and wished it was ten minutes ago, when she'd thought her painful past was a casualty of fate.

But the petition said otherwise. It said that her father had signed away his rights knowing full well that she would slip into foster care. Shock and hurt quickly gave way to anger. A deep, red-hot rage that demanded to know one thing.

Who does this to a child?

Especially when he'd clearly had the means to care for her.

As if on cue, Charlotte heard the hiss of air brakes. Through the large picture window in the living room that looked out to the street and the Puget Sound beyond, she could see a bright yellow school bus stop in front of the house. Its doors whooshed open and a half dozen kids spilled out, wearing raincoats and rubber boots, whooping with joy as their backpacks bounced with every step that took them back to waiting parents and warm, dry homes.

That could have been her.

That could have been her!

"Why?" she choked out, not trusting her voice to form full sentences.

Why would her father not claim her?

Was there something wrong with her?

She didn't realize she'd spoken the words out loud until the attorney gently slid the folder from her grasp and thumbed through the documents.

"Here," he said, pressing something into her hands.

An envelope, its ivory paper thick and expensive. *Dr. Charlotte Owens* printed on the front.

"Maybe this will explain things," he said, his tone gentle and sympathetic for the first time since they'd met.

Charlotte stared blankly at the letter, as if she had forgotten what envelopes were for. She felt utterly uncertain about what to do next. She considered the contents of the envelope. Good grief, was this her father's attempt to explain himself? To make things right? How dare he? He'd had years to write, call or find her. To do something. To do *anything*! And now he was going to put this on her? Just leave her a letter so he got to have his say while she had none?

The very thought repulsed her so much, it felt like she was holding a snake. She pushed the letter aside so vehemently it would have slid off the counter had Jeffery not caught it first.

"Sell it." Her voice was flat, but steely, her hands curled into fists.

Jeffrey looked at the letter. "Sorry?"

"The house," she clarified. "Just sell it and donate the money to charity."

She wanted nothing to do with anything her father had touched. Why had he even bothered to leave her this house? Was it some kind of torture to make sure she understood all that she had been denied?

She checked her watch and gathered her things. This trip had been a waste of her time. But it wasn't too late to salvage her vacation. If she was lucky, she might catch a late flight to San Francisco, so she could start the long trip to Sydney the next day. With any luck she'd be able to join her friends by the weekend. She could really use some time on a beach chair with a fruity drink before she started her next assignment as ship physician aboard *The Eden*, a massive cruise ship that traveled the Caribbean.

"Wait," Jeffrey said, combing through his briefcase. He fanned a stack of documents before her. Home inspection reports, market analyses, and other incomprehensible paperwork that seemed irrelevant to Charlotte. Until he explained that, despite its desirable zip code and near-perfect facade, the home had been neglected for quite some time. It needed a new roof, there was pervasive mold in the basement, and some structures on the property, like the greenhouse and the pool house, had fallen into such disrepair it was considered hazardous for anyone to enter.

"I'm sorry, but I don't see what this has to do with me." Charlotte shook out her coat, preparing to leave.

The lawyer tidied the pages into a neat stack before clipping them together. "To be blunt, you can't sell the home. I mean, you can try, but no insurance company will cover a house with these problems. And without homeowner's insurance no bank will issue a loan. So, unless you have a cash buyer, this house can't be sold."

Charlotte frowned, her mind racing. "So, are you saying I'm stuck with his house?"

The attorney flicked some invisible lint from his jacket. "Not necessarily. You could sell the property 'as is' to a real estate investment firm. You'll only get a fraction of the home's market value, but you'd be free and clear in a few weeks. In fact…" he rummaged through his seemingly bottomless briefcase "…our firm has an investment division that would be happy to take this property off your hands."

He pushed yet another document her way.

Charlotte's heart leapt at the chance to escape. Just one signature and she could join her friends in Sydney, where the steady tempo of the surf would chase her stress away. Warm sun, cold rum, and friendly locals would help her forget everything that had happened here.

But when she saw the offer amount her pen froze mid-air. She knew a steal when she saw one. Even in its current condition, this house was easily worth three or four times what the firm was offering.

So what? You're going to donate the money to charity. Why do you care?

Maybe that was why she balked. Because this money could do some real good. Charlotte didn't know much about her father, but if he could live in a house like this and not claim his daughter she doubted he had supported many charities. Selling his home and donating the money might be the first good he'd ever done in his life.

It would be wrong to let this attorney lowball her out of the home's true worth. Jeffrey's financial gain wouldn't benefit anyone other than opportunistic investors.

But giving up her travel plans to oversee the renovations felt like a handful of salt in a wound that had never healed. When she'd turned eighteen and aged out of foster care she had vowed that *never* again would others decide her fate. No more social workers and no more donated suitcases. Now she went where she wanted, for as long as she wanted, and stayed only as long as it felt right. That was the beauty of being a traveling doctor. No long-term commitments and she was in total control of her fate.

But what if she had a reason to stay in Seattle beyond renovating her father's home? A purpose that would allow her to leave Seattle with some sense of closure for the harm her father had done? What if she spent *his* money and *her* time helping kids who were in the same situation she'd once been in—alone, vulnerable, scared. Then maybe she would feel justice had been done.

Surely her recruiting agency could help her find a short-term assignment here in Seattle. There had to be a public health clinic or community hospital that could use an extra pediatrician for a few months. If not, she would just volunteer.

Either way, she'd be able to board *The Eden* with a sense of pride. She didn't need her father's wealth, but she could make damn sure that his money would benefit teens who needed it.

She pushed the contract back to the attorney. "Thank you for the offer, Jeffrey. But I have other plans."

The Sunshine Clinic for Kids was a humble brick building that claimed the corner of Fifth and Monroe. Charlotte's heels clicked against the aging sidewalk where stubborn weeds managed to grow in the cracks formed by years of Seattle's rain and low-grade earthquakes. This part of the city was old and industrial, with little concern for aesthetics.

But Charlotte wasn't focused on the factories or the weeds. She was more interested in the clinic itself. The stout little building didn't have the same left behind feel of its neighborhood. Its glass door was polished and flanked by two blue ceramic pots that were spilling over with lush verbena flowers. Lace curtains softened the windows, and in a burst of creativity someone had drawn a bright yellow sun above the clinic's name. There was a relentlessly optimistic feel about the place that appealed to Charlotte. As if the clinic refused to be dragged down by its shabby surroundings.

"Good for you," Charlotte said out loud.

She didn't normally talk to inanimate buildings, but the past few days of being stuck in her father's house was making her a little crazy. Every minute there was a reminder of her father's utter disregard for her well-being when she was still a child.

But finally, she could put all that behind her. The recruiting agency had been thrilled to place her with The Sunshine Clinic, a satellite clinic of Seattle's main hospital, dedicated to providing care for the city's at-risk and homeless teens.

She didn't know why her recruiter had been having a hard time finding an interim pediatrician for the clinic, but she was more than ready to lose herself in the demands of a busy day seeing patients. Work and travel had always been her escape from stress and painful emotions. That was how she had sailed through high school with top grades and landed full scholarships to college.

Today was special, so she had chosen her favorite dress. It was light blue, fell just below her knees, and had been handmade by an artist in Sedona, Arizona, where Charlotte had worked at a pediatrics clinic for one summer. When she hadn't been treating the tourists' kids for sunburn and dehydration, she'd used her free time to hike and explore the legendary red rocks of a mountain town reputed to be home to four powerful energy vortexes. Wearing this dress felt like a promise that as soon as the house was ready to sell she'd be back to living life on her terms again.

She struggled to open the clinic door, one arm balancing a box of office supplies and framed diplomas.

"Hello!" she called, but the security system chirped at the same time, obscuring her greeting.

A man was hunched over the reception counter, his back to her, with a phone pressed to his ear, oblivious to her presence. She took in his dark jeans and motorcycle boots, along with a leather jacket that strained to contain his broad, muscular shoulders. Was he a patient or an employee of the clinic? She couldn't tell. But the open ladder near the counter made her think he might be something to do with maintenance.

Whoever he was, he was not having a good day.

"But Mrs. Winthrop, at least she used her words, right?" The man forced a chuckle. "No, I agree. It's inappropriate for an eleven-year-old to use *those* words." After a few *mm-hmms* and *yes, I sees*, he suddenly straightened. "Oh, no, that won't be necessary." There was a silence as he pressed the phone harder to his ear. "Well…yes, but you see…" His shoulders slumped in defeat. "Mrs. Winthrop, please. I'm begging you. This is Piper's third school this year…" There was a long pause before he suddenly brightened. "Oh, thank you! I appreciate that." He ran his thumb along the edge of the counter, smoothing an imperfection that was invisible to Charlotte. "I promise that we *will* be working on this at home."

His leather jacket shifted when he hung up the phone, revealing the V-shape of his back and waist. Charlotte bit her lip as she watched him pinch the bridge of his nose. It was obvious she had overheard a private phone call. She hated to intrude on his apparent distress, but today was her first day and she didn't want to be late. She needed to report to Dr. John Bennett, the clinic's director, as soon as possible.

She cleared her throat. "Hello?"

The man spun to face her. For several long seconds Charlotte felt a kind of shock to her system that momentarily stole her words and purpose. The strength she had seen his leather jacket struggling to contain was also found in the thick muscles of his chest and neck. He had a handsome, honest face and wore his chestnut-brown hair long to his collar, the waves still shower-damp. He was rugged and masculine, and maybe a bit intimidating with that intense scowl.

Or maybe it was his eyes that pinned her in place. Greenish gold, like the eyes of coyotes and cougars, his gaze was so intense she felt like a rabbit that had wandered too far into apex predator territory.

She swallowed hard as she noticed the stethoscope around his neck. Though he bore little resemblance to the bland headshot posted on the hospital's website, this was Dr. John Bennett, her new colleague.

For heaven's sake, Charlotte. Stop staring and say something!

But he saved her the trouble. He folded his arms across his impressive chest and assessed her with a measured stare. "Dr. Owens, right? The locum doctor?"

Charlotte wiggled the lapel of her lab coat where her name was embroidered in black thread. "Guilty as charged!" she said, hating her too-cheerful tone.

The first day of a new job was the worst. She loved the freedom that came with being a traveling doctor, but being "the new doc" took its toll.

"Paperwork, please," he said, finally shifting his focus from her to rummage through his toolbox. "So we can get you on your way." He found whatever he was looking for and started to climb the ladder.

"Paperwork?"

"You know... Whatever the courts gave you to track your community service so you can get your medical license reinstated. I'll sign off to say that you're making a good faith effort to find a service site and you can be on your way."

Charlotte had felt off-kilter ever since she'd walked through the door. This conversation was not helping. "I'm sorry, I don't know what you're talking about."

He paused, a screwdriver gripped between his teeth. He removed it to ask, "Then why are you here?"

Charlotte was starting to wonder if Gina, her recruiter, had made a mistake with this assignment. Only that would explain this surreal conversation.

"Because you need a locum pediatrician. At least that's what I was told."

Her new colleague chuckled and shook his head. "Depends on who you ask, I suppose."

As if that should satisfy her curiosity, he tucked the screwdriver in his back pocket and climbed back up the ladder.

What did that mean? And what was she supposed to do

next? The box she was holding was growing heavier by the minute. She'd like to set it down on the counter, but the strange man was occupying that space, so she chose one of the orange vinyl chairs near the picture window instead. Then she found her phone and contemplated calling Gina, to make sure she was in the right place. But she'd worked with Gina for years, long enough to know that Gina double-checked every detail before sending one of her doctors to a new assignment. There was no way she was in the wrong place or had the wrong information.

Whatever was wrong here, her new colleague seemed to be at the heart of it.

John Bennett started whistling a tune—something familiar, but she couldn't quite place the melody. And she didn't care because she was getting annoyed. For Pete's sake, she was standing right here. Why was he refusing to talk to her or deal with her?

Before she knew exactly what she was going to do, she strode over and gave the ladder a tiny shake. "Hey!"

"Hey!" he yelled back. "Do you mind?"

"Actually, I do. Do I have a job here or not?"

She braced herself for a fight, but from this angle, looking up at him, she could see a slight crook in his nose, hinting that he was no stranger to fights much worse than what she was bringing.

He leaned one arm on the ladder and studied her like she was a specimen under a microscope. "Well, that depends. Because so far everyone interested in the job has been a pretty desperate character. Either they need community service hours to get their medical license reinstated or they are serving probation for some kind of legal trouble." He tucked the light fixture back in the ceiling and started tightening screws. "We don't need any of that nonsense around here."

"I'm not a desperate character!" Unless you counted her desperation to get away from her father's house and all of its painful memories.

John paused his tinkering long enough to indicate her entire person with a wave of his screwdriver. "I don't know about desperate, lady. But that dress definitely makes you a character."

A flare of heat bloomed in her cheeks as she realized this John didn't want her in his clinic. Just like her father hadn't wanted her in his life. Which was fine by her. She was sick of being pushed around by the inexplicable whims of men who wielded their power with a reckless disregard for how they hurt others.

She stalked back to the window and grabbed her box of personal belongings. A familiar bravado infused her core. Gina could find her another noble cause to keep her busy while she was stuck in Seattle. Or maybe she should abandon this plan to do some good while she was here. It wasn't too late to follow her first impulse and sell her father's house "as is" and get her derriere over to Sydney.

She was halfway to the door when she spied that shaky yellow sun hovering above the clinic's name. Who had drawn that? Had it been one of the teens who'd passed through here, desperate for something pretty and warm to brighten the world? Or an employee—perhaps the same employee who had planted flowers at the front door and hung lacy curtains in the windows?

Someone was working awfully hard to make this clinic a refuge for the teens who found their way here. It wasn't Dr. Sunshine-on-a-Ladder over there, that was for sure. But someone here had known darkness and loss. And also that the tiniest gesture of hope could pull you through the darkest nights.

Her shoulders slumped as the fight left her. What kind of

doctor would she be if she turned her back on vulnerable teens after a little friction with a grumpy doctor? She huffed an exasperated sigh as she set her box back down on the orange vinyl chair.

John was off the ladder now, rummaging through his tools. If he'd noticed her near-exit, he was keeping a pretty good poker face about it.

"So." She crossed her arms. "Where's my office?"

He glanced up, a tiny glimmer of surprise in his eyes before he recovered his stoic expression. Had she had surprised him? If so, good. John looked like he needed someone to rattle his cage once in a while.

He closed his toolbox and latched it shut before turning back to Charlotte, arms folded across his chest. "If you're going to stick around, we have to fix this first." He indicated her entire person with a chin-thrust.

"Pardon me?"

His gaze moved like an elevator from her head to her shoes before he shook his head. "Didn't the agency tell you how to dress?"

Her urge to snipe back was strong, but if they were going to get anything done they needed to have an actual conversation.

"Here, give me that." He proffered his hand, clearly wanting something from her, and she detected a hint of his cologne. Clean, with musky male undernotes and hints of spice and surprise.

"Give you what?"

"Your lab coat." He beckoned with a quick wave of his fingers.

The man made less sense by the minute. Why on earth did he want her lab coat? Still, he was at least speaking to her now, and that seemed like progress.

She shrugged off her coat and handed it over.

"Do you have anything else you could wear? Something less…bohemian?"

That familiar quick flash of anger flared again. "This isn't bohemian. It's practically a work of art. It was hand-stitched in Sedona by a textile artist whose work is in high demand."

But that wasn't why she'd bought it. She just loved the whimsy of a blue dress printed with sycamore trees, pink owls tucked in their branches.

"Is that so? Well, you don't see many hand-stitched works of art around here, which means you're going to stick out. Not the effect we're going for, Dr. Owens, so please, follow me."

Curiosity compelled her to follow him down a narrow hallway to a storage closet where he dragged out several boxes labeled *Donations*. Then he dug through the clothing, checking tags and tossing items aside, until he held up a pair of faded green cargo pants. "These might work," he said.

Charlotte hooked a finger through the belt loop. "For what?"

He didn't respond. He was too busy digging through the box until he found a salmon-hued graphic tee shirt. After years of washing, its letters were faded and peeling, but she could still make out *Fort Lauderdale, Florida. Est 1911*.

He pointed to a door behind her. "You can change in there. But I can't help you with the shoes."

Charlotte looked down at her simple flats.

"From now on you need to wear closed-toe athletic shoes."

Her head was spinning. What was happening here?

He grabbed a box of baby wipes from the shelf. "The lipstick—it's got to go. And the earrings. And the bangles." He paused and assessed her with a critical eye. "And your hair." He indicated her long, dark hair, which she wore in loose waves past her shoulders. "Just try to draw less attention to yourself. Be like a lamppost—there, but not really seen. Okay?"

"You want me to look like a lamppost?"

He shook his head, exasperated. "No, I don't want you to look like a lamppost. Just be less…striking, okay?" He groaned as if he hadn't meant to say that, running a rough hand through his hair.

Charlotte caught a glimpse of herself in the hallway mirror, crumpled clothes and baby wipes in her hand. "Dr. Bennett, this seems very unprofessional."

His green eyes softened for the first time since they'd met. "Good. Then maybe the kids will talk to you. Tell you where it hurts."

He headed back to the waiting room, leaving Charlotte alone. She went into the small bathroom and tried to recover her equilibrium. It wasn't like she'd expected a parade just for showing up. But she sure hadn't expected to be butting heads with her new colleague on day one.

She puffed an errant strand of hair away from her eyes. "So much for saving the world," she said to her reflection.

Was this why Gina had had such trouble filling this position? Who knew how many well-meaning doctors had been here before her, wanting to help, only to get run off by a good-looking but grumpy doctor?

She slipped off her dress, trading it for the tee shirt and cargo pants. John had guessed her size just right. She liked the shirt, soft and cozy after years of washing, but it was hard to shake off the unwanted flashback to her younger self, when she'd had to take whatever hand-me-downs were given to her.

"So go," she whispered to her image. "You don't have to stay…"

Easy-breezy was her life's motto. *Travel light and keep things casual and fun.*

That was how she'd stayed one step ahead of the heartbreak and loss that had stained her teen years. But Dr. Bennett looked like he was anything but easy-breezy.

Conflicting thoughts swirled in her head. This assignment was going to be tough, for sure. But life was full of tough challenges. That was what it took to reveal true character. And if she missed this opportunity to make a difference in the lives of teens who needed her, then she'd be a lot more like her father than she wanted to admit.

She took a deep breath to steady herself, then started arranging her hair into a French braid.

She wasn't going anywhere—whether John liked it or not.

CHAPTER TWO

JOHN CLIMBED BACK up the ladder to finish his repairs. He didn't have time for these extra tasks, but filing a work order with the hospital's maintenance department meant waiting weeks for someone to show. Out here, deep in Seattle's industrial district, his little satellite clinic wasn't a big priority for the administrative types.

Which was fine by him. If being the king of his clinic meant doing the maintenance, so be it. It kept the top brass from breathing down his neck and let him do things his way. The same way he'd been doing things since his father had walked out on his family, leaving John charged with keeping his little brother Michael out of trouble while their mom worked two or three jobs to keep their heads above water. Not an easy task for John—especially with Michael's iron will and mad Houdini-esque escape artist skills.

But Michael wouldn't be escaping anytime soon. He'd been sentenced to five years in prison on drug charges, making John the legal guardian of Piper, his eleven-year-old niece. But, despite his best efforts, Piper was not settling into her new life with her bachelor uncle on his live-aboard sailboat very well. She was frequently in trouble at school, which meant now the hospital was breathing down John's neck plenty, on account of his many missed shifts so he could meet with Piper's principal or fill in when an exasperated sitter quit on the spot.

Those missed shifts had eventually caught the attention of the chief of pediatrics, who'd decreed that adding a locum doctor to the clinic would be better than relying on on-call doctors to fill in. John had done his best to assure the pediatric team that he had everything under control. The last thing he needed was another doctor in his space, messing up the systems that he and Sarah, his receptionist and medical assistant, had spent years perfecting.

And most of the locums who had applied so far had had their own agenda—like documenting community service hours to get a medical license reinstated. He had worked too hard to earn the trust of Seattle's vulnerable teens to let anyone like that through the front door. And the good doctors just didn't stick around. The long hours and limited resources made it too tempting to accept positions with the main hospital or pediatric private practices.

So he probably didn't need to worry about the tall brunette who was now carefully folding her dress. Two weeks—four, tops—and she'd be one more doctor who'd ghosted him for a better opportunity, leaving him alone to take care of everything.

At least she looked better now that she had changed. Not that she'd looked terrible before. She was actually quite stunning, with that Grecian profile and soft blue eyes. But the rumpled tee shirt and casual braid made her more approachable, which the teens needed. Many had trust issues with adults, so he had learned to ditch anything that made him look like an authority figure.

She hoisted the box and turned to face him. "Where's my office?"

So she was sticking around despite his unsolicited wardrobe consultation. *Interesting.*

"You don't have an office. Sorry." He'd had to sacrifice his own to create a second exam room for the steady parade of locum doctors who had come and gone before her. He folded the ladder and leaned it against the wall. "But I can add some shelving to your exam room if you want."

"Where am I supposed to do my charting? Or phone in scripts and consults?"

He pointed behind the reception desk, where he had set an old door across two sawhorses. Two computers and a single phone marked the office space.

She narrowed her eyes and he braced himself for another clash. He liked how her blue eyes darkened when she was irritated. A man could learn to read a woman like that, he thought, the same way a sailor could read the skies for signs of trouble.

But Sarah saved him from the impending squall by breezing into the clinic. She hustled behind the front desk, organizing her coat and purse before she noticed Charlotte.

"Oh, honey!" she exclaimed. "You must be the new doctor!" She set Charlotte's box on the counter so she could pull her into one of the famous Mother Bear hugs the teens loved. Then she stepped back, her hands cupping Charlotte's shoulders. "Ready for some coffee and a tour?"

Now, why hadn't he thought of that? Coffee and a tour would have been a far more civilized way to start the day.

John half listened as Sarah led Charlotte on a tour of the real-estate-office-turned-medical-clinic. They had maximized their small space by using office partitions and creative design to create two exam rooms, an onsite pharmacy and lab, and a food pantry where kids could grab snacks and drinks to go. It was half as much as John had wanted when he'd started the clinic five years ago but, as Sarah often reminded him, Rome wasn't built in a day.

"And here we are, back where we started," Sarah said, her hands set low on her hips.

Charlotte rounded the corner and he caught her eyes for a moment. Everything about her—from her resume, which read like a travel brochure, to her sun-kissed smooth skin—hinted at freedom, wanderlust, adventure. She was like a telegraph from his Before Times, when he had been free to spend his time as he liked. Mostly that had translated to long hours at the clinic, then spending his free time rehabbing *The House Call*, the sailboat he called home, to prepare for his next trip into the open waters beyond the Puget Sound. It was a little too easy to imagine Charlotte's long, lithe body at the helm of *The House Call*, the wind whipping her dark hair and her eyes wild with delight.

But there would be no voyages now—nor wild-eyed women on his boat or in his bed. Not with Piper as his charge. The mistakes he had made with his brother had robbed Michael of his freedom and his future. Mistakes he would not repeat—which was why it didn't matter that Charlotte smelled like jasmine and rain. He'd be sticking to his side of the clinic until the trade winds that had blown her into Seattle blew her somewhere else.

By noon, the clinic was in chaos. The waiting room was standing room only, with teens laughing and buzzing like a swarm of cicadas. A tower of mail and magazines threatened to spill off the reception counter. Sarah was running triage, somehow taking calls and screening walk-ins without losing her mind.

John walked his last patient to Sarah for checkout just as Charlotte left her office. She had Matthew with her, a quiet boy John knew from his previous visits. Something about Matthew's uneasy expression and the stack of prescription slips in his hand tripped John's radar.

"For starters," Charlotte said, "you'll need to avoid triggers like smoke, pollen, and cold weather."

John willed himself to stay on his side of the clinic, as he had vowed. He didn't need to get in the middle of every single thing that happened.

Matthew squinted at one of the slips. "What's a nebulizer?"

Okay, maybe he did. Cripes, she'd prescribed a *nebulizer*? Didn't she know some of these kids didn't have…?

No, of course she didn't. This wasn't her world—it was his. And whether he wanted a partner or not, he had one now. It was up to him to make sure she understood what she had signed up for.

He joined them at the reception counter. "May I see those?" he asked, indicating the prescriptions. He thumbed through them one by one. "Advair disks…excellent choice." He crumpled the slip and stuck it in his pocket. "If state insurance covered them."

Charlotte's brow furrowed.

He looked at the next slip. "Steroids—good. Let's add an antihistamine and a generic bronchodilator. Sarah can find those in our pharmacy." Which wasn't a pharmacy at all, but a storage closet stocked with the medications they prescribed most often. "Now, let's talk about your digs."

Sarah swiveled in her chair, a phone receiver pressed to her ear. "I've got the House of Hope on the line. He's got a bed."

"And a caseworker?"

"Working on it!" She patted the chair next to her, indicating Matthew should sit with her while she worked.

Suddenly Charlotte's hand was on John's arm, squeezing hard. "How am I supposed to help these kids if I can't give them what they need? You know as well as I do that Matthew needs more than steroids and allergy meds!"

The intensity of her expression matched the pressure of her grip. Was she a Type A person, then, intent on excelling at whatever she tried? Or did she actually care if Matthew got the help he needed?

John sighed and slid his pen behind his ear. "You prescribed a nebulizer, right? Which requires electricity?"

"Of course."

"So, does Matthew have consistent access to electricity?"

She frowned. "I don't know."

"And the Advair disks? Insurance doesn't cover the branded version, so he'll need the generic—which we don't stock. So where is the closest pharmacy? What bus routes does Matthew need to get there?"

Her grip on his arm loosened. "I don't know that either."

He reached behind the counter, then slid a bus route planner in front of her. "Well, study up, Doc. Because this is part of your job too."

She looked up at him, her hand still draped on his arm, her eyes shiny—with anger or distress? He couldn't tell. "Why is he even on the street? Why not in a shelter or a foster home—someplace safe?"

Because life was inherently unfair. End of story. There was no point dwelling on *who* or *why* or *should* and *could*. All that mattered was being there for the teens who needed them and doing what they could for as long as they could.

"Kids like Matthew have it tough. There are only a few shelters in Seattle that are certified to accept unaccompanied minors, and they have long waiting lists. That's why they need meds they can stuff in their pockets or shoes. It's not ideal—I know that. But if we can help, they'll start to trust us. That's when we can make a difference."

Charlotte stepped away, her gaze avoiding his as her fingers fidgeted with a loose thread on the hem of her shirt. Her forehead puckered, as if she was working something out. He'd seen that look before, in the doctors who had come before her.

He braced himself for The Talk, full of reassurances that *It's not you, it's not the kids...it's me.*

But she surprised him.

"You know what we should do? We should set up an area where kids could come by for breathing treatments when we're open." She was stalking the clinic now, looking through doorways and assessing every room.

John felt like a puppy as he trailed her. "I'm sorry...what? We don't have the budget or the space for..."

"And we should stock more brand-name drugs. Pharmaceutical companies donate drugs all the time. I'm sure there's a process—and lots of forms, of course. But we can figure it out!"

We? When had they become a "we"?

John cleared his throat. "I appreciate your enthusiasm, Dr. Owens. But we don't have the space to add a breathing treatment area. And Sarah doesn't have the time to set up and monitor a drug donation partnership."

"Just Charlotte is fine. It won't be difficult, I promise. If we move a partition here or there we can make the space. Then we could contact the university and become a practicum site for nursing students. They could oversee the breathing treatment area in exchange for getting firsthand experience in community medicine."

She was bold—he had to give her that. Bold and provocative and a little sexy, with those intense and determined blue eyes.

"These are very ambitious ideas, Dr. Owens, and I appreciate—"

"Charlotte," she corrected him again.

"Charlotte, I appreciate your enthusiasm—I do. But we have our hands full providing the services we already have."

Not that he didn't want to offer the teens more. When he'd started he'd been full of ambitious plans to grow the tiny storefront clinic into a full-service medical, dental, and behavioral health clinic, able to provide all the care Seattle's vulnerable teens deserved.

But there was only so much that he and Sarah could do on their own. And, while Sarah had been nagging him to start thinking about how he would replace her when she finally retired for good, he could not imagine entrusting the clinic and its teen patients to anyone other than himself and Sarah.

"I couldn't possibly ask Sarah to take on more—"

Charlotte flashed him an absolutely brilliant smile. "Sarah doesn't have to do a thing. You have me now! I'll start researching the medication program tonight."

Then she powered up her computer tablet and scanned the day's appointments as if she'd worked there all her life.

John stood for a moment, hands fisted at his sides, thoroughly annoyed at the flare of attraction that bloomed in his chest. Everything she'd suggested was exactly how he wanted to grow the clinic. Could it be different if he had a partner? Could someone like Charlotte figure out how to overcome obstacles that had stymied him?

For one long minute it was tempting to lean into the hope he felt stirring in his chest.

But no, he wouldn't do it. It was too risky. The teens and the hospital relied on him to keep the clinic running, day after day. The last thing he needed was to build something with Charlotte, only to have her take off when wanderlust struck, leaving him to pick up the pieces. It was better for him to stick to what he could manage on his own, year after year.

His musings were interrupted when the front door was flung open hard and fast, hitting the wall at the same time as the security alarm chirped twice.

"Hey, Doc!" a girl's frantic voice called. "This kid needs help!"

John knew who it was without looking. Angel was a frequent visitor to The Sunshine Clinic, often dragging along a kid who needed help while refusing any for herself.

Today was no different. She had one arm slung around the shoulders of a freckle-faced boy who wiped his nose on his sleeve, looking more confused than sick.

Sarah peered at the girl over her bifocals. "The door, Angel. We've discussed this, remember?"

"Right!" Angel dashed back and shut the door quietly, her long ponytail swinging wildly with every step. "Sorry."

Sarah oversaw the check-in process for the boy, Bruce, while John contemplated how to handle Charlotte's plans for the clinic. He didn't want to crush her enthusiasm for helping the teens, but he wasn't going to start anything with Charlotte that he couldn't finish.

"Angel, would you please take Bruce to Exam Room Two?" Sarah said.

John's head snapped up. That was Charlotte's exam room.

John willed himself to wait until Angel had led Bruce out of earshot. "Sarah, what are you doing? Angel's case is far too complicated for Charlotte's first day."

"Angel?" Charlotte asked, clearly confused. "I thought Bruce was the patient?"

Sarah explained Angel's habit of bringing other kids to the clinic. "But we're worried about Angel."

"Or whoever she is," John continued. "We don't know, because she won't tell us her real name. What we do know is that sometimes she presses her chest, as if it hurts. And she's admitted to having a few dizzy spells. She won't consent to an exam, but even if she did I can't treat her until she qualifies for state medical insurance."

Charlotte bit her bottom lip as she listened. "And you can't get her qualified for insurance without a real, legal name, right?"

"Right," Sarah confirmed. "That's why I think you should

be the one to see her. You're brand-new here. Maybe there will be something about you that will get her to open up."

"But this is Charlotte's first day!" John protested. "She doesn't know anything about Angel's case. More importantly, Angel doesn't know her. There's no rapport there…no trust."

"I know she trusts you, John, but despite your best efforts you haven't been able to get Angel to consent to a physical exam. If we don't make progress soon, whatever's wrong with her could get a lot worse."

Every cell in John's body was on alert. It had taken him months to build a rapport with Angel, but despite his lectures and gentle cajoling Angel still would not agree to an exam or reveal her name.

Sarah was right. For Angel's sake, he had to give Charlotte a chance to get past Angel's defenses.

He gave a quick nod of agreement. "But be careful, Charlotte. No pushing her, okay? If she wants to talk—" *she wouldn't* "—great. But if not, just back off. Otherwise she'll run away and we may never see her again."

Charlotte nodded and headed down the hall. John followed close behind, feeling jittery with frustration. He knew Sarah was right to see if Charlotte could have a breakthrough with Angel, but it felt like just one more area of his life where he was losing control.

Not that his life before getting guardianship of Piper had been perfect. He'd worked long hours at the clinic and sailed alone on the sea. But it had been *his* life to live the way he saw fit, and he'd liked it just fine.

Now he felt his world churning beneath his feet, as if a fierce storm was headed his way.

Charlotte closed the door behind her and assessed her young patients. Bruce sat on the exam table, relaxed and curious.

Angel stood in the corner of the room, her back up against the wall, arms crossed across her chest, her expression suspicious.

"Where's Dr. J?" she demanded.

"Busy with other patients," Charlotte answered truthfully, because the waiting room was about to burst at the seams. "I'm Dr. Charlotte Owens."

Then she cringed, because that sounded so formal. Was it better to introduce herself as Dr. C, borrowing the teen's shortened name for John? That didn't feel right. She realized she had no idea how to get things off to a good start with kids who didn't trust her as readily as the patients she usually treated.

It would be nice to ask John for some guidance, but apparently she didn't know how to get things off to a good start with him either. Was he this unfriendly to all the locums who'd come before her? Or was there something special about her that brought out his snarky side?

"So tell me, Bruce, what brings you in today?"

It wasn't Bruce who answered, though. Angel immediately responded, describing Bruce's sneezing, watery eyes, and occasional cough. She seemed very comfortable in the medical setting. *Interesting*, Charlotte thought. Angel had clearly been mothered by someone who'd taken her to the doctor. So where was that parent now?

"Well, let's take a look, shall we?"

Charlotte soon ruled out any serious infection or a virus. Bruce didn't have a fever and his lymph nodes were just slightly enlarged. Enough to indicate his immune system was on alert, but not fighting anything serious.

"Looks like seasonal allergies, Bruce," Charlotte said, making a note in his file.

"So he'll need antihistamines, then," Angel said, still serious and motherly. That was another surprise, because most teens didn't talk like that.

How old was she anyway? Charlotte did a quick visual.

Angel wore a lot of makeup, had big hoop earrings, and carried herself tall and strong. Late high school was Charlotte's best guess, maybe close to graduation. Charlotte remembered what it had been like to be on the cusp of graduation, on the verge of losing the fragile support she'd had through foster care. It hurt her heart to think that Angel was already fending for herself when she was still in high school.

"That's right, he will. Do you prefer chewable or can you swallow pills?" Charlotte asked Bruce.

"Pills."

She typed up the visit notes along with an order for a month's supply of allergy medication. "Bruce, take this to Sarah. She'll get your medication and get you checked out."

Angel stood to follow him and Charlotte held her breath, hoping for the best. "Hey, Angel, would you mind sticking around for a minute?"

Angel paused, her hand on the doorknob. She gave Charlotte a long, appraising look before she slowly walked back and stood in the corner, recrossing her arms against her chest.

Charlotte slowly exhaled with relief. Finally, she had a chance to make a difference here—which was the whole reason she wanted to work at The Sunshine Clinic.

"What do you want?"

Charlotte took care to keep her distance, positioning herself away from the door so Angel knew she could leave whenever she wanted. But Charlotte hoped she wouldn't.

"I just wanted to talk a little, if that's okay."

"About what?"

"About you, I suppose."

Angel's eyes narrowed. Everything about her, from her tensed body to her focused gaze, spoke of distrust and fear.

"Dr. J told me that your chest hurts sometimes. And you also get dizzy?"

Angel shrugged. "It doesn't happen that often."

"That's good. But you're pretty young for chest pain. How old are you anyway?"

Angel gave her a knowing look and shook her head. "Nice try, Doc."

So Angel was withholding *all* personal information, not just her name. Did she not want to be found? Was it possible she had a head trauma or an illness that affected her memory so that she truly didn't know who she was? Or had she found one small way to seize control of something in a world that had spun hopelessly off its axis?

Charlotte continued. "Angel, there's a lot of reasons why you might have these symptoms, like dehydration, stress or fatigue. But there's also some pretty scary ones. I'd like to do an exam, if that's okay, or at least listen to your heart for a bit."

That only seemed to make Angel double down on her tough girl facade. She jutted her chin forward, more determined than ever. "I'm not scared."

But there was a flicker in her eyes that said otherwise, and she was starting to cast side glances at the door.

Charlotte's stomach fluttered with alarm. How was she going to help this girl if the mere mention of a medical exam triggered her flight response?

Stay calm and think. Find a way.

Then Charlotte noticed Angel's necklace. She wore a pendant with four interlocked hearts. The first one was solid gold while the others were hollow. A hazy memory from Charlotte's foster home days slowly rose to the surface.

"That's a sister's necklace, right?"

Angel's hand reflexively flew to her neck. "I guess."

"And you're the oldest, right? That's why the first heart is solid?"

"Yeah."

Charlotte's mind sifted through the possibilities for connection. It was clear that Angel's need for control was too strong for her to accept help. Not for herself, anyway.

But maybe for her sisters, she would.

"I'm worried about them, Angel. Your sisters, that is."

Angel's brows furrowed. "Why? You don't even know them."

"True. But I know that many heart conditions are hereditary. So, if you're sick…"

"My sisters could have it too?" Angel's defiant expression melted into worry.

"It's possible. The only way to know for sure is to find out if your heart is healthy."

A great war of emotions played out across the canvas of Angel's face. Charlotte bit her lip, hoping against hope that her love for her sisters was enough to push her beyond her comfort zone.

"Okay, fine." She turned and jumped up on the exam table.

Charlotte quickly completed the exam, limiting herself to what was essential. Angel was thinner than Charlotte would like, and she would have loved to check her blood cell counts and nutritional status. But Charlotte limited herself to focusing on Angel's heart, warming the stethoscope drum before laying it against the girl's thin chest. She took her time, listening from all angles to make sure she was right.

"Thank you, Angel." Charlotte stood and draped her stethoscope around her neck, considering her approach.

"So?" Angel asked, adjusting her shirt. "Am I okay?"

Charlotte smiled. "Overall, you look really healthy, Angel.

But your heart is beating faster than it should. We need to fig-ure out why."

"Can't you just give me a pill or something?"

"That might be an option, once we know what's wrong. That's why I need to refer you to a cardiologist for an EKG." Charlotte silently chided herself for the doctor talk. "In other words, I'd like you to see a heart specialist. They'll want to do an EKG, which is a painless test that gives us more infor-mation about how your heart is working."

Angel avoided Charlotte's gaze as she jumped off the table and headed for the door. For one moment, Charlotte feared Angel would just walk out the door and never return.

But Angel paused, her hair falling to block her face. "This would help my sisters?"

Charlotte's heart clutched with compassion. She wanted Angel to know it was important to help herself too. "It would be a good start. But it could lead to more testing to figure out what's really wrong."

For several long seconds, Charlotte stayed perfectly still, waiting to see what Angel would do.

Come on, girl. Take a chance on me. I won't let you down.

"Maybe," Angel whispered, before slipping out the door.

That was not the answer Charlotte wanted to hear. Tachy-cardia could be caused by a lot of things, some of them quite serious. If Angel had a congenital heart issue, her heart could be a ticking time bomb, just waiting for a day when she exer-cised too hard or was otherwise stressed to go into full car-diac arrest.

Where did Angel go? When would she come back?

Would she ever get another chance to help her?

Charlotte dropped her head to her hands, overwhelmed with the weight of this work. She'd come here determined to make a difference in the lives of teenagers who had no one looking out for them. But how could she help kids who didn't have a permanent address or phone number? Or a clean place to sleep or safe places to store their medicine?

And could she even help a girl so determined to live like a ghost?

Charlotte made her way back to her makeshift office. John was already there, recording his notes on the computer.

Charlotte dropped into the chair next to him.

"So, how did it go?" he asked.

Charlotte let her head drop back until it rested on the back of her chair. She didn't want to tell him he was right. But he was. "Exactly the way you said it would. Except..." She held up an index finger to mark her point. "I did get her to consent to a basic physical exam."

John's fingers hovered over the keyboard. "And?"

"You were right again. She has significant tachycardia that needs to be checked out by a cardiologist."

John spun in his chair to face her. "And she agreed?"

Damn it. Every cell in her body wanted to say she had made the connection with Angel that John thought was impossible. For Angel's sake, of course. But also to prove that she belonged there, to John and maybe even to herself.

"No, she didn't," Charlotte conceded. "But she didn't say no either. In fact, I got a 'maybe' before she left the office. Kind of in a hurry."

"Was she freaked out?"

"Not freaked out. Just not happy."

John rubbed the back of his neck and looked off into the distance, as if he might be able to catch a glimpse of Angel before her tiny frame disappeared into the city.

"So what does that mean? Will she come back?"

Judging from his worried body language, John didn't know either. And that was when Charlotte realized she had signed up for something she didn't understand. How was she going to make this grand difference in the universe when she didn't even know who her patients were or when they would come back?

"All we can do is earn her trust over time…on her schedule," John said.

His sigh was heavy as he turned his bulky frame back to the tiny keyboard and resumed his hunt-and-peck technique. He was so earnest as he studied the screen, deliberately typing each word. It was tempting to tease him a little, but she wasn't sure if John was the teasing type. In fact, she knew very little about him.

If she was going to have any chance of making a difference at The Sunshine Clinic, she needed to understand the kids who came here. One person in this place clearly had that gift, and he was currently squinting at the screen with a pencil clasped between his teeth.

"So…" Charlotte said, fiddling with the pocket on her cargo pants. "If—I mean *when* Angel comes back, we should have some sort of plan for her EKG, right? Maybe we could work together on making that happen?"

John looked her way, a flicker of surprise in his eyes. He really was a handsome man when he wasn't scowling. Intelligent green eyes, smooth, olive-toned skin. And a sculpted jaw that would make Michelangelo weep.

Charlotte willed herself to look away, but her gaze lingered on his mouth a beat too long and her cheeks grew warm when he caught her staring.

Sarah paused in typing away on her keyboard and spun her chair to face them.

"Oh, John, you should take her to Guido's for lunch. It's been ages since you've had a real break from the clinic. And I think it would be lovely for you two to get to know each other."

Something in Sarah's tone sounded slightly provocative, like she was suggesting a date rather than a working lunch between colleagues. Good grief, did John think that was what she was thinking? Because she wasn't! She just wanted to talk about Angel and how to get her to a specialist.

Did he feel put on the spot too?

If so, he didn't seem bothered. If anything, his moss-green eyes seemed a bit softer now as he studied her. Making her feel less like a specimen and more like a…a friend?

"Sure," John agreed affably. "I'd love to get to know my new colleague."

CHAPTER THREE

IT WAS MORE than a week later before they could carve out some time for their lunch date. John kept a tight schedule, often skipping lunch so he could fit in one more appointment or spend extra time with a teen who had complex medical needs.

By the time they set out on the short, four-block walk to Guido's Mexican Cantina, Charlotte had been thinking about their lunch for days. John's plan to earn Angel's trust over time wasn't sitting right with her. Not with Angel's fast heart-beat and dizzy spells. They needed to be ready to help her as soon as she returned, whether she shared her real name with them or not.

Despite it being early, the cantina was crowded when they arrived. With its ombre orange walls and wrought-iron decor, the café felt like a Spanish Gothic man cave. On the back wall, near the kitchen, a stenciled jet-black bull posed, its nostrils flared, with one menacing hoof poised to stamp.

John found a wrought-iron table at the back of the café. It was tiny and seemed more suited to a streetside coffee shop, but it was the only table available. Charlotte slid into one chair while John disappeared to place their order.

John glanced her way as he waited in line. He gave her a little nod. What that meant, she couldn't say, but it unleashed a flurry of goosebumps down her back. She smiled in return, then dove for her water glass to relieve her parched throat. Why was she so nervous about this lunch? She'd completed dozens of assignments as a traveling doctor. Meeting new people, fitting in—it was all old news to her. So this edgy feeling she had around John made no sense.

It was also annoying, because she had some ideas for helping Angel get her testing done faster. She needed to stay focused if she was going to get past John's territorial tendencies, not stutter her way through her speech because of nerves.

Reflexively she groped through her handbag until her fingers found her lipstick and compact. She flipped it open to check her appearance and was just about to freshen her lipstick when she paused.

What are you doing, Char?

Her gaze shifted from the mirror to John, who had made it to the order counter and was oblivious to her gaze. He was a solidly built man, that was for sure, with a cool, streetwise vibe that the teens gravitated to. The woman taking his order was giving him lots of big smiles while twirling a strand of her hair. Even at this distance, it was obvious she was flirting.

Charlotte could see the appeal. John was a strong, attractive man, with a no-nonsense attitude that could make a girl feel a bit invincible by his side.

Her gaze shifted back to her mirror. Was that what she was doing too? Flirting a little with her attractive, vigilant colleague?

She paused to consider that scenario, then felt a rush of heat as she realized it was true. She snapped her compact shut. No need to give anyone the wrong idea—including herself. She had one simple rule when it came to romance on the road, designed to keep her career intact and her reputation stellar. *No. Dating. Coworkers.* As a traveling doctor, she needed excellent recommendations to secure her next assignment. She couldn't afford loose ends, bad breakups, or misunderstandings in her line of work.

So John could keep that stacked body of his on his side of the clinic—because romance was not in the cards.

Nor was it the point of this lunch!

She shook her head in frustration.

Focus, Charlotte.

She closed her eyes and mentally reviewed the lines she had practiced all week.

John, I know I'm only here for a few months. So, I hope you won't think I'm speaking out of turn when I say that I don't think we can just wait for Angel to be ready to trust us before we refer her for testing. There must be some other way to get her EKG done...something we can work out with the hospital. I don't know exactly how yet, but I'm just not willing to take no for an answer...

"Take no for an answer to what?"

John was back, holding two chilled fruit sodas in one hand and a basket of just-fried tortilla chips in the other. His bulky frame was less intimidating, now that it was paired with his relaxed, friendly smile.

Her flood of goosebumps returned, making her wonder if it really was nerves that made her body react this way.

Embarrassed, she grabbed a chip, eager for an excuse not to talk. "Mmm..." she said, waving her chip like an idiot. "Delicious!"

She moved over as far as she could to make room for him to settle into his chair, but his knee jammed hard against hers anyway. He muttered an apology as he moved left while she went right, both doing their best to navigate their postage stamp of a table. Despite their amateur gymnastics, she could still feel the heat of his leg next to hers, his jeans tickling her ankle. That set off another hot explosion of nervous energy that she couldn't seem to tame.

John used the heel of his hand to twist the metal caps from their glass bottles, then handed one to her. The strawberry-lime fizziness was a sweet, cool contrast to the salty chips. John took a deep draw from his soda, then set the bottle down to study her. She felt like a spotlight had suddenly been aimed her way, making her wish she had freshened up that lipstick after all.

"John…" she began—because that was the way she'd practiced it in front of her bathroom mirror that morning.

"I suppose I owe you an apology," he said, at the exact same moment.

"I know I'm only going to be at The Sunshine Clinic for a few… Wait…what?" she stuttered, flabbergasted that the prickly pediatrician she'd met a week ago was even capable of an apology.

He leaned in close enough to stir the hair at her temple when he spoke, launching her heart into a swift staccato.

"Listen, I probably shouldn't tell you this." He looked over both shoulders as if checking for eavesdroppers. "But The Sunshine Clinic…"

"Yes?"

"We're not really a medical clinic."

"What are you talking about?" Hints of sandalwood and orange spice from his aftershave were confusing her even more than this strange conversation.

"Remember those makeover shows? Where the show's producers took average people and gave them glamorous makeovers?"

She couldn't imagine where this was going. But it was interesting, so she grabbed another chip and waited.

"We're doing a show like that at the clinic. Hidden cameras and all that. But we're targeting medical professionals. It's called *Medical Makeovers 911* and you were our very first wardrobe intervention!" He leaned back in his chair, leaving a cool rush of air in his wake. "What did you think?"

His demeanor was typical Dr. J—calm, cool, unflappable. But there was an unmistakable glint of mischief in his gaze and she rather liked it.

She tapped her chin with one manicured fingernail, thinking fast on her feet. "Tackling the profession's lab coat problem? I see…"

"Exactly. They're so predictable."

She tilted her head, taking in this new, unexpected side of her colleague. So Dr. John Bennett had a sense of humor. Who would have guessed? Not her. But now she wanted to keep the game going, so she could tease out the smile making the corners of his mouth dance. "So donated cargo pants and faded tee shirts are…what? Med Chic?"

His eyes widened with delight at having a sparring partner. "Maybe Retro Rounding?"

"On-Call Casual? But wait…" She indicated his dark jeans and leather jacket with a wave of her hand. "What do you call this?"

"This?" He opened his jacket to check himself out. "I call this Hip-Hop Doc." Then he looked down at his red tee shirt, featuring a garish cartoon picture of a burrito. "With a side of kitsch."

She shook her head in mock disapproval. "Looks more like Grunge G.P. to me. With a side of goofy."

And then he laughed—a wondrous, husky sound that made Charlotte feel like she had won a fabulous prize. He tapped his bottle against hers.

"Touché. Sorry for the corny attempt at humor. Just my way

of trying to make up for your first day getting off to such a rotten start. That was entirely my fault."

For the first time since she'd started working at the clinic, the pins-and-needles anxiety that she felt in John's presence faded. The whole world felt new and shiny, like Seattle's streets after a spring rainstorm. But dangerous too. Because it would be harder to stick to her No Dating Coworkers rule if her colleague was as charming as he was handsome.

She took a quick sip of her soda, hoping her attraction didn't show. "Well, it did seem like you were having a bad day."

John tilted his head with a soft half-smile.

"You were talking to someone when I came in," she clarified. "It didn't sound like it was going well."

He was thoughtful for a moment. "Oh, right! That was the principal at Piper's school." He dragged a hand down his face. "That kid's gonna be the death of me."

"I saw her picture on your desk. She doesn't look that scary."

"No?" He chuckled. "Try this on for size." He ticked a list off on his fingers. "Three schools and four nannies in seven months."

Charlotte finished her soda and set it aside. "She works fast. I'll give you that."

John's expression grew serious. "It's not her fault. My brother got himself into some trouble last year. He's been sentenced to five years in prison on drug charges. Because of that, my eleven-year-old niece must live with her bachelor uncle on his tiny sailboat."

Bachelor uncle.

So, he was single. Interesting…

Not interesting! Irrelevant!

"She doesn't even have a room to call her own. I've listed the boat for sale, and I have been looking for a new place. Something cozy, not too far from the clinic, with a little backyard where we can grow a few vegetables. Maybe even get a pet, like she's been begging for. But between my clinic hours and taking care of Piper, there hasn't been much time for house-shopping."

"So, that's why I'm here?" Charlotte deduced.

"That is indeed why you're here. Though I'm not used to sharing my turf with other doctors." He gave her a wry smile. "As you may have noticed."

"Yes, I may have noticed that," Charlotte agreed solemnly.

He tilted his soda bottle her way. "Enough about me. Just who exactly are you?"

"In case you've forgotten, I'm Dr. Charlotte Owens…"

He waved her off. "Not the boring stuff. I want to hear the good stuff. Like why a doctor who graduated top of her class has a resume full of locum assignments. And how you wound up in my little clinic, with nothing but an old wood door for your desk and a surly doctor in your face?"

She chuckled, enjoying their new camaraderie. "The old wood door is growing on me."

And maybe the surly doc was too.

She gave a casual shrug before delivering the canned description of her nomadic life that she had perfected over the years. "It's a great way to see the world…" *pause for a moment…* "without paying for an expensive hotel room!"

Perfect. Now laugh and toss your hair over your shoulder, just like the carefree girl you are.

John nodded but his gaze was serious, not quite joining in the fun. "So, you're a destination doc, then? I've read about that—doctors who use locum tenens assignments to see the world, complete with travel stipends and per diems for meals."

She shrugged. "It keeps the bills paid, right?" Charlotte reached for her soda again, but it was empty, which gave her hands nothing to do. "Just trying to keep life casual and fun, you know? No worries about hospital politics or microman-aging supervisors. I help where I'm needed, then spend my free time on the slopes or in the surf. The whole work-hard-play-hard thing, right?"

It was enough to leave it at that. He didn't need to know the truth. That she couldn't settle down in one place for long before she got an itchy sensation at the nape of her neck. Like a warning that something dangerous was headed her way. He didn't need to know why she couldn't have a favorite pie café, or a puppy, or spend the weekend painting her living room.

Because once upon a time, she'd had all those things, only to have them snatched away in the middle of the night by a police officer with a kind face who'd knocked on the door, then shattered her world.

She'd survived that once and learned how to live a life that couldn't be taken away.

Because she always left first.

By now people had usually asked all sorts of questions about her travels. Then told her how they wished they could go back in time, be a little more adventurous before the pressures of work and family settled them into rigid routines. That had in-spired her to launch her travel blog, where she posted the pic-tures and stories of her travels around the world.

"I'm surprised you landed in Seattle," John said, his gaze intense and watchful. "Not exactly an international destina-tion, is it? Unless you're an avid skier or snowboarder?"

Under different circumstances, Charlotte would have loved to take her snowboard out to one of Seattle's many ski runs. But that was not what this trip was about. "Seattle's my home-town, actually. I just came back because my father left me his house."

"I'm so sorry. I didn't realize you'd lost your father."

"Thanks, but I didn't really know him. He and my mom broke up before I was born."

John's brows narrowed. "Yet he left you his house? Why?"

It was a great question, but she had no idea why he'd left her his house. The letter the attorney had given her, with its promise of explanation, was still sitting in her kitchen, on top of the toaster oven where she had warmed her English muffin that morning.

"He never married or had more kids, so maybe I was his only choice."

That was just about all the personal chit-chat she cared to share. It was time to get back to the reason for this lunch—Angel's need for an EKG.

She took a deep breath. "John, I know I'm only here—"

"So it's just you and your mom, then? Or do you have siblings?"

The question stumped her for a minute. She couldn't understand why he was so interested in her family. "It was just me and my mom. But she died when I was thirteen, and I didn't have other family so I grew up in foster care."

Time to lead him back to safe territory. Where was their lunch, anyway?

"So, I've been thinking about Angel and—"

"What was she like? Your mom?"

Goodness, were they still talking about her? She'd much rather show him her latest social media posts, pictures of a mountain resort ski clinic in Colorado where she'd spent a month working. But something about his intense gaze made her doubt she could distract him so easily.

"She was...you know...nice. Like most moms are, I guess. Anyway, we don't have much time before we have to get back to the clinic, John, and I really think we should discuss—"

John leaned back in his chair and folded his arms in a relaxed, easygoing pose. "We've got plenty of time, Charlotte. All the time in the world, if we need it."

Charlotte bit her lip, out of ideas for how to get John to focus on anything but her. It was unnerving being the center of his attention. The way he was looking at her. Something about his gaze made the world feel like it had narrowed to just the two of them.

"Well, she was a single mom, you know. Things weren't easy for her…raising me on her own."

She waited for some kind of response, but he was placid, waiting for her to continue. She huffed an impatient sigh.

"We didn't have a lot of money, but I remember these silly little traditions she created for me. Like my birthday. Every year, on the night before my birthday, she'd let me stay up until midnight. We'd go to the local diner and have a midnight milkshake party so we could celebrate the exact moment I turned one year older."

These were memories she hadn't thought about for a long time. She smiled reflexively, remembering her mother's irrational excitement at sharing a simple milkshake with her.

John smiled in response, revealing a pretty irresistible dimple. "She sounds lovely, Charlotte."

Charlotte spun her empty soda bottle between her palms. "She was."

And I miss her a lot.

But she didn't want to dwell on that. Her life worked best when she stayed focused on the future, filling it with the destinations and assignments that kept her mind busy and her heart full.

She took a sip of water to regain her equilibrium. How did he do that? Somehow, in the space of five minutes, she had told John more about herself than she'd told anyone else. Unnerving, for sure.

It was high time to get back to the matter at hand. She cleared her throat and tried again. "John, I know I'm only here at The Sunshine Clinic for a few months—"

But then she felt a strange buzzing sensation under her hands, which she had splayed across the table.

"Sorry," John muttered, reaching for his cell phone. "Dr. Bennett speaking."

Maybe she should just send him an email. She was giving up hope that she and John were ever going to talk about Angel and how to pay for her EKG.

"Mm-hmm... Just a few hours, then?" John frowned and ran a hand through his hair. "Well, that's better than nothing, Cassie. And good luck with your exams!"

When he hung up, his relaxed vibe disappeared. He rubbed his forehead as if he had a headache. When he finally looked up, his face was tense in a way that was very un-Dr. J.

"That was my sitter," he explained. "I have been thinking about Angel's EKG. I want to be ready when she comes back to the clinic so we can get that test done quickly. We have a charity fund at the hospital that might cover Angel's testing. But the application is long, and I can't access her file away from the office, so I need to stay late to get it done. I was hoping my sitter would do a few nights this week, but she's studying for college entrance exams and can only give me one evening."

Just then, the server who'd taken John's order appeared with two red baskets. She was young and prettyand seemed to dawdle at their table just a bit too long, paying far more attention to John than was strictly necessary.

Charlotte could hardly blame the girl for flirting. John was a sexy catch and now, after chatting, she knew he had a heart of gold too. What girl wouldn't want to make a guy like John hers?

But that didn't justify the flare of jealousy that knotted her stomach. John was her colleague—and a temporary one at that. She shifted in her chair, trying to get comfortable, and that sent her knee crashing into John's again.

She should pull back into her tiny sliver of space.

But she didn't want to.

His leg was solid and warm. In some small way, her knee against his felt like she was laying claim to him. Even if it was just the claim of having a private lunch date.

"Nice to meet you," the server said, letting her hand trail against John's shoulder as she left.

Charlotte reached for another chip, desperate to burn off some angsty energy. But the basket was empty. John was watching her now, his expression both curious and challenging. But he didn't move away. If anything, his knee seemed to be returning the pressure.

What on earth was she doing? This was a working lunch—nothing more! Why on earth was she flirting with him?

She shifted her attention to her burrito, hiding any expression that would reveal the riot of emotions doing battle in her body. She tried to saw into her burrito with her plastic fork and knife, but the thick tortilla shell made a mockery of her efforts.

"That won't work. You gotta just go for it. Like this."

John demonstrated the technique by taking a huge bite of his burrito, making Charlotte regret her order. It was always awkward, eating in front of coworkers, but even more so when the stoic coworker in question had a smoldering sex appeal and was leaning his knee against hers.

She didn't want to think about that for too long, so she mimicked John's burrito technique, and the next thing she knew she had unleashed a hot, delicious mess of charbroiled pork and spicy red sauce all over her fingers. Before she could blush again, John laughed with abandon, making everything—the stress of her new job, the messy burrito, her unexpected jealousy—seem miraculous and wonderful.

She couldn't help but join in. Maybe everything was going to be okay. Surely these strange reactions to John would quiet down soon, and they would settle into a sensible friendship.

But then John passed her a stack of napkins, and his fingers grazed hers. That was when she knew she was wrong. Terribly, horribly wrong. Because that barely noticeable touch sent a hot charge of electricity racing from her fingertips to some place deep in her core. The sensation was not friendly. It was hot and demanding...impossible to ignore.

She couldn't downplay her body's reactions to John anymore. There was something about him that sent her body into a mutinous riot every time he was near.

Charlotte had a sudden unbidden image of John working alone after hours in the dark clinic, with nothing but empty takeout containers to keep him company. The urge to offer her help was so powerful she had to bite her lip to keep herself in check. Staying after-hours at the clinic with a colleague she found insanely attractive was a terrible idea. Quite possibly the worst idea of her life. If she wanted to get back some semblance of self-control, she needed to keep her distance and stick strictly to business. No more lunches alone, no more talk of anything other than clinic business, and certainly no being alone with John after hours.

No. Dating. Colleagues. Remember that simple but oh-so-effective rule, Charlotte?

John wadded up his napkin and placed it in the now-empty basket. "Well, it was just an idea. We'll just have to hope that Angel finds her way back to the clinic soon and is ready to give us her real name."

That was a long shot and they both knew it. But obviously John was concerned for Angel too and had found a way to get her EKG covered. Without charity funding, there was little they could do for Angel unless she literally collapsed on the street and needed emergency care.

So, while keeping her distance might keep Charlotte's heart safe, it would do nothing for Angel, who was at a great deal more risk.

"I could help," Charlotte blurted, and then squeezed her eyes shut, wondering if John would be shocked at her boldness.

But John didn't look shocked. If anything, he seemed pleased. "Are you sure?"

Invisible hands pushed her from behind.

Go for it! some long-dormant voice screamed in her head. *You know you like him. Maybe something good will happen.*

Or maybe things would end badly and she would ruin her professional reputation.

But her next assignment was already set, and the tiny dimples that shadowed his smile were making all her reasons pop like bubbles in the sun.

"Yeah, I'm sure," she said quickly, before she could change her mind.

CHAPTER FOUR

JOHN SURVEYED THE preparations for his after-hours meeting with Charlotte. For the millionth time, he wished for a proper conference room, or even just an office.

Rome wasn't built in a day.

For Pete's sake, Rome wasn't his problem right now. What *was* his problem were these jittery, restless feelings that were driving him mad as his workday ended. He was spending entirely too much time double-checking that he had every form and supply they could possibly need. Not to mention stressing about whether he should order dinner in, or if that would look too much like a date.

Because this wasn't a date. This was strictly two professionals collaborating on a difficult case.

Oh, what a load of bunk. He spent entirely too much time thinking about Charlotte to believe that he wasn't interested. Of course he was interested—what man in his right mind wouldn't be interested in Charlotte? She was beautiful and smart, naturally warm, and adventurous. With little hints of vulnerability that she thought she kept hidden. So endearing.

Before John could stress on any more details, Charlotte showed up.

"Very efficient," she said, nodding to the supplies he had organized with military precision.

She brushed his shoulder as she passed, and the faint hint

of her touch, plus her unique jasmine-infused scent, did nothing to quiet his nerves. If anything, her proximity set off an increasingly familiar war between his heart and his head, with his heart taking a strong lead today.

Sarah appeared in the doorway. "Do you two need anything before I go?"

It was kind of her to offer. But, as much as John appreciated Sarah's help, he also craved time alone with Charlotte, without the constant interruption of phone calls and texts and questions and emergencies. Even their lunch date had been a noisy, cramped affair, but it had also been intriguing. He couldn't stop thinking about the press of her knee against his. Had that been intentional? Maybe not. That table had been tiny—it was probably just logistics.

But he didn't think so. There had been something challenging and exciting in her eyes when their knees touched, and he strongly suspected she had been flirting.

That possibility had haunted his thoughts ever since the lunch and he was beyond annoyed with himself. He needed to focus on Angel's funding, not wonder if Charlotte had the hots for him. In another time and space, yes—he would pursue Charlotte with all he had. But that time and headspace belonged to Piper now, and it wasn't fair to start something with Charlotte that was destined to end badly.

The lunch date had been good. They had broken the ice and were on a friendlier footing now. No need to hope for anything more than that.

John separated the application form and handed her half. "We don't have much time, so I thought we could each take half and help each other as needed. I've got to warn you, though—this could take some time."

As John handed her a pen, a terrible thought occurred to

him. Seattle was Charlotte's hometown, surely full of friends, classmates, and maybe a former lover or two?

The sudden hot rush of raw jealousy that roiled in his gut was ridiculous, but he had to ask anyway. "Unless you need to leave soon because someone is waiting?"

Charlotte's pen stilled, but she didn't look up. "Nope," she said, and it seemed a bit too cheerful in John's opinion. "No one is waiting for me."

Good grief, what was wrong with him? The rush of relief he felt was just wrong. Someone like Charlotte should not go home to an empty house. She was beautiful, and smart, with a huge, warm heart for teens like Angel. But he couldn't deny that it pleased him to know that she was free. John had his faults, but dishonesty wasn't one of them.

Charlotte and her pen got back to work. He should do the same. But his mind was in a state of mutiny and his gaze lingered on her profile. He felt an invisible current buzzing between them that made him hyper aware of everything about her. The heat of her body, the rise and fall of her chest, the way she pursed her lips just so when she worked... His gaze lingered just a breath too long and she looked up to catch him staring.

Time froze for a moment, maybe two, before she gifted him a sweet, spontaneous smile. Then she shook her head in a scolding fashion and glanced him with her elbow.

"Come on, lazy bones. Get back to work."

A very sensible idea. He should totally do that. But the black squiggly marks on the pages before him could not compete with Charlotte for his attention. He shook his head to clear the fog.

"So, how did you end up living on a sailboat?" she asked. "It sounds quite romantic."

He laughed, thinking of his tiny living space, anchored just feet from his neighbors, with the constant briny scent of old boats and sea water.

"It started as a way to save money on rent while I was in med school. And I don't know about romantic… Last week I had the scare of my life. I woke up in the wee hours of the morning to a terrible commotion on the deck. I thought someone was trying to break in! Piper hid in the bathroom while I went to check it out, baseball bat in hand."

Charlotte waited, her eyes wide. "What happened?"

He laughed. "It was just a sea lion, looking for shelter from predators. Or a free meal."

"A case of barking and entering, then?"

"You could say that." He chuckled.

She shook her head as she refocused on the paperwork before her. "You know, in all the travel adventures and mishaps I've written about on my blog, I don't believe I have a sailing story. Maybe I could interview you sometime? Get a few pictures and put it on my blog?"

Before John could think it through, he blurted, "Better than that—I'll take you sailing!"

Her laugh was spontaneous and relaxed. "That would be great."

John was sorely tempted to bang his head against the table a few times. Maybe that was what it would take to knock some sense into him.

He quickly changed the conversation to keep himself out of trouble.

"But, as much as I love sailing, *The House Call* is no place for a tween girl to grow up. She needs privacy and space…a backyard. Even that pet she's been begging for."

And as much as he hated the idea of being anchored to a mortgage and property taxes, Piper's need for stability was more important than his whimsical dreams of adventure.

He hated it, but a familiar pang of nostalgia roiled in his gut. Nostalgia for his life before Piper, when he had been free to live as he pleased. With his mother gone and his brother grown, it had felt like the past was finally behind him. Finally, it was time for him to pursue his own dreams, with no fear of hurting or disappointing anyone.

But, like the Greek god Icarus, his dreams had taken him too close to the sun, searing his wings until they could hold him no more. It was his brother, though, not him, who'd crashed to the earth, no longer buoyed up by John's promise to be his keeper.

What a terrible thing it was…watching others pay for his mistakes.

Charlotte laid her pen down and tilted her head. "So, do I have this right? You started to take care of your brother when you were probably still wearing action hero pajamas. Then you started a clinic to make sure Seattle's homeless teens received good medical care. And now you're raising your niece."

He felt hypnotized by those indigo-blue eyes. Utterly incapable of looking away.

"I have to ask…" She leaned forward, and the slight movement was enough to stir the air between them, filling the space with her intriguing jasmine scent. "Just who takes care of Dr. J?"

Long-buried emotions rumbled deep in his gut. Her question touched a soft, raw place in his heart that was best left alone. In all the years he had tried to fill his father's shoes no one had ever asked about him, or the sacrifices he'd had to make. When kids his age had been buzzing about baseball tryouts or running off to spend a hot summer day at the nearby creek, he'd had to focus on his little family, making sure Michael was safe so his mother could work hard…so hard…making sure they had a roof over their head and some food in the refrigerator. It had never occurred to him to want more. Or maybe it had and he'd just learned to be numb long ago. Because there hadn't ever been any "more" to be had.

Charlotte was waiting patiently for answers he didn't have. Everything about her felt receptive and warm. She wanted to know him—and, as much of a revelation as that was, it was even more of one to realize he wanted to be known by her.

He coughed and shifted in his chair. "No one, I guess. It's just me and Piper."

"And before that just you and your brother?"

He nodded. It was just the three of them when his dad had skipped out, leaving his mom three months behind on rent and a boatload of bills. But he didn't want to dive into all that. It was getting late, and he wanted to focus on Angel's application—not the mess of responsibilities that his father had left on his young shoulders.

When they'd finished the application John walked Charlotte to her car, grateful for her help but still haunted by her question.

"Just who takes care of Dr. J?"

All his life he'd done his best to fill the void his father's absence had left behind. It was second nature for him to take care of Michael, the teens, and now Piper…to make sure she didn't fall into the same abyss as her father.

He had no regrets for his decisions so far, but was this his destiny? It often seemed that way. He was Piper's guardian for the next few years. Then Michael would return and need help getting his life back on track. The clinic would always need him to fight for money and resources. And someday Sarah would retire, leaving him without a trusted partner to figure this out.

Charlotte glanced up at him as they walked. She was wearing a wool pea coat, dark leggings, and black boots. Her hair was pulled up in her trademark messy bun that left tendrils of loose curls framing her face. Beneath the weak lighting of the parking lot's lamps, her blue eyes were as dark and stormy as the sea he loved. She gave him a little smile and then he knew. He wasn't imagining things, and her knee against his had not been an accident. That electric buzz he felt when she was near…? She felt it too. He was sure of it.

Her car chirped twice as she unlocked it with her remote and the interior lights came on. She arranged her things in the passenger seat, then met him at the driver's side. She reached for the door handle, then paused and turned back, her eyes wide with questions. She seemed less confident out here in the dark, just the two of them alone, the moment full of possibility.

Her question still lingered in his heart. What about him? When *would* it be his turn to find happiness?

He stepped forward, drawn to her warmth, wanting to touch her, hold her. Maybe now was his time. Right now…with her.

His cell phone beeped twice—the distinctive tone that signaled a text from his sitter. A sign that he was lingering too long in this quiet space with Charlotte. And a reminder of what was at stake. He was Piper's guardian because of the mistakes he had made with her father. He had to do better by Piper. He just had to.

Maybe later would be his time. When Michael came home. Or when Piper was older.

His jaw clenched with frustration. Yes, that was what he had. A whole basket of *maybes* to keep him warm at night.

Charlotte was practically in his arms, her gaze raking his face, trying to make sense of the emotions he couldn't hide. But as much as he wanted to feel her warm body against his, he needed to do the right thing—because following his desires would only hurt her in the end. After years of practice, he thought he'd become numb to the resentment of turning his back on what he wanted. But the effort of leaving Charlotte had his fingers curling into tight, hard fists.

Deep breath. Count to three. Then open the car door and send her off with a brisk goodnight.

Quick and painless. Like ripping off a Band-Aid.

But in the end his body betrayed him. He found himself bending to graze her lips with a featherlight kiss, stealing something small and warm for himself. Her lips were soft and receptive, a safe harbor on this bitterly cold night. His hand wandered of its own accord, finding her hair, then her neck, trailing over it with his fingers, setting loose a flurry of goosebumps in his wake. Her gloved hand found and grasped his, as if steadying herself. How his body raged for more—a deeper kiss, a longer night...

But he had to put a stop to this. He'd already gone too far.

"I'm sorry," he whispered, though he lacked the strength to explain why.

Before his heart could make more trouble, he turned on his heel and strode back to the clinic. An icy wind kicked up, slicing through his thin tee shirt and raking his face with its cruel, cold claws.

Her car door slammed, making him pause at the clinic's entrance. When her engine revved, he fought off the urge to call her back. Instead, he channeled his frustration into a ferocious pull on the clinic door that made it bang against the cement support post with a satisfying crack.

Then he ducked back into the clinic.

Back where he belonged.

Charlotte stopped by the coffee station before her last appointment of the day. It had been a long, grueling day, thanks to an influenza outbreak. But Sarah had made things a little better by leaving a basket of home-baked treats near the coffee pot.

Charlotte was unwrapping an enticing blueberry muffin when she heard John approach. Her spine spontaneously stiffened at the sound of his footsteps.

All weekend she had been unable to escape her thoughts of John and that phantom kiss. She could still feel how his lips had brushed hers, so light she'd wondered if it was a dream.

It made her feel foolish to be thinking this way, unable to shake thoughts of him no matter what she tried. Her weekend had been a frenzy of cleaning and organizing, followed by long runs through the upscale neighborhood of her father's home. All so she could escape the awful yearning that his teasing kiss had left behind.

But even when she had worn herself out she'd still been able to remember the way she'd felt, pressed to John's chest. Like he was a mighty fortress, sheltering her from harm.

This must stop.

That was what she had vowed that morning on her way to work. She needed to come to her senses and put a stop to whatever this was between them. Infatuation? A crush? Whatever. They were both adults with sexual needs. Obviously they had developed some harmless attraction. So what? Attractions weren't destiny. They could be fun, or they could be annoying, but they were always meaningless so long as you didn't act on them.

From now on she would stick to her side of the clinic. No more lunches with John. No more after-hours work sessions. She would just focus on her patients and confer with John only when absolutely necessary.

And now here he was, standing behind her, his breath stirring her hair. Ready or not, it was time to put her new resolve to the test.

"Afternoon," John said. "How was your weekend?"

He reached across her for the cream and sugar packets,

sending notes of sandalwood and citrus into her space. Her traitorous body went on full alert, forcing her to close her eyes against the rush of desire.

Sticking to her side of the clinic was going to be a challenge. "Very busy," she croaked.

Her hamstrings still ached from the long miles she had logged, trying to outrun her thoughts of him.

For a long minute John doctored his coffee with two creams and one sugar, as was his habit. Charlotte willed herself back to her office, where she'd be safely sheltered from his tempting masculine aura. But her body seemed frozen in place, forcing her into an inner battle of self-control.

Just when she'd mustered enough willpower to grab her coffee cup and leave, he stopped her with a question.

"Do you have a moment? There's something I'd like to discuss."

Alone? In your office?

Her resolve was too new and shiny for this level of challenge!

"Of course," she whispered.

She followed him on autopilot, trying to ignore how the soft, well-washed denim of his jeans hugged every masculine curve of his backside.

He closed the door behind her. For one wild moment she thought he might push her up against the wall, crush her mouth with his, and finish what he'd started in the parking lot last week.

And if he did? Would she politely demur and explain her new sensible plan for self-preservation?

No, she would not do that. She would lose her ever-loving mind—that she was sure of. And then she would need a new plan.

What on earth was wrong with her? Vowing to retreat one minute...willing to toss the rules out the window the next.

Casual and fun!

That was her motto when it came to romance.

Easy-breezy, no promises, no demands.

But when it came to John, what she felt was anything but casual or fun. It was intense and greedy…like a wild animal she couldn't control.

John leaned against his exam table. She stood near the door and felt a brief impulse to bolt before things got any more complicated.

She took a deep breath to steady herself.

It was just a silly little kiss, she chided herself. *He probably doesn't even remember it.*

"Thanks for your time," John said. He crossed his arms over his chest, making his leather jacket strain against his bulky arms. "We should talk about what happened last week. After we finished Angel's application."

Crap. He wanted to talk about the kiss.

"Okay," she whispered.

"I was out of line, kissing you like that. I apologize for being inappropriate, and I genuinely hope I didn't make you uncomfortable."

Uncomfortable? No, sir.

There were a lot of things that kiss had made her feel, but uncomfortable was not one of them.

"Listen, Charlotte… I hope I'm not out of line to say this. You're a beautiful woman, and I'm very attracted to you."

She bit her lip, unsure how to respond. Of course, she knew he felt something for her—that was obvious from the kiss. But hearing him say it out loud…even the way her name rolled off his lips…she felt a strong desire to throw the rules out the window and just let her body take the lead.

The only thing that stopped her was his expression. He

didn't look like a hopeful lover confessing his feelings. More like a fugitive confessing his crimes.

"But I have Piper in my life now. She's still adjusting to the trauma of what happened with her father. It's just a terrible time for me to be…"

Charlotte felt her heart sink. Which made no sense since she had come to work determined to keep her distance from John.

But there was a tiny piece of her heart that had spent the weekend wondering if John had thought of her half as much as she had obsessed over him.

And now she knew. He *had* been thinking about her. A lot.

About what a mistake it had been to kiss her.

He didn't want her in his bed, or maybe even in his life.

She could practically feel her heart latching every window and bolting every door. Every beat screamed *Mayday! Mayday! Mayday!* as her body stiffened for battle.

She jutted out her chin and sharpened her sword. "It's fine," she said coolly. "I didn't think it meant anything. In fact, I hardly remember it."

John stuffed his hands in his pockets and looked down at his shoes. "Right… I'm glad you understand."

Charlotte fought off the urge to snort. She understood just fine.

Inconvenient. Unwanted. Go away.

Sarah knocked and poked her head around the door. "Sorry to interrupt. Dr. Owens, your patient is ready." Then her gaze ping-ponged between them. "Unless you want me to reschedule?"

Charlotte pushed herself off the wall. "No need, Sarah. I think we're done here."

So done.

But she couldn't help but steal a glance at John. He had his back to her, hands still stuffed deep in his leather jacket as he looked out the window. She heard his long, audible sigh just before she left.

He was probably relieved that it was over.

Well, she was too. This was what she got for even *thinking* about breaking the rule that had kept her heart safe all these years.

Lesson learned—thankfully before any real damage had been done. She should be dancing a jig down the hall. *GypsyMD* was a free-spirited gal. No strings holding her down, thank you very much.

But instead of relief or joy she was left with a bitter taste in her mouth and one burning question.

Why did getting what she wanted feel so bad?

CHAPTER FIVE

CHARLOTTE STOPPED BY the coffee station for the cup of coffee she hadn't got. Drat, the pot was empty. She didn't have time to make another, so she headed to her exam room where Sam, a fifteen-year-old boy complaining of headaches, was waiting.

Sarah had put an asterisk next to the symptoms, which was her way of signaling that the teen was making a complaint about one thing but probably needed to be seen for something else. This sometimes happened when a patient had a private concern or didn't know exactly what they needed.

Sam was seated on the exam table facing the door when Charlotte entered. He wore combat boots and camouflage pants—the sort of things he could find at a military surplus store. His sweatshirt was zipped up, the hood pulled far over his head. It looked like he had created a safe cocoon for himself.

"Hey, Sam."

She was about to ask about his headaches when she noticed a strong odor in the room. Infection? Poor hygiene? No, more like decay. And the closer she got to the thin boy with the big brown eyes, the stronger the scent was.

"So, Sarah tells me you're not feeling well."

Over the past few weeks Charlotte had learned to keep her questions open-ended, even if her patient had written something specific on their intake form. It allowed the teen more space to share what was wrong, and often one symptom was really three or four.

The boy bit his lip and looked away. "My feet hurt."

"Okay. Let's get those boots off so I can take a look."

Charlotte kept her voice as light and casual as she could, trying to distract herself from the overpowering odor. Her brain was already reviewing the possibilities. He could have an out-of-control fungal infection. Or boots that needed to be replaced. Maybe a bacterial infection that had gotten out of hand.

The boy just sat there, looking straight down at the floor, not moving. His hood was draped over his face now, hiding him from the world and from her.

She washed her hands slowly, planning how to proceed. Charlotte was accustomed to having parents in the room with her patients, who could provide a full medical history and ensure compliance. But here it was just her and Sam.

Her first instinct was to lecture him about all the bad things that might happen if she didn't treat whatever problem he had. But nothing about his body language or demeanor said that he was resistant or rebellious.

Instead, he looked ashamed—which broke her heart. Why should he feel one second of shame for something that wasn't his fault?

What would John do?

She was surprised when that thought jumped into her head, considering how infuriated she'd been with him just a few minutes ago. But whatever her personal issues were with John, he was a hero to the teens who came to the clinic. They trusted him implicitly, and he'd earned that trust by being honest and reliable. If John were here, he wouldn't lecture Sam—that was for sure. He would slow things down...way down...so it seemed like he had all the time in the world to spend with the boy.

That was probably why he was always running late. But it was also why the teens trusted him so much.

Time to borrow a page from John's playbook.

"Sam, I'm going to take your boots off now, okay?"

Charlotte took one foot in her hands. Sam didn't resist or pull away, so she felt she was on the right track. The boot was old, and very worn, the sole pulling away from the upper. She untied the laces slowly. She would have liked to keep up a steady stream of mindless chit-chat to set his mind at ease.

So, how's school? What's your favorite subject? Do you have any pets?

But none of those questions felt right. She didn't know if Sam had a bed of his own, let alone pets or the ability to get to school every day.

As soon as she tried to remove his boot, she saw Sam's first problem. The boots were at least two sizes too small for him. As she tugged and pulled on the boot Sam winced in obvious pain.

"My goodness, Sam! How do you get these off every day?"

He shot her a deer-in-the-headlights look. That was when she realized he probably didn't take his boots off every day. Because it was too painful.

"I'm sorry…this might hurt a bit. You ready?"

He peered at her through long bangs, fear shadowing his eyes.

"I promise you'll feel better when this is done. Okay?"

He bit his lip, then looked away. He gave her a faint nod again.

She applied steady, even pressure as she pulled and wiggled. Eventually the boot gave way—at the same time Sam cried out in pain. Any feeling of triumph that she might have felt at winning the boot war was instantly overshadowed by waves of the strong smell of infection. Charlotte forced herself not to react. Sam knew darn well the odor was coming from him. He didn't need her to remind him.

"Okay, Sam, one more time."

She repeated the process for his other boot, then began her assessment.

Sam's socks were in tatters, barely covering the sores that covered his feet. The sores had broken down the skin and were causing tissue loss, which was the source of the odor. She couldn't imagine how Sam managed to get around on feet that were in this condition.

Charlotte could feel Sam's eyes on her, fearing judgement or ridicule. This, she realized, was the moment when John had the most impact on the teens. When someone had revealed their greatest source of shame and pain, what did you say?

She slowly and gently released his feet, then looked up at him, feeling the weight of the world—Sam's world—on her shoulders. He just wanted to hear that everything would be okay. That was all any of the teens who came to the clinic wanted.

Charlotte shrugged and smiled. "I can fix this, Sam. No problem."

Sam bit his lip again, then nodded and visibly relaxed. Charlotte started by soaking his feet in an Epsom bath to help with the inflammation. He had a severe case of trench foot—a condition she'd honestly never expected to see outside of a medical textbook. But it made sense. Winter was Seattle's rainy season. And, while Charlotte loved to listen to the sounds of a rainstorm while she cooked dinner or read a book by the fire, days of rain were a nightmare for homeless teens. Their clothing, sleeping bags and footwear all got soaked. If they didn't have a safe, dry place to go, and extra pairs of dry socks and shoes, this was what happened.

She gently toweled his feet off, avoiding the blisters. "Does this hurt, Sam?"

He shook his head. "Not really. My feet used to hurt a lot, but then I decided to keep my boots on all the time. Pretty soon I stopped feeling anything at all."

That was not a good sign. Losing feeling meant his feet had been wet long enough to cause damage to his circulation and nerve function. As he healed, the feeling would return with a vengeance, which meant days of intense pain.

Charlotte sprayed his feet with antibiotic, then handed him a pair of new, clean socks. "I'm going to give you several pairs of dry socks, Sam, and we'll find some shoes that fit you from our donation box. You're going to need to keep your feet clean and dry, so they can heal. I'll make sure you get some antibiotic spray, too, and some pain relievers. I'd like to see you again next week, if that's all right?"

"Sure."

He slid off the table and gingerly landed on his feet. She handed him a pair of throwaway slippers to wear with his socks. Not a fashionable look, but that was probably all he could handle until his feet were in better shape.

"The best thing is to keep your feet clean, elevated, and exposed to the air for healing. Are you staying someplace where you can be warm and dry, Sam? In a shelter, maybe? Couch surfing with friends?"

His lips were a flat, tight line again as he shook his head.

"Let's go see Sarah, then. She has a way of finding shelter space when no one else can."

Sam's medical needs would help him get placed higher on the waiting lists too. With any luck he'd have a safe place to be while Social Services worked on finding a longer-term solution for him.

Charlotte left Sam with Sarah, after a hug and a reminder to schedule his follow-up for the following week.

Sarah looked more frantic than usual. "Oh, honey, have you heard the news?"

"No?"

"It's Piper. She's had some kind of accident at school. John dashed off to meet the ambulance at the hospital. I'm afraid it's too late to have an on-call doctor fill in. Can you manage these last appointments on your own?"

There were two teens in the waiting area. One was stretched out on the vinyl chairs, grabbing a nap, while the other flipped through the pages of a magazine that was probably two years old.

"Of course—but what happened?"

"I don't know yet. John tore out of here twenty minutes ago." She waved her cell phone. "I'm going to wrap things up here, then head to the hospital. Want me to wait for you? Or will you meet us there?"

Charlotte froze with uncertainty. No matter how angry she had been at his apparent rejection of her as a romantic partner, she knew how much John loved his niece. Seeing her injured and in pain was probably killing him.

But that didn't mean he wanted her at the hospital. He'd made it clear that they were workmates, nothing more.

"I'm not sure yet," Charlotte said, still not able to give a firm no. Because, as much as she wanted to push him away, she couldn't forget how he'd looked when he'd ended their kiss that night at the clinic. And that strange apology that didn't make sense... Was he really sorry he had kissed her? Or sorry that he had to stop?

She didn't have to decide right now. She could see these last two patients while Sarah went to John. Maybe Piper's accident wasn't that serious. Or maybe John would make his intentions known with a text or a phone call.

Sarah promised to let her know any news, then left for the hospital. Charlotte locked the front door behind her before returning to her exam room. She tried to focus on her last two patients, hoping that work would be her refuge from intrusive thoughts about John. Her heart might be closed off to any romantic entanglements with him, but that didn't mean she didn't care. He was a genuinely good man, who gave his best to everyone who counted on him. He deserved the support of friends at a time like this.

But did she belong at the hospital while he was facing a crisis? Well, the answer to that was probably no. He hadn't texted her since he'd left the clinic.

Besides, this was a family emergency—and she wasn't family. That was the price of being the Queen of Easy-Breezy. No messy commitments…no risk of loss. Just the way she liked it. But it also meant that no one ever thought to call on her for help, because she was always on her way somewhere else.

After she'd seen her patients, she locked up the clinic and headed to her car. It was strange, not seeing John's black SUV in its usual parking spot.

He's fine. You're fine. Everybody's fine. Just go home.

But it was impossible to imagine being back in her huge, empty house with a takeout order. Acting like it was just a normal night.

But that was what he wanted. For them to be just colleagues. That was what they both wanted.

You can't have your cake and eat it too, Owens.

A funny little phrase that meant she had to accept the limits of being colleagues. A sensible and wholly unsatisfying arrangement.

She made her way through the parking lot to the exit.

Turned her left-hand signal on and waited for an opening in the traffic.

And then her phone chimed.

A text message. From John.

Hey.

That was all.

It was enough. She changed her turn signal from left to right and headed to the hospital.

Charlotte found John in the pediatric waiting room. Her heart gave an involuntary squeeze when she saw his bulky frame folded into a hard plastic chair. His eyes were closed, and he had his head resting on one hand, a day's worth of beard shadowing his jaw. All traces of the calm, cool and collected doctor she worked with every day were gone. He just looked weary and vulnerable.

She touched him lightly on the knee. "John?"

He woke up, dazed, looking at his surroundings in confusion.

Charlotte slid into the chair next to him. "What happened?"

John rubbed his eyes. "Bike accident at school. Piper was messing around, I guess, and went over the handlebars. Compound fracture of her fibula." He sighed and leaned back in his chair, the very image of weary exhaustion. "She'll need to stay a night or two for observation after her surgery, to make sure she doesn't have head trauma too. Then I can take her home."

Sarah appeared with a tray laden with mugs of coffee and half a Boston cream pie. Charotte had worked at the clinic long enough to know that in Sarah's worldview, there wasn't a problem in the world that couldn't be improved with hot coffee and a slice of pie.

"Home?" Sarah snorted. "To what? That sardine can you call home?"

"Yes, back to *The House Call*. Where else?" John clutched his coffee mug like it was a life preserver.

Sarah was having none of it. "That is a terrible place for Piper to recover. She has a broken leg, for Pete's sake! How is she going to get on and off the boat?"

"I'll help her."

Sarah rolled her eyes. "And what about bathing? She needs a bathtub where she can soak but keep her leg elevated and dry. And how comfortable is she going to be on a tiny little berth instead of a real, soft bed? What about the damp? And the mold?"

Sarah made good points. Charlotte had seen firsthand at the clinic how much longer it took their patients to recover from viruses and injuries because they didn't have the right environment to rest and recover.

Just then Charlotte looked up to find Sarah pinning her with a pointed stare. A *very* pointed stare.

"If only John had a friend with a spare bedroom or two. That sure would be helpful."

Charlotte felt her eyebrows dart upwards. Good grief, was Sarah suggesting that John and Piper stay with her?

No. That was crazy. Especially after they had just agreed to stay in their professional lanes. She and John barely knew each other. And Piper didn't know her at all. It would be strange, and awkward, and the complete opposite of keeping their distance as they had agreed.

It would also be helpful and kind and generous. All the things she had wanted this forced trip back to Seattle to be about.

Sarah was right. She had heard Charlotte complain enough about her father's home and its endless renovations. Every problem solved seemed to reveal two more. But renovations or not, the house was massive, with plenty of room for John and Piper. They could even have their own bathrooms, complete with luxurious marble baths and heated floor tiles.

She had no excuse not to offer the use of her home—except for her bruised ego and her desire to keep complications to a bare minimum.

She took a deep breath, then jumped in with both feet. "You could stay with me."

John looked up from his coffee, stunned and confused.

"My father's house—I mean, my house. It's huge and… Well, wait…"

She found her phone and navigated to the professional photos her real estate agent had sent a few days earlier in preparation for the house sale.

She flipped through the photos with John. "There's a bedroom off the kitchen that would be perfect for Piper, with its own bathroom. I could ask the work crew to add handrails to the bathtub if you want." She scrolled to the photos of the owner's suite. "And you could have this room…just down the hall from Piper."

"I don't know, Charlotte. This seems…"

"Weird?"

Because it was. It was extremely weird to invite a coworker of any kind, let alone one she had kissed and then agreed to avoid, to share her home for a few weeks.

He smiled. "Yes, but I was thinking more that it's an imposition."

"Not really. Honestly, the house is so huge I'll probably hardly know you're there."

Oh, so not true.

She would be acutely aware of his presence, but he didn't need to know that.

"I don't know… Maybe I could find a short-term rental for a month or two."

"Oh, John," Sarah huffed, crossing her arms across her chest. "You are not going to find a short-term two-bedroom rental on short notice. Stop being such a stubborn mule."

Emotions played out on John's face like a movie screen. *Stubborn, protective, uncertain, confused.*

She knew what he was feeling because she felt it too. Inviting him to stay with her after they'd agreed to ignore their attraction felt like asking for trouble. But there were bigger issues at play than their feelings.

"Listen, John. This house I've inherited… Well, it's complicated. Let's just say that I've learned that my father chose his wealth over me when I was young. So I have resented the hell out of this house and all the suffering it represents for me and my mom."

She spontaneously grabbed his hand for emphasis, feeling strength in his broad palm and fingers.

"Using the house to help you and Piper would make me so happy. In some small way, it would make up for my father's selfishness, if that makes sense."

John's eyes were full of questions that she couldn't possibly answer right now.

He opened his mouth to protest, but then his shoulders slumped in resignation. "Maybe you're right. It would be good for Piper."

For the second time that day Charlotte got her way, yet she felt no sense of triumph. Already her emotions were a jumble of attraction and fear of getting hurt. Sure, they had agreed to keep things professional, but that was going to be a lot harder if John was showering and sleeping and living just down the hall from her.

A doctor in green scrubs approached. "Dr. Bennett?"

John jumped to his feet. "That's me."

"Piper's out of surgery. Everything went very well. Would you like to see her?"

"Yes, please!" He turned back to Charlotte. "One more thing... Thank you."

The next thing she knew he had drawn her to him, enfolding her in a warm hug that seemed to narrow the world down to just the two of them. She tried to return the hug like a friendly coworker would, but when she felt the tension coiled in the muscles of his back her hands just itched to massage his worry away.

"For everything," he whispered against her ear.

Then he released her and followed the surgeon, leaving her to wonder what else he was grateful for.

CHAPTER SIX

HOW HAD HE made such a mess of things?

Charlotte's kitchen was in total chaos. John had used every surface to make the dough and homemade sauce for his infamous pizza recipe. The kitchen was warm and infused with the tantalizing aroma of cheese and pepperoni. The price of his efforts was flour spilled on the floor and tomato sauce splashed on the counter.

But that wasn't the mess he was worried about.

That particular complication was still at the clinic. He and Piper had moved into Charlotte's home during the day, while Charlotte was at work. Because he had taken family leave as soon as Piper was injured, he had not seen Charlotte since the night at the hospital when she'd invited him and Piper to stay with her while Piper recovered.

That must have been so uncomfortable for her. He knew Sarah had strongarmed her into the invitation. It was for Piper's sake that he'd agreed to stay, but he was still looking for a short-term rental. It was the right thing to do—especially since he had made such a huge deal about sticking to the boundaries of their working relationship.

What a hard conversation that had been. The last thing he'd wanted was for Charlotte to feel he was rejecting her— he wasn't! And he didn't want her to think he regretted that kiss. He just regretted the timing. Had they met last year—or a few years later, when Michael was reunited with his daughter—maybe a relationship would have worked out.

But Piper had to come first. She was just a kid, trying to make sense of a world that had turned upside down on her. If he hadn't gotten so caught up in his dream of starting The Sunshine Clinic maybe he would have seen the signs that his brother was in trouble. It was his fault that Piper had lost the dad she loved with all her heart, if only temporarily. He couldn't take the chance that surrendering to his chemistry with Charlotte might make him miss signs of trouble with Piper too.

But he could at least apologize for making such a mess of things with Charlotte. Hopefully his homemade pizza and a nice bottle of Chianti would smooth things over. Put them back on good footing as colleagues and hopefully even friends.

"More pizza?"

Piper didn't even look up. She was sitting on one of the stools that flanked the kitchen bar. She had a laptop balanced on her lap and her leg, now wrapped in a new white cast, was propped on the chair next to her. Her fingers flew over her keyboard as she played some online game.

He sighed, missing the chatty girl he'd used to visit in California. There was little chance she'd want to watch a movie or play a board game with him tonight. Not with the fate of the universe playing out on her computer screen.

The oven alarm went off, signaling that the last pizza was done. This one was for Charlotte—his attempt to mimic the spinach and feta pizza she sometimes ordered for lunch at the clinic. Not quite as obvious as a big bouquet of flowers, but hopefully the effect would be the same.

He slid the pizza off the pizza stone and onto a large serving platter. Then opened the bottle of Chianti so it could breathe before Charlotte got home.

"Charlotte will be here soon. Do you want to stay and hang out with us?"

Piper looked up and seemed to give it a good think. But then she bit her lip and shook her head. She tucked her tablet under her arm and slid off the stool, refusing his offer to help her back to her room.

Damn, he wished he could connect with her somehow.

"Hey," Charlotte said from the doorway.

John had seriously underestimated how seeing her again would affect him. She had her hair pulled back in a casual ponytail, revealing the sharp curve of her jaw and the length of her smooth neck. Her cargo pants hugged her curves just right, and her soft, peach-toned tee shirt brought out the color in her cheeks.

"Hey, yourself," John said, resisting the urge to welcome her home with a soft, warm kiss.

Exactly the kind of urge he'd feared when Sarah had proposed this arrangement.

Her gaze slowly scanned the kitchen. John hoped she wouldn't take offense at the mess of flour and sauce and pans all over her counters. But when her gaze settled back on him, she just smiled.

"This is nice, John. The house actually feels cozy."

He knew just what she meant. Once Piper was settled in her room, he had taken a tour of the downstairs. He knew Charlotte's home was under renovation, and he wanted to know which areas were too dangerous for Piper to navigate on crutches. Thankfully the crew seemed to be focusing on Charlotte's basement this week, working to remedy some water damage.

The house was just as Charlotte had described—spacious and grand in many ways, but also cold. Maybe it was because many of the rooms were empty, cleared of furniture in preparation for the eventual house sale. But in a way John couldn't describe, the house felt like an empty shell. As if no one had ever really lived there. It troubled him that this was where Charlotte ended her days after caring for their patients at the clinic.

John held up the pizza. "Made your favorite."

She cocked her head. "You made a pizza just for me?"

"It was the least I could do, considering Piper and I have taken over your castle."

She smiled as she looked around. Piper's homework waited on the counter…a single shoe had been kicked off by the door. "I like what you've done with the place. Speaking of Piper— where is she? I'd love to meet her."

"She's either battling aliens or role-playing in an alternative universe at the moment. I'm sure she'll join us later, when she sees the chocolate eclairs we're having for dessert."

John reached into the glass display case that was suspended over the kitchen island. He found two wine glasses among the stacks of porcelain dinnerware and poured her a glass of wine. He detected a hint of her perfume as she took the glass. Something sweet and mysterious, plus those jasmine notes that always trailed after her. For just a moment, he could imagine this as his life. Making dinner for Charlotte, with Piper safe and sound down the hall. Just like a real family.

Whoa! What on earth was he thinking? He and Piper hadn't even spent a night in Charlotte's home and he was already thinking of them as a family! He turned away from Charlotte, hoping she wouldn't see the intense emotions playing out in his heart.

"I have some good news," she said, reaching past him for plates.

Her arm brushed his as she passed, setting every hair on his arm to attention.

"I could use some good news." John busied himself with

finding cutlery and napkins for dinner. He had to get these unruly emotions under control.

Charlotte added pizza slices to two plates. "The chair of pediatrics signed off on Angel's charity application. It's being forwarded to the financial services department for processing. Once we get official approval, I'll set up Angel's EKG."

That was good news indeed. But the rush of relief he should have felt was muted from the stress of his week.

Charlotte took a small bite of pizza, then closed her eyes with pleasure. "*So* delicious, John. I think this is the first homemade meal I've had since I came to Seattle."

"Seriously? You don't cook?"

"I move around too much to justify hauling around heavy kitchen mixers or a full set of saucepans. Besides, there's no better way to experience a new place than through its food." She set her glass down and crossed her arms on the counter. "I thought you'd be more excited about Angel's application. Is something wrong?"

Was something wrong? What a funny question. Six months ago, his life had been simple enough. He'd worked too much, then spent all his free time preparing *The House Call* for its next adventure. Now he was living as a guest in the house of a colleague he was incredibly attracted to, thanks to his failure to keep his niece safe, no matter how hard he'd tried.

"No, everything's fine."

Because it had to be. His life and his problems had nothing to do with Charlotte. She was a free spirit, destined to spend just a month or two in Seattle before she flew off to more exciting destinations and assignments. She didn't need to be burdened with his problems.

"I see." She drummed her nails against the counter. Then she cocked her head and smiled playfully. "Don't mind if I do."

He mimicked her head-tilt. "Don't mind if you do, what?"

"Have that second glass of wine you want to offer me."

She peered past his shoulder to the half-full bottle of Chianti he had placed out of reach.

He shook his head with chagrin. "What is it about you that makes my manners disappear?"

That was a rhetorical question, of course. He knew exactly why he acted like an angsty teen whenever she was around. Because he liked her. A lot. She was beautiful, smart, and when he wasn't acting like an idiot, they had a really cool vibe between them.

He poured her another glass of wine, then topped off his own. He kept her company while she ate a second slice of pizza and caught him up on the clinic's schedule for the upcoming week.

When she'd finished, she blew him a chef's kiss. "That was delicious, John. Thank you." She folded her napkin, pushed it aside and leaned back in her chair. "All right, Bennett... Start talking."

"About what?"

"About whatever's making you look as mopey as a hound dog, as Sarah would say."

"Do I?"

He ran a hand across his jaw, stubble chafing his palm. He'd been too busy tending to Piper to focus on himself for these past few days. Charlotte waited, both hands cupping her wine glass. Her expression was patient and attentive. For one moment John was so tempted to let down his guard. To share his worries about Piper and his fears that he would fail as her guardian. But that wasn't fair to Charlotte. Why would a free spirit like her want to get wrapped up in his problems?

"I'm probably just tired," he said, offering his best attempt at a smile.

She eyed John for a long minute, as if she was weighing the

merit of his reply. Finally, she shrugged and swirled the wine in her glass. "Sorry, Bennett. I just don't buy it."

John chuckled, surprised at her response. "Don't buy what?"

"The baloney you're peddling here. I know you're upset about something."

John couldn't imagine how she was so certain.

Reading his expression, she clarified. "It's this funny thing you do with your eyebrows when you're upset. You kind of squash them together…like this."

She mimicked the look for John, pushing her eyebrows to-gether furiously while pursing her lips at the same time. She looked like one of the angry characters in Piper's video games.

John couldn't help but laugh. "I do not look like that!"

She sat back with an amused smile. "Yeah, you kind of do. But it's okay. You're still my favorite workmate."

He shook his head as he looked down at his glass. She was teasing him, and he rather liked it. It felt good to have some-one in his life who knew him well enough to tease.

She leaned forward, resting her chin on her hand. It only made her look even more enticing. "Sometimes sharing our burdens makes the load a little lighter, yes?"

Why did she have to be so beautiful? Everything about her was warm and appealing. It was almost impossible not to lean into the moment. Maybe he could allow himself the indulgence of believing, just for an hour or so, that he didn't have to bear his burdens alone.

"Piper goes back to school on Monday," he said.

"And this is a bad thing?"

"Normally, no." The truth was he was dying to get back to the clinic. "But Piper didn't have a bike accident at school. She ran away."

Cripes, it was awful saying the words out loud.

"She showed up for her first period class, so she was there

for the attendance check, but then she and a friend slipped away before the next period. They rode their bikes over a mile to a local bike park, to try out some tricks they saw on social media. It was all fun and games—until Piper's bike went one way and she went the other."

He closed his eyes against the image of her flying over the handlebars to land against a concrete barrier.

"John, that's terrible. But she's all right now, right? And what about you? Are you okay?"

"No," he shot back, immediately regretting his sharp tone. "How could I let this happen?"

Charlotte's brows knitted in confusion. "I don't understand. You weren't even there. So, how could this be your fault?"

"Because it's my job to protect her! It's up to me to choose the right sitter, the right school, the right…everything! If the school failed to keep her safe, then I failed her too. Because at the end of the day I'm all she has."

And that was his fault too, but his throat and chest were so tight he could hardly speak, let alone tell Charlotte the role he'd played in Piper's new reality.

John stood abruptly and cleared their dishes. He knew he was being too rough, clashing cups against plates and making a terrible racket. But it was oddly satisfying, the way the external clatter matched his inner turmoil. He felt Charlotte watching him, but she didn't say anything. What could she say? These problems were his to bear, and he shouldn't have burdened her with them at all.

He dropped the dishes in the sink and turned the water on full blast. Soon he had a sink full of hot, soapy water. Charlotte appeared at his side and cupped his shoulder with her soft hand. He closed his eyes against the swell of emotion her touch inspired. Somehow she was slipping past his defenses into the closed-off places of his heart, surprising and jarring him at the same time.

"Look, I don't have kids, or anything, so maybe I'm out of line here. But it seems to me that you've done an amazing job of being her safe place to land after her father went to jail. She's still grieving about her father and the loss of the home she knew. What about a therapist? Someone she can talk to and sort things out?"

John fiddled with the cloth napkins now stained with pizza sauce and wine. "We've tried a half-dozen therapists. She won't talk to them. She just clams up and stares out the window."

"Maybe you haven't found the right therapist?"

"Maybe," John muttered, then set about cleaning up the mess he had made.

Charlotte joined him, silently drying dishes while he worked out his frustrations with soap and a cleaning wand. He shouldn't have unloaded on her like that. Just a few days ago he'd been insisting that they needed to stick to being work colleagues, and now he was using her as a sounding board. This wasn't what she'd wanted when she invited him and Piper to stay here, he was sure of that.

When every dish was washed and put away, John checked his watch. "It's getting late. I'll get Piper to join us for eclairs and coffee."

"Looking forward to it!" Charlotte said.

But John didn't find Piper sprawled on the bed with her computer or her books, like he'd expected. She wasn't in the bathroom either. The bed was still made and her suitcase sat next to the dresser, still waiting to be unpacked. But her shoes and jacket were missing.

John's heart jumped into his throat. Had she run away again?

He dashed back to the main living area, hoping against

hope that Piper had somehow transported herself to the living room without him noticing. His mind was working overtime. She had a broken leg, for Pete's sake—how far could she go?

Unless all that time on her computer meant she'd been talking to someone online? Someone who could pick her up and…

John shifted to emergency mode. "She's gone!" he shouted. His throat was tight with terror.

But Charlotte was gone too.

"Out here!" he heard Charlotte call. "Bring your coat!"

John dashed outside to find Charlotte sitting in an Adirondack chair, wrapped in a plaid blanket. She was watching Piper approach a scraggly cat.

Charlotte smiled warmly at John and tapped the chair next to hers.

John sank into the chair, feeling a little wobbly with relief. "So, who's this?"

"I just call him Cat. The lawyer doesn't know if he belonged to my father or not. He visits every day, but he won't come into the house."

"What's wrong with his eye?" Piper studied the cat like he was something foreign and exotic.

Now that he was adjusting to the dimmer light outdoors, John could see what Piper was talking about. It was a tabby cat. Not young, but not a senior either. It was thin enough to count its ribs, and one eye had been scarred shut.

"I'm not sure. Maybe a fight. Or an accident. Doesn't look like he had proper veterinary care, so the eye is permanently damaged."

Piper was quiet. Then she reached out to touch the skinny creature.

"Don't!" John cried.

One bite and Piper could get Cat Scratch Disease, or rabies, or an infection of her bloodstream.

Charlotte laid her hand on John's to calm him. "Put your fingers out so he can sniff. Cat will let you know if he's feeling social or not."

John would still rather shoo the cat away, but before he could say so the cat began rubbing his face all over Piper's fingers and hand.

Piper looked up with a delighted smile. "He likes me!"

"Indeed, he does," Charlotte said. "And so far you are the *only* one he likes."

"He won't let you pet him?"

"Nope. I'm only allowed to feed him, and even then he seems to think he's doing me a favor."

The tabby was going mad on Piper now, even allowing her to scratch under his chin. A distinct rumbling sound rose from the cat's skinny belly, making Piper smile wider than John had ever seen. It was good to see her happy, even if it took a down-on-his-luck cat to make it happen.

"Why doesn't he have a real name?"

"I guess because I can't keep him. Seems better for his future family to have the honor of naming him."

Piper's smile faded. "Why can't you keep him?"

"Because soon I'll sell this house and get back to my real life. It's hard to have a pet when you move around a lot."

And there it was. The reminder he needed. Charlotte was amazing as a colleague and a friend. Her generosity in sharing her home with him and Piper was more than he'd ever expected. But he couldn't lean into this. As wonderful as it was to share an evening with Charlotte, this was just a sabbatical of sorts. He had a real life too, and it couldn't include Charlotte. He was the oak tree, deeply rooted to the earth, while she was a bird that flew where it wished. Their time together would be wonderful, but short, because that was what they were made for.

Charlotte's expression had turned thoughtful. "You know, Piper, seeing how Cat seems to like you so much, maybe you can help me..."

She cast John a sideways glance that made him wonder what she was up to.

"Cat's not going to get a good home if he's dirty and un-friendly. He obviously likes you, so maybe you could help me earn his trust? Then I could take him to a veterinarian for some good medical care. And together we could help him gain some weight, brush out his coat, and learn some basic manners."

John instantly understood her plan. When the doors to someone's heart were locked up tight, like Piper's after what had happened with her father, sometimes you had to find an-other way in. Piper wasn't willing to talk to a therapist about her adjustment issues, but maybe she would open up to Char-lotte. Especially if the goal wasn't for her to open up, but just to help a scruffy old cat who had given up on people.

Piper was somber as she considered the offer. "He needs a better name."

Charlotte's laughter was lovely and spontaneous. "Are you negotiating your terms? Okay, it's a deal. You can name the cat whatever you want if you help me get Cat ready for his new forever family."

Cat stood and arched his back, then dropped to his forearms for a deep stretch. Maybe that meant he liked the deal too.

Piper followed Cat to the edge of the yard, watching as he easily scaled the fence and disappeared.

Charlotte called out a warning for her to stay away from the dilapidated greenhouse which clearly had not been used for a decade or more, then whispered under her breath, "Maybe the best therapist for Piper has four legs and a tail?"

Maybe so. But how was Piper going to help with Cat once they moved to a short-term rental?

She wouldn't. Not only would it be awkward and uncomfortable to set up frequent visits, there was no guarantee that Cat would be in a social mood when they visited.

So if he wanted Piper to have a chance to connect with Cat, and maybe even Charlotte, he was going to have to spend just about every minute of his day in close proximity to the woman who had captivated his imagination but was strictly off-limits.

Charlotte's hand still warmed John's arm, triggering that feeling he couldn't quite name. He searched his memory bank for another time in his life when he'd felt like this, but he came up blank. There was a sense of relief, yes—but why? And it was mixed with some emotion that made him feel warm despite the chilly night air. As if they were a team, dedicated to helping Piper. Which meant he didn't have to go it alone.

"I think you're right. Sometimes we find help where we least expect it."

John tucked her hand into his chest, then closed his eyes and let the warmth infusing his body chase the evening chill away.

Charlotte broke down the last cardboard box and stacked it with the others for the recycling bin. The clinic's supply closet was restocked, ready for the week's work. She stretched her back and hamstrings, then grabbed a bottle of cold water from the kitchen.

She still needed to finish the draft of a federal grant report by the end of the week. John hated the mandatory reporting that came with federal funding, and she kept messing up her billing codes, so they had agreed to trade their most dreaded tasks.

Charlotte thought ahead to the end of the day, when her work would be done. Her travel journal had been badly neglected since she'd come back to Seattle. The house renovations would be done in less than a month, around the same time Piper's cast should be off. It was high time for her to start researching everything the Caribbean cruise ship had to offer.

She also needed to update her blog, *GypsyMD*. She didn't have a million followers, but those who did follow her were loyal, and loved following her adventures as a traveling doctor. If she couldn't give them an exciting glimpse into her nomadic life now, she could at least give them some teasers for her forthcoming exciting travels aboard *The Eden*.

It would be a welcome distraction from the simmering tension she felt with John in the house. It was one thing to work with him at the clinic, when they were both busy and focused on their patients. Quite another to see him padding about her house barefoot and wearing fitted jogging pants low on his hips. More than once she'd had to take a cold shower after work to get her mind out of the gutter.

Charlotte found Sarah and John in the lobby. John was sorting medical supplies into piles, while Sarah filled plastic sandwich bags with handfuls of supplies. Once a month The Sunshine Clinic closed early, so John could do street call work, where he went deep into Seattle's industrial district looking for homeless teens, sharing information about the clinic and providing medical care if needed.

John noticed her. "Hey, could you hand me those flyers?"

He pointed to a table behind Charlotte. She handed him a stack of blue flyers secured with a thick rubber band.

"Fifty!" Sarah said with finality.

She scooped up handfuls of the filled sandwich bags and dropped them into an open backpack at the end of the table.

"Perfect," John said. "We'll leave half at The House of Hope and place the others at gas stations and convenience stores in the area."

He finished stuffing the backpack with clean socks and toiletry kits.

Charlotte took a closer look at the bags Sarah was holding. They were filled with travel-sized medicines and ointments, along with a toothbrush, alcohol wipes, and a business card with the clinic's address and operating hours.

"Hey, this is your cell phone number!"

She was incredulous that John would share his personal number, rather than using the clinic's answering service for emergencies.

"If a kid needs us, I want to know. Not rely on an operator to decide if their call is important enough to page me." He shrugged on his backpack. "Ready?"

From beneath the table he hoisted a second backpack, already filled with supplies, and held the straps out to Charlotte.

She shrugged on the backpack and groaned under its weight.

"Sorry!" John chuckled. "You're carrying the bottled water."

"Thanks a lot," Charlotte mock-complained, but she was secretly glad.

The struggle of hauling water bottles all over Seattle would be a welcome distraction from her frequent thoughts about John.

They headed into the street while Sarah stayed behind to handle phone calls and walk-ins. John gave Charlotte a lanyard that identified her as medical staff. He was hauling a wheeled blue ice chest, filled with more cold water and snack packs of apples, string cheese, crackers, and peanut butter.

Their first stop was The House of Hope, where they dropped off flyers and first aid kits. The shelter was decorated for Valentine's Day, with pink and white hearts taped in the windows. Charlotte couldn't see the kitchen, but she could smell the sweet scent of fresh-baked cookies and hear teens chattering and laughing amid the clatter of dishes being washed.

The shelter director insisted they take a few cookies for the road. Charlotte's frosted sugar cookie had *Be Mine* shakily piped by a young baker's hand. John's had a chubby Valentine cherub, his bow and arrow pointing Charlotte's way.

Not that he needed any help from Cupid. Ever since John's SUV had joined her rental in the garage, her feelings of agitation and restlessness had only multiplied. She wasn't herself when he was around. She felt awkward and overly self-aware.

John was walking ahead of her now, hauling the cooler and considering their next stop. Charlotte gazed down at his backside, admiring the muscular curves that flexed the limits of his denim jeans. *Damn*. She couldn't help but remember the night they'd worked late. That passionate but fleeting kiss... the feel of her fingers kneading his thick, silken curls.

She forced her gaze back to the work at hand. These distractions weren't going to help anyone. John had made his feelings perfectly clear. He might have enjoyed that kiss as much as she had, but moving forward was not an option.

They headed deeper into Seattle, stopping at churches, gas stations and the community center to drop off flyers and first aid kits. Clerks and volunteers suggested places where they had seen teens who might need their help. Charlotte had to walk fast to keep up with John, as he seemed determined to investigate every lead before dark.

The sun edged closer to the horizon. Charlotte jiggled her pack. "I have a few water bottles left."

John rubbed his chin. "One last stop, then—the skate park. We'll pass out the rest of our supplies, then head back to the clinic."

Despite the waning sun, the skate park was in full swing. Kids gathered in big and small groups, boasting and laughing, skateboards resting under skinny arms or leaned up against the fence. John focused on two girls near a cherry tree, its branches bare for a winter rest.

The girls, wary at first, soon warmed to John's gentle curiosity. The taller girl in skinny jeans said she knew about the clinic but didn't have plans to visit anytime soon.

"Keep the card," John said, pointing to the kit. "In case you need us."

She tucked the card in her back pocket. "Okay. But you guys should check on Tommy."

The shorter girl, with chipped, bubblegum-pink nail polish, pointed to a white cargo van. "Yeah, he's pretty sick."

The van was parked at the back of the parking lot. Based on the flat rear tire and the tall weeds growing through the front fender, it seemed it hadn't been moved in a long time. The rear door was open and Charlotte could see a boy, lanky and thin, lying on his side with his back to the world.

She and John approached the van slowly, calling the boy's name. It took almost a dozen attempts before Tommy moaned and turned their way.

"Hey, Tommy." John's voice was warm and soothing. "My name is John. I'm a doctor, and so is my partner, Charlotte. Your friends are very worried about you."

The boy opened his eyes but seemed too exhausted to keep them that way. He threw an arm across his face. "Man, I am *so* tired. I've been sleeping for *days*."

Charlotte scanned the boy from head to toe, assessing his condition. Her first impression was that he was a fast-growing adolescent who needed more calories than he was getting. His sandy brown hair needed a shampoo, and his jeans were frayed at the bottom. But what really concerned her was the beads of sweat on his forehead and his too-pale skin. Tommy was a very ill boy.

"Okay if I check you out?" John asked.

But Tommy didn't answer. He had already slipped back into unconsciousness.

Charlotte fished the blood pressure meter and thermometer from her pack. She accepted a pair of latex gloves from John, then took Tommy's temperature. One hundred and one degrees. Elevated, yes, but not dangerous. Ditto for his blood pressure and heart rate.

John gently pinched the skin on the back of Tommy's hand. It stayed tented. "He's dehydrated."

Charlotte draped her stethoscope around her neck and considered the boy. Tommy's eyes, when open, were vacant and confused. He clearly needed more than fluids and rest, but his vitals were that of a relatively healthy teenager. What could be wrong?

If only she had an army of highly trained doctors and nurses, ready to run any test she wanted. Or the benefit of a full medical history delivered by a parent or guardian who was intimately familiar with his history. But out here, bent over a sick boy in a rusty van, all she had was her intuition and the equipment she could carry in a backpack to save a boy who was deteriorating before her eyes.

But she also had John.

"Let's try an orthostatic," she said.

"That's pretty old school."

"I know, but it's worth a shot."

Tommy was beyond the typical age range, but it was possible that his body retained a child's ability to hide symptoms of serious infection. If so, getting him to stand would overwhelm his defenses and reveal how sick he really was.

John helped her to get Tommy to struggle to his feet. He was so weak John had to support his full body weight while Charlotte checked his vital signs again. She frowned at the new numbers. His blood pressure had plummeted while his heart rate had soared to one hundred and fifty beats per minute.

Alarm bells rattled her core. "Sepsis," she muttered.

John's gaze darkened. They both knew that without immediate medical intervention the inflammation raging through his body could damage his internal organs to the point of death.

Charlotte reached for her cell phone to call 911, but John growled, "No time!" All traces of the easygoing Dr. J were gone.

They maneuvered the moaning boy back into the van, barely aware of the growing crowd of teens gathered around watching them, silent and somber.

Charlotte dug through the cooler for the IV bag of antibiotics and saline, while John started a large bore catheter. They worked carefully, laser-focused on starting the IV fluids that would fight off whatever systemic infection was shutting Tommy's organs down.

John held a stethoscope to Tommy's chest while Charlotte called for an ambulance. Soon she heard the high-pitched wail of a screaming siren headed their way. Tommy's breathing had slowed ever so slightly. There was even a hint of pink in his cheeks. Charlotte allowed herself a tiny sigh of relief. Tommy was still in danger, but this baby step of improvement was a relief.

The ambulance crew arrived, and John completed the handover, squeezing Tommy's hand as he was loaded into the ambulance. The teens drifted away slowly, murmuring in hushed whispers.

With the crisis behind them, Charlotte's adrenaline rush was soon replaced by a crushing fatigue. She dropped like a stone onto a rickety wood bench. John sat next to her, the bench groaning under the extra weight.

"Will we ever see him again?" She felt cold and numb as she contemplated the near tragedy.

"Probably not."

Her stomach clenched with delayed fear. "That was too close, John. We almost lost him."

To her dismay, her voice was shaking, betraying emotions she couldn't control. She didn't realize her hands were shaking too until John folded both of his around hers, buttressing them against the late-day chill that seemed to rise from the damp earth beneath their feet.

"I know."

His voice was so calm. Like he had seen this a thousand times before—which maybe he had. But how could he stand it?

"I don't get it, John. What happened? How can a boy be *that* sick with no one to care for him?"

John's jaw clenched for just a second. "I don't know, Charlotte. Asking why too often can drive you crazy. These kids are like ghosts. You see them going to school, working a part-time job, trying to fit in. They work hard to hide what they lack. Teenage bravado, maybe, or an instinct to hide weakness on the street. I don't really know."

His grasp tightened around her hands, and she looked up to see his clenched jaw.

"But I do know this. They're worth saving. Every last one of them."

John released one hand so he could trace her cheek with his finger.

"What about you, Charlotte? Are you worth saving?"

Charlotte gasped at his question. "What are you talking about? I'm nothing like Tommy! He's completely alone in the world, with no one to look out for him except us. I have..."

She trailed off. Who did she have? Who could she count on to come to her aid at any time of the day or night, no questions asked?

She had thousands of followers who loved to live vicariously through her travel blog. But they didn't know her.

Even the friends she met every year or two for an exotic vacation didn't know her all that well.

Certainly not well enough to drop everything in their life for her if she were sick or injured.

Which was by design—so that she didn't have to feel the pain of saying goodbye to someone she cared about.

But she had never asked herself why she kept saying goodbye in the first place.

"So who would be there for you if you were as sick as Tommy? Who would refuse to leave your side until you were strong enough to take care of yourself?"

"I *am* strong enough to take care of myself!" She always had been—ever since her mother had died.

That was enough to trigger the memory of that terrible night. First the policeman, who'd delivered the terrible news. He'd asked if there was anyone he could call for her, but there had been no one. It had always been just her and her mom. A tiny family of two, complete in and of themselves. But she was gone and so the social workers came.

She had only been allowed to take what would fit in the trash bag they gave her. She'd packed as if she'd be gone for just a night or two, leaving so much behind. Pictures and collected seashells. Her mother's recipe collection and Charlotte's saved art projects. Ticket stubs and favorite slippers and the soft blanket they'd snuggled under for their movie nights.

John's steady gaze was stripping her bare. All he wanted was her truth. But she wasn't sure she knew it anymore.

She was certain of one thing. She was tired of running. She could feel it in her bones.

Because what was the worth of a life spent living like a tourist? That was what she was, essentially. What was she missing by being always on the road, never dug in? Was she happy never making a difference in anyone's life because she was always on the move, always planning her next adventure, always one step ahead of heartbreak and hurt?

Instead of a family she had a travel blog. Instead of love she had a well-worn passport.

It had been enough for a long time...when she was defining herself after her years in foster care.

But what about now?

She sighed and looked down at the hands that enveloped hers. Hands that belonged to a good man who always stayed, no matter how it might crush his heart with despair.

She checked her neck—there was no itching, no feeling of imminent danger. For the first time in a long time, maybe forever, she felt like she was right where she wanted to be.

CHAPTER SEVEN

BY THE TIME Charlotte and John got back to the clinic, it was long past dark. The clinic was locked and Sarah's car was gone. Charlotte had barely spoken after Tommy's perilous rescue and now, under the parking lot's lamps, John noted dark shadows under her eyes. He didn't press her for conversation as they unpacked the coolers and prepped for the next day.

"See you at the house," she mumbled as she rooted through her purse for her car keys.

John's stomach fluttered with alarm. Everything from her slumped shoulders to her slow gait screamed fatigue. His partner was far too tired to be behind the wheel of a car.

"Let me drive you home," he said.

"I'm fine," she countered, but it sounded like a reflex.

John paused, considering his options. Just long enough for her to unsuccessfully smother a huge yawn.

She gave him a sheepish half-smile. "Maybe you're right."

She dropped her keys into his hand and followed him to the car. John slid into the driver's seat and pressed the car's ignition button. The radio picked up Charlotte's playlist, playing an R&B song that was a soothing balm after their long day.

John turned on the car's heater, then checked his texts. Piper had gone to a friend's house after school, her first ever playdate since she had moved in with John. Living with Charlotte and finding camaraderie with a cat who didn't know where he belonged either had helped her find her bearings a bit, and helped John to see that in his desire to protect Piper he might have accidentally smothered her. If she was going to heal, he had to help Piper find her own village of friends and caring adults. And maybe a dumb cat too.

John texted the friend's mother to let her know he was on his way to pick up Piper.

She was blossoming at Charlotte's house. Sometimes John woke on his days off to find Piper's bedroom empty. Instead of the rush of alarm he'd felt that day when he'd been having pizza with Charlotte, he knew exactly where to find her. In Charlotte's kitchen, perched on the counter, helping to stir eggs or just chatting away while Charlotte made breakfast. Sometimes they both worked on the cat, brushing his fur out or showing him the joy of feather wands.

Their work seemed to be paying off. John could no longer count Cat's ribs at a glance. Cat was filling out with a steady diet of good food and extra treats.

In time, it had become natural to start their mornings in Charlotte's kitchen, with sunlight streaming through the windows while soothing music played on the speaker. Charlotte and Piper had little jokes that he didn't understand. But he liked to watch them while he pretended to read the news on his phone. Their easy camaraderie and quick laughter mixed with the music and the smell of coffee brewing and the sizzle of eggs and bacon on the stove. They were like threads in a tapestry, all woven together into something that felt warm and nurturing.

As they left the clinic, John realized he was famished. Charlotte must be too. Had they eaten lunch? He couldn't remember. But it was far too late for a restaurant, and local fast food was awful. They needed something simple, but quick. He spotted a coffee shop ahead, its interior lighting glowing amber against the dark, wet streets of Seattle, and drove in.

The aroma of fresh brewed coffee and sweet treats paired with the intense grinding and hissing of professional-grade coffee machines met him at the door. A glass display case was filled with croissants and bagels, sandwiches, fruit tarts, and a dizzying array of baked goods. John had no idea what Charlotte liked, so he chose a little of everything, then capped it off with two herbal teas.

Back in the car, Charlotte sniffed the steam escaping the takeout lid. "Mmm, chamomile," she breathed. "Perfect choice."

Just then it started to rain. Huge, fat drops that thumped on the windshield and roof of the car. He dialed the heat up two degrees and headed for their shared, temporary home.

The tea seemed to revive Charlotte. She peered into the backseat. "What smells so good?"

His best guess was the toasted buttered bagel, because the smell of it was making his stomach growl too.

She reached for the bag and the next thing he knew she was offering him half.

She groaned with pleasure at her first bite. "It's like you picked my favorite before I even knew it was my favorite!"

Was it ridiculous to feel this much pride at pleasing her? Maybe so, but he couldn't deny the shiver of pleasure that spiraled up his spine.

When they picked her up, Piper was equally pleased with the bag of goodies. She happily snacked on the chocolate chip muffin he had selected just for her and spent the trip home regaling them with stories of her adventures with her new best friend.

John guided the car out of the rain and into the garage. He silenced the engine, then checked the backseat, wondering what had happened to Piper's happy chatter. She was sleeping, curled into a tight ball, still holding her half-eaten muffin.

"Out like a light," Charlotte whispered.

"She must have had fun."

John plucked her from the backseat while Charlotte held her injured leg for support. They worked silently to tuck Piper into bed.

"Wait," Charlotte whispered. "I have something for her."

A few minutes later she was back, with a small gift bag that she gave to John.

"That's really thoughtful, but shouldn't it wait till morning?"

Charlotte shook her head with a smile. "She needs it now."

It was a nightlight in the shape of a lighthouse, its beacon providing a soft amber glow to illuminate the nooks and crannies of Piper's room.

"Ever since you and Piper moved in, I've been searching for a sailboat nightlight, to remind her of *The House Call*. But when I saw this one, I thought it was a good second choice." She looked down at the sleeping girl between them. "I like lighthouses. They can guide you back home, wherever that home might be."

They unloaded the car, and he followed her to the kitchen, where Charlotte busied herself with gathering up the takeout order and her purse.

Just when John was about to wish her goodnight, she held up the takeout bag.

"Want to join me for dinner?"

It was the exact opposite of what he should do. He liked her too much...was too keenly aware of her scent and her movements, the tiny freckle on her chin, her favorite music and how she liked her coffee.

But the stress of Tommy's rescue lingered in the knotted

muscles of his shoulders and neck. It had been a close call—far too close for John's comfort. It would be nice to share the end of the day with someone who understood.

He must have hesitated a breath too long, because she looked down with a pained expression and toyed with a thread on her pants. He could hear what she didn't want to say out loud.

She didn't want to be alone.

"Of course," he said, aiming for the same casual tone. "I don't want to be alone either."

Which was a funny thing. Between Piper, the teens at the clinic, Sarah, and his colleagues at the hospital, John was rarely physically alone. But sometimes he felt like being in a crowd only amplified how isolated he felt. He was there, but not truly seen—or understood. It hadn't been until Charlotte joined the clinic that he'd had reason to question the grind of his life. Charlotte and her piercing questions had let him know she saw exactly who he was and what he had sacrificed to be what others needed him to be.

When Charlotte was close, he felt like he was more than a doctor, his brother's keeper, Mr. Responsible. She made him feel like he was a man with dreams of his own that mattered.

Charlotte set the café bag on the marble countertop and began searching for plates and cutlery.

They usually used the kitchen for their breakfast dates, but he wanted something more intimate and comfortable for tonight. He looked past the kitchen into the family room. It was smaller and seemed less formal than the great big room at the front of the house. There were pretty French doors that opened out to the lawn and the woods beyond. And a brick fireplace—though that had been painted white too. Still, this was a space he could work with.

He found a plush navy-blue comforter and a few candles in the hallway linen closet. In just a few minutes he had started a fire and lit a row of candles on the mantel. He shook out the comforter and laid it on the floor, just as Charlotte rounded the corner holding a tray laden with food.

"Voila!" John said. "Who says you can't have a picnic in the rain?"

She froze, considering the scene, and for a moment John feared he'd made a mistake. But her surprise quickly warmed into a smile.

"Lovely!" she pronounced. "I didn't think this house could be cozy, but you pulled it off."

"At least in this room." John settled on the comforter. "So, do they have any leads?"

She joined him. "Leads…?"

"The police. I imagine they must have an all-points bulletin out on your missing furniture."

She laughed, and John decided he could happily spend the rest of his life making that happen.

"No, it's all gone. I sold it—as per the plan. The last thing to go is the house." She bit into a berry tart and sighed with pleasure.

John chose a turkey sandwich from the serving tray. "When will you sell the house?"

"When we don't need it anymore."

When *we* don't need it anymore. He realized what was holding her back. "You're waiting because of me and Piper?" Guilt overshadowed the pleasure of being alone with her.

But she waved off his concern. "Don't be silly. I'm thrilled to see this house put to good use. You can stay as long as it takes for Piper to heal. I don't start with *The Eden* until the spring, so there's plenty of time."

Her mention of her next adventure was an unwelcome reminder of the invisible clock that held power over his life. Funny how he had balked at the prospect of sharing his clinic with another doctor. Everything was so different now. It was getting easy to imagine Charlotte as his partner at work.

And now, with the firelight casting a soft glow on her hair and the curves of her face, it was getting easy to imagine her in his bed too.

"So, why do you think he left you all this—after years of...?" His hand found her knee, embraced its curve.

"Of wanting nothing to do with me?" She smiled and stretched. Her hand found its way to his, landing light as a butterfly atop the one he had clasped around her knee. "I really don't know. I imagine it's in the letter."

"What letter?"

"The letter my father left for me. It's in the kitchen, on top of the toaster. Maybe I'll read it someday. Then again, maybe not."

"You don't want to know?"

She plucked at a loose thread on the comforter, her jaw tight with tension. "If I read his letter, it feels like I'm letting him have his say. I'm not sure I want him to have that space in my head." She took a deep breath and softened. "I don't know. Maybe in time I'll get curious. But for now, I just want to sell this monstrosity of a home so I can donate the proceeds to charity."

And get back to my real life.

He heard the words, even if she didn't say it out loud.

"So, no settling down for you, then? White picket fence, two-point-five kids, that sort of thing?"

Why on earth should his body be so coiled with tension? Her future personal plans were none of his concern. But once again his body was betraying him, revealing the disconnect between his sensible thoughts and what his heart truly wanted.

"When I was young I was rather angry about how my life had turned out. Bouncing from house to house in foster care was rough. But when I learned about locum tenens jobs, and how I could help kids anywhere in the world, I realized those foster care experiences could be turned into something positive. Not everyone can live like a nomad, with their whole life stored in a single suitcase. But thanks to those foster care years, I can."

"And being such a wanderer…does it suit you?"

The fire had warmed the room now. Its flames were casting dancing shadows on the wall. A log snapped loudly and shifted in the grate. The candles flickered in time with the steady beat of the rainstorm outside. This moment felt insulated and private, as if he had somehow managed to stop time so that the entire world had narrowed to just the two of them in the little cocoon he had created.

Maybe it was this sense of otherworldliness that made it seem so natural for him to brush an errant strand of hair from her eyes. She didn't flinch a bit. She just held his gaze, steady and thoughtful. Her chest rose and fell with each breath, her gold pendant reflecting the firelight.

"Until now," she whispered.

"Charlotte?" His heart was a thief, stealing the moment to claim its deepest desire. "Did you really forget our first kiss? That night at the clinic?"

She tilted her head, baring her delicate throat. "I thought it was a dream."

John leaned into her. Close enough that he could feel her breath as her chest rose and fell. "I think I want to renegotiate the terms of our agreement."

She closed her eyes, her soft, pink mouth waiting. "What agreement?"

"Exactly."

Charlotte felt his lip brush hers. His mouth was firm and warm, with a touch of intensity that quickened her pulse. She shifted toward him, felt his hand find her waist, his heat radiating through her thin shirt. It was gentle, this kiss, more like a gift or an offering than a runaway train of fiery passion. But Charlotte was keenly aware of everything about him. The musky sweet taste of his kiss. The scruff of his beard against her soft skin. The press of her breasts against his solid chest.

Her hand found the curve of his shoulder, followed it to the nape of his neck. Her fingers buried themselves into his hair, mapping him like he was a treasure to explore. Long-buried desires rose from deep in her core and rippled through her so that she opened to him fully, kissing him deeply. Their passions rose and she craved the feel of his bare skin. She wanted the length of his naked body pressed against hers so that there was nothing between them.

He had exposed what she wanted most. Someone who would touch her, love her, like this. Make her believe, even if it was just a dream, that she might be worthy of someone like him.

As if she had spoken aloud, he pulled her closer, tucking her into the curves of his body, and their tongues slowly danced as she wished the moment would never end.

But it did end—though not for long minutes—with Charlotte pulling away to catch her breath. She reached for her tea, needing something to soothe her parched, dry throat. But the tea did little to dampen the fire his touches had stoked.

She risked a glance at John, feeling as naked as if he had stripped every garment from her body. Their former agreement, as flimsy as it had been, was officially null and void. If they weren't coworkers committed to keeping their attraction in check, what were they?

She opened her mouth to ask, but something in John's expression stopped her. He was listening to something beyond the room.

"Piper? I'm in here."

She appeared at the door a moment later, rubbing her eyes, clearly a bit confused as to where she was. John rose to his feet and met her at the doorway.

"I had a bad dream," she said, on the verge of tears.

John swept her up for a hug and murmured comforting words. He gave Charlotte an apologetic smile as he took Piper back to her room, promising he would stay with her until she fell asleep.

Charlotte stayed behind to watch the fire slowly die. What on earth were she and John doing? He was committed to his niece and she was a mere visitor to Seattle and his clinic.

If this were just a fling, she might not feel this angsty mix of desire and apprehension.

If she had any sense at all, she'd put a firm end to whatever this was between them.

But she couldn't. Not after that kiss. John had set something loose in her that was not willing to be shut away again.

The time for good sense had come and gone. From here on out she was in uncharted territory.

CHAPTER EIGHT

"GOOD MORNING, DR. OWENS. This is Julia, with Seven Seas Cruise Line International. We emailed your employment contract two weeks ago but have not received your signed copy. Could you please complete that at your earliest convenience?"

The cruise ship human resources director left her contact information and hung up.

Charlotte deleted the message and drummed her fingernails against her desk. Her assignment as ship's doctor for a major cruise line was less than a month away. By now she should have a full itinerary planned for herself, detailing all the excursions and sights she wanted to see while she cruised the Caribbean.

She wrote herself a reminder note and pinned it to the bulletin board above her desk. This weekend. She would definitely look at that contract this weekend.

From the corner of her eye, movement caught her attention. A paper plane had landed on her desk. Its pilot followed close behind and dropped into the chair next to her.

"Guess what that is."

"The winning lottery numbers?"

John groaned. "I wish… That, my friend, is everything you never wanted to know about the hospital gala."

Charlotte unfolded the airplane. It was John's invitation to the hospital's thirty-seventh annual fundraising gala, with all funds raised going to support the hospital's outreach programs—including The Sunshine Clinic.

John looked less than pleased.

"That bad, huh?"

"Tuxes are involved."

Charlotte thrilled at the image of her scruffy colleague all packaged up in a smart tuxedo. "I think I'd be willing to pay to see that."

"You don't have to pay. Just say yes."

"To what?"

"Come with me to the gala. Be my date. You don't even need a pumpkin carriage. The hospital has negotiated a corporate rate for hotel rooms, so guests won't need to drive if they've had a drink or two."

"What about Piper?"

"Sarah's practically begged me to let her stay overnight with her. A chance for her to spend time with her 'adopted grandchild' before she moves south to be closer to her children when she retires."

So, they would be alone for the night…

Their gazes met and held a second too long. Ever since that kiss by the fireplace John had been extra careful about Piper. With her father in jail and having had two moves in one year, he was cautious about revealing their status as a couple.

Which made sense to Charlotte too. It wasn't fair to let Piper get invested in them as a couple when it was destined to end in a few weeks. So that meant, other than stolen kisses when Piper was busy or in bed, their love life was mostly a cauldron of barely repressed desire.

A night away in a hotel room sounded very good to Charlotte.

But John misread her long silence. "Of course, you'll have

your own room. At my cost. My way of saying thank you for accompanying me."

That wasn't what she was worried about, but this wasn't the time or place to discuss it. Not with Sarah manning the front desk behind them and a whole waiting room full of noisy teens.

The front door flew open and crashed against the wall.

"Hey, Doc! I got a kid who needs help here!"

Charlotte felt a rush of adrenaline at seeing Angel again. Finally! She and John had been waiting weeks for her to return to the clinic. Now that her charity funding was approved, all they needed to do was get her to see the cardiologist.

But that would have to wait. Angel had a girl with her. Fourteen, maybe fifteen years old, was Charlotte's best guess. And very sick. Even from a distance Charlotte could see from her hot cheeks and glassy, unfocused gaze that she was in a lot of pain.

"I'll think about it." Charlotte said. She patted John's shoulder, then went to the girls.

"This one needs help for real," Angel said. All her swagger had disappeared and she seemed genuinely afraid for her friend.

"I can see that," Charlotte said. "Come on in."

She led them to her room and asked the girl to get on the exam table.

She took her vitals, noting her high temperature on a chart.

"What's your name, honey?" she asked as she checked the girl's lymph nodes around her neck. The swelling there indicated her immune system had been working overtime to fight off some kind of infection or virus.

"Lily," the girl whispered. She was cradling the right side of her head in one hand and looked absolutely miserable.

"Does your head hurt?"

Charlotte cataloged the possibilities. She worried Lily had

meningitis, and the swelling around her brain and spinal cord was causing extreme discomfort. But a bad virus could cause nasty headaches and a fever too.

"My ear…" Lily whimpered.

Charlotte's heart squeezed with sympathy for this girl who was suffering.

"We'll get you something for the pain in just a minute," she promised as she retrieved the otoscope.

Lily was hesitant to stop guarding her ear, but Angel turned out to be an unexpected ally.

"It's okay," Angel soothed. "Dr. Owens is one of the good ones."

Charlotte blushed with pride at Angel's compliment. Earning the trust of a streetwise kid like Angel was no easy feat. She just hoped Angel would trust her referral to a cardiologist too.

Lily's ear was practically on fire with infection. The delicate tissue of her middle ear was red-hot, bulging with inflammation. Despite Lily's whimpers, Charlotte gently moved the otoscope up and down, to the left and right, exploring the extent of the infection.

"Lily, could you wait a moment? I need to consult with my partner, Dr. J."

My partner.

Two words Charlotte had never said in her adult life.

John joined her in the hallway for an impromptu consultation.

"I'm pretty sure she has mastoiditis," she told John. "I didn't think that happened outside of medical school lectures. Can you confirm?"

John followed her back to the exam room and examined Lily's ear for a second time. He sighed deeply and clicked off the otoscope.

"I'm sorry, Lily, but we can't treat this here. You have an ear infection that has spread to a hollow bone behind your ear called the mastoid bone. Now it's filled with infection, and it could rupture any minute. If that happens, the infection could get into the covering around your brain and cause meningitis."

Lily was in so much pain she didn't care what happened next so long as they didn't touch her ear again.

John called for an ambulance to transport Lily to the hospital, leaving Charlotte free to focus on Angel.

"Thanks so much for bringing her in, Angel," she said. "She really needed a friend like you."

Angel gave her a shy smile.

"I'm really glad to see you again. How have you been feeling?"

Angel bit her lip. "I still get a little dizzy sometimes."

"Well, then, I hope you'll think this is good news. The hospital wants to pay for your EKG testing, and we have a cardiologist who can see you on short notice. In fact, she could see you today."

Charlotte hoped that wouldn't scare Angel away, but she had to ask. Lily's ear infection was just one more example of what happened when kids didn't get good medical care fast enough.

Charlotte beamed when Angel sheepishly agreed to go.

She would have loved to drive Angel to the specialist herself, but hospital rules made that impossible. Instead, she gave Angel a bus pass and directions to the hospital. She watched Angel head off for a long multi-bus trip on her own, carrying a plastic bag that Charlotte had filled with chilled water and snacks.

Free transportation
In-house EKG testing

Charlotte mentally added two more items to her running list of services she would like to add to the clinic. She didn't know why she did this, except that she kept discovering more hidden needs in this little medical center.

But that was just the beginning. She'd been there long enough to know the kids needed far more than medical care to get their lives stabilized. They needed help getting proper identification, mental health services, and a nutritionist who could address the malnutrition that afflicted nearly every kid she worked with.

Sarah interrupted her musings. "Charlotte, I don't know what to do. Piper's school is on the phone and I can't reach John."

Charlotte felt her chest tighten. "Is Piper okay?"

"She's fine…she's fine. But she's gotten herself into another scrape at school and the principal wants her to go home. John's still at the hospital with Lily. They weren't too keen about admitting one of our patients without a consult from the emergency department attending."

"When will he be back?"

"No telling, love. Hospital admissions can take—"

"Forever," Charlotte finished.

Charlotte texted John but didn't get any more of a response than Sarah had. He was probably focused on getting Lily admitted as quickly as possible.

"Page the on-call pediatrician and ask them to come in. I'm going to get Piper. Tell John if you see him first."

John had added Charlotte to the school's list of Piper's "safe persons," so the principal was able to give Charlotte a report on Piper's latest scuffle. This one had earned her a three-day suspension from school, and the principal said she would like to see John "at his earliest convenience."

That does not sound good.

Charlotte knew that Piper's future at the school was hanging on a thread.

She took Piper home and headed to the kitchen, where she kept the first aid kit.

"Let's take a look, okay?" She indicated the scrapes on Piper's arms and knuckles.

Piper shrugged and hoisted herself up to sit on the kitchen counter.

Charlotte used antibacterial soap to clean her scrapes. "What happened anyway?"

"Some girl said something I didn't like."

"If anyone at school is bullying you, your uncle will help you. You know that, right?"

Piper jutted her chin and looked away. "No one's bullying me."

"So what happened, then?"

Piper shrugged. "I just didn't like the way she looked at me."

"That's it? All this because someone looked at you funny?"

"I guess…"

Charlotte rinsed the cuts with disinfectant, then applied a thin layer of antibiotic ointment while she tried to understand this version of Piper. With Charlotte, she'd always been a sweet kid. Gentle with Cat, helpful at home. Always polite, though a bit subdued. This combative side of Piper just didn't make sense.

Charlotte used her knuckles to gently guide Piper's head up and her gaze to her own. "Hey, kid. What's happened here? Why are you in trouble all the time?"

Piper's eyes brimmed with tears. "It won't make sense."

"Try me."

Piper took a deep breath, looked out the window. "I don't mind being in trouble."

"How come?"

"Cause if I get in enough trouble, they'll have to send me to jail." Piper shifted her gaze back to Charlotte. "Then I could be with my dad."

Understanding rolled through Charlotte's body like a gentle wave. Everything—the fighting and rule-breaking, even Piper's running away from school—made sense when viewed from the limited perspective of an adolescent girl's view of the world.

Charlotte set the last Band-Aid in place. "Does your Uncle John know that's what you want?"

"No, but he never asks either."

With that, she slid off the counter, tucked Cat under her arm, and went to her room.

By the time John got home, Piper had fallen asleep, with Cat tucked in a tight ball at her feet. Charlotte warmed up some leftovers and kept John company while he ate. She filled him in on Piper's troubles at school and what she had learned from their talk.

"Has she seen her dad since he went to jail, John?"

John's expression was pained. "I haven't wanted to do that to her. I see Michael every month, but the whole process of getting through security...the environment...it's all so bleak."

"To you and me, sure. But she needs to see him, John. And he needs to see her too."

"I know." John sighed and let his head fall back to rest on the couch.

Charlotte settled in next to him. "What are you afraid of?"

"That she'll blame me for her father being there."

Charlotte handed him a glass of wine. She studied his profile, illuminated by the cozy fire that John had started when he got home. "Why would she blame you, John?"

John exhaled in a long, low sigh. "When our mother died, she left us a little money. Michael used his to go to art school in

California. I used mine as seed money for the clinic. I thought that we were all grown up, and it was safe for me to focus on my dreams. Michael came home after a year, bringing baby Piper with him."

He smiled at the memory and Charlotte could see he loved being an uncle.

"But he seemed different. Moodier, and more prone to angry outbursts. I thought it was due to his breakup with Piper's mother and that he'd get better in time."

"But he didn't?" Charlotte surmised, hoping her patient demeanor would encourage conversation.

"No, he didn't. He got a lot worse over time. I saw him and Piper as often as I could, but the clinic was just taking off and I wanted it to be a success."

He set his wine glass on the table and leaned forward, rolling his neck to release the tension stored there.

"What I didn't realize was that Michael was undiagnosed bipolar. And his wild mood swings were driving him to spend more time with people who weren't good for him. One night..." John paused to gather his thoughts. "One night he called me for help. Said he really needed to see me. But it was the night of the hospital gala, and the chair of pediatrics wanted me to represent the clinic. I was already in my tuxedo, and the mayor was going to be there. There was no way I could skip the event."

Charlotte felt dread rolling off John in waves. It was clear he hated even thinking about that night, let alone speaking of it out loud.

"That was the night Michael was arrested. If I had just answered his call instead of letting it go to voicemail! If I had just listened more, or been a better brother, maybe I would have realized Michael had bipolar disorder! Instead, it took a prison psychiatrist who doesn't even know him to diagnose what was in front of me all along."

John rolled his head to look at her. She saw hints of the boy he'd once been in those eyes, forced to grow up too fast. He was drop-dead handsome, but that wasn't what pulled at her heart. It was the vulnerability that he was too tired to hide. She never saw this side of him at the clinic. He was too busy being strong for the teens.

She reached out to cup his face with her hand, felt his stubble rough on her palm. He laid his hand over hers, capturing her. Then brought her hand to his mouth. She could feel his warm breath as he kissed her fingers, one by one.

She waited until he seemed calm. "That's a sad story, John," she said. "And I'm sorry that happened to your family. But just because you *feel* guilty, it doesn't mean you are."

Something that looked a little like hope sparked in his eyes.

"Thank you," he said. "I just wish things could have been different."

John turned her hand, revealing her wrist so he could kiss it, then followed a path up her arm, leaving gentle kisses in his wake. She could see a tiny scar on his chin and she itched to trace it with her fingers, hear the story of its origin.

"What's the story with this necklace?" John said, thumbing the pendant lying against her chest. "I've never seen you take it off."

Her hand flew to the pendant, as if making sure it was still there. "Really? I'm sure I have."

"You haven't." He pressed her hand to his heart. "I'm very perceptive about these sorts of things."

"It was my last birthday gift from my mother." The pendant featured a moon tarot card—a reminder that in the face of uncertainty, she should trust her intuition. She moved away from him and thumbed it unconsciously…her version of a worry stone.

John said nothing but his gaze was kind and patient. She knew he was waiting for more. And if the man had the courage to share his most painful secret with her, she supposed she could do the same.

"I was thirteen when she died."

He whistled, soft and low. "That's a tough age to lose a parent, Charlotte. That kind of thing can leave some emotional scars."

She shrugged and swirled her wine glass, watching the ruby-red liquid cling to the glass. "I suppose…if you let it."

He cocked his head. "Why did you grow up in foster care? Couldn't Social Services find your father?"

His question took her by surprise—so direct and to the point. She was tempted to evade the question, just so she wouldn't have to tell him the truth, but that didn't seem fair after he had just bared his soul.

"A couple of months ago I would have told you no. But I just recently learned that my father did indeed know that I existed and that my mother had died." She drained the last of her wine for a bit of courage. "He opted to terminate his parental rights."

John's eyebrows rose perceptibly. "Are you serious?"

When she nodded, his usual calm, tell-me-anything demeanor disappeared. He leaned forward and took her hand in his again, grasping it firmly as if he feared she might float away.

"That's awful, Charlotte. No man should ever abandon his child. You did not deserve that."

Charlotte shrugged. "It worked out okay in the end. Because of my foster care years, I've built a pretty exciting life for myself as a traveling doctor. I'd say that's a win-win."

John's eyes never left her face. "Losing your mother as a

teen and having your father's rejection send you into foster care is not a win-win, Charlotte."

She was about to come up with another quip, to lighten the moment, but his expression said *Don't.* So, she sat frozen, not knowing what to do other than sit there with the truth that she had just shared. Her father hadn't wanted her—even when she'd needed him very badly.

John didn't say a word. It was uncomfortable at first, just sitting in silence, letting the pain of that admission swirl about in her chest. She was gripped with a strong impulse to get up and get busy. Clear the table, stoke the fire, build an addition to the house... Anything other than just sit and feel the pain of abandonment.

John stroked the back of her hand with his thumb, and she took great solace in his quiet way of saying she wasn't alone. But his words were the sweetest balm of all, letting her know that he saw what she truly feared.

"There was nothing wrong with you, Charlotte." His gaze was serious, piercing. He spoke slowly, emphasizing every word. "That was all on him. It had *nothing* to do with you."

Charlotte's pulse quickened at his perception. His eyes were as intense as she had ever seen them. As sexy as she had always found him, this level of connection was a whole new level of temptation.

Which brought its own set of problems.

She didn't think she'd be able to get by with stolen kisses and furtive glances for much longer.

Not when their attraction was deepening into something that she found quite irresistible.

CHAPTER NINE

CHARLOTTE STOOD IN front of the floor-length mirror in her hotel room, fearing she might have made a mistake. When shopping for a dress for the hospital's fundraising gala, she'd thought the floor-length, off-the-shoulder black crepe gown was a sensible choice. Paired with a little purse and crystal-embellished silver high heels, she'd thought she would make an elegant but feminine statement.

And she had achieved that for sure.

With a serious side dish of sexy.

A slit in the dress ran from the hem to her hip, much higher than she remembered when she'd tried it on, and it would undoubtedly afford a generous view of her leg as she danced. The sleeveless top showed off her neck and shoulders, along with a tantalizing glimpse of cleavage.

This was a far cry from the donated cargo pants and faded tee shirt she had worn on her first day at the clinic. Maybe too far.

She loved the way the crepe whispered when she moved, but the way it hugged and amplified every feminine curve was making her doubt herself. This dress didn't hint at exotic travel and rugged adventure. It spoke of romance and intrigue, fantasy and fascination. It felt a little dangerous, this dress. Like it could take her places she'd never gone before.

Stop, she whispered to her reflection.

This dress symbolized her new mission of pursuing the life she wanted, not just running from what she feared. And tonight she wanted to feel elegant and pretty.

She swished the dress some more, just for the fun of it, then started working on arranging her hair into a French braid updo. She felt like a princess tonight. A princess who wasn't going to wait for the king to rescue her. She was going to save herself, slay her dragons, and then claim her prize.

She was setting the last pin in place when there was a sharp knock at the door.

She strode to the door, feeling the cool air of the hotel room on her exposed leg.

"Good evening, Dr. Bennett."

She had no idea why she went all formal like that. Maybe because she was wearing formal wear. Or maybe because the man on her threshold oozed class and elegance in a tuxedo that had been perfectly tailored to his masculine, bulky build. Powerful, sophisticated, and elegant, this new version of her colleague left her speechless.

John seemed to be having trouble finding his words too, because he just stood at the threshold of her room, his mouth open, while he scanned her from head to silvery strappy toe.

"Dr. Owens. I mean, Charlotte. I think… Wow." He shook his head and tried again. "You look quite stunning, Charlotte."

An all-glass elevator was their carriage as they traveled down from Charlotte's room to the gala downstairs, affording a generous view of the hotel's lobby as they descended. Women in beautiful gowns roamed the halls and the boutique had stayed open late, offering high-end accessories and expensive jewelry. She thought she recognized one of the women as an on-call doctor who sometimes helped at the clinic.

"Oh, look. Isn't that…?"

But John wasn't paying any attention to the activity in the

lobby. Instead, he was focused on the small stack of notecards in his hand. It must be the notes for his speech as he whisper-practiced the words that he hoped would inspire donors to support The Sunshine Clinic and the other outreach programs of the hospital.

The champagne reception was in full swing when they found their way to the ballroom. Waiters swooped here and there with trays full of champagne and hors d'oeuvres, while a lone pianist played smooth background music. John flagged down a waiter and took two tall flutes of champagne for himself and Charlotte.

"Come on, let me introduce you to some people," he said.

They moved from group to group, meeting the many specialists who made the hospital one of the top-rated in North America. Then they found their way to one of the round tables, where placards printed with their names marked their assigned places.

John and Charlotte took their seats. A server soon appeared, pouring ice water into their glasses and offering a basket of assorted breads and butter. Introductions revealed that they were sharing their table with a heart surgeon and her husband, a nurse practitioner who worked in cancer care, and the Pattersons, who had an entire wing of the hospital named after them for their generous donations.

"I'm sorry, dearie, what did you say your name was?" Mrs. Patterson asked, leaning in toward Charlotte. She cupped a hand around her ear, clearly hard of hearing.

"Dr. Charlotte Owens. I'm a locum pediatrician at The Sunshine Clinic for Kids."

"Oh, that's nice. How many kids do you two have?" she asked, her fingers curved round the top of her purse.

"Oh, no!" Charlotte laughed. "We're not married."

Mrs. Patterson beamed. "Aw, you're newlyweds, then? The babies will be here soon enough."

Charlotte just smiled back. There didn't seem to be any point in correcting her again.

John leaned over and kissed her cheek, which made Mrs. Patterson beam even more.

All too soon, the chairman of the hospital board introduced John. Charlotte gave his hand a little squeeze for good luck as he headed for the stage.

John scanned his notecards one last time. This event was all about asking the community to support the hospital with generous donations. He didn't know why the chair of pediatrics had asked *him* to be the keynote speaker this year. Asking strangers to donate thousands of dollars was way outside his comfort zone. As was admitting that he couldn't do the important work of The Sunshine Clinic on his own.

But the teens needed him to be their voice.

He arranged the cards in a neat little stack, tucked them in his pocket and adjusted the microphone.

"My name is Dr. John Bennett and I really hate asking for help. When I was young, asking for help was terrifying. I was afraid my family might be split up if anyone knew that we sometimes couldn't pay the phone bill or afford more than the basics. Now I'm a doctor, and I take care of kids who also hate asking for help. But unlike me, who at least had a family, they're alone in the world and don't know who to trust. I want to be that person for them. The one who helps them see they deserve so much more than just basic survival. That it's safe for them to dream and set goals. That they can count on us to be there. Ultimately, I want them to understand that it's not just okay to ask for help, it's their basic human right to get it. But to do that work, I have to ask for *your* help. Because I can't do it alone—no matter how much I think I want to."

John went on to describe the vision he had for The Sunshine Clinic. Expanding it into a one-stop health clinic able to address all the medical and mental health needs of teens in crisis. Finding ways to expand its reach in Seattle and beyond, so more teens could get the support they needed. He finished by telling them about Matthew and Sam and Angel, giving human faces to the dry statistics he had captured on the index cards in his pocket.

He refocused on the audience. He felt utterly drained after exposing his deepest thoughts and desires to virtual strangers. But he also felt liberated. Whatever happened next would be what it was.

He was about to leave the stage when, from the back of the room, he heard the sound of someone clapping. Soon it was followed by another person, and then another. One by one, everyone in the room rose to their feet, clapping and smiling. There were more than a few hankies out, dabbing at damp eyes.

John was mystified. It took him a full minute to realize that the standing ovation was for him.

His throat grew tight with emotions he was having a hard time containing.

He saw Charlotte standing next to Mrs. Patterson, patting her shoulder as she dabbed her eyes with a hanky. Charlotte gave him a shaky smile through her own shimmering tears as she clapped. *Well done*, she mouthed, and he suddenly felt blissfully, crazily, unbearably happy.

With the speeches done, the lights were dimmed and the on-stage curtains parted to reveal a DJ with her equipment surrounding her. She played songs that were energetic, with a strong background beat for dancing.

John offered Charlotte his hand. "Dance with me?"

For the next hour, they burned off the nervous energy of the night, dancing and spinning and singing along with the lyrics. Charlotte pulled out the pins that held her French updo in place, letting her dark waves spill down over her shoulders and driving John crazy. It felt so good to let himself go, to dance and move with Charlotte until they were both damp with exertion.

There was a slight pause, and then the first notes of a slow ballad played. Charlotte gave John a small smile, then nodded toward the table, indicating that she was ready to head back. She was probably right. This was a professional event. The two of them slow-dancing together would definitely activate the hospital's gossip network. But he was surprised at the sudden wave of resistance that washed over him. He was so tired of ignoring his heart's deepest desires.

He stopped in his tracks. "No, please stay," he said, catching her hand.

She gave him a nervous smile. "With all these people?"

"Why not?" he said, tugging her to him. "You are my wife, after all."

She hesitated for a moment, then her eyes lit up with understanding. "That's right—we're newlyweds! At least in Mrs. Patterson's mind."

"That's good enough for me."

She laughed, and then she was in his arms. John felt her hand curve over his shoulder as he claimed the small of her back. Their free hands met, their fingers intertwined, and then they were dancing to the music, their bodies in perfect sync.

As they circled the floor—first right, then left, then right again—John felt her body slowly melt into his.

She pulled away from his shoulder to look up at him. Her mouth was candy-apple-red, plump and full. An irresistible feast waiting to be devoured.

"We danced like this at our wedding reception, didn't we?"

she said. Her eyes were hesitant, as if she was not sure he'd want to play the game.

He lightly traced the curve of her jaw with his finger. "We did. And we were perfect, Charlotte. As if we'd been dancing together for a thousand years."

The dance floor was more crowded now. He tucked her closer and her body became like a reed, bending and swaying with his as they smoothly moved between the other couples.

Charlotte moved so elegantly with the music. There was something very ethereal about the way she danced, as if she were a mirage that could disappear at any moment.

Please stay, he thought.

A yearning rose from deep in his heart—for what, he couldn't say, but he knew it was awfully important. His heart beat faster with the wanting of her.

Charlotte was gazing at him with a wistful look in her eyes. She caught her bottom lip between her teeth before asking, "And our wedding night…were we perfect then too?"

His heart literally stopped for a full beat as he realized what she was asking. There was a hint of challenge in her eyes mixed with nervousness. Because it *was* a challenge—and he knew it. They had been dancing around the question of their relationship ever since they'd met. John knew their attraction was undeniable, but so was the force of the fears that repelled them when they got too close.

They moved in rhythmic circles, gazes locked, bodies melded. She matched his movements perfectly, so that he couldn't tell if he was leading or following. Everything blurred together—he and Charlotte, the past and the present, hopes and fears…

He took a deep bracing breath and stepped into the unknown, with all its wild, sweet possibilities. "Better than perfect, Charlotte. We were real."

He heard Charlotte's breath catch in her throat. He could practically feel the want humming in her body, vibrating into his. She stopped dancing for a moment, gazed at him directly, without artifice or fear. For a moment he feared he had taken the game too far and she would disappear in his arms like smoke.

But instead she raised herself on tiptoe and whispered in his ear. A sudden hot rush of desire swept through his body like a tsunami. He nodded and led her to the edge of the dance floor. He knew they should probably say their goodbyes to co-workers and donors.

John hovered between responsibility and desire.

Oh, to hell with doing the right or proper thing. All he wanted was Charlotte.

He grabbed Charlotte's hand and led her out of the ball-room, letting his heart guide the way.

CHAPTER TEN

MERCIFULLY, THEY HAD the elevator to themselves. John punched the button for their floor. For a moment they stood side by side, shoulder to shoulder, watching the numbers climb on the indicator. Soft music played in the background—something kind of jaunty. The entire scene was surreal, and out of sync with the urgent, pressing need she felt deep in her belly.

Neither reached for the other's hand or stole a kiss. Which was good, she thought, because just one touch would be like dropping a match on a pile of dry kindling. It wouldn't surprise her if they both went up in flames.

At last, there was a soft *ding*, signaling their floor, and the elevator doors slid open. Then John grabbed her hand and led her down the hallway to his room. With one quick swipe of his key card, the door swung open and John pulled her across the threshold.

Finally, they were alone.

As soon as the door clicked shut, John's hands found her waist and guided her backwards, until her back was pressed up against the door. His mouth, hard and needy, found hers, shocking her breath into silence. Her body instantly responded to his. Her mouth opened to him, tasting a hint of whiskey on his lips and beneath that, the taste of him. Wild and masculine, thrilling and real. It was almost too much, all these sensations at once, and she whimpered against his mouth, needing more.

Her hands moved of their own accord, traveling the length of his arms to the breadth of his shoulders, the strong muscles of his back. But that wasn't enough—not nearly enough—and she tugged at his shirt, freeing it so she could slide her hands beneath to explore the warm, firm flesh of his belly and back.

John groaned against her lips, his breath jagged and harsh. "I've wanted to make love to you since the day you walked into my clinic."

Charlotte took a ragged breath. "Really? Because I thought you hated me."

John nipped her bottom lip, making her gasp with the shock of it, then followed with light kisses and nibbles that made a shiver of pleasure race up her spine.

"None of that is important now. Only this. Only us."

He braced both of his arms on the wall, creating a cocoon just for them, then moved his mouth over hers. She closed her eyes and let him take her deeper, until all she could see and sense was him, all around her.

She opened her eyes to find his gaze, steady and strong. He encircled one of her wrists and guided her to the sleeping area. She followed him to the foot of the king-sized bed that dominated the room. He kissed her again, this time gently, with great deliberation.

"I want to take this slow, Charlotte. I've waited so long to touch you. I need to know you, see you… I don't know if that makes sense, but…" He trailed off as he bent to kiss her again, his hands reverent as they cupped her face.

So, this was what it felt like to be cherished. To have someone make you feel like you were the most important person in the world. It felt good to be seen, but also vaguely dangerous. She stood on tiptoe, her hands on John's as they framed her face, as if he were her only chance of surviving the raging rivers of doubt that threatened to drown her.

And then he was undressing her. Slowly spinning her till her back was to him, finding the zipper cleverly hidden in the side seam of her dress. There was a sharp, hissing sound, then her dress fell in a crumpled heap at her feet. The cool air of the room rushed over her body, tensing her nipples and sending goosebumps down her back.

John's mouth found her flesh...the graceful curve where her shoulder met her neck. His mouth was warm...so warm compared to the cool room. His fingertips stroked the delicate flesh over the curve of her breasts, teasing the place just above her lacy strapless bra. It made her shiver with pleasure again.

"Look at us, Charlotte," John said, his voice husky. "We're perfect."

There was a mirror across from the bed. There she was, nearly naked and wrapped in John's arms. They fit together so perfectly, her head to his shoulder, his strength to her grace. She felt the symmetry of them, and it was so tempting to lean into him and this image, believing it would be enough to sustain them.

She turned away from the mirror, offering her profile. "The light... Can we turn it off, please?"

Not because she was ashamed, but because she wanted to block out the entire world so that all she could feel and taste was John.

He switched off the table lamp, then opened the heavy draperies so the soft glow of Seattle's nightlife was their only illumination.

Then he was back, pulling her to him, and she had her chance to even the playing field. She quickly unbuttoned his shirt, sliding her hands up and over his shoulders, letting the shirt slide from his back to finally reveal the strength she'd lusted for these last long months. He was as beautiful a man as she'd ever seen, his muscles full and firm, his belly taut with tension.

He guided her to the bed, following her down till they lay together. He continued his slow, deliberate exploration, his tongue finding the soft flesh curving up from her bra, driving her crazy with little licks and nibbles. She arched her back, silently begging for more, and he obliged, unclasping her bra and then flinging that useless garment across the room. It made her laugh a little, his wanton playfulness, but when his mouth found her breast and began a careful exploration of her hidden pleasure points she couldn't laugh anymore. She could barely think.

Had she ever been loved like this before? Definitely not. It was like he was creating her with every touch, every kiss, every stroke of his fingertips. Finding everything good and tender she'd kept hidden away and sculpting it out of the raw material that was her life. She felt found, and she knew it was because John was the first to ever look.

She moaned as his thumb found her nipple and teased even more pleasure from her already heated body. Such a flood of sensations—the roughness of his fingers, the softness of his tongue, the solid weight of his body on hers, the beat of their hearts together... The air seemed to crackle with electricity as he hooked her lace panties with his finger and slid them off her legs. Then his hands were everywhere, exploring, finding, teasing, setting off a deep ache that started in her core and rolled out in gentle waves to every inch of her body.

He strummed her desire ever higher, till she was fisting the sheets beneath her, arching toward a release that seemed tantalizingly out of reach.

"John...!" she cried out, and she didn't know if she was begging for mercy or begging for more. "More..." she panted into the night, her skin slick with sweat.

More sensation, more pleasure, more touch and more tingles, and more long, slow, wet kisses that wiped her memory clean.

I want more, she thought.

So much more that all her doubts and fears were overcome by the raging desire she felt for him. But she couldn't say all the things in her heart. All she could do was call his name.

And then he was there, as if he had read every thought in her head, stretching the full length of his body with hers, the weight of him so reassuring in the midst of this storm that was sweeping through her, threatening to sweep her out to sea. She grasped tight to his body, finding refuge and calm there in his steady heartbeat and patient hands.

More...

John eased her onto her back. She could feel the heat of his body under her hands, hear his jagged breath against her ear. Proof that he wanted her as much as she wanted him, and it only made her crazier.

"Please..." she whispered against his kiss, and she couldn't stop herself from grinding against him, which made him growl with need.

She hooked one leg over his, felt his body shift under hers as he reached across the bed. She heard a drawer open, then the rip of foil, before his weight was fully on her again. With the moonlight bathing their bodies in a luminous glow, he found her, and she arched to meet him. The sensations that followed were so sublime Charlotte felt utterly incapable of speech or thought. Gentle and slow, he rocked her into the night. Every sigh took her home, back to a place and time when she'd felt loved and protected.

He gathered her close and rocked her until her mind was quiet and her heart full. So full she feared it would explode into a thousand points of brilliant light. And when the warm feelings in her body heated to their inevitable flashpoint, it was his body she clung to. Every shuddering wave wiped her slate clean, leaving her raw and exposed, defenseless in his arms. He cried out her name soon after. She opened her eyes and found his gaze, deep and intense, his pupils dark with pleasure.

Later, when their hearts had slowed to a normal rhythm, he spread the comforter over both of them and tucked her into the curve of his body. She listened as his breaths grew long and deep. It was tempting to let the rise and fall of his chest soothe her to sleep…

But this wasn't her room. She didn't belong there—not all night. Somehow falling asleep in his arms seemed too intimate despite their intense sexual encounter.

The digital clock marked another minute's passing.

One more minute. I'll leave when the clock is at the half-hour.

Sixty seconds later, she swore she'd leave when five minutes had passed.

But it was many minutes later when she sighed, knowing she couldn't linger in John's warm bed any longer.

He was surely deep in sleep by now.

It was time for her to go.

As if reading her mind, John tightened his arm around her, pressing her against his chest.

"Just stay," he whispered against her hair. "All you have to do is stay."

Charlotte's body went still, but her mind was running wild. It was so tempting to stay there, curled up against John. His body was warm and she could smell his uniquely masculine scent on his skin and her pillow.

"Just stay" was closing her eyes and drifting into sleep, safe and peaceful in John's arms.

"Just stay" was sharing coffee with him the next morning,

planning their next date and sending sexy text messages between patients.

"Just stay" was having a future, adopting a puppy, spending their weekends painting the living room.

But *"just stay"* could also be police officers and stolen fu-
tures and having everything she knew and counted on wiped
out in a split second. There was no way she could have love
without accepting the risk of losing it forever.

Her body remained rigid as her mind battled furiously with
itself. Want versus need…hope against fear.

The room's heater clicked on. Beyond the door she could
hear a faint peal of laughter as other hotel guests found their
way back to their rooms.

He doesn't mean forever. Just for tonight.

She could do this… just for tonight. She let herself slowly
relax into John, melting into the warm cocoon he had created
for her. And as the sun's first rays cast a faint, pink glow in
their room she finally closed her eyes and drifted into sleep.

A week later found John in an exceedingly good mood. He'd
come to work late, on account of taking Piper to the doctor
to have her cast removed. She'd lost a little muscle tone after
weeks of resting her leg, but that didn't stop her from jumping
out of his SUV and skipping her way into school.

John's gait was positively jaunty as he crossed the waiting
room. "Morning, Sarah," he said, swinging his backpack up
to land on the reception counter. "What have I missed?"

"Not much," Sarah said. "Charlotte seems to have things
under control this morning. Now, what's happened to put you
in such a good mood? You look like the cat who's just eaten
the canary."

"Which would not be good news for the canary, now, would
it?" John said, his body pulsing with anticipation.

After weeks of consideration, he'd finally made a grand decision. There was no point in trying to hide it from Sarah. She was the eyes and ears of the place, able to ferret out anything out of the ordinary.

John opened his backpack and carefully withdrew the forms he'd spent the previous night working on. He handed them over to Sarah and waited for her response.

She popped her bifocals on the end of her nose and perused the documents, then handed them back. "It's about time, if you ask me."

He should have known better than to expect flattery or compliments from Sarah. She was old-school about that sort of thing, believing that excessive praise made a person go soft.

Still, he had thought she would be a little more excited, considering how often she had harped at him to add a second doctor to the clinic.

"It's not official, of course," he cautioned, tapping the forms into a tidy stack. "I need to talk to Charlotte first, before I submit this to Human Resources. I don't want just any doctor to work here on a permanent basis. So if Charlotte's not interested in staying long-term, then these forms will wind up in the trash."

It felt like a long shot—maybe the longest shot he'd ever taken. But after the night they'd spent together after the gala, he couldn't imagine living life as if everything was the same. These past few weeks of living with Charlotte and Cat had made him realize that maybe all his protectiveness over Piper was a mistake. All this time he had thought that he needed to ignore his growing feelings for Charlotte, so that Piper would be safe. But Piper was healing much faster now that they lived with Charlotte. Maybe, he thought, his job wasn't to protect her from anything that might hurt her. Maybe his job was to help her find a tribe of friends and family who would pick her up if she took a fall.

Sarah crossed her fingers for good luck for him as she reached to take a call. "Oh, one more thing," she said. "Your first patients of the day are waiting in your exam room."

John nodded and headed to the workstation he shared with Charlotte. Soon he'd be able to trade the old wood door for a real built-in office area. He had gathered all the supplies and just needed to carve out some time on the weekend to get the work done.

Still whistling, he carried on preparing for the day. He stopped by the coffee station first, then reviewed the day's cases.

He was just about to set off for his exam room when he noticed a bright pink note pinned to Charlotte's bulletin board.

Return cruise ship contract ASAP!

It was written in Charlotte's neat script. There were about fifty exclamation marks for emphasis.

He stopped whistling mid-note and his heart took a nosedive toward his stomach. He plucked the note from the board and examined both sides, though he had no idea what he expected to see.

So, she was still excited about working on the cruise ship. She hadn't spoken of it in so long, he'd thought maybe she was losing interest in the prospect. An assumption on his part and apparently an incorrect one at that.

He put the note back and slumped in his chair to recover. Was everything just the same for her, then? Their night at the hotel had meant nothing?

Not that she owed him anything after their shared night together. They were both grown adults, free to spend their nights where they wished. But for John, going back to the status quo was not going to be easy. He was falling for her, pure and simple. And now that he had seen how well Piper was doing with Charlotte in their lives, his fear that falling for Charlotte might hurt Piper was losing its grip on him.

He sighed and scrubbed his face with his hands. He had patients waiting. He couldn't mope here like a lovestruck teenager, hoping for a different outcome if he waited long enough.

He looked at the forms he had so meticulously completed the night before, asking the hospital to make Charlotte's job permanent.

Should he even ask her if she wanted to stay? Or were the fifty exclamation marks on that note all the answer he needed?

He contemplated that for a long minute—then dropped the forms in the trash can next to his desk.

CHAPTER ELEVEN

JOHN WAS IN LOVE.

She was beautiful and funny and had the cutest one-toothed smile he'd ever seen.

Babies weren't John's usual patient demographic, but this particular baby was snuggled in her big sister's arms. Rosa was seventeen years old and had brought baby Anna to the clinic because she was worried about her.

"She does this strange eyelid fluttering thing," Rosa said, her brow furrowed with worry. "It used to only happen when we were outside, on sunny days. But now it happens a lot inside too, especially when she's first waking up in the morning. I've rinsed her eyes and tried some of those eye drops made for babies from the drugstore. But nothing is helping."

John gently took the baby from Rosa. His heart went out to the girl. She looked as nervous and worried as any mother would. Speaking of mothers—where was Anna and Rosa's mom? That was always a tricky question, and one he'd have to approach carefully.

John lay Anna on the table and started with a basic exam. The baby girl was in excellent health. Her cocoa-brown skin was smooth and nourished, and her plump, round belly said she was getting plenty of calories every day. He noted her tiny clean white socks and the warm yellow sweater over her jumper. Someone was taking very good care of Anna.

"Sorry, Miss Anna, but I have to shine this bright light in your eyes," John crooned to the baby.

Anna flailed her arms wildly and blew a raspberry kiss, which John took as her tacit approval. Shining his ophthalmoscope in each of her chocolate-brown eyes, he determined that her basic brain function was fine and she didn't show any signs of neurological disease. The eyes themselves were fine too, without evidence of injury or disease.

But during the exam Anna had had several short episodes of her eyes rolling upward, paired with rapid-fire eyelid flutters. Each episode lasted just a second or two and didn't seem to bother Anna in the slightest.

"Does Anna ever seem spaced out to you? Like she's daydreaming and you can't get her attention?"

Rosa nodded. "Yeah. Sometimes when I'm feeding her she'll just stare off in the distance for a little bit, like she's thinking about something. Is that important?"

"It could be." John finished the exam and passed Anna back to Rosa for snuggles. Anna giggled wildly when she saw her sister, clapping her chubby hands with delight.

"Silly girl," Rosa said, giving her sister a gentle nose-bop with her finger. "I never left you!"

And you never would, John thought, instinctively knowing that for some reason Rosa had stepped in as Anna's mother and was doing the best she could with only the knowledge and resources she had as a teenager.

"So, what do you think is wrong?" Rosa asked.

Baby Anna began fussing in Rosa's arms. The long wait to see John had surely extended into her lunchtime. Rosa opened her backpack with one hand and tugged out a small cooler where a chilled bottle waited. She shook it to mix the formula, then offered it to Anna, who greedily sucked at the nipple.

John made some notes in the baby's brand-new client record before focusing on Rosa. "There's a couple of possibilities. Your sister's eye-blinking could be a sign of a behavioral tic. Most kids outgrow those in a year or less. But if not, she could have a condition of the nervous system called Tourette Syndrome. But the fact that your sister also had periods of spacing out makes me suspicious that she's having seizures. Those spacing out spells could be absence seizures, which are like brief electrical storms in the brain that impair your sister's consciousness for anywhere from ten to forty-five seconds. The blinkies might only be eyelid myoclonia, a small seizure that doesn't impair her in any way, but all that seizure activity is not good for her brain."

Rosa was wide-eyed now, and clearly afraid. "Is she going to be okay?"

"I think her prognosis is excellent. But we need to get those seizures under control—and that means she needs to see a neurologist for testing and treatment."

Rosa's expression fell. "Oh, I don't think my family has the money for anything like that, Dr. J."

John closed his laptop and rolled a stool over so he could meet her eye to eye. "Well, let's talk about that, Rosa. And then let's talk about you."

A half-hour later John walked Rosa to the reception area and asked Sarah to set up a neurology appointment for Anna. The baby was asleep now, her dark lashes like fringes on her tiny, plump cheeks.

"And let's reach out to the hospital's Social Services, too," John told Sarah. "I'd like a social worker to contact Rosa regarding subsidized childcare options for Anna." He turned to Anna. "No more skipping school to take care of your sister, okay?"

Rosa's eyes were shiny with misty unshed tears. "Thank

you so much, Dr. J. I don't know what we would have done if you weren't here."

John squeezed her elbow. "That's what we're here for."

John returned to his desk to type up the notes from the appointment. Seeing Rosa had triggered so many memories for him. He was glad he could be there for her, but it brought back memories of all his lost years. How much he had given up to try and protect his brother as best he could.

He thought of Rosa and the worry that had etched her young face. Would she blame herself for Anna's seizures? When in fact the culprit would be a rogue gene, either inherited or mutated, that had set the path in place before Anna was even born.

There wasn't anything Rosa could do to change her sister's fate. Was it possible that there wasn't anything John could have done to change his brother's fate either? Maybe Michael, like Piper, needed more than just John in his life, trying to shoulder all the burdens on his own.

Maybe he needed more in his life too. More love, more connection, more community, more support. Certainly the last few months with Charlotte had opened his heart to magical new possibilities. Thanks to her, he had been able to speak from the heart at the gala about the work they did at the clinic, garnering historic levels of donations for The Sunshine Clinic. Thanks to her, Piper's laptop sat ignored for much of the day while she played with Cat or invited a friend over for manicures and "girl talk"—whatever that was.

Was he really going to let all that walk out of his life without a fight?

The papers he'd discarded before seeing Rosa were still in the trash. He pulled them out, smoothed the corners with the palm of his hand. His heart wavered. This was a crazy idea. Did he seriously think that *GypsyMD* would want to trade her life of exotic travel and adventure for a grounded life in Seattle with him and Piper?

But he couldn't forget how it had felt to hold Charlotte in his arms that night at the hotel. To feel the struggle in her body for so many long minutes when he'd asked her to stay. He'd feared she might just flip the covers back and leave anyway. But though she'd never said a word, he'd felt the answer in her body as she'd finally softened against his chest. It had stirred his protective side, knowing that she was choosing to trust him, and he'd wanted to be worthy of that trust that night and for all the nights ahead.

That was the part of him that knew he had to ask Charlotte to stay—even if it ended in rejection. Because he deserved to have this chance. And so did she.

John slid the paperwork back inside his backpack. He would ask Charlotte tonight, after Piper went to bed, if she would consider staying in Seattle permanently.

But, drat, it was Thursday—the day he played basketball with the teens at the community center after work. He rarely missed these games. The kids had come to count on him being there every Thursday—it was a sort of unofficial office hour, when they could ask questions or check him out in a more relaxed setting.

Trust was so important in his work with these teens. Making those games every Thursday was one of the ways he earned that trust.

Okay, tomorrow, then. He'd take the paperwork home but wait until the next day to ask Charlotte to consider staying in Seattle.

Charlotte's pink note fluttered when the heat pump clicked on. It felt like a taunt. Was he sure he had until tomorrow? This note was pinned to her bulletin board to make sure she didn't forget. That meant she was going to sign that contract soon.

But if it was still taped there, she hadn't signed it yet. He still had a chance.

Enough contemplating, it was time for action.

He borrowed her notepad to write her another note.

You are cordially invited for a sunset cruise aboard The House Call. Dress is resort casual. Dinner will be served. Don't be late!

He taped that note on top of hers, to make sure she noticed it first. Then added fifty-one exclamation points for good measure.

Mickey's Café and Tiki Bar was a harborside restaurant located at the marina where John docked *The House Call*. He and Piper were frequent visitors. Piper loved the strawberry milkshakes and John loved the breathtaking views of the harbor, where he and Piper would watch various water vessels come and go. Making up outlandish stories about the people aboard and their adventures was their favorite game.

But tonight it was just him and Charlotte. He had asked Sarah if she would mind keeping Piper at her place overnight again, so he and Charlotte could sail alone.

He could feel the cold bottle of champagne he had stored in his backpack pressing against his spine. The paperwork he needed to submit to make Charlotte's position at the clinic permanent was safely stored in a different pocket. With any luck, he'd be able to pop the champagne later, to celebrate the start of a new adventure for both of them.

But first dinner. John ordered several sandwiches and side dishes as part of the café's signature "picnic to go" special, which they offered to their seafaring customers. Everything was packed into an adorable wicker picnic basket which, it was understood, customers would return to the restaurant on their way out of the marina.

John watched Charlotte as they headed toward the dock where his boat waited. With her hair down and the breeze rustling its loose, dark waves, she was truly stunning tonight.

Moose, the marina cat, was serving his self-appointed role as sentry. He was perched on a post, big, fluffy and regal. Local lore said that petting Moose before a trip would keep sailors and boats safe at sea. Charlotte obliged with a long session of ear-rubs.

John and Charlotte held hands as they followed the walkway to John's boat. It was six-thirty—half an hour past the time he usually went to the community center. Some of the regulars would be there by now, warming up and trading friendly taunts for the game ahead. More teens would trickle in over the next half-hour, greeting each other with hearty jests or tentative smiles. John knew he was the glue that held the whole evening together, helping shy kids find their place on the team and giving the strongest players a good workout.

Charlotte put her hand on his arm. "You good?"

He was doing it again—ruminating on all the people he wanted to save instead of just being with his people.

Tonight was about him and Charlotte. And Piper too, even though she wasn't there.

Charlotte spun so that she was facing him, blocking his path. "We don't have to do this, you know."

"What are you talking about?"

"Sailing. I'd love to go, but I have a feeling you'd feel better if you were at the community center."

He started to protest but realized it was pointless. Charlotte could read him like a book. "How did you know?"

"It's this funny thing you do with your face when you're worried. Want me to demonstrate?"

He laughed, remembering her demonstration of his scowling face. "No, thanks. I'm good."

John contemplated the possibility of making it to the community center to check on the teens and then getting back in time for a quick sail around the bay. He couldn't deny the nagging feeling that he was letting the teens down.

He shook off these familiar demons. He loved those weekly basketball games, but that didn't mean he should be there every single week. If he was going to build a bigger life for him and Piper, and eventually his brother, he needed to stop carrying the weight of the world on his shoulders all the time.

He gave Charlotte's hand a little shake. "Come here."

He pulled her in close and circled his arm around her waist. He could feel her smooth, warm skin through her shirt. He nuzzled her neck, deeply inhaling the sweet scent of Charlotte mixed with jasmine and the briny scent of the sea. All his favorite things mixed together in one intoxicating fragrance.

"This is the only place I want to be." He pulled back so he could see her eyes. "Okay?"

"Okay," she said, leaning into him until her forehead rested against his chest.

He stroked the back of her neck for a moment, feeling a new warmth take root in his heart and expand to fill his entire body. It chased away the guilt and fear, so that all that was left was a profound gratitude that of all the clinics in all the world, this gorgeous woman had found her way to The Sunshine Clinic.

"All right," he said, placing his knuckles under her chin so he could guide her gaze to his. "Are you ready to learn the ropes, so to speak?"

"Sure!" She laughed. "I've had a lot of travel adventures in my life, but this will be my first time sailing."

They boarded *The House Call* and he showed her how to prepare the ropes for their voyage. Then he used the onboard motor to navigate out of the marina and into the harbor.

If he had more time, he'd take her far beyond the harbor.

Past the sea lions basking on buoys and the seawall that protected the shoreline from storm surge flooding. Past the sailboats and houseboats and the seaside mansions. And past the fishing trawlers, their nets heavy with catch. He'd take her out to the Puget Sound where, if the winds were favorable, he would shut off the engine and hoist the sails and harness the power of nature to explore the islands and ports off the coastline of Seattle.

But there was little wind, so Charlotte's first sailing lesson couldn't include hoisting a sail. She accepted the consolation prize of navigating via the onboard motor while John set out their picnic dinner from Mickey's Café. With their plates full, and the boat floating far from the shoreline, they sat on the deck to eat dinner, their legs dangling over the water.

John didn't think this moment could be any more perfect. There was the feel of Charlotte's hip and shoulder against his, the distant lights of other ships in the harbor reflecting off the water, and the very light breeze that rippled the water and made Charlotte shiver in the night. All the things he'd always wanted…all in one place. There was only one thing that would make this night more perfect.

He was about to reach for his backpack, with its contract and champagne, when Charlotte glanced up at him, her shoulder pressed to his. Their gazes met and something in her eyes made his pulse quicken. There was a sultry glint to her eyes that made it too easy to imagine her naked in his berth, stretched out on the navy-blue comforter, her hair wild and tousled against the pillow.

Oh, what he would give to have the length of her gorgeous naked body pressed against his in the same bed where he had spent so many lonely nights. He could imagine it all quite perfectly—and suddenly it was all he wanted.

He raised his fingers to stroke her cheek delicately, as if she were a very fine statue meant to be kept safe behind velvet ropes. He felt that way sometimes…that she was not really for him. Then he dropped his head to kiss her, deliberately and carefully, with great reverence.

Her lips were warm against the cold night. The soft meeting of their mouths made his soul sigh with pleasure. How could he ever doubt that she was for him? They fit together too perfectly and understood each other too well. Even their jagged edges were like the pieces of a puzzle, fitting together to make sense out of the fragments of their past.

Charlotte scooted closer to him, eventually working her way into his lap. Now she was everywhere…in his arms… deepening the kiss…asking for more. And he wanted to give her everything he had—tonight and all the nights after. His mouth became hungry and hot. He wanted to somehow pull her into his very soul. Charlotte was here, in his arms, filling all the empty places in his heart and soul.

I believe in this. I believe in us. I believe in forever.

"John…" she whispered against his ear.

Her hands had burrowed their way beyond his coat, under his shirt, and were now stroking his skin, taking his temperature higher. He knew what she was asking of him and he wished he could figure out a way to hoist both of them up from where they sat so he wouldn't have to let her go.

"Mm-hmm…" he replied.

It was all he could manage. Because Charlotte was kissing him everywhere now, and it felt so good to be loved this much. He believed that was what this could be. Love—pure and simple.

"Make love to me again…" she breathed, stirring all those lovely memories of their night at the hotel, when she had thrilled him just by asking for what she wanted.

Oh, he should do that. They should make love tonight,

and then in the morning, and probably midday tomorrow for good measure.

He whispered against her lips. "Charlotte?"

"Mm-hmm…?"

He stopped her gently, pressing his fingertips against her chest with just the tiniest bit of pressure.

She broke away, but her eyes were hazy and unfocused with desire. "Hmm…?"

He traced his thumb against her bottom lip, willing himself to propose the idea of her staying long-term. But she was doing something with her fingers, tucking them into the waistband of his pants, finding the warm, hidden skin there with her sea-cooled fingers. It made him burn all over for her, and to wish for a better space to continue their explorations.

"Hold that thought," he said—then crushed her mouth with his. He felt like a starved man who would never get his fill.

Somehow they struggled to their feet without breaking their kiss. Charlotte wrapped herself around him, matching his hungry kisses with her own before leading him downstairs to his berth.

Then she jumped on the bed and landed on her knees. And she laughed and laughed, telling him to, "Get in here, slow-poke!" She pulled her sweater off in one fluid motion, revealing her luscious curves and the sweet tease of her white lace bra.

He unbuttoned his shirt as fast as he could, but the last button was stubborn. He had no choice but to pull his shirt apart with one ferocious yank, sending the button flying across the room to land with a soft *plink*. Her eyes widened with delight as she moved aside to make room for him in the berth.

But before he could join her there was a ferocious buzzing in his back pocket—the insistent chime of a five-alarm fire bell. It was the distinctive tone he had chosen for calls from the hospital.

Charlotte froze on the bed. Their gazes met and locked. They both knew this wasn't any routine call from the hospital. Not this late on a weeknight.

He answered it. "This is Dr. Bennett."

He listened for many long minutes, asked routine questions about the patient's status. Eventually he turned away from Charlotte, so she wouldn't see what this call was doing to him.

"Thanks for calling. I'm on my way."

John disconnected the call and paused, taking one last minute for himself. One last minute of feeling loved and hopeful about his future. One last minute of living in a watercolor dreamworld where he had a vibrant, if hazy, future with Charlotte.

"What is it, John? What's wrong?"

He darkened the phone before sliding it into his pocket. He felt the mask of Dr. J slipping back into place.

"We have to head back."

"Why?" She held her sweater to her chest. "What's wrong? Is it Piper?"

John made the adjustments that would fire the engine back into life. He didn't want to talk. He just wanted to get moving...get back to work. It seemed to be the only thing the universe was willing to trust him with.

"John?" She was more insistent now, sensing the magnitude of the change in their tiny space.

"It's Angel. She went to the community center looking for me because she was feeling very sick."

"Is she okay?" Charlotte slipped her sweater back on.

"I don't know. She collapsed at the center and was rushed to the emergency room."

CHAPTER TWELVE

THE HOSPITAL'S WAITING room was filled with teens that Charlotte recognized from The Sunshine Clinic. She wanted to go with John to get an update on Angel's status, but seeing the stress and worry on these young faces, she knew she needed to stay with them.

Unlike on most of her temporary assignments, where she was the outsider looking in, the teens here had adopted her as part of their ever-shifting, highly flexible family unit. Not a family like any she had seen in movies or on television, but a family all the same.

Maybe that was why she hadn't responded to *The Eden* yet. The beauty and adventure of the Caribbean still called to her, but she felt a strange and utterly unfamiliar pull to stay in Seattle. She was falling for John—she knew that—and for his precocious, lovable niece. But there was more holding her in Seattle. Forces she couldn't understand, but which made it impossible for her to just board *The Eden* and leave it behind.

She didn't know exactly what she would do, but she knew she needed to call the cruise ship's human resources department and ask for an extension before signing her contract. It would give her more time to think and decide what she wanted to do.

Now, looking at the pale, strained expressions of the teens who had witnessed Angel's collapse, she finally understood why she felt pulled to stay. She was needed here. Piper, and the teens, and even that silly Cat, all needed her.

The only person she wasn't sure about was John. He was so self-sufficient…so insistent on doing things his way and on his own. Would he welcome her decision to stay in Seattle? Or was their love affair nothing more to him than a fling with a doctor he was sure would leave?

But she pushed those thoughts to the back of her mind as the teens told her what they had seen—how Angel had gone to the community center, pale and confused, looking for John. How she'd left and some of the teens had followed her, sensing something was wrong, and how they'd found her in the parking lot, unconscious and cold.

"It was so scary," one of the girls said. She had her arms wrapped around herself, rocking back and forth.

"Where was Dr. J anyway?" one of the boys demanded. "He's always at our Thursday night games!"

John returned to the waiting room and the teens gathered around him for news and information. He did his best to get them caught up on Angel's status, assuring them that Angel was going to be okay.

He caught eyes with Charlotte and nodded toward the nurses' station.

"I'll be back in a second, kids. Let me just get Dr. Owens caught up."

Charlotte followed John to a quiet alcove near the nurses' station.

"The EMTs said when they found Angel she was unconscious but breathing on her own. Other than her fast heart rate, her other vital signs were good. She regained consciousness on the way to the ER, but complained of dizziness and a small headache. The ED attending wants to keep her for a few hours for observation. But if she remains medically stable, they plan to release her by morning."

Charlotte grabbed his arm. "We can't let them do that, John. Angel could have a genetic heart defect. Maybe Brugada Syndrome? I don't know… But I do know that if they release her tonight without more testing her heart could be a ticking time bomb in her chest."

John ran a hand through his hair. "I know. But without a full family medical history they're not going to admit her to the hospital for testing. Especially not without health insurance."

"I'm going to talk to the attending," Charlotte snapped.

John caught her arm at the wrist before she could stalk down the hall.

"Hey." John pinched the bridge of his nose. "I think it might be time for me to take over Angel's care again."

"What are you talking about?"

John slipped his hands into his leather jacket. "I feel that I've been losing sight of some of my priorities, you know? That I might be getting out of touch with the teens. Your house will be done in the next few weeks. Who knows what's next for you?"

Charlotte's brow furrowed in frustration. "I haven't signed my contract."

"I know. But you could if you wanted to. You can go anywhere you want, Charlotte, or you can stay right here. I don't have those choices. I've got people who count on me to be there for them, and lately—like tonight—I've been letting them down."

Charlotte felt a familiar heat creeping up the back of her neck, and that prickly, itchy sensation following close behind.

"Having you here these past few months has been…" John stopped to cough, his voice breaking. "Amazing. Charlotte, I can't thank you enough for all you've done for Piper, Angel, the teens…and me."

Charlotte wanted to press her hands to her ears.

Please stop talking…please stop talking…please stop talking.

"I don't ever want my life to be the way it was before, Charlotte. Falling in love with you has made me realize that I deserve more. The trouble is, I don't know how to get what I most want—you—without hurting someone. Like I did tonight."

Toughen up, Owens. This isn't your first rodeo. Yes, he said he loved you, but now he's changed his mind. So what? It's not like you haven't been here before. If your own father didn't want to claim you, why would John or anyone else?

"Now that Piper's leg is healed, she and I can move back onto *The House Call* tomorrow. It will make it easier for me to get the work done on it so I can list it for sale and buy a proper home."

That bitter voice was back in her head.

I told you so. I told you so. I told you so.

Then suddenly he was in front of her, cupping her face between his hands, right there, where everyone could see them.

"Charlotte, listen to me. This isn't goodbye. I just need a little time to straighten things out."

She took his hands from her face, put them back at his sides. "It's all right, John. I understand just fine. Take all the time you need. I'll wrap things up at the clinic this week and let the cruise ship know that I've completed my assignment."

"Wait… You're leaving?"

"Yes—that's generally what people do when they're no longer needed."

"I never said that."

"You don't have to say the words out loud, John. It's written all over your face. You might love me, but you're never going to trust me. Not with the hard stuff. Not with the people who matter to you. You want to save the world all alone, like some kind of superhero. But I never wanted a superhero, John. I just wanted you."

She gathered her purse and coat, eager to escape with her dignity intact. She did not want to weep in front of John or any of the hospital staff. That would have to wait until later, when she was far away from here and could put all this behind her.

John stopped her before she could storm down the hall. "Maybe you didn't want a superhero, Charlotte, but did you really want me? Imperfect, fallible, sometimes not sure what's the right thing to do? Because you sure seem willing to bolt as soon as things are less than perfect."

Charlotte looked down at his hand on her arm. "Well, I guess we've both had a chance to speak our mind. I'm going to go see Angel now. Even if she isn't my patient anymore, I still care what happens to her."

"Charlotte!" John protested.

But then the attending appeared at John's elbow, ready to discuss Angel's case.

John looked helplessly back and forth between the attending and Charlotte. "Just…wait for me, okay?" he said.

He followed the attending out of the waiting room, all of his attention concentrated on being briefed about Angel's progress.

Charlotte watched him leave, her heart breaking into a million tiny pieces.

She made it past the reception desk and the triage area before the tears she'd held back spilled down her cheeks. She needed a few minutes to pull herself together before she saw Angel.

She paused in the hallway outside the treatment bays, leaning against the wall, her jacket folded over her arms. A nurse passed by and gave her a compassionate smile and squeezed her arm. She probably thought Charlotte had just received some terrible news about a family member. And that wasn't too far from the truth. Because what she'd had with John and Piper over the past few months had been the closest thing to family she'd had since her mother died.

"Dammit," she said, searching her bag for a clean tissue.

How many times would she have to learn the same painful lesson over and over again? Love didn't stay—at least not for her. Her fate lay in pursuing adventure, not sticking around and waiting to be rejected. She'd *known* this when she'd come here, yet she'd insisted on taking a chance.

Charlotte checked her appearance in the glass window of a treatment room. Her nose was red and her skin a bit blotchy, so she dusted some powder over her face and fluffed her hair until she felt presentable. Then she searched the emergency department until she found Angel's room. She looked tiny and wan on the hospital gurney, her face the same pale shade as the white blanket draped over her thin frame.

"Hey, Angel," Charlotte said, sitting at the end of her bed. "How are you feeling?"

Angel took a deep sip of the soda that a nurse must have given her. "Mostly good," she said, her voice lacking its usual bravado. "Maybe a little dizzy. And I have a headache."

Definitely symptoms of Brugada Syndrome, the genetic heart defect that Charlotte had feared Angel might have. But the only way to know for sure was to have Angel admitted to the hospital for extensive testing.

"The doctor said I could go home tonight. That's good, right?"

Charlotte tilted her head with a soft smile. "Usually that would be great news, Angel. But in your case that's not what I want for you."

Charlotte explained the medical condition that might be causing Angel's symptoms.

"But the only way we can get these tests done is if you let us know who you are. Then we can get a full medical history. That is, if you're okay with us talking to your family?"

Angel's expression darkened. "I don't want to be a burden to them."

"Why would helping you be a burden to your family?"

Angel looked away, out the window, her hands moving restlessly over the blankets that covered her legs. "I have three sisters, and my mom was having a hard time taking care of all of us. I thought it would be easier if I left. I'm almost fifteen now...old enough to get a job, take care of myself. It's one less mouth for my mom to feed, right?"

"Does she know where you are?"

Angel's jaw quivered. "No. I don't want her to worry. I can take care of myself now."

"Based on what you've told me so far, Angel, I'm pretty sure she wants to hear from you. And I'm certain she would want you to get help with these heart problems you're having." Charlotte pulled a pad of paper from her purse, and a pen, putting them in front of Angel. "I don't know exactly why you don't want anyone to know your real name, but I know the power that comes with seizing control of something when your world feels like it's spinning out of control. Not showing your true self does protect you from being hurt again. But it also makes you invisible. And invisible people can't be loved, because no one knows who they really are."

Angel met her gaze now, and Charlotte felt like there was a flicker of understanding in her eyes.

"Let me help you, Angel. Me and Dr. J and all the doctors here. We all want you to be safe and healthy."

Angel took a deep breath, then picked up the pen and began

writing, the pen's nib making scratching sounds against the paper. Then she handed it to Charlotte.

Charlotte read the paper and smiled. "It's nice to finally meet you, Kaitlyn Webb."

A few hours later, John left the emergency room feeling like a bus had run over him slowly and repeatedly. It had been a long, grueling night of trying to convince the attending that Angel's case was more serious than simple fainting.

It was only because Charlotte had got Angel's real name that he'd been able to call her mother and get a full medical history. Learning that her father had died in his forties of a heart attack had been enough for the attending to order more testing. Thankfully Angel would spend the next few nights in the hospital, where she would be safe and sound.

He had immediately looked for Charlotte, to share the good news, but she'd been nowhere to be found in the hospital. She hadn't responded to his texts or calls either. His last hope had been to find her car next to his at the hospital, where they had hurriedly parked when they'd come back from the marina.

But her car wasn't there.

He felt his blood run very cold. Memories of their fight about Angel's care had haunted him all night. Had he really needed to make his stand so soon after learning the news of Angel's collapse? He'd been shaken and worried, not in the best frame of mind to tell the woman he loved that he needed a little time and space to straighten out his life.

But he did. He had been living in a strange limbo for years now, and he'd never seen it until he'd fallen in love with Charlotte. Only then had he seen how his old, limiting beliefs were holding him back from living the full life he deserved. So long as he felt it was up to him and him alone to care for the teens and for Piper, he'd never be able to make room in his life for anything more interesting than a houseplant.

He checked his phone again—still no response to his texts. This was unlike Charlotte, who was as obsessive about returning calls and texts as he was. He started his car and headed for her house. Suddenly it felt very urgent that he find Charlotte right away.

Charlotte's car was in the garage. That was a good sign. But he felt very uneasy at finding her in her bedroom, with a suitcase on the bed.

"How's Angel?" she asked. But she remained where she was, her back to him as she gazed out the window.

Something wasn't right.

He moved slowly, assessing the situation. "She has an excellent prognosis, thanks to you getting her real name." His eyes roamed the room, saw the empty hangers in the closet and the counters cleared of perfume and makeup. "What's going on, Charlotte?"

She turned to him, her eyes red and puffy. "I have to go, John."

He took it all in. This seemed like an awfully strong reaction to him asking for a little space to get his life straightened out.

"I thought your assignment with *The Eden* didn't start until next month."

She sniffed and turned away. "I never signed the contract."

"So, where will you go?"

"I don't really know."

John had a well-honed radar after years of working with teens who were too young or too traumatized to verbalize their needs. He was good at reading between the lines…hearing the truth in what wasn't spoken aloud.

All this time he had believed Charlotte was someone with

wanderlust in her soul—*GypsyMD*, keeping life casual and fun. But now he thought she might be something different.

"A little Greyhound therapy, then?"

She sniffed again. "What?"

"Greyhound therapy. That's what we call it at the clinic. Some of our kids think if they pack up their stuff and jump on a Greyhound bus they can leave all their problems behind. Start fresh somewhere else."

"I don't think that."

"No? Then what's happening here?"

She sat on the bed, her fingers curling round the mattress edge. When she spoke, her words were too soft for him to understand.

He took a step forward, straining to understand. "I'm sorry… You don't know how to…what?"

"I don't know how to *stay*!" she exploded, and the tears started again.

She resumed packing, channeling her nervous energy into cramming sweaters into her large suitcase. "I'm just not built like you, John. If I stay in one place for too long I start to get nervous and jumpy. Like I'm a fish in a blender…just waiting for fate to push the button. I love you, and Piper, and the teens—and even that crazy Cat who won't go away. But I'm not sure that's enough."

None of that made sense. They had worked together for months and she'd seemed perfectly comfortable at the clinic and at her house. The big change had come tonight, when he'd asked for space to straighten out some of the messes in his life. Which made sense, considering she had been doubly traumatized at a young age. First, by losing her mother to a car accident and then by her father's rejection.

What better way to make sure she was never abandoned again than to refuse to stay? Charlotte didn't travel because she had wanderlust in her soul. She traveled to avoid the connections that would break her heart if she lost them.

Every cell in his body wanted him to gather her into his arms and promise her that she was safe. That he wasn't going anywhere, and she could stop running now.

But he doubted she would listen. Not when she was this upset.

John considered his options, then headed over to the chair she had in her bedroom. He pulled it away from the wall, sat down and stretched his legs out. He opened his phone and navigated to the apps. Soon the room was full of the sound of bells and dings and whistles.

Charlotte stopped packing and looked at him. "What are you doing?"

"Some fruit-matching game that Piper taught me."

"What?"

The sounds of several bells chiming at once filled the room. "See, I just matched five lemons there—so now I have five hundred points."

Charlotte stood across from him, her arms full of sweaters. The expression on her face was pure confusion.

"Just something to do. You know... While I wait."

"Wait for what?"

He laughed. "For you, of course. Oh, wait—I need this pineapple." He made a few finger-swipes and then there were more bells and whistles. "See, the way I figure it, you can go as far away as you want. Travel all seven oceans...cross the continents. Hell, you can go to the moon. But when you've gotten all that out of your system you *will* come back to me. Because there is nothing in this universe that is stronger than the love we made the night of the hospital gala. Nothing, not even your fear, can overpower that. So do what you must. I'll be right here waiting for you. For as long as it takes."

For several long minutes Charlotte stood staring at him in disbelief. John willed himself to focus on the stupid game. Whether she left or stayed—that was up to her. But he wasn't lying. He really would wait for her. Even if he was an old man when her stubborn heart finally accepted what he already knew was true.

There was no other woman on this earth for him but her.

After a very long, uncomfortable silence, she set the sweaters down. Not in the suitcase, he noticed, which seemed like a good sign.

She finally looked at him. She looked exhausted and a little fragile.

He dropped the phone and went to her, gathered her in his arms, ready to buttress her against all the hurts of her past. She lifted her head and waited. He bent his head to kiss her, long and slow. He wanted to soothe her pain away, calm her stormy emotions and welcome her home.

But there was a strange and bitter taste in this kiss.

He searched for the sweetness he always found in her, but found only sadness, longing, and goodbye.

Disbelief churned in his gut, making him feel sick and sad. He wanted to shake her and beg her to stay. She didn't have to go, no matter how many times she told herself she did. She could stay if she wanted. Didn't she know that? She could break the rules that were holding her hostage.

He pulled away and searched her face. That was when he knew he wasn't going to win this fight. Her mind had been made up ever since she'd left the hospital...maybe ever since she'd arrived in Seattle.

She stepped away. Touching her fingers to her mouth. Pressing her lips as if imprinting their last sad kiss there. Then she turned back to her suitcase, pushed the sweaters down, and zipped the mammoth case shut.

Every cell in his body wanted him to fight for her. But that would mean fighting *against* her, because the enemy he wanted to defeat was buried deep in her heart.

Just stay! he wanted to scream. *That's all you have to do... just stay!*

She wrestled the suitcase off the bed.

This was happening whether he liked it or not.

He sat helpless and stunned as she escaped the room and his life. There wasn't a thing he could do to change her mind. He knew better than to even try.

All he could do was wait. And hope that the trade winds would soon blow her back to him.

CHAPTER THIRTEEN

CHARLOTTE TOOK A break from eating to stretch. Her body was so achy these days. She often wondered if she was coming down with a cold, but the sniffles never came. She was probably just tired from the last few weeks.

It had been a whirlwind of goodbyes as she'd ended her assignment at The Sunshine Clinic and put her father's house on the market. She had opted to stay at a hotel until John moved out of the house and into a cute little brick house near the hospital, with plenty of room for Piper and Cat.

Charlotte had seen Angel—now Kaitlyn—one last time before she'd left for *The Eden*. Angel had come by with many of The Sunshine Clinic's regular patients to say goodbye to her. She'd had her aunt with her, with whom she was now living, and was sporting a new pacemaker that protected her heart from going into cardiac arrest. Testing had revealed she did indeed have Brugada Syndrome, and it was probably the reason her father had died so young.

But all that was behind her now. *GypsyMD* was back! Traveling the Caribbean on an unbelievably swanky cruise ship that provided every luxury and amenity she could imagine.

She looked at the dinner her medical assistant had brought. Caesar salad and roasted chicken with a few petits fours for dessert. All perfectly prepared by an award-winning chef.

But absolutely nothing looked appetizing.

"You need to eat something," her assistant had urged.

Charlotte knew she was right. She had lost ten pounds since leaving Seattle and judging from the total loss of her appetite she might lose ten more. Now her cute summer dresses just hung on her frame, when she bothered to put them on at all. All she really wanted to wear was her gray sweatpants and an old band tee shirt she'd found at the thrift store.

All this because she had tried giving up her nomadic ways to give love a chance and it had failed spectacularly.

When she had accepted the cruise ship assignment, she had planned to lose herself in everything the Caribbean cruise had to offer. Surely a few days of sea mist and warm sun would restore her soul? Then she would be ready to take advantage of the many port excursions and tours that were part of cruise life. She just had to pick which ones.

She pushed her untouched dinner away and thumbed through the brochures listlessly. Cave tubing. A historical Mayan ruin site tour. Barrier reef snorkeling. A jungle Jeep tour.

She didn't know what was wrong with her. By now her notebook should be full of ideas and itineraries, all arranged in priority order because there was never enough time to do everything she wanted. But her notebook remained blank. All she could think about was how much Piper would love cave tubing if she were here. Or how John would make his corny jokes during the Mayan ruin site tour to keep things lively.

Nothing sounded good unless she could share it with her people.

She shook off the thought. She didn't have people anymore, but what she did have was a tidy sum of money from the sale of her father's home. The money was sitting in her account, waiting to be donated to a worthy charity. She opened a new page in her notebook and wrote *Charity* across the top. If she figured out where to donate the money, maybe that would clear her head to focus on her next adventure.

There was a knock at the door. Her medical assistant said, "Dr. Owens, we have a patient complaining of chest pain."

That wasn't good. So far Charlotte's work on *The Eden* had been fairly uneventful. Plenty of sunburn cases, indigestion, and a few folks who had forgotten to pack their medicines. Nothing truly serious had happened while she was onboard, and she was hoping to keep it that way.

"Okay, please put them in Exam Room One."

"I did that. But just so you know, she's brought her husband and family with her."

"Good. I'm glad she has support." Charlotte closed up her notebook and draped her stethoscope around her neck.

"Her *very large* family," the medical assistant said with a wink.

Sure enough, the hallway outside the exam room was packed with family members of every age. The youngest was a baby, who had fallen asleep on her mother's shoulder. Everyone was wearing Hawaiian-themed shirts—which would have been a festive sight if it hadn't been for the worry on their faces.

"Excuse me," Charlotte said repeatedly as she pushed through the small crowd.

She finally made it into the exam room where an older lady was lying on the bed, her eyes closed, holding hands with a gentleman who looked to be around her age and very worried.

"Mrs. Patterson?" Charlotte said, recognizing the elderly woman who had shared her table at the hospital's fundraising gala.

The man at her side gave her shoulder a gentle shake. She opened her eyes and said, a little too loud, "What?"

The man gestured to her ear, then made a hand sign as if turning a dial up.

"Oh!" the woman said, before reaching behind her ear. Lily could see the half-moon shape of a hearing aid perched on her ear and knew Mrs. Patterson was adjusting the volume.

"The doctor's here," the man said, before taking her hand in his.

he woman squinted her eyes before she smiled in recognition. "Ah, the newlywed lady doctor. How's your husband?"

Charlotte's heart squeezed hard with a fresh wave of pain. Just seeing Mrs. Patterson brought back a flood of memories of that night with John…especially the way they'd danced together in the ballroom, and how they'd spent their time later, in his room.

Charlotte just smiled to hide her distress. She didn't want to spend time explaining her situation. Especially when Mrs. Patterson was complaining of chest pain.

"I think what's important here is you, Mrs. Patterson."

Her husband had both of his hands clasped around hers. "She started complaining of chest pain about an hour ago. We had such a lovely dinner, and then we did some dancing."

"A lot of dancing!" Mrs. Patterson laughed.

"We're celebrating our fiftieth anniversary," Mr. Patterson explained. "Our family planned this cruise as a kind of family reunion and wedding anniversary celebration."

"How lovely," Charlotte said. "I'm sure you don't want to spend your anniversary down here in the medical clinic, so let's get you checked out and on your way, shall we?"

Mrs. Patterson's vital signs were all quite stable, which made Charlotte feel a lot better. If Mrs. Patterson was having a heart attack she would likely have an irregular heartbeat, clammy skin, or shortness of breath. Still, heart attacks could be sneaky, with no warning signs, so she'd need to do an EKG to monitor Mrs. Patterson's heart activity.

The cruise ship's medical clinic had a portable EKG monitoring system that was easy and compact to use. Recordings were stored on the cloud, so if it was necessary to arrange a helicopter evacuation to a land-based hospital, a patient's test results could easily be accessed by the hospital's emergency room. This was the kind of technology that Charlotte had wanted to add to The Sunshine Clinic. But it was expensive, and few teens needed an EKG on a regular basis, so hospital funding would never include these types of extra services.

"So, tell me how you two lovebirds met," Charlotte said as she set up the electrodes that would monitor Mrs. Patterson's heart.

She would need to be monitored for at least an hour, so Charlotte wanted to keep her mind busy and distracted from the testing at hand.

"Well, we very nearly didn't!" said Mr. Patterson, giving his wife a sweet smile. "Thanks to my wife's stubborn streak."

Mrs. Patterson laughed and waved him off. "Heavens, am I ever going to live that down?"

Charlotte pulled up a chair and made herself comfortable. "You'd better tell me the story now. You've piqued my curiosity!"

"It was all my fault," Mrs. Patterson said, folding her hands across her chest. "I went to a Halloween party with some friends in high school. When I walked in the door there was the most handsome cowboy I'd ever seen, dancing his heart out in the living room. My own heart quite literally skipped a beat when he looked my way. But he was dancing with two witches at the same time. Beautiful girls, hanging on his every word, and I decided right then and there that he must be some kind of heartbreaker who collected girlfriends like trophies."

"So when I asked this beautiful lass out on a date the next weekend she roundly turned me down," Mr. Patterson said. "And the next time and the next time and the time after that. It was embarrassing!"

Mrs. Patterson fixed her pale blue eyes on Charlotte's. "I was certain that he was only pursuing me for the challenge of it. That as soon as I said yes he'd pull his love-'em-and-leave-'em routine on me too. A routine I hadn't actually seen, by the way, but was sure he was guilty of." She patted her husband's hand affectionately. "As it turned out the two beautiful ladies he was dancing with were his cousins, visiting from out of town for a long weekend."

"I've never collected girlfriends!" Mr. Patterson said indignantly. "I've got my hands full with this one!"

The long-married couple gazed at each other as if they'd just met a few hours earlier. Charlotte smiled at their obvious love for each other.

"And to think," Mrs. Patterson said, "if I hadn't ever learned the truth about you, none of this would have happened!" She waved her hand to indicate the family members who were standing around or sitting on the floor, waiting for news of her health.

An hour later, Charlotte removed the electrodes and gave the Mrs. Patterson the good news that her heart was strong and healthy. "You may have just overdone it with the anniversary celebrations," she told her. "Take it easy for the next few days, don't hit the all-you-can-eat buffet too hard, and come back to see me if anything seems amiss."

The Pattersons and their multi-generational family left the clinic in much better spirits than when they'd entered. And Charlotte's heart felt lighter too, now she knew the couple would be able to enjoy their anniversary trip and hopefully many more years together.

Charlotte closed up the clinic and headed back to her cabin. Her mind was full of the story that Mrs. Patterson had shared. Especially how the Pattersons' love story would never have happened if she hadn't learned the truth about her hopeful suitor.

Then she thought of Angel—Kaitlyn—and how she'd risked her health because she'd thought she was a burden to her family.

And Piper, who'd assumed that getting herself into trouble at school would get her reunited with her father.

And John, who'd thought asking for help for the clinic would be a sign of weakness, when in fact the Seattle community very much wanted to take care of its at-risk teens.

How many self-destructive things do we do when we don't know the truth? Charlotte wondered.

Which made it impossible to avoid thinking about her own decisions—especially the ones that had led her here.

"This isn't goodbye, Charlotte. I just need a little time..."

John had straight out told her what he needed. But all she'd heard were echoes of her father's rejection and abandonment. She hadn't been able to get past her own fears and really listen to what John needed. So she had made decisions for him, for both of them, that were really just about protecting her ego.

It's too late. He wouldn't want to see me now after what I did to us.

And there they were again. Her assumptions and beliefs about what John would do, without ever giving him a chance to speak for himself.

The truth was, she didn't know what he would say. Maybe she was right. Maybe he never wanted to see her again.

It would break her heart if that were true, but she still had to try.

She had to be stronger than her fears if she ever hoped to

have a real life for herself. A life that looked like the Pattersons', full of love and a devotion so strong that it created two more generations.

But before she went back to Seattle there was one more truth she needed to face. One more person she had not allowed to have his say.

Charlotte closed the door to her cabin and went to the closet. She had packed up in a hurry once her father's house had sold, so she wasn't sure what documents had come with her and which ones were packed away in storage. She flipped past her medical license, the house sale contract, her employment contract with *The Eden*. Towards the back, she finally found what she was looking for.

She held the envelope, its ivory paper thick and expensive, for several long minutes. She ran her finger across her name, *Dr. Charlotte Owens*, written in her father's script across the front. It felt like her entire life had come down to this one letter.

She took a deep breath and flipped it over, running her finger under the seal to break it.

The new built-in desk was an excellent addition to the office, giving John and the clinic's second doctor a dedicated space for their computer and files. Much classier than the old door he'd lain across two sawhorses.

He wished Charlotte were here to see it.

The very thought of her was enough to form a thick lump in his throat. His body still felt utterly exhausted from the hard work of grieving over their breakup.

He'd kept hoping she'd come back, or call, or in some way reach out to him…give them a second chance. But she was gone in every sense of the word.

She hadn't even updated her travel blog, which had worried him at first. But the hospital had assured him that they had spoken to her when she'd ended her assignment, so he knew she was okay. She just didn't want to speak to him.

Sarah poked her head into John's office. "Don't forget that meeting with the chief at two o'clock this afternoon!"

"I won't," John assured her. "Now go on with yourself. There's a retirement with your name written all over it."

He got up to walk her to the door, knowing that otherwise Sarah would find a hundred more little tasks she needed to do before she officially retired.

"Oh, John…" Sarah lamented. "I can't imagine not seeing you and the kids every day. Are you sure you're going to be all right?"

John stooped to give her a kiss. "I'll be fine, Sarah, though I'm sure going to miss you. Without you, I don't think The Sunshine Clinic would ever have happened."

Sarah reached out to give John one of her signature bear hugs, and he gratefully accepted.

"You would have found a way, John. You always do."

John walked Sarah to her car and wished her well. He had a new medical assistant now, and a new receptionist to replace Sarah now she'd announced she was finally ready to retire. She meant it this time.

There had been other changes to the clinic too. Like the breathing treatment area that Charlotte had suggested, and a steady stream of nursing students who worked every afternoon to earn practicum hours toward their degrees and provided John with free staffing. There was a nutritionist who came every Friday afternoon, and there were plans to add a dentist and a hygienist two or three days a week.

But the best thing of all was the ten-year plan that the hospital had developed for The Sunshine Clinic, with John's input taking priority. In due time, the clinic would move into a bigger building that could accommodate more doctors, nurses, and other specialists, who would provide all the services John had always dreamed of.

It was like a dream come true, and it had all started the night he'd given his speech from the heart at the fundraising gala.

As it turned out there were a lot of doctors and administrators who wanted to help Seattle's disadvantaged teens. They just hadn't known that John needed more donations, more volunteers, and a bigger budget—because he had never asked. Now that the hospital's board of directors were aware of his ambitions and needs, a lot more funding and support had been sent his way.

Which was why he had a monthly meeting with the chief of pediatrics to discuss the clinic's progress and growth. But the chief's emails had been rather cryptic of late, hinting at some new initiative the hospital had in mind for the clinic. Despite his best efforts, John hadn't been able to get his boss or any of his colleagues to spill any beans about this new plan.

John gathered his files and notes for the meeting. Then paused in the hallway outside the door he still thought of as Charlotte's office. But Charlotte wasn't there anymore, and she wasn't coming back. He had a new part-time pediatrician now, who worked a few afternoons a week, and on-call doctors filling in the rest of the time. It was more help than he'd had since he started the clinic, but it wasn't Charlotte…

John usually made good use of his driving time by listening to pediatric medicine podcasts, so he could keep up with the latest research and treatment options. But he just wasn't in the mood today, so he searched the radio until he found a smooth jazz station. It reminded him of the night he had driven Charlotte home from the clinic after their street call work. It had felt so good to take care of her when she was so exhausted after Tommy's close call with death.

But it didn't feel good to remember their fight at the hospital when Angel had collapsed.

"You might love me, but you're never going to trust me... not with the people who matter to you."

A superhero. That was what she'd called him. She'd said that he just wanted to save the world alone, like some kind of superhero.

That was crazy, he'd thought when she'd first left. The last thing in the world he felt like was a superhero of any kind. Superheroes didn't have brothers who fell apart right in front of them, or nieces who wanted to fight their way into jail.

But that had been a few months ago, and he saw things differently now. Especially now he knew how much his colleagues wanted to help the clinic once he had told them the truth during his speech at the gala. He really couldn't do everything he wanted for the teens all by himself.

So, Charlotte was right.

He had fallen head over heels in love with her. But he hadn't been willing to fully trust her with all of his vulnerabilities. To let her know that he needed her at the clinic and in his life.

John pulled into one of the parking spaces at the hospital for medical staff and made his way to his boss's office. Her assistant directed him to the conference room and offered him a coffee while he waited.

"She'll just be a few moments. She's invited a guest to join you today. Someone who is familiar with the new community initiative the hospital wants to explore."

It was really driving John crazy that no one would tell him what was going on. It had been like this for weeks—ever since the hospital had gained a new donor who was apparently putting some stipulations on their donation. John hoped it wasn't going to become a problem.

Eventually John had waited long enough to need a refill on his coffee. He was doctoring his coffee with two creams and sugar when he heard the conference room door open.

"Hey, Dr. Fagan," John said, without looking up. "Can I get you a coffee?"

"Sure. Two creams, please. But I guess you already know that."

John's world froze as he recognized her voice. He slowly turned and faced her. She was even more beautiful than he remembered, her long hair falling in waves around her face and her skin now tanned from the time she had spent in the Caribbean.

"What are you doing here?" he managed to say, amazed that his brain was still able to form words.

"I have something to show you," she said, tucking her hair behind her ear.

"I can't go anywhere right now. I'm about to have a meeting with the chief of pediatrics and a new donor to the clinic."

She smiled and, damn, if his heart didn't skip a beat. "I believe I *am* that donor, John. And I'd like to show you what I've donated."

This entire situation had rendered John mute, and he had no choice but to follow her like an obedient puppy. She led him out of the conference room to the elevators outside the chief's office. It was too soon and too awkward for any kind of conversation, so he simply stood in silence next to her, smelling that jasmine-scented perfume she favored, which stirred memories of their last elevator ride together.

Those memories were too provocative, so he forced himself to concentrate on the ever-decreasing floor numbers as they descended to the parking garage.

"Where are we going?" he asked, as she walked him out of the garage toward a fenced lot next to the hospital. This was where the hospital's ambulances parked when they were off duty.

"This way," she said.

When they rounded the corner, John was shocked to discover the chief of pediatrics was there, along with other colleagues from the pediatrics department. And Sarah too.

They were all flanking a large blue vehicle that John had never seen before, but which bore the name of his clinic. Only it said *The Sunshine Mobile Clinic for Kids*.

John looked to Charlotte. "I don't understand…"

Dr. Fagan appeared at his side, all smiles and handshakes. "Congratulations, John. You're the proud owner of a new forty-foot mobile health clinic, equipped with two exam rooms, an onboard laboratory, and telehealth equipment so your patients can access specialists all over North America. All thanks to the extremely generous donation of your former locum tenens Dr. Owens. I've been trying to woo her to come back and work for us full-time, but she's playing hard to get. Maybe you'll have better luck."

With that, Dr. Fagan opened the door to the mobile clinic so that the pediatric team could get their first tour, leaving John and Charlotte alone.

John searched for the right words. "This is amazing, Charlotte. Thank you so much. But I don't understand…"

"It was my father's letter, I guess."

"You read it, then?"

"Yes, and now I want to read it to you."

She led John by the hand to a picnic table under some trees and sat across from him. She pulled a letter from her purse, then smoothed the paper with her hands. Her voice was shaky but clear as she read to him the words she had avoided for so long.

Dear Charlotte,

Words cannot express my regret at having to write this letter. If I had lived my life properly, a letter such as this would never be necessary. Unfortunately, I made choices I deeply regret. And, while I can never take back the harm I have caused you, I can at least give you a full accounting of the details.

I met your beautiful mother the summer before I went to college. I was bright and energetic, destined to attend a good college and become a good attorney, like my father and his father before that. Your mother waited tables at a café my friends and I liked to visit, and I thought she was just about the most amazing creature I had ever seen. What started as a harmless flirtation blossomed into a full-blown love affair. She was all I could think about every minute of every day.

A few weeks before I was scheduled to leave for college, we discovered your mother was pregnant. And while I was thrilled, and confident we'd find a way to raise you while finishing our educations, my parents had a very different reaction. They gave me an ultimatum—I could choose you and your mother and forfeit the family trust fund that would pay for my college. Or I could walk away from both of you and everything would be as if it had never happened.

I think my choice is obvious, and I will never be able to make up for the hard years you and your mother endured. There is no excuse for what I did. I was young and afraid and convinced I couldn't survive without my family's support.

Years later, when your mother died, I forfeited my parental rights rather than face you. I couldn't imagine that you wouldn't hate me for my choices. I foolishly as-

*sumed that you would be placed with a relative on your
mother's side. That was not the case, as I learned much
later, when making plans for my estate.*

*In the end, Charlotte, all of my choices were for
naught. The legal career I valued above you failed me
when my business partner embezzled funds, leaving
our firm destitute and in legal jeopardy. Everything I
worked for slipped through my fingers like sand. And
why shouldn't it? A house that's built on a shaky foun-
dation is destined to fall in times of trouble.*

*Now, at the end of my life, all I have left in the world
is this house, and it's in about as good of shape as I am.
I hope in some small way it will bring good to your life.
And I hope that you'll be smarter than I was.*

*Charlotte, when something—or someone—good
comes your way, you grab on tight and don't ever let it go.*

Charlotte folded the letter into thirds and slipped it back
into its envelope. John noticed how worn the paper was and
suspected that she had read and reread the letter many times.

"It was Mrs. Patterson who inspired me to read the letter.
You remember her from the gala, right? She was on a cruise
with her family on *The Eden* and had a bit of a health scare.
She was fine, thank goodness, but talking to her and her husband and meeting her family made a bit of an impression on
me."

Charlotte paused to tuck some errant strands of hair behind
her ear. She seemed different now, he noticed. More confident
than he remembered.

Despite their many months apart, John had the strongest
urge to pull her into his arms, tuck her against his chest. He
knew how hard that must have been for her, reading a letter
from the man who was responsible for the hardest years of

her life. But she wasn't his to comfort anymore, so he willed his hands to remain at his sides while she spoke.

"I'm afraid I'm guilty of making the same mistakes as my father," Charlotte said, her blue eyes dark and solemn. "I fell in love with you and Piper and The Sunshine Clinic. I knew you were my home, John, and that I belonged here. But at the first sign of trouble I dived back into the life I knew instead of doing what was right. I should have been there for you after Angel's collapse, even if you needed some space to deal with your emotions. Instead, I balked and bolted, so I didn't have to risk you rejecting me."

"I was never going to abandon you, Charlotte. I just didn't know how to love you without someone getting hurt or overlooked."

She reached out for his hand. "I know that now. Which is why I wanted to donate the proceeds of my father's house sale to The Sunshine Clinic. Now you can bring those corny jokes to even more at-risk teens in Seattle, whether they want to hear them or not."

He pulled her to him now, close enough that he could see the dark circles of her pupils and the lush, full lips that he longed to kiss. "I don't suppose I could interest you in an exciting travel assignment on the streets of Seattle?"

She tilted her head up in an unmistakable invitation to pick up where they had left off. "I don't suppose you could keep me away, Dr. Bennett."

Finally, she was his. Really, truly his. And it seemed like the heavens should open so that legions of angels could tumble from the sky and serenade them where they stood. But that didn't happen, so he settled for a long, sweet, slow kiss that would start the next chapter of their lives.

EPILOGUE

One year later

CHARLOTTE HAD JUST smashed a perfectly good bottle of champagne.

It was a beautiful Saturday in June, and John and Charlotte had invited all their friends, who were really their family, to join them for an official christening ceremony for their new sailboat, *Two Docks and a Boat*.

Piper was hosting her first playdate on their new, larger sailboat. She practically beamed as she showed her friend how to dock and tie off the boat, along with all the other boating chores she'd learned since living with John.

Piper's friendships were blossoming at school, and playdates like these were becoming a regular occurrence in her life. She and John were visiting Michael regularly now and had invited Charlotte to join them for their next visit. Charlotte was looking forward to meeting her future brother-in-law, and eventually helping him start his life over with her and John for support.

John was busy on the deck of their new boat, cooking burgers for a summer picnic. Charlotte went up behind him and gave him a hug. "Look what we've done here," she said.

John paused in his work and watched the party unfold. The

air was filled with the chatter of excited teens, many from the clinic, catching up with Angel/Kaitlyn and her new life.

Seagulls circled overhead, hoping for their chance at a stolen hamburger bun, while the sun shone over it all.

"We made this," Charlotte said, her heart full to bursting. "Our own little family."

John slipped an arm around her and grazed his lips against hers. "You think you'll miss jungle tours in the Caribbean? Or snow-skiing in Vail?"

Charlotte chuckled. "Definitely!" She looked down at the hand that John had splayed protectively against her belly. "But I think our little guy will provide enough adventure for me for quite some time."

John nuzzled her ear. "Should we tell everyone now or later?"

She leaned back against him, loving the solid strength of him. "Later, I think."

For now, she wanted to bask in the quiet refuge of his arms, safe in the knowledge that she had found her way home.

* * * * *

COMING SOON!

We really hope you enjoyed reading this book.
If you're looking for more romance
be sure to head to the shops when
new books are available on

Thursday 28th March

To see which titles are coming soon, please visit
millsandboon.co.uk/nextmonth

MILLS & BOON

MILLS & BOON®

Coming next month

FORBIDDEN NIGHTS WITH THE PARAMEDIC
Alison Roberts

He wasn't about to put any pressure on her, but he wanted Jodie to know that, if he had seen behind her mask, she could trust him not to use it against her or even mention it.

That she could trust *him*.

Maybe his lips curved, just a little, but it was Eddie's eyes doing most of the smiling and Jodie caught her bottom lip between her teeth.

Eddie was still holding her gaze. Or maybe Jodie was holding his. Maybe it didn't matter because something bigger was holding them both. The air in this small room with its shelves so tightly packed with medical supplies and the heavy, security door firmly closed seemed to be getting heavier. Pressing down on them.

Pushing them closer together.

Neither of them said a word. They didn't seem to need to. By whatever means, whether it was body language or telepathy, apparently the desire was expressed, permission sought – and granted.

Jodie slowly came up onto her tiptoes. Eddie bent his head just as slowly, turning it in the last moments, just before he closed his eyes and finally broke that contact, so that his lips were at the perfect angle to cover Jodie's with a soft, lingering touch.

When he lifted his head, he found Jodie's eyes were open before his. Maybe she hadn't closed them at all? Because of their soft, chocolate brown colour, he could also see that her pupils were getting bigger fast enough to tell him that she had liked that kiss as much as he did. That quick intake of her breath suggested that she wanted more.

Eddie had played this game often enough to be an expert. He knew there was an easy way to find out…

This time, the kiss wasn't nearly as soft and her lips parted beneath his, her tongue meeting his almost instantly.

Oh, yeah…

She wanted more.

So did Eddie. But not here. Not now. Not just because they'd be breaking all sorts of rules and it was a bad idea, anyway. No…he had a promise to keep to someone else and Edward Grisham never broke a promise.

He broke the kiss, instead.

'I have to go,' he said.

Jodie's gaze slid away from his. 'Me, too. We're done here.'

But Eddie was smiling as he turned away. He spoke softly but he knew that Jodie would be able to hear him perfectly well.

'I'm not so sure about that,' he said.

Continue reading
FORBIDDEN NIGHTS WITH THE PARAMEDIC
Alison Roberts

Available next month
millsandboon.co.uk

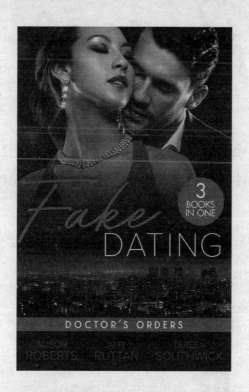

LET'S TALK
Romance

For exclusive extracts, competitions
and special offers, find us online:

f MillsandBoon

X @MillsandBoon

◉ @MillsandBoonUK

♪ @MillsandBoonUK

Get in touch on 01413 063 232

MILLS & BOON

THE HEART OF ROMANCE

A ROMANCE FOR EVERY READER

MODERN

Prepare to be swept off your feet by sophisticated, sexy and seductive heroes, in some of the world's most glamourous and romantic locations, where power and passion collide.

HISTORICAL

Escape with historical heroes from time gone by. Whether your passion is for wicked Regency Rakes, muscled Vikings or rugged Highlanders, awaken the romance of the past.

MEDICAL

Set your pulse racing with dedicated, delectable doctors in the high-pressure world of medicine, where emotions run high and passion, comfort and love are the best medicine.

True Love

Celebrate true love with tender stories of heartfelt romance, from the rush of falling in love to the joy a new baby can bring, and a focus on the emotional heart of a relationship.

HEROES

The excitement of a gripping thriller, with intense romance at its heart. Resourceful, true-to-life women and strong, fearless men face danger and desire - a killer combination!

From showing up to glowing up, these characters are on the path to leading their best lives and finding romance along the way – with plenty of sizzling spice!

To see which titles are coming soon, please visit

millsandboon.co.uk/nextmonth

GET YOUR ROMANCE FIX!

Get the latest romance news,
exclusive author interviews, story
extracts and much more!

blog.millsandboon.co.uk